AF424607

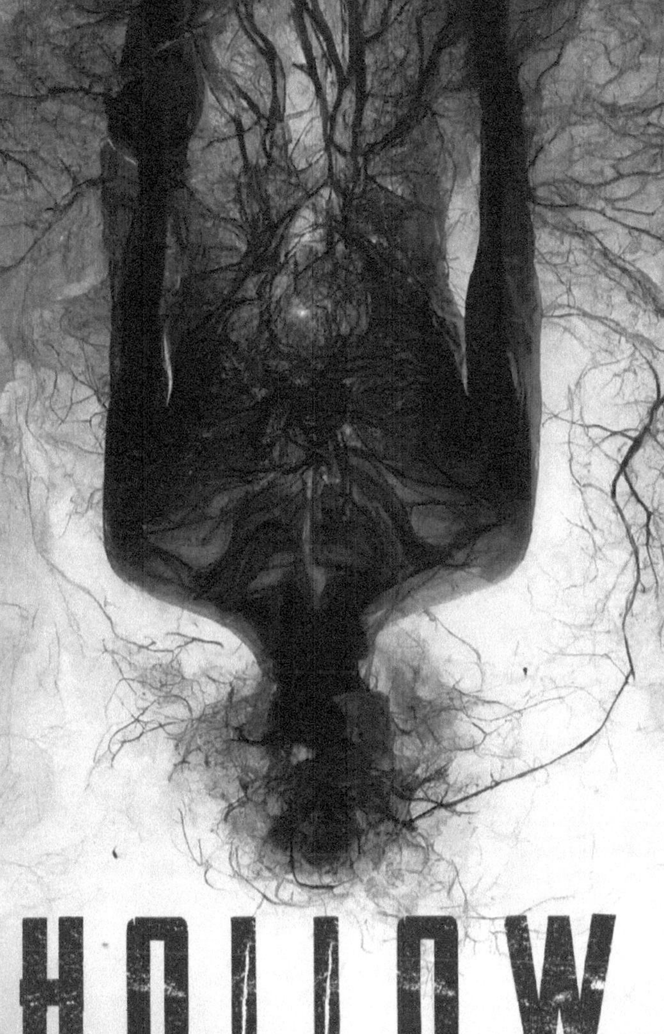

# HOLLOW

## DAVIDE TARSITANO

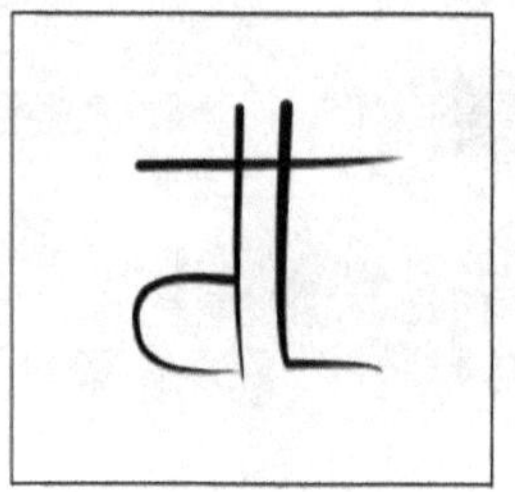

# DAVIDE TARSITANO

# HOLLOW

## A NOVEL

Copyright © 2023 Davide Tarsitano.
The right of Davide Tarsitano to be identified as the author of this work
has been asserted.
All rights reserved.
No part of this book may be reproduced, stored in a retrieval system, or
transmitted, in any form, or by any means (electronic, mechanical,
photocopying, recording or otherwise) without the prior written
permission of the author, except in cases of brief quotations embodied in
reviews or articles.
It may not be edited, amended, lent, resold, hired out, distributed or
otherwise circulated, without the publisher's written permission.
Permission can be obtained from:
www.dtarsitano.com

This book is a work of fiction. Except in the case of historical fact, names,
characters, places, and incidents either are products of the author's
imagination or are used fictitiously. Any resemblance to actual persons,
living or dead, events, or locales is entirely coincidental.

Published by Davide Tarsitano

dtarsitano.com

**ISBN: 979-8-9881921-0-7**
Cover design: Innsanctum Design
Interior formatting: P.J. Blakey-Novis

*This book is for you, Grandma.*
*You were ready*
*I was not.*

*What looked like morning was the beginning of endless night*

*William Peter Blatty*

*There are horrors beyond life's edge that we do not suspect, and once in a while man's evil prying calls them just within our range*

*H.P. Lovecraft*

# Part One:

# The Phone Call

# 1

Rosa Cortez brought her car to a halt, parking the gray Dodge Caravan on the driveway like she had on Monday, Wednesday, and Friday of every week for the past thirty-five years—occasionally on some weekends when the Hansons were out. She had always been a creature of habit, a valuable skill for her job.

Among the mansions she had to attend, her favorite was Jane's, with the beautiful courtyard they had built together in the front of the house. She looked proudly at the neatly trimmed bushes of white roses, the peonies, the Russian sage, and the sunflowers. They offered a natural frame to the yard's borders and followed the path of flagstones all the way to the front porch of the house. Their colors blended in harmony with the tones of the fall, shyly peeking into the last ripe days of summer.

Rosa opened the rear sliding door of her van and grabbed a brown bag of groceries, then walked to the front porch, rummaging through the pocket of her jacket with her free hand. As she climbed the wooden steps, she glanced at the garage window.

Every Monday, Mr. and Mrs. Hanson usually had breakfast on Main Street and wouldn't be home before ten, at the earliest. But today, both cars were there.

Rosa looked at her watch: 9:00 a.m.

And the door had been left ajar.

She got in and closed it behind her.

All the blinds in the living room had been shut. The only daylight came through the white curtains in the kitchen, on the other end of the open space. The staircase separating the library from the den was swallowed in darkness.

"Jane? Anyone home?" Rosa asked in a trembling voice.

She called for them again, louder this time, after clearing her throat.

No response. The house was filled in a smothering silence.

They must have walked to Main Street this morning and left the door open by mistake. But why shut the blinds? And with such a gorgeous day outside? Rosa's mind could understand a slight variation of the routine, but this felt past her threshold.

She walked to the kitchen and placed the brown paper bag on the marble counter. Everything seemed to be in place, as usual, but at the same time, she couldn't shake off the feeling that something was off. Rosa put the groceries away, then walked back to the living area, opening all the blinds and two of the front windows. The daylight and the crisp air of the morning flooded the room and made the house look a little more familiar.

Rosa went to grab the vacuum and the cleaning products she needed from the under-stair closet, but she stopped at the bottom of the staircase, looking up at the gloom of the second floor.

Her heart quickened. Grabbing her phone, she dialed Jane's number. No doubt hearing her voice would make Rosa feel more at ease.

One ring.

Two rings.

At the third ring she heard a sound coming from upstairs, and the blood froze in her veins.

Jane's phone.

At first, Rosa thought it was possible Jane had simply gone out for breakfast without her phone—perhaps intentionally, or maybe not. But the oddities kept mounting up to a point Rosa felt was unsustainable. Something was wrong. Everything in the house was trying to warn her. Ignoring it was not a possibility at this point.

With her heart pounding inside her chest, she started to climb the steps. The old hardwood planks creaked under her weight, echoing threateningly in the still house.

She had loved that house. It was a place of light and colors, of open windows and moving air. But today, the place was different. Gloomy and gray, filled with spoiled and still air.

When she reached the top of the stairs, the atmosphere was heavier.

"Jane?" The word barely escaped Rosa's throat, coming out in a choked whisper.

A muffled sound came from the master bedroom, and she turned toward it in the dark hallway. All the doors were closed, except for that room. As she walked forward, the sound became more defined.

Flies buzzing.

The realization unlocked other senses that had previously been numbed, and an intense smell reached Rosa's nostrils.

Spoiled meat. Rotting flesh.

She brought her forearm to her mouth and breathed into the soft fabric of her cardigan, hoping to find some relief from the horrible stench. Her hand clung to the pendant cross she wore around her neck, and Rosa shook her head, as if that could magically drive away the thoughts forming in the back of her mind.

Something horrific. Something she was not ready to accept.

Crouching, she clutched her knees with her arms, rocking back and forth to calm down. On the wall at the end of the hallway, a tall shadow loomed in the darkness. Rosa closed her eyes and prayed. Prayed for this to be a dream, to wake up and to realize this wasn't real, that everything was fine, for her routine to be back, for the sound and the smell to go away. She wished to reopen her eyes to find the shadow gone, that light, piercing with strength from an open window, filled the room. To find Jane and Bill downstairs, sipping coffee around the kitchen island and teasing each other over silly things.

Rosa opened her eyes again, only to see that nothing had changed.

She sat there for ten long minutes, working on her breathing in a desperate attempt to recompose herself. When she felt a little better, Rosa slowly stood and rested both hands on the walls, as though they provided some sort of comfort, a lifeline in the tempestuous ocean this day had brought in her life.

The answer was through the master bedroom's door, but the last thing she wanted to do was see it. Rosa longed to escape, to leave the house, to jump in her car and drive away as fast as she could, beyond the speed limit she always respected. But she couldn't bring herself to leave. Was it curiosity? Was it the utter repulsion she felt toward negligence? Rosa didn't have an answer, but she knew leaving was not the right thing to do. She had to see this through.

So, she dragged herself closer to the doorway.

The stench turned up a notch. Her heart galloped with full steam, and she took a deep breath, trying to ignore the sweet notes in the air. Rosa decided to count to three, then she would enter the room, no matter what she was going to find.

One.

Images flashed in the darkness of her eyelids. Jane sitting near her in the courtyard, her gardening tools scattered on the dark fertilizer.

Two.

Bill resting on the back porch, reading a book and sipping a beer.

Three.

Rosa stepped inside the room and knew, in that very moment, what she saw would haunt her for the rest of her days. Some things were not meant to be seen.

She wanted to scream but couldn't. Nothing came out. Rosa felt paralyzed in her own body. It failed to respond and refused to do anything.

Bill and Jane Hanson's lifeless bodies lay in bed, raided by a cluster of flies. Crawling in and out of their mouths and nostrils, strolling on their glassy opened eyes.

Rosa crashed to the floor, kneeling and calling the Lord for help. She wasn't new to the sight of a corpse—their stillness was not the cause of agitation inside her. Afterall, Rosa had had to bury her husband, who lost his life on the job, so dead bodies didn't bother her too much. She had seen the cold shells of her parents, her brother, lying in caskets, distant reminders of the souls once inhabiting them. There was nothing to fear from the dead.

What bothered her were the faces…

Their features were eternalized in awful screams. The jaws opened so far, Rosa thought they had been broken. The dull eyes were also wide, unwilling to believe in whatever had been in front of them when the moment came, when life was about to slip away. Inside that last expression was the inability to comprehend, to accept that whatever they saw in that instant could exist. There was no relief, no peace in those eyes and in those soundless wails.

"Oh! Lord. Oh God! Please help me." Her voice finally came out, and with it, tears flowed freely.

Rosa cried, then screamed and prayed out loud. And the words got lost in the deafening buzz of colliding flies.

Then she called 911.

# 2

The lips of the woman in front of him moved, but he could barely hear what she said.

"Mr. Hanson?" The voice seemed to come from a remote place, delayed, invisible in the thick mist his mind had fallen into.

The woman handed him a piece of paper. Her eyes were an intense shade of blue, and she wore her hair in a tidy and tight bun. The red of her lipstick framed a gleaming smile.

For a moment, Peter thought he was dreaming. It would have been nice to dream a bit, to get out of that intolerable numbness. Or maybe not. Maybe it would have been better if this was a dream. To wake up and realize it was all smoke. That would have been the best option by a nautical mile.

The sound of a phone ringing brought him back to reality, breaking the fog, sharpening everything around him again.

"Mr. Hanson. I need a signature for the room deposit. Your card will be charged three hundred dollars, which will be refunded after checkout," the woman said.

"Oh yeah!" he uttered, looking at the document clipped in the cardboard holder. A pen hung from a chain connected to it. "Absolutely!"

Despite his numbness, the yellow highlighted field at the bottom of the paperwork was easy to locate. Under normal circumstances, Peter would have taken his time to read anything he had to sign. Under normal circumstances, he would have signed with his full first and last name. But these weren't normal circumstances, so he quickly scribbled something and returned the cardboard holder to its owner.

"Thank you. I appreciate that." She returned her focus to the screen in front of her, the mouse clicking as she quickly maneuvered it. "The refund of the deposit should go through within five business days.

"Here are your keys. Two copies. Room 217." The woman handed him a key holder containing two room cards. "Breakfast is between 6:00 a.m. and 9 a.m. You will find the instructions to access our complimentary Wi-Fi inside the room."

Peter Hanson nodded.

"Anything else I can help you with?"

"Actually, yes. I might need to prolong my stay."

"Oh, for sure. Do you already know your new checkout day?"

"Not yet."

"Just let us know when you do. There should be no problems extending your stay."

"Thank you."

He walked toward the car parked in front of the hotel's main entrance and stood on the sidewalk, still trying to process the storm of thoughts raging in his mind.

It was a beautiful Indiana afternoon in mid-September, and the sun was setting at the horizon. Sparse clouds moved quickly in the blue sky, pushed by a light breeze. The world was trapped in a mystical limbo with the seasons transitioning into one another. From the woods on the other side of the interstate, he could already smell the damp and earthy aroma of the mushrooms, the compost, and the sweet decay of the already fallen leaves. At the same time, the sun's warmth still caressed his skin, and the smell of the grass, freshly cut in the morning, lingered.

Peter debated whether to bring the suitcase in the room now or later. He opted for the latter, so he jumped back in the car, where Luna panted with excitement, tail wagging. She was on an adventure, her first road trip. Peter pet her, making sure to scratch her in the spot behind her right ear. Luna tilted her head and licked his arm with approval.

"At least I've still got you, princess," he said, envying Luna's unawareness.

The drive to the house was brief. The familiar road unwound from Main Street to the Speedway, home of the Indy 500. As he drove through one of the cross streets, he looked at the houses around him and was hit by memories of his childhood. This place seems so different. Or most likely, it looks like that because I am so different now. And right after came the first big wave of grief. It filled his eyes with tears, spilling and rolling down his cheeks when he blinked. Chills crossed his whole body, along his spine, goosebumps on his arms, and he tensed on the steering wheel.

Peter parked in the driveway of the house where he had grown up, then got out of the car and opened the passenger door to let Luna out. He took his glasses off and dried his eyes with the lower part of his gray T-shirt.

The dark siding, the large and modern windows on the first story, the tree whose branches reached out to the window of his old room upstairs…Countless times he had risked breaking his neck to walk from the ledge onto that branch, sturdy enough to hold his weight—a friend he could count on in the summer days, his favorite place to sit while reading a Stephen King book, hidden by the taller branches and the leaves, protected from the rest of the world, safe in its shade.

The yellow ribbon the Indianapolis Metro Police Department had placed around the front porch of the house fluttered in the breeze of the late afternoon. He climbed the porch steps and crouched to pass under the tape, then stopped. A white piece of paper with the IMPD logo had been taped on the door, declaring the house inaccessible until the end of the investigation.

Peter got close to the window and put a hand on his forehead to peek inside. In the strange stillness of the house, now uninhabited, he caught a glimpse of the big chandelier hanging in the living room. He pictured his dad on a stepladder, replacing a broken bulb, and his mom looking up at the ceiling, pointing out he had picked the wrong light color.

Cold instead of warm.

They would argue about it for hours, all the way through dinner. Just when things had started to get tense, they would burst into laughter and hug each other. His parents would stand side by side, one washing, one drying the dishes, while whispering things to one another. And it didn't matter to them that Peter mentioned they had a dishwasher.

That was Bill and Jane Hanson, back when they were.

But now, they weren't anymore, and that was the precise reason why Peter was here.

Because they had been found dead three days ago, under circumstances no one had explained yet.

He reckoned he had never been in such a place of gloom, of confusion and despair. The thought of the shift his life had taken was impossible to accept. Not fully. He had replayed over and over in his mind the events that shook the foundations of his whole existence. They were still scattered and unclear in the fog, but the more he recollected, the more details emerged.

Two days earlier, he had received the phone call that changed his life forever.

Peter had been sitting at his desk, just like every morning from 8:00 a.m. to 12:00 p.m., working on his next novel—bleeding on the keyboard, as Frank Price, his literary agent, always said. When the phone buzzed loudly on the mahogany desk, Peter got mentally ready to tell Price he would have the first part of the manuscript ready by the end of the week. He had frowned, realizing it wasn't Price calling him, but a number with the Indianapolis area code. Peter had looked at the phone vibrating in his hand, pondering if it was one of those robocalls.

After two more rings, he picked up.

On the other side of the phone was a deep masculine voice. "Hello, am I speaking with Mr. Peter Hanson?"

"Yes, that's me."

"Mr. Hanson, this is Detective Robert Cooper from Indianapolis Metro Police."

For a brief moment, Peter had thought it was a prank call. Yet his senses sharpened all of a sudden, and he found himself holding his breath, unsure how to respond.

"Yes. Good morning."

"Mr. Hanson." The man paused for a moment. "I'm not sure if this is a good moment for you to talk."

"It is. How can I help you, Detective?"

"Just to confirm. Are you the son of Bill and Jane Hanson?"

"Yes, I am." Peter's heart accelerated. Something was not right.

"I'm afraid I have bad news concerning your parents."

Those words had been hard to make sense of. His mind couldn't really comprehend what was happening and tried to protect him from the trauma. The conversation had gone on for a while, but Peter couldn't remember what had been said. It was as if the reset button had been pressed, and that part of the conversation was still missing from his recollection.

An amnesia that, for now, didn't bother Peter a bit.

"We need you to come to the station for some questions. Then I will escort you to the Marion County Morgue for the identification process," the detective had said.

"I'm in New Orleans," Peter replied in an absent, empty voice, staring at the bookshelf on the other side of his office.

"I am aware. There is no rush. When do you think you might be able to get here?"

There had been a long pause. Peter's focus kept going to the spine of a yellow paperback. Without his glasses, he couldn't read the title, but he knew it was The Parable of The Sower, by Octavia Butler.

"Mr. Hanson? Are you still there?"

"Yes. Uhm. Yes, I am. A couple of days, probably." The air was thicker in the room, harder to breathe.

"Okay. That will work. I will be waiting for you on Thursday morning at the station."

"Okay."

"Mr. Hanson, I'm really sorry for your loss. I really am."

"What happened?"

"We don't know yet, but I hope to give you more information by the time you are in town. All I can say at this time is that they were found in their bed."

"Did it happen in their sleep?" Peter asked, his voice sounding choked.

"I am afraid I don't have an answer for you on that. If you have any questions or need anything, please don't hesitate to call me at any time. Night or day. Again, I'm truly sorry."

The detective had provided him with his personal phone number, and that put an end to the conversation.

Peter had thrown a few changes of clothes into his gym bag, gathered Luna's things and his laptop, and packed his car. He pondered if it was a good idea to drive in that state of mind, but he did anyway. It wasn't as if he had any other choice. Flying was not an option, not with Luna, and he hadn't wanted to leave her with Melissa, the girl he had been dating for a few months.

So, he jumped in his car and drove until he couldn't anymore, stopping somewhere in Tennessee to break up the trip. Slept a few hours, navigating through the nightmares and the random panic attacks that had forced him to stop along the way. Then he had finally arrived in Indianapolis, where he stood now, in front of the same house that looked so different.

He felt the urge to sleep again. It seemed the only thing that made any sense—the instinct of preservation kicking in, trying to survive the unbearable weight threatening to crush him.

# 3

Peter arrived at the police station ten minutes earlier than the time he had scheduled with Detective Cooper. He kept tapping the right pocket of his jeans, feeling the edges of his pack of cigarettes through the denim's fabric, just to make sure they were still there. Peter didn't know how he was going to bring himself to do this, but there was no other option.

It was a necessary step for the bodies to be released and sent to the funeral home for the final arrangements. But never, not in a million years, had he pictured himself identifying his parents' bodies—lying cold on silver metal tables, covered by white sheets. That's when all those movies and true crime novels popped into his mind. White tags hanging from their toes…He thought he was going to vomit, so he was glad he hadn't eaten in a while.

Peter fished the Nicorette pack from his black leather jacket, opened the lid, and let one drop on his tongue. He chewed it five times, then placed it between his upper gum and the side of his mouth so the nicotine would kick in quicker. After checking the time on his phone, Peter walked through the main entrance. He stepped into a long and narrow room with waiting seats on one side and reception stations on the other, protected by bullet-proof glass. Two officers checked people in, and the other three seats were empty.

The female officer at the end of the room gestured for him to come forward.

"How may I help you?" she asked in a listless and annoyed tone.

"I'm here to see Detective Cooper."

"Can I see your ID, please?"

He pushed it through the small slot at the bottom of the glass. She looked at the card, then at him, and back to the ID. The officer grabbed the phone receiver on her desk and waited a couple of seconds, looking up and cursing—probably for the hundredth time—whoever had let that workday start for her.

"Cooper at reception," she finally said, hanging up without waiting for an answer. "Please have a seat."

Peter had been sitting down for not even a minute when the heavy door on the wall buzzed and turned on its squeaky hinges.

"Mr. Hanson. Welcome and thanks for coming over. Please follow me." Cooper held the door and gestured for Peter to come through. The depth of his soothing voice brought Peter back a couple of days earlier, back to that terrible call.

Detective Cooper was a tall black man and wore his hair very short. Peter judged him to be at least six two and in his forties. He wasn't wearing a uniform, but a pair of caramel trousers, a blue shirt with the sleeves rolled-up half the length of his forearm, and black suspenders. On his right side, he had a holster with a 9mm resting in it.

They stopped at a small scanning station, which looked exactly like the ones at the airport TSA checkpoints. The detective passed through one side of the scanner and waited for Peter to empty his pockets and walk through behind him. They took the elevator, and Cooper pushed the button that would bring them to the first underground floor. After walking through a couple of hallways with closed doors on both sides, they finally stopped in front of a door with a white plaque on it: "INTERROGATION ROOM 7."

The room was way less fancy than the ones shown in movies and TV shows. No team of investigators was anxiously waiting behind a one-way mirror for the suspect to confess, no modern dark colors on the walls. The room was bare and old. Two discolored vomit-green chairs had been placed on both sides of a very old white table filled with crevices. The walls needed a refresh—some large pieces of plaster had come off them. A few of the ceiling covers were missing, and the ones still there were stained from years of leaks.

Cooper dragged one of the chairs without lifting it, so it produced a horrifying screeching sound on the epoxy floor. Then he gestured for Peter to take a seat across from him.

"Mr. Hanson, I am so very sorry for your loss."

Peter didn't respond but acknowledged with a composed nod.

"As I mentioned on the phone, you are here for a formal identification of what is believed to be the bodies of Bill and Jane Hanson. But before we get to that, I wanted to read you the summary of our preliminary report, if that's all right." Cooper opened the file holder on the desk and flicked through a few pages.

Peter wondered how many of these meetings Cooper had had during the course of his career. How many cases had he worked? Whatever happened to his parents must have seemed pretty normal to him.

"Yeah. That's all right."

"At 9:32 a.m. on September 20, a call to 911 was made by Rosa Cortez. According to her deposition, Mrs. Cortez came by to work around the house. She claimed to have a copy of the house keys, in accordance with your parents. Do you have any knowledge of such an agreement?"

"Yes. Of course. She has been the housemaid since before I was born. She is part of our family." Peter tried to ignore the ache those words gave him. *Our family.* He watched Cooper take notes.

"According to her statement, approximately ten minutes after she entered the house, we received the call from dispatch. Officer Spencer and Torrance were patrolling the area at the time of the call. They arrived at the site at 9:41a.m. Your parents, Mr. And Mrs. Hanson, were found in their bed and—"

"Detective, I hate to interrupt, but is there any chance we can cut to the chase here? I'm assuming all this information will be in your report. It's been a really long couple of days, and all I can think of is that I'm going to have to ID my dead parents. I would really appreciate it if we could get this over with so I can make arrangements for their funeral."

"Yes, yes, of course. I totally understand. I must ask one more question, though."

Peter gestured for him to go on.

"To the best of your knowledge, were you aware of any…psychological problems your parents suffered from?"

"Psychological problems? What do you mean?"

"An inspection of the house's gas system has not revealed any leak or damage, but the fire department has found signs of potential tampering of the furnace."

"What is that supposed to mean?" But Peter knew exactly what it meant. His mind was just busy trying to process how it could have happened. The majority of these accidents seemed to occur in the winter, when the temperatures dropped, not in early autumn.

"Mr. Hanson, my job is to make sure we learn what happened to your parents. In order to do that, at this point of the investigation, we need to look into any possible scenarios. We cannot rule out—at least not yet—that what happened to your parents was not the result of an accident, but a premeditated action. I want you to be prepared for the possibility this might be a case of suicide."

# 4

Peter hopped into the passenger seat of Detective Cooper's car, still trying to make sense of the information he was given. The nauseating smell of Royal Pine Little Trees filled the air, but in the background lingered the stale smell of cigarettes. Peter wondered if Cooper still smoked and, for a moment, contemplated sharing his own attempts to quit. He clamped his mouth shut and looked out of the window when Cooper drove south away from the station. Neither one of them talked during the short ride.

A few blocks after, the detective pulled into a narrow driveway on McCarty Street and parked in the closest spot. Peter jumped out, glad to get rid of that chemical pine fragrance. Cooper led the way toward the entrance of a two-story, squat building, sided with discolored and pale-yellow bricks. On the right side of the door was a white, rusty sign reading: "Marion County Coroner's office."

Behind the reception desk was an incredibly skinny man in his forties, wearing glasses with very thick black frames. He reminded Peter of Martin Scorsese.

"Morning, Russ!" Cooper greeted him, putting the documents on the desk. "Did you watch the Cubs last night? Pretty good game, huh?"

"It was all right," Russ said mechanically, typing something on his keyboard. He sprang up in an unnatural twitch, told them to wait there while he retrieved Dr. Rigg, then disappeared down the hallway.

Peter's heart was racing faster than ever. He couldn't believe what he was about to do. A deep wave of sadness mixed with helplessness assailed him. A few months back, at the peak of the summer, he had come home to visit, when his parents were alive. They had had a good time together, seemed to be doing really well despite the pandemic. Both looked as good and relaxed as he could ever remember them being. And now, they were lying a few feet from him, somewhere in a refrigerator, gone forever. Peter tried to remember the last thing he said to them on that video call a few days back, but he wasn't able to. And he couldn't decide if that was a good thing or a bad one.

Russ came back and gestured for them to follow him. They reached the elevator at the end of the hallway and went down to the basement. It was a large open space with ten rows of metal tables, which felt cold even just by looking at them. Each one was equipped with a tiny faucet and a sink—immaculately clean, but for some reason, Peter pictured them dripping with blood and other organic fluids. The temperature in the room was low, sending sudden chills down his spine, and it smelled of chemicals and disinfectant.

In the middle was a bald man wearing green scrubs, intent on putting on a pair of blue latex gloves. He nodded to Detective Cooper.

"Morning, Julian. This is Peter Hanson. He is here to ID Bill and Jane Hanson."

"Julian Rigg," the man said, reaching for Peter's hand. "My condolences, Mr. Hanson."

"Thank you, sir."

Rigg walked toward the wall on the left side of the room, where three rows of five white square doors were arranged in a disturbing symmetry. The doctor stopped between the last and the second to last columns of refrigerated cells and turned the handle of the two doors in the middle row. The locks snapped open with a loud metallic sound that made Peter flinch.

Cooper put a hand on his shoulder and said gently, "Take your time. We just need a verbal confirmation."

Peter looked at him and for a moment, seeing what looked like sincere sorrow, or was it pity, maybe?

The doors sprung open toward the top. The doctor turned, facing them, then grabbed the metal handles and pulled, walking away from the wall. Two metallic beds rolled forward, clattering on the old rails.

Two human shapes, covered by white sheets.

Peter followed the outlines; from the bumps their feet produced all the way up to the rounded bulges of their heads. The doctor walked on one side of the first corpse and grabbed the ends of the sheet, then looked at Peter, awaiting his permission to proceed.

"Mr. Hanson, I want to warn you. The rigor did not allow us to change the facial expression of the bodies, besides closing their eyelids. The funeral home will take care of that."

Peter took a deep breath, then nodded his approval.

Dr. Rigg rolled the sheet down, just enough to uncover a familiar face once belonging to Peter's mother.

Peter didn't even see the tears coming. They just instinctively filled his eyes and then dripped down his cheeks. He grimaced at the sight of her, almost as if trying to mimic the expression frozen on her face. Pain stabbed him in the back when he saw her gaping mouth stretched in a terrifying scream, so wide he could see her tonsils in the back of her throat.

*How could this have happened?* Peter fought against that unexpected look. He had imagined her passing away in her sleep, peacefully fading away. But there was no peace in that scream. He turned toward the detective with interrogative eyes.

"We'll know more when the autopsy report is finished and the forensic results are back," Cooper told him softly, as if he could read his mind.

Peter turned back to the body.

The pallor of her skin didn't take away her delicate features. Her lips were dark, and the outsides of her eyelids were a mix of gray and purples.

Peter put a hand on her shoulder and felt the endless cold of death pervading him. His mom's warmth was gone. She wasn't there anymore. He turned to Cooper and looked at him with swollen eyes, laden with tears.

"It's her. My mother," he eventually said, remembering the detective had asked for verbal confirmation.

Dr. Rigg rolled down the other sheet, and Peter saw his dad. His heart wrenched once more at the sight of the stillness clashing with that horrible, soundless scream. Peter's dad had always been his compass, his North Star. And now, he had faded away, leaving Peter in darkness and confusion.

He sobbed and hid his face in his hands, then turned again and confirmed the identification to Cooper.

The doctor covered his dad's face and pushed them both back into their cells. Peter felt like stopping him; he wasn't ready to let them go.

Dr. Rigg approached Peter with a freshly printed sheet and a pen and asked him to sign it.

"By signing this, you confirm the identification," the doctor said dryly, keeping his head slightly down as a sign of respect.

Peter scribbled something in the appropriate field at the bottom of the paperwork.

"Thank you, Mr. Hanson. Again, my most sincere condolences. The autopsy has been conducted, and you will receive a summary. It should contain the toxicology report and the lab results performed on the sample of tissues we used."

Peter nodded absently.

He walked back to the parking lot with Cooper. The detective lit up a cigarette in the chilly air promising the coming of fall.

"You can now make the necessary arrangements for the funeral. Just remember to let the funerary services know to contact the morgue." Cooper passed a business card to him. "The coroner will make sure your parents are transferred to their facility as soon as they make the call."

Peter nodded, looking at the card.

"Oh! I almost forgot. The forensic team has collected all the evidence at your house. The fire department has checked the gas system and the furnace and have deemed it safe. Tomorrow morning, you will be able to regain access to the house. An agent will be there at 8:00 a.m. to check the premises with you and remove the seals."

"Thank you, Detective." Peter shook Cooper's hand and started walking away.

"I can drive you back to your car…"

"Thanks, but I think I'll take a stroll," Peter said, resuming his walk.

A few seconds later, the detective's voice reached him again, deeper than ever.

"I know what you're thinking."

Peter turned. The detective couldn't possibly know what he was thinking, for the simplest reason: Peter could *not* think. His mind kept spinning like a top.

"You are wondering why their faces were…Why they looked like…*that?*" Cooper took a few steps toward him.

"Do you have any theories? Why were they screaming? Let's say it *was* a gas leak…Why couldn't they move and open a window? What were they scared of?"

Cooper took a long draw of his cigarette, then flicked it in the middle of the street.

"I don't know. Not yet. But I'll be damned if I'm not going to figure it out."

# 5

When Peter arrived at his childhood home the following morning, the police officer Cooper had mentioned was already there, waiting patiently, having refrained from stepping on the front porch until Peter showed up.

As Peter stepped out of the car, it occurred to him the house was now his, a thought that brought more anxiety and sadness than anything else. He grabbed his brown leather bag from the passenger seat and walked on the broad flagstones leading to the front porch.

"Mr. Hanson?" the officer asked rhetorically, offering him his hand. "I'm Officer Carson."

Peter shook the man's hand and nodded in return.

"I'm here to check the premises and formally remove the seals from the house. I believe you have been informed of such a procedure by Detective Cooper, correct?"

"Correct."

"I'm going to need to see your ID and a couple of signatures."

They went through the formalities, and after the officer collected Peter's signature, he started removing the yellow ribbons from the porch, then walked to the front door, where he carefully removed the tape and the seal. The officer extracted the house keys from a brown evidence bag. Peter recognized the silver skull hanging from the keychain. That had been a gift he had given to his mother a few years back.

Carson looked at Peter as if waiting for some kind of silent approval, then used the key to open the front door's deadbolt and turned the knob. The officer removed the key from the lock and handed it to Peter.

"I'll check the premises and then be out of your way, Mr. Hanson. Please wait here until I am done."

Carson stepped inside the house, and Peter lifted the keychain, studying the silver skull dangling in front of his eyes, which filled with sudden tears. He walked back to the front yard and looked around. The neighborhood seemed as if nothing had changed in all those years, immutable to the passing years, carved into a timeless dimension of existence. How could everything change so abruptly, Peter wondered, and yet remain exactly the same as always?

He looked at Luna through the car window he had left open. She seemed to sense the sadness looming upon him, upon the place. Luna sat quietly in the car with her head slightly tilted, helpless in her unconditional love for him.

His train of thought derailed when a familiar old minivan pulled into the driveway and parked behind his car. The sight of the woman behind the wheel opened an unexpected crack of light in a day that couldn't possibly get darker. It thawed his heart, and he found himself crying all over again, crossing his arms on his chest.

Peter realized altogether the fragility of the place he was at. It didn't matter what kind of emotions he felt—positive or negative. The wound that kept ripping his heart apart was too extended and too fresh for him to be able to discern between the two. Everything ached, even the good stuff.

"Peter, oh, Peter. My boy." The woman got out of the car and clumsily ran toward him. She threw herself forward, reaching up and putting her arms around Peter's neck, abandoning herself in a long hug. Rosa wailed on Peter's shoulder as he held her tight.

Peter felt all the tension she had been carrying in her body. Rosa had been the one who had found his parents, the one who had to witness the horror of that discovery, in what must have been a perfectly ordinary day for her otherwise.

"I'm so happy to see you," she whispered, in a voice broken by sobbing.

"It's good to see you too, Rosa. I wish it was under different circumstances." He bent over slightly to compensate for the difference of height between them.

"I'm so sorry," Rosa continued, unwilling to end the hug, tightening her grip. "Are we allowed to go in? The house must be a mess. All those cops going in and out."

Peter smiled. Only Rosa could think about the house in a moment like this.

He freed himself from the hug when Carson reappeared in the front doorway and walked toward them.

"The house is all clear. Here is a carbon copy of the document you signed before. I also want to mention that the fire department has thoroughly checked the furnace and ruled out any possible risks. Do you have any questions?" Carson asked.

"Thank you, Officer. I'll bring my stuff in."

"I'll be out of your way. Have a good day."

The officer walked to his car parked on Fifteenth Street, fired up the ignition, and disappeared behind the tall trees.

Peter looked at Rosa, who was trying to dry a thin tear of mascara that had dribbled on her cheek.

"Do you want to go in?" he asked.

She grimaced at the memory of the last time she had been inside. Peter couldn't blame her. He didn't feel any more ready to go in than she did.

"Let's go in. I will fix some coffee and see what kind of mess the police have left."

Peter grabbed his stuff from the car, let Luna out, and walked inside the house. The air was warm and still, in clear contrast with the cooler temperature outside. It gave him a sense of smothering vacancy. The house smelled of dust, damp wood, and chemicals, presumably used by the forensic team when they collected evidence and scanned for prints. He stopped and looked at the staircase, feeling goosebumps appearing on his arms.

It had been hard to step inside that empty house, but upstairs? That seemed like a completely different challenge. One he wasn't at all ready to face.

The image of his parents' mouths, trapped in those awful screams, flashed in front of his eyes.

"Are you hungry?" Rosa's voice came from the kitchen. "I brought you some food."

For some reason, he felt guilty to admit he was starving. Hunger hadn't exactly been a concern in the past days, but just like any other animal, the instinct of self-preservation started to kick in, and he was glad there was someone to take care of it for him. Even the thought of defrosting a TV meal in the microwave seemed an impossible task. All he wanted was to lie down on the couch and sleep.

But there was a component of shame in all this. It was the urge to make sure his mom and dad were taken care of. It seemed silly to believe they were still there, in those cold bodies, feeling discomfort or being cold, but that was the only thing he had left of them, and he didn't want them to stay in a refrigerator, if he could do something about it.

What were their last wishes? Did they even want a funeral? How in the world was he supposed to figure that out? They had been in shape, happy, finally enjoying their retirements, taking the trips they couldn't before. His parents weren't exactly planning their wills, that he knew of. They had so many more years ahead.

Sadness and confusion came together, mixed with anger and hopelessness. The emotions came and went in waves, each of them bringing a sensation of cold and loneliness. He guessed that was the way grief worked, but the reality was, he had no idea if this was even grief yet. Maybe he was just in shock. Grief might be a far more terrifying beast than he could imagine now.

"I need to take care of the funeral," he said, dodging Rosa's questions.

"Of course, of course. But why don't you relax on the couch for a little while? You must be exhausted. Let me warm up that casserole. I'll bring you something to eat before you know it." She walked briskly to the kitchen.

Peter smiled and did as she asked. He sat on the couch, and Luna immediately hopped on it and curled next to him. He pondered how much information was necessary to share with Rosa. What was the point of stabbing her in the heart once more, he wondered, passing on the information he had learned from Detective Cooper? Hadn't she already gone through enough trauma?

Rosa wasn't only the keeper of the big house Peter's family had lived in. She was family. She was a second mom to him. In that moment, it occurred to him that his parents would never be able to talk to Rosa anymore. *How absurd is that?* They just can't. They wouldn't be able to do anything. His parents were just bodies now, still blocks of decomposing flesh and bones.

The image of their wan, screaming faces flashed through his mind again: the thick layer of frozen ice on his father's beard, their eyelids fading into purple, the fear elongating their lips…

A few minutes later, Rosa came back with a tray. She placed a kitchen towel on the coffee table in front of the U-shaped sofa and put a cup of steaming coffee beside a plate of reheated casserole.

"I'll go to the grocery store later, but this will do it for now." Rosa sat on the short leg of the sofa.

"This is perfect, Rosa. Thank you so much for this."

"I still can't…" She paused in an attempt to control the wave of emotions coming at her. "I can't believe it. I just can't."

"I know. It's pretty surreal."

"Did you talk to the police? I mean…What did they say?"

"They are still working on it. They are not sure." Peter spared her the details, the terrifying hypothesis that might be behind his parents' deaths.

Rosa grabbed a Kleenex from the box on the table and dried her tears without asking for more information.

Peter turned the TV on. There was a baseball game on ESPN that neither of them had any interest in. It was probably the last channel his dad had watched before going to bed that night, to never wake up. Peter felt like crying again, but he didn't want to. Crying required effort, and he was too tired to do that now.

They watched the TV in silence while he devoured his meal. When he was full, Peter got up to bring the plate into the sink, but Rosa didn't let him. She put everything on a tray and went back to the kitchen, jingling the dishes together as she washed them. When she was done, she sat right next to him and held his hand.

"Your mom was the one that managed all the bills and the paperwork. Your father didn't want anything to do with them." She looked up and giggled.

"Yeah, I can kind of picture that," he said, smiling at her.

"You know…She was my best friend, your mom." Tears ran down her cheeks, and she tried to take some deep breaths. "If I can help you in any way right now, please just let me know."

"What do you think they would have wanted me to do in this kind of situation?"

"It's hard to tell, but I'm sure we can find out. Your mom kept all her most valuable things and documents in the safe in the office upstairs. Your mom was the most scrupulous woman. If there is something, it will be in there."

Peter followed Rosa upstairs to the studio once belonging to his parents, thinking about one of the conversations he had had with them a few years back, in that same room. It was always about trying to convince him to stay. They had offered to make that room his personal writing dungeon, were ready to move out of the house and give it all to him if that meant he stayed.

*What's the point of going to Louisiana?* He remembered his dad asking. A raging sense of guilt assailed him all at once. Peter had had his reasons to go away from Indianapolis. New Orleans had conquered a special place in his heart since the first time he visited with his parents. He must have been sixteen or seventeen when they had all spent the weekend there. The city was wrapped in the mysterious veil that only places with troublesome history possess. Its streets were pregnant with stories, voodoo folklore and a sense of mysticism that Peter felt would be the perfect incubator for his work. Since the moment he walked the streets of the French Quarter, something had clicked, something that was impossible to shake off. But there was another reason, something that had more to do with his incapacity to face difficult situations than with his professional ambitions, a reason he had never found the courage to talk about with his parents. New Orleans was the perfect place to run, once he couldn't face the guilt of his ghosts in Indiana. He felt responsible for what happened to them. Peter knew it wasn't a completely rational thought but couldn't completely dismiss the idea that things could have gone differently if he hadn't left.

*Carbon monoxide. Suicide. Murder-suicide.*

His dad had struggled with his mental health after he retired, but

Peter couldn't possibly imagine him doing something like that. Not taking his wife with him. Not like that. It just wasn't possible. And their faces…Those weren't the faces of people who had wanted to die…They had seen something. But what?

Rosa opened the door—with her usual rushed but composed pace—and walked to the safe hidden behind a family portrait. She stopped and looked at it, her hands crossed on her waist, almost as if she were paying them a tribute.

In the picture, his mom wore her favorite dress, a light turquoise mixed with purple stripes along the long sleeves. Peter sat on her lap and wore a red shirt and a Cubs cap. She was holding his hand, as always. His mom must have said something funny because he was captured with a smirk, almost to the verge of exploding in loud laughter, and she had a grin on her face. The kind you have when you know you've made someone happy, mixed with pride.

His dad was bent forward, one hand on the back of the chair she sat on and the other hand on her shoulder. He wasn't looking at the camera, but down to the two people he loved the most.

The picture was far from being perfect. Nobody was focused or ready for it at the time it was shot. But that was exactly the reason his parents had wanted it framed. It was the perfect expression of their family.

Rosa lifted the frame from the bottom corners, unhooking the wire in the back from the nail on the wall. That revealed a small, rectangular black safe with a keypad. Rosa looked at him and gestured for him to go ahead.

Peter approached the safe and typed the six-digit combination, then turned the knob lock to the left. There was a neat clacking sound, and the safe gently opened.

"Your mom…" Rosa stopped and took a few deep breaths to control her emotions. "Your mom just needed to always have a plan in case things went south. My son always tells me I'm a control freak. I think I got this from her." She smiled at him.

Peter started going through the papers stored in the safe. There were a lot of them, way more than he could have imagined. Rosa observed from across the desk, keeping a little distance. Peter assumed she didn't want to invade his privacy but still wanted to be there to support him.

After a little digging, Peter found a green folder labeled: "For Emergencies Only." He recognized his mother's sharp-cornered, neat handwriting. Inside, just as Rosa had predicted, Peter found all the information he needed, including the life insurance policy, which covered full funeral services for all the members of the family. Rosa had burst into tears when she found out Bill and Jane had also extended it to her and her son.

Among other documents, there was a small white envelope in the safe with Peter's name on it. He contemplated if he should open it. His heart was racing in his chest.

But he opted not to. Peter put it in one of the desk drawers and tried to forget about it for the time being.

He just wasn't ready.

# 6

After Rosa left, Peter spent the rest of the day on the couch. Sleeping was probably the only thing that made sense to him at this stage, the only source of relief. The rest was needed—and though he hadn't endured any physical effort in the past week, he still felt drained of all his energy—but the escape from his thoughts was the best part of his naps. Not that he was ever completely able to escape from all of them. What he thought could be put to bed for a while ultimately returned in some form in his dreams.

A repeated scratching sound awakened him. Still half asleep, he looked around. The house was dark, illuminated only by the TV he had left on. Peter got up from the couch and followed the noise all the way to the kitchen. The digital clock on the microwave read: 8:21 p.m.

Then the scratching again. This time, really close.

He looked over the kitchen counter in the middle of the room and found Luna sitting in front of the glass door. The silver light of the moon outside flooded her curly black fur, gleaming on her nose. Her ears were raised, and she was on alert. Luna looked outside as if she were in some sort of trance. Her paws timidly reached for the door, producing the scratching sound.

"Baby. You okay?" Peter asked. His concern grew when Luna didn't turn to him.

Peter walked slowly toward her.

"Luna?" he called softly for her. "Do you need to go potty?"

Luna kept staring outside with wide eyes and high ears. When Peter got close, he petted her gently. All of a sudden, she turned on him, confused and disoriented. Luna began panting and threw herself at him, licking his face and whining.

"Hey, hey. It's okay, baby girl. Were you dreaming? Let's go outside. Shall we?"

Peter walked out on the back porch with Luna and glanced at the darkness of the woods behind the house. The tops of the tall pine trees swayed, moved by the breeze. The lawn extended in length for a hundred yards, about fifty yards wide, ending at the tree line. There were no fences between his property and the neighbors', so he could clearly see the playground the Meyers—on the right—had built for their grandkids—a couple of swings, a slide, a small playhouse, and a red trampoline.

He sat at the table underneath the pergola his mother had been so fond of, and for good reason. The vines she had planted came down from the top, all the way along the posts. The flowers they produced were white, half closed in the lack of light. He could almost hear his mother's voice telling him how the flowers would open during the day, following the path of the sun.

Peter fought the temptation to light up a cigarette. He had gone two years without smoking but always had his pack with him. The Nicorette gums had become a good stopgap, but now, more than ever, he felt like he could burn through a few cigarettes.

He gazed around, looking for Luna, not wanting her to adventure too deep in the yard and into the woods this late at night. Peter almost flinched when he saw her sitting down, staring at the house to the left side of the yard, back in that odd state of unresponsiveness.

"Luna?" This time, his voice was louder and clearly more alarmed.

The dog didn't move a muscle. She was still in a frightening way, her head slightly tilted to the side, and she emitted a low whimpering sound.

Peter looked, trying to detect whatever was stealing her attention.

The house on the left side of the yard was a large two-story with white siding. It belonged to the Harris family.

Then he saw it.

A shadow stood still in front of the attic's window, the contours of a human figure looking out, immersed in the feeble orange light of the room. The shadow was still, and just like Luna, it seemed to be frozen, an ominous statue.

Peter's first thought went to Lynn Harris's mannequin, which had practically lived in the attic. He knew that house like the back of his hand. Peter had spent uncountable days and nights there since the age of five, hanging out with Will.

Will Harris was Lynn and Frank's son. He and Peter had been practically inseparable. Peter remembered when they were in high school, smoking a joint in the attic, and Will had set fire to the wig Lynn had placed on the mannequin's head. They were terrified but couldn't stop laughing. Eventually, that had resulted in them being grounded for two weeks and banned forever from the attic—a prohibition Will and Peter had never really taken seriously. Even the thought of that funny event didn't really help Peter, not coming close to relieving the sense of dread he felt now, looking at the shadow in the window. A sense of guilt surged inside Peter as he thought about his old friend. Will had always been the introverted one, even when he pretended to be the one who wasn't afraid of anything, or the one who was always comfortable with new situations, his innocence belied that facade of the tough guy. He still remembered the hesitation in Will's eyes when he offered him weed for the first time. There was a hint of fear in his features, the kind that accompanies the sense of unknown when experimenting something prohibited.

He glanced at Luna, who was still whimpering and shaking, seemingly unable to move or bark or do anything. Peter crouched and held her in her arms, petted her, and walked back to the porch.

When he turned one last time to the Harris house, the shadow at the window was gone.

"What the fuck?" he whispered, looking at the light as it extinguished in the attic, consigning the house to a still darkness.

Peter decided it was time to get back inside. The slight anxiety the shadow had given him was turning into fear now that he couldn't see it anymore.

*There must be an explanation*, Peter reasoned with himself. But the only idea that came to him was the shadow belonged to Frank Harris—given the size of the silhouette, it couldn't possibly have been Lynn. But what was Frank doing up there? And what was he looking at?

Peter went inside and prepared a bowl of kibble for Luna, then spent the rest of the night unpacking his stuff and doing a load of laundry. He thought about getting his laptop and checking his emails, maybe writing a bit, but both ideas died, crushed by the next unrelenting wave of grief.

Luna, sitting next to him as he lay on the couch, kept staring in the direction of the kitchen and the glass door, letting out a whine here and there. He turned on the lamp on the side table next to the couch and grabbed the book he had brought, opening it to his bookmark and hoping some reading would help him doze.

But sleep never came.

When he decided to get up and fix some coffee, he glimpsed the microwave digital clock: 3:15 a.m. Peter made his coffee and sat at the kitchen table, looking out the glass door and wondering what Luna had seen.

The Harris's attic light was back on, and the human-shaped shadow in front of the window was there once more, eerily still in the bleak silence of the night.

# 7

Franklin Funeral Home was just about three blocks away from the Hansons' residence—now just an empty shell hosting an orphan and the housekeeper, both dealing with the very first moments of the grieving process in their own ways.

Rosa had offered to go to Franklin Funeral Home with Peter since she had used their services already to bury her husband. So, on the following day, they got the papers ready and walked together.

The morning's beautiful colors contrasted with a cloudless deep-blue sky.

Dead leaves rained down, carried by the wind. An army of squirrels wandered in the front yards, and flocks of birds were getting ready to move somewhere warmer. They walked silently, taking it all in, feeling the weakened sun on their skin, listening to the sounds of the fallen leaves crunching under their steps, and smelling the sweet scent of the wood's decay, mixed with the smoky smell of the bonfires from the night before.

Suddenly, Peter thought about all the times he had refused his mom's invitations, asking him to join her in her daily walks around the neighborhood. Now, he would trade everything to have her at his side, but it was too late. There wouldn't be any more walks.

Peter took a deep breath and put his shades on to mask the redness he felt start to invade his eyes. He looked at Rosa, feeling deep gratitude that she was there with him.

"What's the point of even having a funeral? Why do we care about what all these other people want? I still think we could avoid doing the service. They weren't even religious." He kept his head down as he talked, but he was certain her eyes were on him.

"I don't disagree on that. But all the people that loved them need to have a moment to say goodbye, don't you think?" Rosa asked.

Peter didn't respond, so she continued.

"When my dear Fernando died, it helped me a lot to see how many people cared for him. How much he was loved. It's a way to celebrate their life."

"There's nothing to celebrate, Rosa! They're gone. When someone's gone, they're gone. What could there possibly be to celebrate?"

She quietly stopped in front of the squat building sided in freshly painted white bricks, dark gray frames around the doors and windows. They both released deep exhales in the impossible attempt to make the boulders they carried on their chests any lighter.

Peter and Rosa stepped into a warm and cozy reception, where two elegant gentlemen respectfully walked toward them. The one on the left was a big guy with a neatly trimmed blond beard. His pal was much shorter, with long black hair cow-licked toward the back. The short one opened his arms to welcome them.

"Mr. Hanson. We were waiting for you. I'm so terribly sorry for your loss. My most sincere condolences," he said in a soothing voice.

"Thank you. This is my friend Rosa Cortez," Peter said, gesturing toward her. "She is the one that spoke with you on the phone."

"Of course, of course." The short man held her hand while slightly bending forward. "Ron Bathurst, and this is my associate, Jim Halloway. Please follow us."

The two men led them into a space filled with scented candles and a few chairs surrounding a small coffee table. Flames from a fake fire danced jerkily in the fireplace in one corner of the room. On the opposite wall were small samples of coffins. They looked like asymmetrical shelves put there by some eccentric designer. Peter found himself strangely comforted by the men's professionalism. They spoke with a tone both empathic and respectful. It was probably the basics of their job, but still, he found a moment of peace.

They sat around the table, and the big guy, Jim, opened a black leather folder Peter assumed contained the paperwork Rosa had emailed them.

When Ron began asking about arrangements for a potential viewing before the funeral—if they wanted a funeral, if they wanted open caskets—that brief sense of peace started to fade away, and Peter's heart started to race again. They were talking to him, but he didn't have any answers.

Peter didn't really know what his parents' will said. He had no idea if they were comfortable with all their friends seeing their dead bodies in their caskets—not that it held any kind of importance now—but the reality was, he couldn't make any rational decisions for them. Everything was just too senseless and stupid for him to process, so Jim and Ron began to address their questions to Rosa, even though they kept looking in his direction, seeking some kind of non-verbal approval.

He nodded, but he wasn't really listening anymore. Peter went somewhere else in his mind, to a place made of guilt, remorse, and cold pain, and he wondered again if the grief process had already started. It was like waiting on a beach during a storm, looking at the horizon to see if the wave that would crush him was already in view.

Ultimately, Rosa made all the decisions that had to be made, with Peter's nodded approvals. They would have a showing for close family and friends but no funeral. Peter opted for the cremation. When it came time to choose the urns and the caskets, they picked the simplest one—cherry exteriors with white cream velvet interiors. Peter wondered how any of that would make any difference, given the fact it was all going to go in a cremation chamber at 2000 degrees, but they had to pick one anyway. Ron asked if they could provide a picture for the fliers to be distributed during the viewing, a small memory to celebrate the Hansons' lives, and Jim had concluded with a composed nod.

When Peter and Rosa left Franklin Funeral Home, the air had cooled quite a bit, and the weather had changed. Big gray clouds were moving fast in the high altitudes, ready to clash into one another. The wind picked up; its gloomy howl raised in the streets. Peter lifted his head to look at the waving trees. Some of the leaves let go, abandoning themselves to the force and randomness of the wind, unaware of where they would end up. Some others held onto the branches and twigs where they belonged. They remained anchored, fluttering around, waiting for the wind to pass.

And he couldn't help but wonder what kind of leaf he was.

Peter went back home, realizing he was completely famished. He grabbed the leftover chicken casserole Rosa had left in the fridge and thawed it in the microwave for two minutes, just as she had written on the yellow Post-It note carefully placed on top of the aluminum foil. There were probably three servings left in it, but he ate the whole thing. His appetite was a surprise for him, just as odd as the sense of peace he had felt for a moment at the funeral home.

As he washed the baking pan in the sink, Peter thought about work for the first time in days. It seemed like a month since he had left New Orleans, since that call had changed everything. Price must have been furious with him, he thought, but then again, his agent wasn't aware of anything that had happened. Price was Peter Hanson's literary agent. They met each other at a panel during a conference in Denver. In that year Peter had hoped to be able to attend the conference in person, but the world was still in the midst of the pandemic so the event unfolded entirely remotely. He still got to connect with a lot of other writers and people working in the industry, including a fifty-year-old agent, with an incredibly witty sense of humor and an immense interest for independent authors. Even though Frank Price and Peter were on the same identical wavelength, it took a few months for Peter to convince him to be his literary agent. He pitched the new story he was working on to him and that did the trick. Until that point, Peter had self-published five novels and, even though he had been able to build a bay of readers and followers that loved his work, he had always known that he had to make the jump, to expand his reach to a much broader audience. The royalties were just enough to pay the bills and he had to keep counting on the support of his parents. He knew they were wealthy enough to help him out, until he found his way. Despite the fact that they had always believed in him and supported him as much as they could, the situation had started to weigh on Peter. He was now under contract with a publishing company in New York, with which he had published his collection of short stories: *Tales from Hell.* The book had resonated very well and had enough success to convince the publishing house to keep working with him for his new release: *The Tenant,* which would finally mark his transition to the horror genre. He was on a deadline for an amended manuscript for February of the next year -the hope was to start the pre-release marketing process by then- and he was incredibly late already.

None of that seemed to matter much to him as of right now.

Peter put the dishes to dry on the rack and looked out of the window toward the Harris house, noticing something that had eluded him the other night.

A dark stain stood out near the attic window—the same one where he had seen the shadow in the glowing light of the reading lamp. The stain looked like mold in the old but still discernible white color of the siding, and Peter wondered how he had missed it.

He kept staring, as if there were an energy to it, as if it wanted to be seen, and he felt extremely sad. It stood there like a cancer on the house, and Peter swore, for a moment, it was alive. He could hear the sound it emanated, but he couldn't quite understand if it was really coming from the spot or if he was just about to have a mental breakdown.

The sound of mournful voices, heart-wrenching weeps.

It was inside his head. A thousand flies buzzing around a carcass, the sounds of death and darkness, until it faded in a soft pitch.

*What the hell is going on? Am I losing my goddamn mind?* He rested on the kitchen counter, lowering his head between his elbows. Peter placed his hands on his ears to make the flies stop, to deafen himself from those tormenting screams.

They went away all at once, and the only noise in the room was Luna's low and steady growl, on alert near the door.

"I'm not delusional," he said out loud, petting Luna. "You saw that too, baby girl, didn't you?"

The dog whined to him in return.

"I need a fucking drink. That's what I need."

# 8

The day of the funeral finally arrived, and it was one of the most gorgeous days of fall Peter had any memory of. The sky carried unique shades of blue, reminding him of the ocean, as if the world had turned upside down—which wasn't completely untrue, at least in Peter's mind.

The air was dry, and it brought the sweet scent of the nearby woods. Peter didn't quite know how to feel about it. A tribute to the lives of his mom and dad? Or rather a cruel way for nature to remind him his parents would never be able to enjoy a day like this again?

*What goddamn difference does it make?* he thought, gazing out of the window. His heartbeat raised one notch when he saw the crowd outside. He wasn't ready for this, not by a long shot. Peter once again questioned why any of this was necessary. Funerals were only really for the close friends and acquaintances coming to pay their respects. It wasn't really for his parents because they were dead, getting colder and dryer in the coffins behind him. And the funeral wasn't really for him either; he was already exhausted from the pressure of the event, which hadn't even started yet.

In addition to all of that, Rosa had insisted on having a gathering at the Hanson home, only for the people belonging to the family's inner circle, as if eating food after burying or cremating someone was something to be expected—another request that didn't make any sense, but that he didn't have the will nor the strength to push back against.

He would have paid a considerable amount of money for all this circus to be over right now…and for a whiskey.

And for a cigarette.

*Damn!* He could have killed for one of those cowboy killers.

Among the people in line to pay their respects, there were only a few familiar faces. The majority of them were just people he didn't recognize, but he was sure he had probably met some of them years before. Maybe he had even known their names once. But not now—now it was all a blur.

"I'm so sorry for your loss," and, "My most sincere condolences," closely followed by, "What a tragedy," seemed to be the most popular sentences. Peter kept nodding, saying thank you and shaking hands.

After maybe ten minutes of anonymous faces, he *did* recognize Luke and Vivian Anderson and felt a dangerous wave of emotions raging. Luke was his father's best friend. They had met during their military service in the Navy and had always been there for each other ever since. Peter remembered going to their home in Florida every Spring Break while he was in school. So of course, Luke was here now, his eyes visibly reddened by tears, his face a genuine expression of real pain. When their eyes met, Luke hugged Peter tight and sobbed on his shoulder for a long time. Luke couldn't quite articulate any words, and that made Peter cry too, breaking the fragile defensive wall he had built for the event.

After them, strangers alternated with familiar faces more or less close to the family. Richard Fritz and his wife, Ellen, college friends of both his parents, came to pay their condolences, as well as a lot of other people he didn't know or didn't have memory of.

The crowd that had knotted his stomach before was now giving him a different kind of emotion. It took him a little bit to realize he was now feeling pride—proud of his parents for having had so many people in their lives. All these people had flown from all over the country for this last chance to say goodbye.

All the love these people were demonstrating toward him and his family made Peter feel guilty. An hour ago, he had hoped for these people to just disappear, to leave him alone with his pain, but now, he wanted to thank them all for coming.

The neighbors came too: the Meyers, the man across the street—who Peter hadn't officially met yet and who introduced himself as Jack Sullivan—the Howards, the Bradleys, and of course, Lynn and Frank Harris.

Tears rolling from her swollen eyes, Lynn opened her arms and hugged him.

"Peter…Oh my God, Peter. I don't know what to say," Lynn said.

"It's okay, Mrs. Harris. I don't know what to say either." Peter felt his eyes filling with tears as well.

But while he continued to shake hands, hug people, and recite his pleasantries, the warm thoughts of love he had started to feel disappeared, replaced by the buzzing of flies and the smell of rot, the stench of the unnatural. The screaming faces of his dead parents flashed through his mind, and he grew incredibly cold.

Peter knew whatever he had felt a few days before in his kitchen was back.

And whatever it was, it was close, calling for his attention.

He looked out of the window over the front lawn of Franklin Funeral Home, where the guests had gathered to talk in small groups.

There was a man in the background, apart from the other folks but still mixed in with the crowd. He stood still in his elegant suit, staring at Peter with a horrifying grin on his face.

Peter recognized him immediately, despite the eyes.

Those eyes were nothing like the ones once belonging to the man. They were not human. They were the eyes of a primitive animal with an ancestral hunger.

In the midst of the group conversations happening outside, Peter's old friend, Will Harris, kept staring at him, as if he wanted Peter to be scared, to feel guilty. Under normal circumstances, Peter would have run over and spoken with him, caught up and invited him over for a beer.

But these weren't normal circumstances.

Will Harris had been dead for almost a year.

# 9

A couple of hours later, Peter and Rosa were in the kitchen of the Hanson home. Rosa was setting up all the food the guests had brought with them.

The murmur coming from the den called Peter back to reality.

*I must be losing my mind,* he thought, trying to make sense of what he had experienced at the funeral parlor. He could still see Will at the back of the crowd, that awful grin, but the detail that really stuck with him were those eyes.

It was the third time Peter had had an episode like that: first, the shadow staring from the attic's window of the Harris house; then the stain that seemed to be alive, calling him—the screaming voices, the flies, the rot, the cold, and the sorrow emerging from it.

He poured himself some Four Roses barrel proof in his Glencairn. It was his dad's favorite whiskey ever, The OBSK. Peter remembered his dad trying to explain to him what those letters stood for. It had something to do with the amount of yeast and rye in the recipe, but he couldn't remember now.

Peter walked into the den, and the chatter stopped for a moment.

Another thing his dad had been really good at, in addition to picking excellent whiskey, was talking in public. Again, that was something Pete had never really enjoyed. He thought he was terrible at it. But his dad was not with him anymore, so he guessed it was on him now to entertain the guests.

Peter didn't need to clink his fork on his glass to call for the guests' attention. He was already fully in the spotlight, and his heartbeat raised up a notch.

"Thank you, everyone, for being here. I'm sure Mom and Dad would have loved to see so many friends all at once." He had to pause for a few seconds. The growing knot in his stomach had started migrating to his throat.

"You know…I'm sure you guys miss them…already as much…as much as I do…You were their family…and that cannot be changed…So keep them alive in your memories…and keep telling all those funny stories about them. Keep them alive. Thank you." He raised his glass to the ceiling, and a single tear slid down from his eye, in the same way the whiskey rolled along the wall of the glass containing it.

And so did the guests, toasting to their departed friends.

Later on, sitting on the lounge chair at the corner of the deck, away from the chatter unfolding inside the house, Peter took a sip and exhaled deeply. He focused near the table, on the empty and still rocking chair where his dad used to sit all the time. That's where they would talk about bourbon. Peter imagined his father's voice telling him about the notes he would get from the Michter's Rye: spice, caramel, and the dust of a barn that had been sitting closed from the sun for years.

He fought the urge to light up a cigarette. One would think it would get easier with time, but that was bullshit. He had never struggled so much since he quit. Peter had a mental routine that normally worked pretty well—he would repeat out loud all the things he despised about smoking. He had written a bunch down in a notebook on the day he quit and had memorized them quickly since he had to repeat them to himself several times a day.

*What is happening to me?* he thought, trying to put a logical perspective to things. *Am I hallucinating?* If he was, he hoped it was due to the shock of the last few days, not some kind of condition he had developed. It had felt so real, so cold and dark. The thought of it only made him cringe.

Peter took another sip, letting the whiskey do the job of calming his nerves, realizing how exhausted he was despite all the sleep. His legs were sore, the way they ached the day after a heavy workout. Adrenaline rushed through them, and the vague bother that had started in the back of his neck was the sudden declaration of a bad migraine.

That's why he sighed when he saw a woman walking on the side of the patio, waving at him. Lynn Harris was a tall and slender woman. Back in the day, when he was a teenager, he had had a crush on her. The years had passed, but that didn't take away any of her beauty. She wore a white linen dress and a blue denim jacket. Her blond hair had thinned, and her skin was showing signs of age. But on the contrary, her blue eyes had never been so deep.

Seeing her smile brought back a bunch of memories Peter recognized, not without a light veil of shame. It made him think about one night, a long time ago, when he was having a sleepover at the Harris house. He must have been fifteen, and Will had invited Jeremy Hall as well. They had played cards and watched a movie in Will's room, talked way beyond normal bedtime.

During the night, Peter had woken up thirsty and went down to the kitchen to grab a glass of water from the sink. On the way back, he heard a soft noise coming from Will's parents' bedroom. He noticed the light coming from the gap at the bottom of the door and had gotten closer to eavesdrop.

Yeah, he wasn't proud of it.

That's when he realized Will's parents were having sex. He had returned to Will's room with his heart beating fast. In the hormonal storm raging inside a fifteen-year-old boy, that must have been the moment he started seeing Lynn Harris in a different way.

"Can I sit here for a minute?" she asked.

"Of course," he replied, nodding toward the chair in front.

"What a gorgeous day it is. It feels wrong, almost obscene."

"I was thinking the same thing this morning. They would have loved it." He took another sip of his whiskey and exhaled, turning toward her.

"You know…when I lost Will…" She paused and looked away, trying to mask the tears. "I was gone for a long time. I mean, I was here, but I wasn't, if that makes any sense to you."

"It does," Peter said automatically. He had no idea what she was talking about, and an unsettling feeling took over. The image of Will Harris staring at him from outside the funeral home was another thing that didn't make any sense to him at all.

"Your mom was my best friend. If I'm here today, with what remains of my sanity, it's because of her heart and kindness. She was a healer."

"Yeah. That she was." He wiped a tear from his face.

"A few months after Will passed, she insisted on taking me on a trip out west. She had planned that trip with your dad for a long time. I refused so many times. I didn't want to ruin their time together."

"Yeah. I remember that." And this time, Peter wasn't lying. He clearly remembered his mom telling him about this over the phone.

"She wasn't going to take no as an answer. So, I ended up going. We met this Native American woman in Utah. She claimed to be a medium. I can't remember her name. She had this fire in her eyes. When she looked at me, it was as if she was looking *through* me. There really was something special about her. Anyway, she gave me something to help me grieve."

Mrs. Harris grabbed the purse she had laid on the deck next to the chair and peeked inside it. Peter cleared his voice, took a final sip of whiskey, and sat back straight in the rocking chair, genuinely curious.

She fished something from the handbag and looked at it for a long time, caressing the yellow handkerchief that wrapped it. There were two twines tied at the two ends. She whispered something he couldn't hear, then joined both her hands—in the way someone drinking water from a fountain would do—and slowly stretched her arms to get the object closer to him, keeping her head down, almost as if she were praying.

*It must be something really important to her*, he thought, given the care she treated it with. Peter picked the object carefully from her hands. It was very light, and the wrap was coarse and dry to the touch.

"Thank you, Mrs. Harris."

She finally looked up at him, her eyes red from crying. Her features were serious for a few seconds, somehow making Peter incredibly uncomfortable. Then she gave him a weak smile.

"This has helped me greatly, in the darkest times. I want you to have it now."

"Thank you. I really appreciate it."

Lynn got up, composed herself, grabbed her purse, and smiled at him again before turning and stepping into the house.

Peter had been tempted to ask about the stain near the attic's window. As a matter of fact, he wanted to ask her if Frank had been hanging out at night around that same window, just as much as he wanted to ask her why in the living hell he had seen her dead son at the funeral home.

He remained sitting on the chair, staring at the object in his hands, applying a gentle pressure to it and trying to feel its shape. The coldness of the thing permeated through the dry, shriveled-up fabric and spread on his palm. For a moment, when he wrapped his fingers around it with a firm grip, he could swear the object was vibrating. There was some sort of energy to it, the kind only truly ancient things have bound to themselves.

He slowly undid the twines on both ends and unwrapped it. The handkerchief came loose in his palm, revealing a pendant made of some kind of metal. That surprised him, considering how incredibly light it felt.

On one side of the metal circular plate was an engraved symbol of a man and a woman. They were both upside down. As if they were hanging by their feet.

Peter suddenly felt uneasy, as if he was being observed. A strong and gusty wind raised, swinging the tall—now almost naked—trees in the wooded area at the back of the house. There was a subtle shift in the air. A hint of ice in it, the promise of the winter cold surrounding him.

He shivered, looking at the relic in his hand once more, feeling the low, pulsating energy. Then he quickly put it back in the wrap and threw it in his jacket pocket.

Someone or something was there.

And he felt paralyzed by the obviousness of it. Peter looked out to the woods but didn't see anything out of the ordinary. Nobody seemed to be there, but he was certain something *was* staring at him from a distant spot.

Peter Hanson was not a superstitious man, nor had he ever been when he was a kid. He had always been naturally attracted to dark things from a very young age, the one in his group telling scary stories and creeping the hell out of all his friends. Peter had loved the mystery, the thrill, the horror. He was naturally drawn to serial killers, monsters of the human kind and of the paranormal variety. Ghosts, spirits, and evil creatures were ultimately the reasons for his life choices, like the one to become a writer.

He had always looked for the darkness and the evil, fantasized over it and tried to put it in words.

But he had never experienced it or had any reason to believe in it…until now.

For the first time in his thirty-five years, Peter Hanson was absolutely sure he was in the presence of pure evil.

He went back inside the house, making sure to lock the door behind him.

# 10

Peter woke up in his bed, covered in sweat. His throat was as dry as sandpaper. He reached out in the darkness with his right arm until he found his water bottle. Still panting, he drank avidly, as if he hadn't had anything to drink in ages. The cold water felt good on the walls of his throat. Peter reached for his phone on the nightstand and couldn't find it. He eventually located it hidden in the blankets next to him.

3:58 a.m. Witching hour.

For a moment, he thought his parents might be alive, sleeping one off in the quietness of their bedroom on the other side of the hallway. Maybe he had just awakened from a nightmare. Maybe the funeral, Will Harris, and the horrible feeling of dread he had experienced in the past days were all just a horrible dream.

Something on his left moved.

He couldn't tell how, since the room was quieter than a tomb, but he did. And then he felt it.

Something was there with him.

He couldn't move, paralyzed. He saw the shadow on the wall through his peripheral. It was darker than the darkness. That's how he knew it was there, and it was waiting for him to see it. The utter silence of the room was unreal. A smothering sense of stillness, a smell of something burnt, charred.

Peter could move, but he didn't want to. He was afraid that the shadow was sensitive to the faintest changes in the pattern of the air.

The silence ceased when someone knocked on the door of his room.

Three knocks he knew very well, three knocks he had known his whole life.

His heart sank in his chest, and he couldn't talk. Peter couldn't move because the shadow was still there on the wall, and if he looked at it, he knew he would never be able to get rid of it. Peter didn't want to see it.

Three knocks again.

The same knocks his dad had used every night of Peter's life, when he wanted to wish his son a good night. Peter started crying, remembering a lot of those times when his dad would just swing by. Sometimes just for a couple of minutes to catch up on things. Some other times for hours, talking about everything. His dad had been his best friend, and Peter missed him terribly.

The door slammed open, and hid dad's shadow appeared at the door. There was a feeble red light behind him, coming from the hallway.

*Peter.*

The voice that came out was not his dad's voice. It sounded

hellish, distorted, as if it came from one of those devices that manipulated voices, like Peter had seen in anonymous interviews.

But it wasn't only that.

The voice wasn't human. It was the least human thing Peter had ever heard. There was a depth to it that vibrated in the room and his chest, the sound of a beast snarling and sniffing.

*Peter, look at me, boy.*

He wished to be dead, right there and then. He couldn't look. Couldn't move.

Peter closed his eyes, like when he was a kid, and wished, whatever it was, that it would go away.

When he reopened his eyes, it was dark again.

The door was closed, there was no shadow on the wall.

He looked at his phone again: 6:29 a.m.

One minute later his alarm went off.

# 11

Luna slept on the kitchen floor, resting her body against his leg. Peter looked at the Word editor window on his MacBook Pro—a graduation gift from both his parents. He could still remember the letter that had accompanied it, the look of pride in their eyes, the wishes of great success as a writer, and his own tears wetting the paper and staining the ink through which they reminded him, once more, of their unconditional love.

It had been ten years ago, and that laptop was the most valuable thing he owned. Especially now that they were both gone. Peter felt as if it was the only thing he had left of them, besides the memories. And those would eventually fade. The memories would start disappearing, and the laptop would stop functioning at some point, but what was going to come out of that laptop would be forever.

Peter had always been determined to make every word written on that laptop count.

He would make them proud.

But not today.

Today, he stared at the screen, reading and re-reading the last few chapters he had written before that damned phone call. How different things had been when he was writing those words and sentences. His life was going well, the words were flowing, and he was full of hope as he worked on his novel.

Then he got the call. And everything changed.

The words were blurry in the chaos of thoughts in his mind. Unable to funnel the words, he stared at the screen with dead eyes. All he could do was try to make some sort of sense of what had happened the previous night. But his efforts were in vain.

Peter wrapped his hands around the cup of coffee in front of him, letting it thaw them. He got up and walked to the window, moving the curtain to peek at his backyard.

The day was gray, and the bare trees in the woods stuck out against the overcast. The few leaves left were not going to last long. They were all down, covering the grass, which had stopped growing and providing fertile ground for the squirrels still busy putting on some fat for the winter. He could hear the fallen foliage crunching softly under their weight.

On the left, his neighbor's garage door was fully open, and Frank Harris worked in it. The whirring sound of the circular saw he used for one of his pet projects....Fresh lumber on the side, ready to be cut...

That was when he felt there was something different about the house. But Peter couldn't exactly pin it down to anything specific. Something was out of place. Something that made him very uncomfortable on a subconscious level.

It came to him…

Peter scanned the side of the house, from the garage door to the second story, focusing on the white siding.

The large dark stain of mold was gone.

It had been there just a couple of days earlier.

What were the odds that Frank had repainted the siding? Slim to none. If Frank had painted it, there would be a visible difference in that area, and there wasn't one. Maybe Frank power-washed it? But Peter abandoned the idea because of the dust and dirt still spread uniformly on the planks. The siding showed its age and dirtiness, just not the stain anymore. It had vanished, leaving no marks or sign of its passage on the house.

Only the memory, which felt alive, carrying an energy to it.

Not for the first time, Peter seriously contemplated the possibility he was about to lose his mind. So he decided to go for a run to clear his head. Back in New Orleans, he had formed the healthy habit of running every other day. It helped his writing, his body, and his mental wellbeing. On top of that, running through the streets of the French Quarter had been a unique sensorial experience. Peter loved New Orleans—every bit of it was poignant with mystery and tradition, with legends and the occult.

It felt strange to get out of the house and run through his old neighborhood. Peter had spent his whole life there, and despite some things being exactly the same, everything felt different.

Everything *was* different now.

He ran east on Fifteenth Street, crossing Main Street, then going north on Crawfordsville Road. His mind went to one of his first dates, when he was sixteen and had just gotten his driver's license. He remembered his dad giving him the keys to his gray Chevy Colorado, repeatedly asking him to drive carefully and to be home by ten. Peter had taken Jennifer Mills to Mug N' Bun for a hamburger and a root beer and then to the park, where they talked, laughed, and made out until it was time to go.

He wondered what kind of life she had now. The thought made him smile, and he wished he could teleport himself back to those days, when everything felt lighter.

Peter turned east and kept running until he crossed the old trail and followed it all the way around. By the time he was back in his neighborhood, his Apple Watch reported he had run a little more than four miles. He stopped in front of his house to stretch and cool down. A man on the other side of the street waved at him. Peter smiled and waved back.

It was Jack Sullivan.

The old man had introduced himself briefly at the Hanson house after the funeral. He was a tall and slender man, with deeply carved wrinkles on his forehead. His hair was white and thin, combed softly backward, making it look as if it were made of cotton. Jack wore a pair of jeans at least one size too large, his skinny legs seeming to swim in them. His blue and white checkered flannel shirt was tucked inside the jeans, and its sleeves were rolled up to the elbows. His glasses hung from a retainer around his neck. The face of a man who had suffered but had been able to maintain a layer of kindness—at least on the surface.

Jack Sullivan's house was across the street from Peter's. The road curved, going west, just on the right, making pedestrians blind to oncoming traffic. His mother's voice emerged from his memories, admonishing him for crossing the road there. Pete was supposed to walk east until the stop sign and cross, where the road was straight and there was enough visibility. He hadn't always followed his mother's recommendations, and that made him feel bad. He wished he could hear her voice once more.

Peter quickly checked on his right for oncoming cars and headed across quickly.

When Jack Sullivan saw he was coming, he left the rake near the neat pile of leaves he had patiently built.

"Mr. Sullivan, how are you doing today?" Peter greeted him with a smile.

"I'm doing good, Peter, and please, call me Jack. No need to make me feel older than I am." He giggled. There was something soothing about the man. His attitude and kindness made him feel like a safe space.

"Can I help you out with those leaves?"

"Oh, don't worry. I got it. It's not that I have much to do these days, and a man can only read so many hours. If you take this task away from me, I wouldn't know how to spend the time anyway." Jack winked at him. "If anything, I was going to propose helping you out with *your* yard work. If you ever need any help, just give me a holler. You know where to find me."

Peter looked at his own front yard and realized it was the only one in the neighborhood still covered with a thick carpet of leaves. He felt a little ashamed.

"Thank you. I really appreciate it. I'm going to have to take care of it sooner rather than later."

Jack Sullivan smiled, gently shook his head, and said, "You know, you were pretty busy with way more important things. Like I said, if you need help, I'm here. Do you want to come in? I was going to make some coffee."

Peter accepted without hesitation. He needed *some* form of human interaction to get out of his own head for a bit, to get distracted, and he felt Jack Sullivan might be his best option. Since that damned phone call and all that had followed, everyone had treated Peter with respect and courtesy—which was great—yet it was soaked in some sort of social convention, as if that were the universally accepted way to be a good neighbor or friend.

But Peter picked up on the distance people put between him and themselves. He didn't blame them for it—he would have reacted in the same exact way. Show your respect, give your condolences, and offer your help. But Jack Sullivan hadn't put that distance between them. He spoke to Peter without pretending to feel his pain, without the need to show how sorry he was for his loss. And this made Peter feel like their interaction was real.

Peter had already been inside Jack's house several years earlier, when the Oakleys had lived there. They weren't exactly the closest friends or neighbors to his family, but they had always been cordial with them and often invited the Hansons over, especially when they put the barbecue to work in the summer. They didn't have any kids, which had always made Peter a little resistant to go there since there wasn't anyone his age to play with. They had eventually moved to Texas.

The house was modest but very well kept. The front door led into a single open space. A small kitchen with a bar-style countertop was set up on the right side, and on the left was the living room. A circular table with four chairs rested in one corner, and further down was a loveseat in front of a fireplace.

Bookshelves filled the walls of the living room, different sizes and styles, housing hundreds and hundreds of books. There was no TV in the room, which made Peter think about one of the things his dad always used to tell him—"Never trust a man whose house has a TV bigger than his book shelves." According to that philosophy, Jack Sullivan was a man to be trusted.

"I like your house. It's very cozy," Peter said, remembering how different that room looked when the Oakleys lived there.

"Thanks. It's way too big and empty for me, and I hardly get any visitors these days, so I use the spare bedroom to store some of the books that don't fit in here." Jack smiled. "No such thing as too many books for me. They are the best company."

Peter was fascinated by how many volumes the man owned, some of which were really rare editions. These were deservedly showcased in the only bookshelf with a protective glass.

"Amen," Peter agreed, kneeling and looking with disbelief at a first edition of Stephen King's *IT*.

The coffee machine started brewing with its steaming sound just as Jack Sullivan returned to the living room.

"So I've heard that you are a writer, huh?"

"Yeah, something like that." Peter answered humbly.

"How's that going for you? Have you published any of your work yet?"

"It's a pretty tough world. I have a few books that I self-published, mainly true crime, but two years ago I signed a contract with a publishing house, they published my collection of short stories last year. It's called *Tales from Hell*. It seems to be doing really well."

"Are you working on a new project?"

"Indeed, *The Tenant* should be out in the fall of next year. It's my first peek in the horror genre."

"Good for you. I look forward to reading it. That sounds right up my alley!"

"Thanks. There are so many of my favorite books on your shelves."

"I read a little bit of everything, but I'm mainly attracted to those kinds of books. And not only fiction. In fact, the majority of my books are non-fiction."

"Why do you think you are attracted to this genre, if you don't mind me asking?"

Jack Sullivan sighed, and the expression on his face shifted, as if he had been reminded of something bad, something that hurt.

"Because I believe in evil things. I have been witness to evil, and it was too close for comfort. So many people read about evil as if it was only a work of fiction, a tale to tell to spook yourself or others. I read about evil because I study it. I need to study it to defend myself from it."

Peter frowned and stared at him, not quite sure how to respond to the statement.

Jack smiled, amused, then walked to the kitchen and came back with a cup of coffee. He invited Peter to take a seat.

"I used to be an exorcist. Back in my days," Jack said. "That's not the best word to describe my previous job, but I found that's the part that most people understand."

# 12

Peter let the hot water of the shower hit him straight in the face. In the storming sound of the water rushing, his mind was still humming from the absurd sequence of events that had happened in the last couple of weeks. His parents were dead, and they probably died screaming at the top of their lungs. Was it a…suicide? Those words he hadn't yet been able to pronounce were still punching hard. *Was it my dad that decided that? Or did they agree on it?* And either way, why would they ever do such a thing? How in the world did they decide it was a good idea to leave him with these questions? How selfish could they possibly have been?

It was impossible to even contemplate. They would have never done that.

Or maybe it *was* possible, after all. Maybe he didn't know anything about his parents. Wasn't there a remote chance they were suffering and he didn't know about it? No answers to be found now, nor in the future. How was he supposed to move on from this?

Then there was the stain on the Harris's house. It had provoked a delusion—he had heard voices screaming and wailing, and the flies, smelled the sweet stench of decay, just after looking at it.

*Maybe the cancer has moved inside my house*, he thought.

There had been the nightmares, the shadow in the room, and the paralyzing fear that came with it.

And then there was Will. Peter had literally seen his best friend staring at him at the funeral parlor, but Will Harris had been dead for a while. Peter remembered the day his mother had called him with the news.

Peter and Will had once been inseparable, one the shadow of the other. Will never had any intention to go to college. Despite his parents' constant attempts to convince him to give it a try, he had always been determined to find a job and start earning, had dreamed about a simple life in his hometown, and was never ashamed of his lack of ambition. The thought of that first joint, when they were sixteen, still lingered in the back of his mind. Some things just have their way of escalating, to slip out of control, and it didn't take long for Will to go from the occasional joint to the regular use and, ultimately, to dealing pot to make ends meet. Money had never been a concern for Peter, but it was definitely tight for Will. Under the thunderous sound of the water in the shower, Peter thought about the day he had decided to go away from Indiana, leaving everything behind, especially that first joint, as if running away would bring Will back on the right track. While Peter had been able to leave that part of his adolescence behind, Will had stuck with it. Undoubtedly, Peter had his small dose of popularity in his senior year and invited Will to a lot of parties. It didn't take long for him to get in contact with way stronger stuff than weed. It helps me to feel more, he used to say when things started to get out of control, when they were still in high school. Peter never thought that Will had any problems in feeling. If anything, it would have been good for him to have something that made him feel less rather than more. Even when Peter was about to leave, Will had pretended to be happy for him. Maybe he truly was, but he struggled to mask the sadness of their paths parting.

"You go on, Peter, and kick some ass," Will had said to him the night before Peter's departure to college. "I'll always be your number one fan. Just don't forget to call me. I want to know everything. I'll be all right here."

And Peter *did* call him, almost every day…at the beginning. Then he met Susan Briggs in his creative writing class. She wrote poetry, and he just amazed by how talented she was. Not even two weeks after they started dating, he was so focused on her and their relationship, the calls to Will became only once a week. Then a couple of times a month. Then none at all.

They would still hang out and see each other every time Peter went back home on one of his breaks, but something had changed. They both knew but never talked about it.

Peter watched his best friend slip away from him. He loved Will, but for some reason, he had known it was inevitable that they would part ways. The boys were growing up, changing, exploring their own paths. And those paths were diverging, getting more and more distant as the time passed.

During the phone calls with his mother, Jane had often told him about seeing Will at the grocery store or just walking home. Will would always wave at her but wasn't stopping anymore to talk and ask about Peter.

"It breaks my heart," she had said once, "to see you guys parting ways. Has anything happened between the two of you?"

His dad had seen Will hanging out with some sketchy people in town. Peter's mom was really close with Will's mother, and inevitably, when things started to go downhill, Lynn Harris had opened up with Jane.

"He's lost a lot of weight, Peter. He rented a one-bedroom apartment downtown and is always asking his parents for money. He might be using, Peter. Would you do me a favor and call to check on him? I beg you, do it for me."

And Peter did call him. When Will answered the phone, Peter could barely recognize his voice. It was coarse and without light in it.

"Hey, Hanson. What's up?" Will had never called Peter by his last name, knowing how much Peter hated it. He didn't seem in the mood to talk, and there was loud music in the background. "I can't hear you very well. I've got a few of my buddies at my place." He was slurring, clearly high on something.

"I'm worried about you, Will," Peter had said.

And as a response, Will had hung up on him.

That was the last time Peter had spoken to Will Harris. One week later, his mother called him in tears to tell him Will had been found dead in his bed, choked in his own vomit.

The guilt came out all of a sudden, and the tears for all his losses poured and mixed with the hot water, but they didn't purge his grieving heart.

Peter had refused to go to Will's funeral. He just couldn't bring himself to do it, despite his mother begging him to come.

And now, the words of Jack Sullivan, a man who had been a witness of evil things, echoed loudly in his head.

A former exorcist.

Peter felt watched, observed.

Was it possible he had become a target of some sort of malevolent entity? Was it possible what he wrote and loved to read so much about had now become a real problem in his life? A fight had started, and it was straining his mind, testing its limits and his own beliefs. It was all so irrational. Nothing made sense, and the only things that seemed to click together were so out of normality, he was scared to admit them to himself.

*I used to be an exorcist. Back in my days.*

The old man's words reverberated loudly in his mind. Peter wished he hadn't left so soon. He had questions that, for some reason, he was sure Jack could answer. Peter just wasn't sure if he was ready to hear them. Whatever the possibilities were, he couldn't quite fathom them, couldn't say them out loud.

Because he was terrified of them.

# Part Two:

# Cooper

# 1

Detective Robert Cooper brought his navy-blue Buick Sedan to a halt in front of the elementary school and looked at the young man sitting on the passenger side. The boy was only seven years old and had just started second grade, but the more time passed, the more Cooper could see his wife's features on him.

"All right, champ! Be a good boy, okay?"

"Dad! You promised we could put the siren on," the boy complained in a whiny tone.

"I know, I know. We will when I pick you up later, okay?"

"Okay." The boy seemed totally unconvinced of his father's promise. He clumsily opened the door and slammed it close, throwing his whole tiny body onto it.

"Aren't you forgetting something?" Cooper said, lowering the passenger side window.

"I love you." The boy rolled his eyes, smiling.

"I love you more. Do good things today."

The boy nodded, turned, and ran toward the school's entrance, merging into a river of other small humans. Cooper smiled proudly and watched him running, his lunch bag swinging back and forth from his hand.

*It doesn't get any easier*, Cooper thought, struggling to accept how quickly the time had flown and how much, day after day, his boy kept growing. It was a bittersweet reminder of the human he and Caroline were bringing up and the relentless, inevitable separation that would come one day.

Cooper shifted into drive and cruised toward the police station located a couple of miles north.

Just like every morning, he raised two fingers over the wheel to Ricky Mortimer, a.k.a. Morty, who promptly raised the parking barrier bar from his station and nodded his acknowledgment. Cooper parked in the third row, got out of the car and walked toward the back entrance. He waved at the agents ending their shifts and going home, and he couldn't help but remember the days he had been on night patrol—how awful his biological clock was during that time.

Cooper badged his way inside the building and went through the metal detector, making sure to place his badge, gun, and wallet in the dedicated circular tray.

When he was cleared, he collected his belongings and turned right, opting for the stairs instead of the elevator.

Two floors later, he walked into the Homicide Division, grabbing a quick cup of joe from the coffee station that had recently been moved about five feet behind his desk—a blessing and a curse at the same time since every detective thought it was also the place where conversations had to naturally happen.

The desk of Jimmy Fowler, his partner, was empty, just like it had been the day before. Jimmy had been put on paid leave the previous week after losing his shit with the captain, basically telling him to go fuck himself. Harry Davis, the captain of the unit, was already working on the paperwork to fire him. Cooper had been able to talk him out of it, blaming the excessive stress the division was under and asking for a personal favor. Eventually, Davis had agreed to put Fowler on paid leave, and Cooper had practically forced Jimmy to take that time off. Fowler had flown to Florida to blow off some steam.

Cooper sat at his desk and logged into his computer, the screen showing the report he had left unfinished the day before. It was a case of domestic violence—of course it was. There seemed to be nothing else lately *but* domestic abuse cases to work on. He gave it a quick read, corrected a couple of typos, and sent it to the printer.

As he walked over to collect it, he saw Davis talking on the phone in his office, waving him over with excessive energy.

Cooper entered the room, and Davis hung up the phone.

"Goddamn." The man brought his hands to the bald top of his head. "Are we ever going to catch a fucking break?"

"What have you got for me?" Cooper asked, trying to conceal a grin.

Davis looked at him for a long time, like he usually did when trying to think about the next move. He was one of the best detectives Cooper had ever worked with, and he was glad to call him his mentor. Everything that Cooper knew about the job, he owed to Harry Davis.

"Two bodies on the west side. I was just on the phone with Speedway Police. They need an expert set of eyes on this one. As if we have people to spare these days. Fucking bodies everywhere." Davis handed Cooper a brown folder.

"And what is so special about this one?" Cooper started to flick through the pages.

"I don't know, and I'm not sure I want to. I'm not even sure if I should be happy or not."

Davis clearly referred to the homicide count that had spiked, especially on the east side of town. There was a shooting between rival gangs pretty much every day.

The problem was that not even ten percent of these homicides were ever solved, and many unsolved cases were really bad news, especially before an election. Davis was under pressure from his superiors to double the ratio of solved homicides by the end of the year.

"I'm on it, boss," Cooper said, leaving the office.

"Keep me posted on this one," Davis yelled from his desk.

Twenty minutes later, Cooper arrived at the scene and parked behind the EMS vehicle and the coroner's white van. Several patrol cars already occupied the driveway, their lights still on. Small groups of people, whom Cooper judged as the neighbors, had formed on both sides of the street, just behind the yellow ribbon establishing the crime scene's perimeter, with concern and shock on their faces.

He exited the car, and everyone turned to look at him: EMS staff, police, and spectators.

There had been a time when Cooper was proud of the attention detectives usually got. It made him feel as if he were respected and recognized, the man in charge of the case, and all the sacrifices he had made were worth it. But now, it was just routine for him. When he walked into a crime scene, the only thing Cooper cared about these days was talking with the people who discovered the body and making sure it hadn't been contaminated by idiots.

Two agents walked toward him when he approached the driveway. He recognized the tall one on the right, Stevenson. The one on the left looked very pale and in apparent discomfort.

"Detective Cooper," Stevenson said, shaking his hand. "Thanks for coming over. This is Agent Gilliam. He is the one that was dispatched after a 911 call made by Rosa Cortez, the maid."

"Tell me everything." Cooper turned to agent Gilliam. "Then we walk the scene."

"I'm not going back in there." As if the sole idea had awakened his memory, Gilliam turned to the freshly mowed grass and retched.

"Jesus Christ, get him out of my crime scene." Cooper started walking to the front door. "Fill me in, Stevenson?"

Stevenson told Cooper everything from the 911 call to the officers approaching the bodies. Cooper nodded and took a few notes in his notebook, then put it back in the inside pocket of his velvet brown jacket. He stopped near the front door to check for signs of tampering, but he could find none.

"Have you talked to the maid yet?" Cooper asked.

"Yes, sir," Stevenson said proudly. "We've got her full deposition."

Cooper looked around at the houses surrounding him.

"This doesn't look like a neighborhood where people lock their doors at night, does it?" Cooper asked with a hint of sarcasm.

"I'm not sure, sir, but clearly, there are no signs of a break-in."

Stevenson led the way upstairs, and Cooper noticed the strong odor of chemicals used by the forensic team. It mixed with the familiar stench of decomposition filling the house. *Some smells,* Cooper thought, going up the stairs, *just never go away.*

At the top were two agents from the Speedway Police Department, staring inside the primary bedroom. One had a large professional camera in his hands, lights flashing at every shot.

Stevenson grabbed his arm before Cooper could step forward. "Just so you know…this is a strange one to see."

Cooper looked at him and nodded. *Is there ever a non-strange one?* he thought, approaching the door. The smell went up a notch.

But he understood what Stevenson had tried to warn him about.

Cooper was stunned, but in a way he wasn't expecting. There was no blood in the room—that was the first shock—yet the scene was extremely odd and disturbing in a very singular way.

The lifeless bodies of a man and a woman Stevenson had called Mr. and Mrs. Hanson were sitting on the bed, legs stretched out and backs on the headboard. They were both naked and wan, but that wasn't odd…

The only thing throwing Cooper off was that both of their faces had remained stuck, paralyzed in what looked like an awful screaming expression. Mouths and eyes wide open. Cooper didn't think he had seen anything like that in his entire career.

He walked inside the room and scanned the scene. One of the guys from the forensic team was collecting a sample of a thick and transparent fluid glaring on the pale skin of both bodies. Cooper looked at the drooling wake following the tip of the swab before it went inside a cylindrical tube, then into a brown envelope with other evidence—all properly photographed and cataloged with numbers.

There were no signs of a break-in on the windows, and Cooper doubted someone could have climbed to them anyway. They faced the tallest part of the house, which Cooper judged to be at least eighteen. He looked down at more police agents searching the side of the yard for evidence.

Cooper turned back to the bodies and sighed.

Whatever had happened in that room, Mr. and Mrs. Hanson had died buried in terror and fear. Their mouths stretched open in what must have been guttural, terrible screams.

Stevenson waved at him from the hallway. "They found something in the basement you might want to see."

"Lead the way," Cooper said, following him.

The basement was finished, with floors covered in soft, clean carpets and walls painted a light cream. All the trims showed no signs of dust or spider webs. The place was either used daily as another living space or had been cleaned very recently, Cooper thought, comparing it with his own dusty and unfinished basement.

An officer from the fire department was pointing his flashlight inside a closet.

"What have we got here?" Cooper asked, peeking inside.

"This might be a sign of tampering on the furnace's exhausts, sir!"

Cooper nodded and remained there for a long time. There was a clear gap between the pipe and the gasket at the end of it.

*Carbon monoxide*, Cooper thought, looking around.

"What about that?" Cooper uttered, pointing at the sensor mounted on the wall near the bottom of the staircase.

"We don't know if the sensor is working. It didn't set the alarm off."

"Make sure you guys take photos of everything," Cooper said, then walked back upstairs and out of the house through the front door.

"What are you thinking, Cooper?" Stevenson asked.

"I don't know what I'm thinking," Cooper responded as he brooded, looking at the people beyond the perimeter line. The spectators had doubled compared to when he had arrived. He noticed the van of Channel 13, the local media channel. Among the crowd, he noticed two women sitting on the step of the EMS vehicle. One was Hispanic, in her late fifties, dark hair worn in a bun. She couldn't stop crying while hiding her face between her hands. The other was white, blonde with green eyes, rubbing her back, trying to console her. Cooper wasn't sure what was wrong with what he was looking at, but he sensed something being off. The blonde woman stared into the void in front of her, almost like she was in a different place. The shock probably, Cooper thought.

"Who are those two ladies in the EMS vehicle?"

"Rosa Cortez, the maid that called 911. The other is Lynn Harris, the neighbor." Stevenson said, looking at his file and pointing to the house next to the Hanson's.

Cooper kept staring at the blonde: her head was slightly tilted to the side while she absently consoled the Hispanic woman. There was something in her eyes that he had never seen before. A sense of madness, despair and utter emptiness twirled around her. It was like looking at a rag doll forgotten on a shelf in a dusty attic.

Cooper's phone buzzed in his pocket. He looked at the screen. It was Davis.

"Cooper."

"I found the son, closest relative. Peter Hanson. He lives in New Orleans. Do you want me to make the call?" Davis asked.

Cooper was tempted to accept his offer, but the years on the job had taught him that it was better to take care of some conversations personally, no matter how tough they were. That was another thing he had learned from Davis. He knew the question was rhetorical.

"I'll do it. Just text me the number," Cooper said. Then, before Davis could hang up, "Hey, boss?"

"Yep."

"Is this the Peter Hanson that I'm thinking of? The writer?"

"I wish I had the time to read. I'll send you the contact right away." Then he hung up.

"I have to make a phone call," he said to Stevenson.

Cooper rested his back against one of the front porch's posts, fished a Marlboro from his pack, and lit it up. He took a long draw, inhaling the smoke deep into his lungs. The nicotine hit his brain in a fraction of a second, and his muscles relaxed. He took a deep breath, ready to dial Peter Hanson's number, mentally preparing himself for the news he was about to share. His news would soon destroy another life, to complete the destruction of the entire Hanson family. He had to have so many of those conversations in his career, but the knot he felt in his stomach was still like the first time.

It never got any easier.

There was never a unique reaction to deeply upsetting and utterly shocking news. Back in his Chicago PD days, he had knocked on a few doors to communicate that people had been murdered or simply found dead. Cooper remembered every single visit he had to pay. He remembered the concern on the faces that so hopefully relied on every word that came out of his mouth. He recalled that hope dimming, crashing against reality, like a beautiful and foamy wave smashing on a rock in the ocean, shattering, dispersing and destroying itself. The hope would die and become incredulity. The human brain was naturally designed to protect an individual from traumatic events. Cooper remembered the people he had to pay a visit to, shaking their heads as if they were desperately trying to wake up from a nightmare they couldn't possibly sustain. Ultimately, the incredulity would morph into something different again. It would become a realization, and it would hit them in the face with the violence of a truck. The realization would crush them, make them faint, or scream at the top of their lungs. The pain was too significant and sudden to be accepted all at once. Cooper remembered people refusing to believe him, calling him names and hugging him. Some people became numb and distant, disconnecting from a reality that couldn't be processed. The news that he brought and the reaction of the people who had to hear the news from him were something that would haunt Robert Cooper for the rest of his life.

He took another long, deep breath and called Peter Hanson while the bodies of his dead parents were carried in black bags on stretchers and loaded into the coroner's van.

## 2

Eleven days after the discovery of Mr. and Mrs. Hanson's bodies, Cooper parked in front of the Marion County Coroner building. The parking lot was empty. He was ten minutes early, so when he turned the engine off, he took his time to decompress, hands still resting on the steering wheel. He was tired and sleep-deprived. This case was very different from anything he had worked on recently. He exited the car and walked inside the building, still thinking about all the evidence, pictures of the crime scene, and forensic discoveries he had repeatedly analyzed in the past days. The only real lead he had was the tampering with the furnace, which might have caused a carbon monoxide leak. The strange fact that undermined the leading theory was the complete absence of CO in the house at the time of the discovery of the bodies. If the leak stopped at any given point, it wasn't entirely unreasonable that the CO had dissipated through the doors' and windows' gaps.

Cooper received a call from the coroner's office an hour earlier to communicate that the final report from the autopsy was ready, and the detective was dying to have new elements that could shed light on the case.

Cooper was waiting in the lobby when a voice called him from behind, making him flinch. He turned and saw Dr. Julian Rigg rushing toward him as he carried a brown paper bag with his lunch and a large soda from Burger King. Cooper had always admired how he could be friendly, extremely cold and professional at the same time. When it came to the job, he was one of the most brilliant in his field.

"How's it going, Julian?" Cooper asked as he waited for him to catch up.

"Going alright. How are you?" he said, completely out of breath.

"Not too bad. You know why I'm here, don't you?"

"Results are in," Julian said, leaning over onto a badge reader. The elevator's door in front of him opened, and once they were both in, Cooper pushed the button that would lead them to the basement. It wasn't a reason for pride, but he knew his way around this building. He had visited it more times than he liked to admit. Cooper hoped the man could answer some of the questions that had been tormenting him.

The main question was, of course, practical: Would the autopsy results reveal some other possibility that didn't involve a suicide? Everything seemed to point to that. He couldn't prove that anyone was in the house with the Hansons at the time of their death. The signs of tampering with the furnace and the psychological state of Mr. Hanson, who Cooper discovered had a prescription for anti-depressants, was a slam dunk for Davis to close the case as a suicide. In his heart, he almost hoped that someone else had killed the Hansons. It wasn't because he had hoped there was a cold-blooded murderer free at large but because it would have made some sort of difference for Peter Hanson. Suicide was something that couldn't be explained or ever understood and fully accepted by the ones who were left behind. Cooper had experienced that firsthand.

And that led to his second question: if it had been a double suicide, or a homicide-suicide, committed by Mr. Hanson, why was no suicide letter found at the scene? From a statistical point of view, it was extremely unlikely for people who died by suicide not to leave any trace of their reasons.

Dr. Rigg walked to his desk, where he left his lunch, then crouched to reach the bottom drawer, out of which he fished what Cooper imagined to be the final autopsy report. It was bound by three staples on the left side. The medical examiner handed it to Cooper, who looked at the many pages of the report and then threw it on the desk.

"Really?" He asked with a sarcastic tone he knew he could safely use with Julian Rigg.

"I figured you wouldn't want to read it," Rigg said, amused. "Patience has never been your forte, Cooper."

"Are you going to give me a summary or what?"

"Long story short, I cannot conclude that these people have died of carbon monoxide intoxication." Julian cut to the chase.

"What?"

"There is a stunning amount of evidence that doesn't support that as the cause of death. The blood results and the toxicology report are clear. There was no trace of high CO concentrations or other drugs in their systems. And that's only one data point." Julian paused to take a sip of his Diet Coke. "In severe CO intoxication that leads to death, we would see evident lesions on pretty much all of the tissue. We would see a triumph of cherry red in the organs. That happens when the carboxy myoglobin is formed in the blood. It's basically CO poisoning 101. There are no signs of that kind of damage in either of the deceased. There is no trace of acute pulmonary edema. These people, Cooper, didn't die because of a leak."

"What killed them?"

"That's where things get interesting," Julian said as he grabbed the report and stopped on one specific page. "Even though we didn't find damage related to CO intoxication, we did find lesions on the heart.

"These," Julian said as he pointed his finger to the report's page. "This damage points to myocardial infarction. And this is not only on one of the deceased but on both."

"A heart attack?" Cooper asked.

"Precisely. A strong one, given the extent of the damage."

Cooper found himself not completely surprised. That could explain the look on their faces, but how in the world did that happen to both of them at the same time? The odds of it occurring naturally were infinitesimal. Something just felt incredibly off. Something he couldn't quite put his finger on yet.

"What's your best guess on the time of death?" Cooper asked, brooding.

"Judging from the rigor and the samples, 3 a.m."

"Is that why they looked like that? The facial expression. Was it the pain from the heart attack?" Cooper asked, without even realizing he was thinking out loud as the memory of the bodies flashed in his mind. They died trapped in a nightmare, trapped in an eternal scream of pain and terror.

"It is possible. I can't quite comment on that, but the heart attack happening on both of them at the same time is absolutely off the chart when it comes to probability. But it's not impossible. I know this will sound absurd, but off the record, it's like they were scared to death."

Those words hit Cooper hard and opened up an endless list of questions.

"Is it possible that they took some drugs that caused it? I mean, at the same time?"

"The toxicology report is clear, Cooper. They were clean."

He took the report off Julian's desk and thanked him for his work, then started to walk toward the door, thinking about the bodies again. He was incapable of explaining the absurdity of their story; the irrationality of it was just mesmerizing. And he was now part of that story. He felt his responsibility to give a voice to them, not to let this be just a crazy story that would one day be forgotten. They did not die in their sleep, but they witnessed something so horrifying that it stopped their hearts.

And they screamed out their pain.

Or perhaps they had screamed out the horror of what they witnessed in front of their very eyes.

# 3

Cooper went back to the station when it was already dark. He walked fast in the opposite direction of the agents and detectives checking out for the day, on their way to their suppers and families waiting for them at home.

When he was at his desk, he sat down heavily on his chair, letting out a prolonged sigh. He was exhausted, but his day wasn't over yet. He wanted to go through everything once more. The puzzle pieces were all in front of him now, and even if the solution looked to be the simplest one, deep down, Cooper knew he couldn't be further away from putting all the pieces together. He felt the urge to do that more than the need to go home to Caroline and Tyrese. He felt terrible about it, but at the same time, he felt as if the Hanson case had reignited something that he thought he had lost. He hadn't felt that spark about his job in a long time. This case was filled with details that didn't quite add up, and that was ultimately what he had missed the most about his old position. He missed the challenge of a real puzzle. This case was far more complicated than what the initial evidence showed and way more complex than what the preliminary elements of the investigation might lead to.

He fished the phone out of the pocket of his velvet jacket and called his wife to tell her he would be late. He was going to start the puzzle right there and then.

That's where Robert Cooper felt in his natural element, in an empty office illuminated only by the orange light of the desk lamps, with pages and pages of statements collected, pictures taken at the scene, coroner's report, and his determination to understand what happened to the Hansons. People always asked him about his job, picturing him in action like detectives were depicted in true crime movies or books. The reality was much simpler and boring. The work of a detective consisted, for the most part, of getting all the elements of an investigation together, building a solid case for the prosecutors, and spending hours, days, sometimes even months, going over and over the same details, hoping to find something they might have missed the first time, something that would connect the dots, something that would help to complete the puzzle. There was beauty in that systematic research; there was dedication and commitment, but most importantly, there was the scream for justice from the victims, a sense of duty in giving a voice to those bodies that couldn't speak for themselves anymore.

After the autopsy results, which ruled out the carbon monoxide poisoning, all the investigation elements pointed to a heart attack. This natural cause could have been enough to close the whole case. Cooper knew that, in the absence of further evidence, the case would be closed soon, but he couldn't ignore the fact that two heart attacks occurring on two individuals at the exact same time were extremely unlikely. While reading his notebook, Cooper found a note about the security cameras. There were two ADT outdoor security cameras connected to the surveillance system that the Hansons installed in their home. The cameras hadn't shown anything useful or substantial from a preliminary analysis. No one attempted to break in, and no cars suspiciously stopped in front of the house. The only person who had been caught on camera before Rosa Cortez stepped into the house on the day of the discovery of the bodies was the mailman, sneaking the mail in the mailbox and leaving right after.

*Then why did they have that look on their faces?* Cooper thought, looking at the pictures that were taken at the scene. That was the question that kept bugging him.

*What scared you so much to literally stop your heart?*

Cooper stayed up all night trying to answer those questions, to come up with some new detail that would shed a different light on the case. But nothing came. It was never that easy. He had to wait until the next morning to check the footage from the security cameras, since no one could grant him access to the evidence room this late in the night.

Just as he was the last one to leave the precinct on the previous night —except for Timmy and his cleaning crew and the agents on the night shift—Cooper was the first to show up at work the following morning.

He knew Davis would come around 9 a.m., and he would want to read his report or at least hear his thoughts. Cooper had put together all the possibilities, but there were still some blind spots and gaps he couldn't fill. And he hoped to do just that in the half-hour he had left.

He walked to the evidence room, which was located on the second floor. Gabby Lauren was sitting behind the plastic glass and looked more energetic than ever. She was a peppery red-headed woman in her late thirties, and, since day one, she had shown her own particular interest in him without much hesitation. If he had to be completely honest, he would sometimes send someone else to collect evidence because her flirting made him a little uncomfortable. This time, he didn't have much of a choice.

Her face brightened as soon as she saw him.

"Good morning there! That's an early morning for ya," she said in her usual high-pitched tone as she gazed at her Apple Watch. "I didn't think you were an early bird."

"Morning, Gabby." He limited himself to that, then looked at her as if he was waiting for something.

"Oh, right! I'm sorry. I'm still waiting for my coffee to kick in. You look like you might need one, too." She handed him the check-in sheet. Every officer accessing the evidence room had to sign in and out.

"You're right about that. I didn't get much sleep last night," Cooper said as he wrote his name on the sheet.

"Well, whoever kept you up all night, I couldn't blame her." She smiled and winked at him.

He ignored her and took a few steps, stopping in front of the evidence room's door. He waited for Gabby to open it. The door snapped open. He went in and shut it behind him.

The room was dark and quiet, just as he remembered it. Hundreds and hundreds of boxes, labeled by date, filled the long metallic shelves that crossed the entire room. Each box contained labeled evidence, numbered and sealed in plastic transparent bags. He walked to the first shelf at the far end of the room, where the most recent evidence was archived. The second to last box had a label reading: Hanson. He passed a finger on it and kept walking. What he was after, he wouldn't find in a box but in the police database, which was accessible by the computer sitting on the table at the end of the room.

Every piece of evidence wasn't only cataloged and physically placed in a box these days but also photographed or scanned— depending on if the evidence was an object or a transcript—and archived on the cloud. The department had a small team of five in charge of this task; two were IT people.

He logged in with his credentials and went straight to the application that managed the database. He typed Hanson in the search field and hit enter.

As he waited for the system to do its job, he hoped that the videos from the security camera had already been uploaded. After a few seconds, the page updated, showing all the results with the desired keyword. There were two video files from the surveillance cameras installed at the Hanson house, one for the front door and one for the back.

The videos covered a window of thirty-six hours, which had been judged to be around the suspected time of death. He opened both files and placed the windows side by side, then hit the fast-forward button until he reached his desired speed.

He looked at the time, running fast, focusing on any movement or unusual thing he might see. He knew there was a chance he could miss something at that speed, but he definitely couldn't afford to watch thirty-six hours of video when he barely had a half hour left, so that would have to do. When the time at the bottom of the screen approached 3 a.m., he slowed the fast forward to 16x and then to 8x. Witching hour, he thought as he remembered his previous conversation with Julian Rigg. Cooper looked at the black and white images running in sync, freezing and, occasionally, going slightly off focus as they tried to compensate for the lack of light with the built-in infrared.

Then something captured Cooper's attention, and he felt a rush of excitement as he rewound to 3:14 a.m., then he played both videos at normal speed. The leaves of the tall ivy that raveled and twisted around the right side of the front patio fluttered in the night breeze. Cooper kept the focus, ready to detect any movement or anomaly on the screen. He stood there for a few seconds, losing his hope and starting to think he had just imagined it, and then he saw it.

It was a flicker of light on the top part of the screen, a glare that confused the camera's auto-focus system for a brief moment. It was on for a few seconds, then went back to dark, causing the camera to re-adjust its focus again.

He played it back and forth a dozen times, checking the camera on the back door around the same time the light appeared on the front camera. Nothing showed up on that one. He then focused exclusively on the front camera and marked when the light appeared on the screen. Eight seconds, and then the light went out.

He wondered where the light was coming from. He played those eight seconds of video back and forth another couple of times, pausing and studying the angles and heights when the camera clearly showed the slit of light. The light didn't come from the Hanson house but from the neighbor's. Someone in the neighbor's house turned on a light for eight seconds, then turned it back off. Was it possible that they heard something and went downstairs to check?

The light came from Lynn Harris's house.

# 4

"Jesus Christ, Cooper!" Davis said, visibly flinching when he saw him sitting in the darkness of his office. "What the fuck are you doing here?"

"Just my job, Harry," Cooper said without looking at him, focused on the blurry frame he printed from the security footage he had just analyzed in the evidence room.

"The Hanson case," Davis said, throwing his briefcase on a chair and undoing the button of his jacket. He wore a blue three-piece suit and a red tie over an immaculate white shirt that Cooper had seen him wearing when Davis had to attend a press conference. Cooper looked at his boss and old mentor and almost felt sorry for him. He was away from the action these days: managing budgets, assigning resources, and navigating the muddy waters of politics. All that crap came with the increased responsibilities in the chain of command, and Cooper had always thought the jump in career and the paycheck wasn't worth it.

"Do you want the bad news or the good news first?"

"You know which one I want first," Davis said as he sat in front of him.

Cooper walked him through the most recent findings from the coroner's report. Davis massaged his chin, brooding when he learned the carbon monoxide theory had faded.

"So they just had a heart attack?" Davis asked.

"That's the official cause of death. Can I speak freely here?"

"I know where you are trying to go with this. What I can recommend is that you stick with the facts that you have."

"Harry! Two people having a heart attack simultaneously is like one chance in one hundred trillion. It's practically impossible."

"It seems pretty possible to me. You know this job is not based on statistics, right?"

"Something doesn't feel right. Look at these photos," Cooper said as he showed the pictures of the couple's faces. "What do these faces tell you?"

"What are you trying to say?" Davis asked, frowning.

"The coroner's report mentions both the victims had a powerful heart attack. What I'm trying to say, Harry, is that the people were literally scared to death when they died."

"I'm going to need you to be more specific than that."

"We can't trust the lead about natural causes. I think there is a chance these people were murdered, Harry."

"Woah, whoa, whoa," Davis jumped out of his chair, putting his hands on the back of his neck. "Back up the bus a bit for me, would you? I thought there wasn't any sign of a break-in. Any luck with the security cameras?"

"I just came back from the evidence room. The cameras on both the front and back door are clean, but I found something that could be interesting." Cooper handed him the print from the security camera.

Davis looked at the area Cooper had circled with a red mark.

"Is that a glare from a light?"

"Precisely. The light is coming from the Harris house. It was turned on and off around the estimated time of death."

"I'm still not following where you are going with this."

Cooper felt a wave of defeat assailing him, and he wasn't entirely surprised. He knew that whatever lead he was trying to chase was very weak, a dead end, most likely. He knew Davis wasn't going to buy it, and he knew that he needed some facts for the press conference. A death from natural causes would be the best possible outcome for Davis. Reassuring the community that these people were not murdered was Harry's highest priority. Unless Cooper found something quickly, the case would be closed in no time.

"Let me talk to Lynn Harris. Maybe she heard something during the night. She could have seen something. After all, the security cameras weren't covering all the possible entrances. Someone could have gotten in from the side, through one of the windows on the first floor."

Davis sighed; he paced the room, looking down for a while.

"Go talk to the woman. See if you can find something else. But frankly speaking, Cooper, this looks like a non-case, especially considering the coroner has ruled out the gas leak theory. You know this place works because we keep the good numbers, cases solved high, and the bad numbers, cases unsolved low. We don't need bad numbers in this department, Cooper, and sure enough, we don't need doubts based on nothing."

"And since when is our job about numbers, Harry? When did we exactly become accountants or goddamn managers instead of policemen? Since when do we treat everything so superficially? Don't you think Peter Hanson deserves something better than your fucking numbers? Are you really going to tell him that his parents just had a heart attack and died?"

"Go talk to Lynn Harris if that makes you feel better, Cooper.

I'm not going to give anything to the press today. I'm not out of my goddamn mind, but our job is to look at the facts. I've always let you go into your rabbit holes and follow your gut feelings. But there is no rabbit hole in this one, Cooper. It actually seems pretty damn closed to me as far as the case goes."

"Fine," Cooper said as he collected his papers and stormed out of the office, slamming the door behind him.

# 5

Cooper parked in front of the Hanson house. It looked so different from the crime scene he had examined almost two weeks before. Without the ribbons and all the emergency vehicles, it looked like a perfectly regular home, agnostic of the death and loss between its walls. Cooper wondered how Peter was doing and was almost tempted to pay him an unannounced visit to check on him, but then he dismissed the idea for the time being. He needed answers for the man. The visit would be more justified if he were lucky enough to get some from Lynn Harris. He walked to the next house, a two-story that was architecturally very similar to the Hanson's. High ceilings on the second floor, a wraparound front porch, and wide windows on the first floor. He looked at the window on the side, then back at the picture he held in his hand, recognizing the angle he had seen in the security footage. The camera was angled down, almost to the deck of the Hanson's front porch, to capture the front entrance in its entirety, but the lens and the field of view were wide enough to capture the bottom edge of the window on the side of the Harris house.

There was a shift in the air, a sudden change of pressure that clogged his ears. It reminded him of the descending phases of a commercial flight approaching its landing. The air had become heavier, smothering, and thicker as the breeze ceased, conferring a bleak silence to the neighborhood. An utter sense of unease and discomfort caught Cooper as he glimpsed at the Hanson house once more. A dark stain—that he hadn't noticed on his first visit—rested at the bottom edge of the external shutters, as wide as the window itself. It looked as if someone had thrown charcoal at it. It was a tumor rotting the house from the inside. Cooper could feel it like it was inside his brain. He heard the buzzing sound of insects as if they lived in his ear drums.

"Can I help you?" Cooper flinched and let out a small scream of panic at the sound of a male voice coming from behind him.

He turned and looked at a tall man wearing faded jeans, a navy-blue sweatshirt that fit way too large, and an Indiana Pacers hat.

Cooper cleared his voice, trying to recompose himself quickly, then fished his badge out of the inside pocket of his jacket and showed it to the man.

"Robert Cooper, IMPD. Do you always sneak up on people like that?"

"Only if they are wandering in my backyard."

"Fair enough," Cooper said, putting his badge back in his pocket. "I'm looking for Frank and Lynn Harris."

"Well, you found them," the man said, shaking the detective's hand.

"Nice to meet you, Mr. Harris."

"Would you like to come in and talk? Lynn is in the kitchen fixing lunch."

"Sure, I won't be long," Cooper said as he followed the man inside.

"Can I get you something to drink?" Mr. Harris asked as he invited Cooper to take a seat.

"Water, thank you."

Cooper wasn't really thirsty, but he always asked for a glass of water during his interviews. It was a habit he had built over the years. It gave him that bit of time that was required to gauge his surroundings. It had always been surprising how much one could learn about someone else just by taking a good look at the place they lived in. A glimpse of the books Mr. and Mrs. Harris showcased on the shelves was enough to conclude that one or both were quite passionate about thriller novels. His gut feeling didn't depict Frank Harris as a big reader. His hands felt coarse when they shook earlier, and despite it being possible that Mr. Harris indulged in some garage projects and a good book simultaneously, Cooper was still betting on Lynn Harris to be the household reader.

Cooper's eyes fell on one of the shelves where a modern wooden frame rested against a pile of books. The picture showed Lynn and Frank on both sides of a young man who resembled both in a perfectly mixed way. His hair was dark, wavy, and long enough to touch his shoulders. He had his mom's beauty and his dad's physical presence. Cooper thought there was something about him that made him look like a rockstar. Maybe it was the hair, the leather jacket he wore in the photo, or the sadness his eyes screamed out despite the wide smile he was showing to the camera.

"Here you go," Frank said, handing him the glass of water. "Lynn will be here in a moment." Then he sat on the chair next to the fireplace.

"Is your boy playing in a band?" Cooper asked as he sat down at the far end of the couch, resting the glass on the small side table next to it.

"He was," Frank said, then put his head down for a long time. "He passed away last November."

Cooper's blood froze in his veins.

"God, I'm so sorry, Mr. Harris. I apologize for bringing that up. It wasn't my intention to..."

"It's alright, Detective, you couldn't have known."

"You couldn't have known what?" Lynn Harris came into the room, and Cooper was so glad that she arrived at that moment. He didn't want to carry that conversation on any longer.

"Good morning, Mrs. Harris," Cooper said, standing up and greeting her with a gentle nod.

"Good morning, Detective," she said in a broken voice. Judging from the redness in her eyes and the purple bags that had formed behind them, Cooper could tell that she must have been crying a lot. Cooper had learned from the report that Lynn Harris and Jane Hanson were close.

"I'm sorry to show up unannounced. I just wanted to ask you a few questions, if that's okay with you."

"Ask away," she said as she sat on the sofa's arm. There wasn't a necklace around her neck, even if her hands tried to reach for it.

"When did you last see or speak with Jane Hanson?"

Mrs. Harris let go of a deep and frustrated exhale. Cooper knew that was probably the tenth time she had to answer that question.

She rolled her eyes and sniffled, then looked straight at Cooper.

"As I mentioned to at least three other officers, I talked to Jane on the phone a few days before Rosa found them. We were supposed to take a walk down Main Street for coffee, but she wasn't in the mood, so we canceled."

"Would you consider yourself and Mrs. Hanson close friends?"

"Yes. The closest kind."

"Have you noticed anything unusual recently? Any change in her behavior? Any event that might have caused such a shift?"

"Not really. She had bad days, just like everyone else. Are we done here? I need to go check on lunch in the oven."

"Of course. I have just one more question, and then I'll be on my way. Did you hear or see anything suspicious in the very early morning of September 17th going on outside of your home?"

"What do you mean? No. Not that I can think of."

"Nothing out of the ordinary? Maybe a noise outside of the house?"

"I think I would remember if something like that woke me."

Cooper nodded, then turned to Frank.

"What about you, Mr. Harris?"

Frank almost flinched when he heard his name, clearly not expecting the interview to shift to him.

"Sorry, what was that again?"

"Did something wake you up in the very early hours of September 17th?"

He shook his head jerkily and then cleared his throat. The man was in evident distress.

"Nope. Nothing at all."

Cooper sprung up, put his notebook back in his pocket, and buttoned up his jacket.

"Thank you very much for your time. I will be out of your hair."

As he walked toward the door, he slowed down as he passed in front of one of the side windows of the living room. He looked outside and saw the security camera on the Hanson's porch. He looked at Lynn Harris. She kept her eyes down, clearly not wanting to meet his.

"If anything comes to your mind, here is my number. You can call me at any time."

She grabbed the business card and stared at it, unable to hide a grimace that was a mix of disgust and exhaustion.

"Will do," she said and walked back to the kitchen.

Frank Harris dismissed the detective with a nod, then gently closed the door as Cooper left the house.

The sky had filled with clouds traveling fast, pushed in a rush by the high winds. The breeze had picked up again, and it felt colder than before.

He fished out a cigarette from his pack and lit it up while still on the Harris's front porch. He looked around at the neighborhood. It looked deserted. There were no cars in the driveways except for a blue Ford Taurus, parked in the driveway of the house right in front of the Hanson's. An old and tall man stood near the car. He had a white beard and long, thin hair combed to the back. A brown paper bag hung from his hand as he stared at Cooper.

When Cooper waved at him, the man, perhaps surprised, made a clumsy attempt to reciprocate. He then walked to the front door and disappeared behind it a few seconds later.

*This day cannot possibly get stranger than what it has been,* he thought as he exhaled the smoke out of his nose.

# 6

It must have been around 5 p.m. when Cooper pulled into the station downtown—this time opting for the front of the building—when he noticed a car leaving the perfect open parking spot for him. He stopped at the bottom of the marble steps of the building, and his brain couldn't help but go straight back to what happened at the Harris house a few hours before.

The thought of the flies buzzing he had heard coming out of the dark stain was haunting him. He knew excessive stress and sleep deprivation could be a powerful cocktail regarding mental health and even delusions. But nothing like that had ever happened to him, and there were times when his stress level had been higher than now. *Why did the stain seem to come alive?* There wasn't any trace of logic in his thoughts, but he could have sworn the stain was pulsing when he had looked at it.

*And even if stress was the cause of it all*—which was still the theory his mind liked the most— *what was he so stressed about? What was it about this case that was hitting him at such a personal level?*

And then it came to him.

*Of course. Of course, that's what it is.* His train of thought was derailed, and memories he had tried to erase from his mind had returned to him all at once. He wasn't sure he wanted to bring all that back from the dark well he had buried deep inside.

But it wasn't as if he had a choice. The memories came out of the well like water out of a broken hydrant, and he felt as if he was going to faint.

He backed to the concrete wall behind him and leaned against it.

And he went back in time to when he was fifteen.

He laid on his bed with his Walkman. He could hear the gut-wrenching sounds of Jimi Hendricks' guitar reduced to faint notes from the headphones resting on his bare chest. It was summer, and it was hot. Air conditioning was something he believed existed only in the movies or in some rich kid's house. Definitely not something that was even remotely possible in Roseland, on the south side of Chicago. The only things that seemed to matter around here were drugs, guns and violence.

Sometimes, he wondered how he was still alive. He would walk to school every day with his friend Paulie, and they would be called the worst kind of names by people who looked exactly like them. Except their eyes burned with anger and desperation. Dozens stared at them and verbally threatened them, but no one ever robbed them, beat them up, or worse.

He knew worse things than being beaten could happen in the streets of Roseland. He had seen them with his own eyes and had nightmares about them: people getting shot in daylight on a curb, kids beating the shit out of a dead cat in the gutter, the shootings with the police, the blood flowing in the drains on a rainy day.

But nothing ever happened to Cooper and Paulie.

He finally understood why he and his friend could enjoy that kind of immunity when his Uncle Roger had picked him up at school and brought him to the corner of South Street for, what he said, was the best Italian beef on the planet.

All the kids on the street would look the other way when his uncle walked by. Some of them would wave at him, and others would almost kneel. His uncle said that was what respect looked like. He also said that he and Paulie carried the light and had to go to school and be good at it to bring the light to the world.

Uncle Roger was the one who had gotten him the Walkman, and he had strictly told him never to bring it outside of his room. He would also get Cooper records, and he would always say that was the good stuff.

In the silence of his room, where the only sound was the muffled music that came out of his headphones, he heard a loud thump.

He stood up and stared at the withered white paint that once covered his bedroom's door. With his heartbeat accelerating, he gently grabbed the knob and opened the door, making sure to apply a slight pressure upward so that it wouldn't squeak on its hinges.

*Did someone break into the house?* He knew that was possible. It happened daily to someone in his building but never happened to them, likely because of Uncle Roger. And in that moment, he wished very much that he was there. He would have known what to do.

The hallway was dark and silent, but he could see his apartment door was closed at the other end of it. He walked barefoot on the uneven planks that creaked under his weight. The thump must have come from his mother's room if nobody was in the house. The door of her room had been left ajar, and a feeble sliver of light came out of it, getting lost in the darkness. He peeked from the opening and saw legs dangling in the air, seeking the ground.

Cooper stood there, paralyzed by the impossible comprehension of the events that unfolded in front of his eyes. His body wouldn't move, wouldn't respond. He stood there, resting on the door frame. He looked at his mother's legs, moving erratically as if they belonged to a marionette maneuvered by inexperienced hands. He watched them reaching, twitching until they swung in the night's still and hot air.

"Mom." That was all that came out of Cooper's mouth in a whisper.

Cooper opened his eyes and gasped for air as if he had just been underwater for a long time. He wasn't in Roseland, and he wasn't fifteen anymore. He looked around and gladly realized none of his colleagues or any other agent had noticed. Life just kept going uninterrupted in the real world.

"Jesus Christ. Get your shit together, Cooper, will you?" he said out loud.

He took another look around, and that was when he saw him.

A man stood on the other side of the street and stared in his direction. He wore a leather jacket. His long and wavy hair fluttered in the wind. He was Lynn's son—the one he had seen in the picture in their living room.

He stood there completely still, a hideous and wide grin painted on his face.

Cooper instinctively started to run towards him for a reason he couldn't logically explain. When the man in the leather jacket saw him on the move, he started walking in the opposite direction.

Cooper went across the street and stopped before a bus ran him over. The man was gone as he reached the other side of the street.

No trace of him anywhere.

# 7

Cooper went up to the second floor to see Davis. That was the last thing he wanted to do. Given the turn his day had taken and the likelihood he was losing his goddamn mind, he would have very much liked to delay that conversation to the following day. Cooper already knew how this was going to go. It was inevitable and, in all fairness, very predictable. It had been that way since the very beginning. He knew Harry always gave him all the freedom he needed in the investigations, and he always appreciated that. But he could see the urgency for closure on the man's face when he walked into his office.

Davis got up and gestured for him to get in and shut the door. Cooper went to the window and pulled down the blind with two fingers, checking the sun setting low at the horizon. Then he turned and saw Davis staring at him with an interrogative air, the one of a man who had been waiting for news all day.

"I don't know what to tell you, Harry," Cooper said as he avoided his gaze. He felt ashamed because he wasn't doing his job. After all, a detective could never build a case on a gut feeling and without a sliver of evidence. That was stuff that happened in the movies or in the true crime books he loved so much. To come to his boss—the man who had taught him how to do the job—empty-handed tasted like shame and failure.

"Did you talk with Lynn Harris?" Davis asked.

Cooper nodded.

"Then why don't we start there, for Christ's sake?"

"Nothing came out of it. They both claim they didn't hear or see anything that morning. Of course, the security footage clearly shows someone waking up in the middle of the night, turning the living room light on and turning it back off."

"Between you and me, never mind the evidence, where are you trying to go with this Cooper? And I mean it as a friend. Help me out here because I honestly have no idea what's happening in your head right now."

"Something feels off, Harry. I can't just ignore it. Those people didn't die of natural causes. I have nothing to back up my theory, but Lynn and Frank Harris are involved."

"And what would the motive be?" Davis asked in a tone that Cooper knew too well. He knew Davis was handling him with gloves; any other detective would have been already kicked out of his office.

"I need more time."

"Well, the thing is, Coop, that's the only thing we ain't got. We need to close this case. I don't have anything in my hand to keep it open." Davis uttered, letting out a whisper and shaking his head. "Why don't you tell me the truth? What is it about this case, Coop? Why can't you just let it go?"

"I'm sorry, Harry. I truly am sorry that we have stopped being policemen and have become goddamn politicians. And for what? To cross a fucking name on a board, to catalog this as a number in the end-of-year stats? So it looks good to your boss when he asks for votes in two months? What the fuck happened to real police work?"

Davis sprung forward, his finger pointed at him and his face going red. The vein on his forehead protruded as if it was ready to burst.

"Hold your horses, Cooper. Police work is backed up by fucking evidence, and if you forgot that, maybe you should take some time off and get your shit together."

Cooper walked out of the office, slamming the door behind him for the second time that day. His fist was clutched with such strength that he could feel his fingernails digging into the skin.  The worst part was that Davis was right, and he knew it. Every bit of what he said was right. Everything he had done was by the book.

Cooper knew about grief that lingers, death without an explanation. He knew the poison that came with it, the anger that never went away, the acceptance that never really came, the necessary burial, and he knew that it could come out at any time, no matter how deep you buried it.

His mind flashed back to the man in the leather jacket. The thought of that horrible grin painted on his face gave him a slow, cold shiver that went through his spine. Cooper had always been a very rational person; he was a die-hard atheist. He didn't believe in the supernatural, in spirits, ghosts, or anything of that sort. He firmly believed in the natural world and its chaotic yet utterly logical fabric.

Of course, Frank Harris might have lied to him about his son being dead, but why in the hell would someone ever do that? Because of his beliefs and mental foundations, the second possibility wasn't really a possibility. If Frank and Lynn Harris's son was dead, it wasn't possible that he had seen him staring at him on the other side of the street.

Which left him with the third and scariest possibility of them all.

That he was losing his mind, that he had become delusional. He knew it was possible; after all, that's why his mom had flicked the switch off. It was in his blood and every cell of him.

And that he wasn't quite ready to accept.

# 8

The digital clock on the dashboard read 7:25 p.m. when Cooper pulled into the driveway. He turned the engine off and closed his eyes for a few seconds, taking slow, deep breaths in and slowly exhaling. These mindfulness exercises had pretty much saved him back in the days when the nightmares and the anxiety were at the highest levels. It was a dark time of his life when he still didn't know how to dig a hole to bury all the poisonous stuff. As time had just proven to him, he hadn't dug deep enough. When all the shit came back out of the hole, his job was to restart from scratch, digging a deeper hole. Considering how long that had lasted, he thought that had worked out quite well. He was aware it would never be a permanent fix. He was pretty confident whatever he was dealing with was practically unfixable, so his exit strategy was avoiding it and hiding it for as long as possible. The problem was that he didn't know how to restart from scratch again. Too much time had passed, and despite his awareness that it would come back at some point in his life, he was shocked to see all that darkness inside him again.

He was starting to feel better, more relaxed, and slightly less negative when someone knocked on his car window.

He let out a choked sound, and his heart leaped in his chest. When he opened his eyes, he saw Caroline's beautiful face smiling on the other side of the glass.

"You'll give me a heart attack one day, you know that?" Cooper said, panting and returning the smile to her.

"Is that right?" Caroline said as she opened the door and kissed him. "And you'll give me a heart attack one day because you never hear your phone. I sent you so many texts. I called you twice. What is wrong with your phone? Or are you intentionally avoiding me?" she teased.

Cooper got out of the car and locked it as he wrapped his right arm around her and brought her close to him.

"You got me. Can't hide anything from you, Detective Cooper," he said as they walked into the house. "Oh, that smells good, baby. Is that what I think it is?"

"It is indeed. Go see your son first. He is already in bed. I'll warm everything up for you."

Cooper went up and gently knocked on the door filled with drawings and the sign Tyrese had painted himself. The pictures were supposed to be reproductions of the Avengers, and the sign stated, in big red letters on a white background, that it was wise for people to keep away from there because that was Tyrese's room.

The nightstand lamp was on, sending a blue light onto the walls and the camping tent Tyrese and he had put together in the far-end corner of the room. They would spend Friday nights in there with a flashlight, telling each other scary stories before bed. Tyrese was really into scary stories, to the point of lying when he was asked if he thought he would get scared from them. He was ready to face adult life and be frightened. This often led to him sneaking into his parents' bed late at night, claiming that would be the last time.

"Hey, Champ. How are you doing there?"

The boy was watching a cartoon on his iPad and was almost about to doze off.

"Hi, Daddy," he said, smiling. He then turned the other way and was out in a matter of seconds.

"Goodnight, my love," Cooper said as he moved his curly hair from his forehead and shut off his iPad.

He kneeled there for a few minutes, looking at him sleeping. There wasn't anything in life that was more worthy of that moment of love. It filled his heart, warmed his soul, and, for a moment, all the darkness of the past days left him. It didn't matter how hard it would be to return to normality. The reason why he had to fight for it was right in front of him.

He landed a kiss on his forehead, then switched the lamp off, and light blue fluorescent lights appeared on the ceiling and diffused the soft glow of the stars.

He went downstairs and ate the delicious dinner Caroline had fixed for him, the Jambalaya recipe from her mother. When he finished, he stepped out of the front porch for a smoke, and Caroline followed him and smoked one with him. She wasn't a smoker, but she enjoyed the occasional one from time to time.

The night was pleasant and slightly cooler than they were used to during the summer, the preface of fall, a time of the year they both thoroughly enjoyed.

"What is going on inside that head? I can tell something is bothering you."

He didn't want to drag her into his misery or his case, but he needed to talk about this with someone and didn't trust anyone more than Caroline. And so he told her everything. He told her about the case, leaving out unnecessarily gory details, about Davis and what all that was bringing back. He was cautious not to mention the dark stain he had seen at the Hanson house or the man with the leather jacket. He wasn't ready to talk about that.

Caroline was an incredible woman for uncountable reasons, but the one that made Cooper feel so lucky to have her was that she was an exceptional listener. She didn't judge; she wasn't there to offer solutions for every single problem or situation. She stood there and listened. They smoked cigarettes and had a couple of bourbons. She was silent the whole time, her eyes focused, absorbing every bit of information he told her.

When Cooper finally finished, she put her cigarette out and looked him straight in the eyes.

"You know, baby, more than a few things cannot be explained in this life. Not rationally, not logically, at least. And I think that's a beautiful thing. It just doesn't pair well with a court of law, but it doesn't mean your gut feeling is wrong. It doesn't mean that *you* are wrong."

"What do you mean?" Cooper said as he exhaled the smoke and looked up at the clear sky. He knew perfectly what she meant but wanted her to expand on her thoughts. The occult had always attracted Caroline. She devoured every book on witchcraft, legends, or haunted houses, both fiction and non-fiction. Cooper had always been a true crime reader, and even though he had enjoyed some books that weren't rooted in reality, he had always wondered why the supernatural element of it attracted Caroline.

"You don't believe these people just died from a heart attack. But the cameras don't show anyone getting in the house. You don't buy the accidental leak theory. You believe that these people were murdered, right?"

"That is correct."

"What if all these things are true? Why are you making it so that if all these things are true, your conclusions are not?"

"I'm not following you, baby."

"I know you aren't. All I'm saying is that when logic and rationality fail to give you an explanation, it doesn't mean that there isn't one. You just have to expand your radar."

"You are saying that whatever killed these people is not logical or rational?"

"I'm saying that some things that happen in this world are not of this world. There are so many examples of it in more stories than you can imagine."

Cooper didn't know what to say. He didn't feel entirely at ease in taking the conversation to this level.

"Like the supernatural? Ghosts and shit like that?"

"I know you can't contemplate something like that. But it doesn't mean that it doesn't exist."

Cooper took another draw of his cigarette and shook his head. He felt stupid for bringing the whole thing up. There wasn't room for any of that in his mind. There never was, even when things were less complicated for him and his mental health. The last thing he needed was to talk about evil spirits, ghosts and the supernatural. For a moment, he imagined the face of Harry Davis and the DA, building a case against the boogeyman.

Caroline hugged him from behind, then forced him to turn and kissed him. He felt the lust on her tongue as she rested her hands on his chest.

"Now, come with me. I've got a few ideas to make you feel better, Detective. If you don't believe in the supernatural, just wait and see," Caroline said as she winked at him.

She then dragged him inside the house using his black tie as a leash.

They made love on the kitchen table, like in the old days when they couldn't get enough of one another. Occasionally, he could still feel the spark of their passion burning hot and hard. They put their hands over each other's mouths, trying to be quiet, hoping that the rattle of the table wouldn't wake Tyrese up.

They laid with their naked bodies pushed against one another, wrapped in a blanket.

They laughed and remembered funny episodes from the past. Cooper wasn't sure he could laugh after a day like the one he had, but Caroline could do that and so much more.

He looked at her, falling asleep in his arms, and carried her all the way upstairs to bed.

He took a shower and laid down in bed, looking at the darkness of the ceiling and wondering if he would be able to sleep.

The sight of his son and the love of his wife had pushed away the dark stuff, but he knew it was just like kicking a can down the road.

The darkness in his mind merged with the one in the room.

When he closed his eyes, trying to focus on his breathing, the only thing he could see in his mind was the man in the leather jacket staring at him from across the street. Cooper opened his eyes. He couldn't stand to see that grin any longer. He tried to focus on something else, one of the happy memories he had discussed with Caroline, but it didn't last long. Peter Hanson came to his mind. Cooper imagined him tormented by all the questions he didn't have an answer for.

It's just an unfillable void.

Just a sense of…

Hollow.

# Part Three:

# Jack

# 1

Jack Sullivan was inches close to completing the seemingly never-ending task of unpacking all the boxes after he moved into his new home. It took him all winter to do it. He had paced himself to have something to do every day during the rigid Indiana winter. Now, well into April, he fished a few kitchen utensils from the last box and drew a sigh of relief, feeling a slight, but not complete, sense of accomplishment. After all, there was no rush. He had learned through the years, despite his age approaching seventy with frightening quickness, that he wasn't scared of death anymore, not after what he had experienced in his long career as an exorcist.

He had pronounced his vows to God when he was eighteen and served as a priest of the Catholic Church of Rome for forty-five years after that. He had formally abandoned his collar at the age of sixty-three.

He didn't leave his position because of a lack of faith but mainly because there was only so much bullshit a man could tolerate before admitting that enough was enough. His beliefs had always been very close to the teachings and the message of Jesus, and that had never changed. What had changed was his awareness and his wisdom that Christianity in America had become the furthest thing from Jesus that he could imagine. It wasn't only the idealization of a white American Christ that had caused the rupture. It was the bigotry and the absolute ignorance about the real message of Christ that he was escaping from. Churches were not places to find peace and comfort anymore. They were practically companies led by fanatics attempting to make radical something that was exactly the opposite of that and to make a profit in the process.

Even after he had officially resigned from his position, with a formal communication to the Vatican, his reputation and knowledge had brought him a lot of requests for consultancy, some of which he had been obliged to attend to.

The faith had never been in doubt. What he had seen, witnessed, and fought in his life was enough for ten lifetimes of enduring faith. His decision to move to Indiana from Chicago, taken a few months before, was his latest attempt to escape. He knew he couldn't escape from it, but he still enjoyed giving himself the illusion that a place existed where his expertise wouldn't be needed, and his bet had been Indiana.

These were his thoughts as he looked at the rare volumes on the bookshelves that he had installed all around the walls of his new living room. His books were the real treasure, his way of living thousands of different lives.

He went by the window and looked outside.

It was cold and gloomy as big gray clouds moved quickly in the sky, threatening to release their content on Earth at any time. There were two houses directly in front of his. The one on the right looked like it had been recently renovated on the exterior, featuring a dark gray color and light wood accents. It was a beautiful two-story house with a big strip of yard in the front. He imagined the backyard would have been even wider, judging from the distance between the house and the wooded area behind it. During his daily walks, he learned that the house belonged to the Hanson family by reading the name on the mailbox.

The other house was equally as large and possessed about the same acreage, but it didn't look as modern as the other one. Its white vinyl planks were showing signs of age. This one belonged to the Harris family.

He hadn't met any of his neighbors yet, but he knew what they looked like from the vantage point of his living room window. He had seen the Hansons leaving together in the SUV parked in the driveway. He had seen them going to the Harris's house, bringing food and various dishes. He had also seen what he believed was Mrs. Harris crying on the front porch or looking absently outside her window. At the same time, Mr. Harris appeared to be absent with his mind and showing the same behavior. He had long wondered what kind of pain was afflicting the Harris family, and ultimately, he guessed right.

There was only one type of pain capable of hurting a family to the point of being intolerable: the loss of a child. He had seen that kind of pain many times, but it still struck him like it had been the first. There was something unnatural about it, something that could never be accepted, something destined to haunt until the last breath of life. Jack Sullivan had researched the obituaries on the internet, and it didn't take him long before finding out that William Harris had died that past November, practically the same week Jack had moved in.

A few hours later, that same day, he received his first in-person visit from his neighbors. Despite never minding his solitude and loneliness, Jack felt excited about it. He thrived through human contact.

He let two women inside his house when he opened the front door. They introduced themselves as Jane Hanson and Rosa Cortez. They both carried round pans covered by aluminum foil. They had brought chocolate chip cookies and a chicken pot pie. Rosa didn't live in the neighborhood, but it was as if she did. She claimed to spend more time at the Hanson's house than her own. From the information she had shared, Jack Sullivan had learned she was a widow, and her son was in college in Michigan. Jane's son lived in New Orleans and worked hard to make a living out of his writing passion. Jack Sullivan had lived in New Orleans for a few months, enough to fall in love with the city and carry its sounds, smells and folklore in his heart forever.

Jack asked Rosa and Jane about the other neighbors, and the conversation inevitably went to the recent Harris tragedy. Jane provided more details about the death of Will Harris and his drug addiction. She also mentioned that she, Bill, and Lynn were almost about to leave for a trip to Utah.

The three of them spoke, sitting around the coffee table for half an hour. Jack shared with them his past as a priest, omitting exactly what his specialty was. That would have to be a conversation for another time. Jack could tell they were anxious to learn more about him, and he realized he had to give them something. He was a good listener but a terrible talker.

"So, what brings you here in Indiana?" Jane had asked at some point in the conversation. "Where were you before?"

"I have to admit I am a bit of a nomad. I have lived in more places than I like to admit. I have no family except for a sister who lives in Arizona. So, I just like to take advantage of my retirement to move around and check out new places. I guess I'm trying to understand if the new place will be better than the last one. My previous stay was in Chicago and Seattle before that."

There were other reasons, of course, why Jack Sullivan had moved from place to place, but that was not a conversation he was ready to have.

Jack Sullivan was quite used to the oddness of the Midwest weather, but he had to admit that Indiana's was probably the oddest he had ever seen, especially during spring. After a couple of false springs, with formidably pleasant and mild weather, the temperatures dropped almost to winter level, only to climb again and re-drop multiple times in a confusing rollercoaster.

A few weeks after the first introduction with Rosa and Jane, when the real spring finally arrived in the month of May, the streets of town started blooming, bringing out people and kids after months of confinement.

The pedestrian trail he walked daily was filled with people walking their dogs, riding their bikes or running. He took a great deal of pleasure from his walks as they helped him focus on his meditation sessions. The air was filled with the smell of wildflowers and freshly mowed grass. Birds of all kinds chirped and flew around, building their nests for the season. People had started decorating their houses and yards with black and white checkered flags and triangular colored ones, getting ready to host the Indianapolis 500. The race track was only a few blocks north of his house. On one of his walks on Main Street, he had stopped at a local memorabilia shop and purchased a book about the history of the Indy 500, which he intended to read shortly.

He passed a small bridge that must have been built very recently, judging from the newness of the wood, and stopped on the side, leaning with his arms on it to look at the small creek that flowed underneath.

On the other side of the bridge was a woman dressed in her workout outfit, sitting on a stone. He recognized the pale features of Lynn Harris, marked by despair.

Mr. and Mrs. Harris were still the only neighbors he hadn't officially met or talked to yet. There had been mutual waving and the occasional greeting from across the street, but they never had any real conversation. And he didn't blame them. He knew what they were going through. It came to his mind that Lynn and Jane must have returned from their trip out west. He hoped it was a good chance for Lynn to distract herself a little.

The woman sat very still and looked as if she was utterly lost in her thoughts. Her eyes were red as if she had been crying. Her fingers were clenched in an angry fist. Jack gently approached her and ensured she could see him with the tail of her eyes before speaking to her to avoid startling her.

"Hello, Mrs. Harris. How do you do?" Jack asked in a soft voice.

She didn't reply or make any effort to make eye contact with him. She just kept looking at the water in the creek, circling away in shock waves from the small pebbles she distractedly threw into it. She played with her necklace, tightly held in the other hand.

"Are you ok?" Jack Sullivan asked again.

"I'm fine," she finally said, annoyed. "I just need to be alone."

"I understand. I just wanted to make sure you were alright. I'm your neighb..."

"Yeah, I know who you are!" She didn't let him finish, and she turned to look at him this time. Her features had shifted from utter sadness and despair to an amused grin and wide-open eyes filled with madness. The voice of Jack's neighbor had shifted as well. What had sounded to him like a fragile, trembling whisper a few moments before had now turned into a hoarse, low-pitched, raging voice. "The unholy priest, right?" she asked, holding that uncomfortable grin and giggling childishly.

Those words hit Jack like a hard slap in the face. He stood there, unsure of how to respond to that. After moments that seemed to last forever, Jack managed to escape the numbness that Lynn's words had thrown him into.

"What did you just say?"

"How are you doing, Father?" the woman asked with a teasing, arrogant tone. "Do you still have wet dreams about the Derringer boy?"

Jack felt his heart sinking in his chest. If he was caught off-guard by Lynn's first statement, this one blew the door off its hinges.

*How did she know about the Derringer family?*

Despite Jack Sullivan's age, he was not naive about the power of the internet and social media. If something had leaked from the time he was sent to the Derringers, it was not unreasonable to think that Lynn could have researched about him and known details about his previous life. He knew such a possibility existed, but, at the same time, he couldn't ignore that the odds of Lynn Harris knowing about what happened to the poor Derringer boy were extremely slim.

"Oh, you look surprised, Father." The woman kept going with hideous confidence.

"How do you know about that?"

"We know a lot of things, Father."

"We?"

"Watch your back, Unholy," Lynn Harris had finally said before turning her attention toward the small creek running below the bridge.

Jack Sullivan turned away from Lynn Harris and resumed his walk, still deeply shocked by what had just happened. That wasn't how he had imagined his first encounter with Mrs. Harris. He put his brain to work. It was the time to think and remember, to go back to a time that he thought he had put behind him. But bad things have a way to re-emerge from the depths.

When Jack formally resigned from his position, many people in the high spheres of the Vatican were deeply unhappy with it. So, it was reasonable to think that someone might have leaked some information regarding the Derringer family and the possession case that came with it. At the same time, the Vatican had always been very secretive about the practice of exorcism. Even though it was the only religious institution that hadn't officially abandoned that particular practice, they weren't proud of it either. It was something they kept very well hidden in a drawer. To discredit Jack's work by leaking information would equate to discrediting the conduct of the Church itself.

His mind went back to six years before when he was contacted by an intermediary of the Vatican to investigate claims about an alleged case of possession of a six-year-old boy in Wyoming.

There were hundreds and hundreds of cases of alleged possessions in the United States every year. The ones that reached the attention of the Vatican went through a very diligent investigation process, and only a fraction of them were looked into further. The goal of the investigations was to collect additional evidence, such as tapes, videos, or recordings of the manifestations. They were then followed by interviews conducted by members of the Vatican. Of the hundreds of claims, only a dozen were investigated, and only two or three were believed to deserve attention.

And that's when Jack Sullivan came into play. His superior was Cardinal Bernard Pruett in Chicago. He had called Jack regarding Joshua Derringer's alleged case of possession.

Jack shivered as he recalled the boy's name and, as if that had turned on a switch, the images of his lifeless body, mutilated and deformed by the evil it had hosted, were still very vivid in his mind—an unkind reminder of his biggest failure.

Then Jack Sullivan started digging, trying to remember things that had been carefully buried deep in the most remote places. He was convinced that some stories would have eventually caught up with him, but he had hoped that day would come later.

How much he had dug to put those stories away didn't matter.

For some stories, no depth could hold them.

# 2

When Jack Sullivan arrived at the Derringer's house years before, he immediately knew that something unusual was unfolding behind its walls. The rain was pouring down relentlessly, and despite the heat and the humidity, a dome of cold air loomed around the house. It was as if he just walked into an open-air refrigerated room.

He heard the screams coming from inside the house. He was pretty sure they were coming out of Joshua Derringer's chest, but they didn't sound like the screams of a six-year-old boy. They were otherworldly and guttural, the snarling sound of a primitive beast. Despite the nighttime, all the lights in the house were off, besides one light on the second story. Jack Sullivan raised his head and watched the rain pouring down the edges of his black hat. He guessed the only illuminated room was the boy's bedroom. Shadows were moving in the room as if someone was passing a hand by the table lamp.

A man was at the front door with a shotgun in his arms. He waved as Jack Sullivan walked towards him. The man wore a red shirt, blue jeans and cowboy boots. He matched perfectly with the surroundings and the ranch house.

Mr. Derringer welcomed Jack into the house and introduced himself as Craig, Joshua's father. Jack noticed he gestured the holy trinity sign, bringing his hand to his head, then to his chest, and finally to his shoulders. He begged him to help his boy. Craig led Jack up the stairs into a dark hallway, at the end of which was a door left ajar. He stopped and invited Jack to go on. The boy's father had seen enough of whatever was behind that door.

Jack felt the knot in his stomach tightening. The house was cold, and the fat raindrops rattling on the roof reverberated hollowly in the hallway, mixing with the screams and bellowing sounds of the monster that dwelled in the boy's frail body. Jack's mind went to the photo that came with his case report. A smiling Joshua was portrayed in it, posing with his baseball glove. His hazelnut straight and velvety hair peeked from the Seattle Mariners hat.

When he entered the room, the temperature went down steeply. A woman was kneeling and praying about ten feet from the full-size bed where Joshua laid, both hands chained to the headboard. The local minister, Father Seldwig, stood, resting his back on the wall on the opposite side of the room. A white rosary hung from his trembling hands. He acknowledged Sullivan's presence with a slight bow. The room smelled of charred wood and ammonia.

"Father, thank God you're here! The boy got much worse in the past few hours."

Father Seldwig wasn't lying, Jack thought as he gazed at the boy.

His body was so thin that it almost seemed to disappear in the comforter that was placed under his body. His rib cage was so far out, stretching the skin, that it reminded Jack of the children of the tribes of Malhua in Liberia. The children Jack had seen were in such bad shape that it was too late to save them because of malnutrition. Even if he wanted to give food to all of them, he couldn't save them. They were slowly waiting for their bodies to shut down completely. That sight, accompanied by their mothers' heart-wrenching crying, was the most horrifying thing Jack Sullivan had ever seen.

Until now.

Now, he stood in front of a boy about to be killed by a different kind of evil. His head was swollen and deformed like something was pushing the walls of the skull out from the inside. It didn't have the shape of a human head anymore. It looked as if he had been stung on his face by thousands of wasps. Purple and blue bumps were moving and growing under his skin, around the cheekbones. His eye sockets seemed to be sinking, and his eyes were as dark as a starless midnight sky. Those radiant eyes full of life and promise Jack had seen in the picture were gone. They trembled in the sockets like dying stars, ready to implode into darkness. His skin was so pale that it was almost translucent. Blue and red veins had popped on his forehead. The swollen face and the incredibly thin body made the boy look like a non-human. Jack Sullivan thought there couldn't have been a more distant thing from humanity than the creature in front of his very eyes.

His body was quite still, except for some sporadic twitch that flashed through the whole body. The chain rattled against the metallic headboard rhythmically at every spasm. The boy's chest went up and down, and each movement was followed by the growling and unsteady sound of his breathing. The white comforter underneath his body was covered in old and dry blood, which had assumed a dark color. The presence of the evil was so strong that Jack could hear it moving around the room as pressure shifted in the air.

The eyes of the demon were still as it stared at Jack Sullivan, using the small space on the bedroom's dresser to set up his equipment. The priest grabbed a rosary, its spheres made of cherry wood and ending in a silver crucifix. He extracted a small bottle of holy water and an old book with a brown leather cover; its pages were thick and ancient, carrying the weight of the years.

"In Nomine Patris, et Filii, et Spiritus Sancti, Amen," Jack said as he observed the demon tensing inside Joshua's boy. It hissed when the drops of water hit the skin.

As Jack started the Roman Ritual, he thought about what he was about to begin. Once more, Jack's moral obligations required that he ascertained, with moral certainty, that the boy was indeed under the devil's assault. There was no doubt that this was the result of evil possession. But the doubt about Jack being able to help and save the boy, to cast out the evil from him, existed and was significant. He thought about his previous exorcism and the time it took him to recover from the guilt and accept that his faith and commitment hadn't been enough. He wondered what the snare of the enemy would be. There was always one. The evil casts doubt and uses it against you, Jack told himself as he turned the page of his book.

Jack started the ritual, mentally picturing the sequence of the rite itself. He began with the prayer of Litany, the Psalms, and the Gospel, which proclaimed the presence of Christ invoking his healing. The boy laid on his bed, belly up, but his head was tilted and focused on the priest. The demon snarled, alternating ominous laughter with bellowing alien sounds.

When the Gospel had been recited, Jack moved quickly toward the boy and pushed his right hand on Joshua's chest, pressing the cross on it. The skin was cold and slimy.

"Behold the Cross of the Lord.

"Be gone, all hostile powers.

"May the Holy Cross be your light and life."

Jack brought his face one inch from the awful grin of the demon. The foul smell hit him fully on his face. The exorcist breathed toward the face of the boy.

"By the breath of your mouth, O Lord,

"Drive out all evil spirits

"Command them to be gone,

"For your kingdom is at hand."

The demon snarled and rolled on the bed, avoiding the exorcist resting against the wall. Jack knew that was the moment to move forward with the Imperative Formula.

He stood up straight and with the rosary in his hands, pointing the cross at the evil he began,

"I charge you, Satan,

"Prince of this world.

"Acknowledge the power and strength of Jesus Christ,

"Who defeated you in the desert,

"Overcame you in the garden,

"Despoiled you on the Cross,

"And, rising from the tomb,

"Transferred your spoils into the kingdom of light.

"Depart from this creature,

"Whom Christ by his birth made his brother,

"And by his death purchased with his blood.

"Depart, therefore, Satan,

"In the name of the Father, and of the Son, and of the Holy Spirit.

"Depart through the faith and prayer of the Church.

"Depart through the sign of the Holy Cross of our Lord Jesus Christ,

"Who lives and reigns forever and ever."

Jack took a few steps back and observed the creature completely still. The demon wasn't facing him anymore but looked at the ceiling in a trance. Jack knew the ritual he had just performed would likely have to be repeated several times. So he went back to the dresser to catch his breath. As he walked, he turned to Joshua's mother and Father Seldwig, and his heart sank in his chest.

The people attending the ritual in the room stared at him with black and empty eyes. The boy's mother stood up slowly, let her rosary fall on the floor and grinned. She had the features of Jack Sullivan's sister, Clara.

"No, no, no," Jack mumbled and closed his eyes, reminding himself that whatever he was seeing was not real. He knew it was probably too late. The demon that Jack had hoped to suffer from his first round of the ritual was counterattacking and, in the subtle and obvious way, that only belongs to evil.

When he reopened his eyes, the woman who once was Joshua's mother and was now Jack's sister had moved closer to him, standing about two feet away from him.

"*Jack,*" she said with the voice of his sister. "*Why didn't you visit Jack?*"

The rest was still a little bit of a blur in Jack's mind. When he regained consciousness, he was lying on the carpet in Joshua's bedroom. A cold and thick liquid dripped on his face. When he opened his eyes, he wanted to scream but couldn't. It was as if life had been taken out of him.

The boy was staring at him from the ceiling with dead eyes. His arms were spread open, and his legs were clenched together.

He had been crucified to the ceiling, his stomach had been torn open, and his guts were hanging low, almost touching the ground.

Blood dripped on Jack's face.

He tried to scream, but he couldn't. He tried to move away, but he couldn't do that either.

That's when he realized the exorcism had failed.

The demon was in control and wanted Jack to watch. It wanted him to know there was no place to hide from it. That it would find him wherever he went after that.

It wanted him to know that it had won and he had lost. And it wanted him to see what would happen next.

The grin on the crucified boy's face started to fade away, and as life left his body, his eyes started to turn from black to white, and his deformed face deflated, almost regaining its original shape.

Father Sullivan saw a shadow coming out of his mouth, nose, and eyes, quickly moving onto one of the walls.

Then, the invisible nails that kept the boy hanging from the ceiling gave up, and gravity won over his body as it fell on Jack Sullivan's.

And that was when he could scream again and cry as his mind tried to reject the horror he had just witnessed.

Then he could move again. He hugged the boy and cried. When he could stand up, he saw the dismembered bodies of Father Seldwig and Joshua's mother on the floor behind the bed.

He called for Mr. Derringer to ensure he was okay, but there was no answer.

Jack Sullivan found him dead at the top of the staircase. The shotgun was straight up, and its barrel, still hot, held what remained of his head.

Everyone was dead. Everyone except him. And to this day, he still didn't know why the demon had spared him. What did the beast get from him? What sort of deal did it make him agree upon? He, of course, had no answers to those questions, but that didn't spare him from some skepticism that had started developing around him in the Vatican.

Jack had eavesdropped on some colleagues of his, talking about him and referring to him as the *Unholy*. The idea of hanging up the collar had become louder in his mind, especially at night when it was time to go to bed. If the transformation of the word of Christ almost into Christian Fascism hadn't been enough, if the sacred institution turning into a business and a race to build the biggest, most gigantic church ever hadn't been sufficient, if the people that were supposed to preach equality, love, and compassion starting to diffuse hate, restriction, and discriminatory concepts weren't enough, the Derringer case was the last straw.

One month after the tragic death of the Derringer family, Father Sullivan resigned from his position.

And the only times where he would look back was to make sure the shadow that had left Joshua Derringer's body on that cursed night was not following him.

# 3

A few days after that first encounter with Lynn Harris on the trail, someone knocked on Jack's front door. He rushed to the door and peeked from the peephole, hesitating for a few seconds after realizing it was Lynn. She was the last person he had expected to see. He had believed they were destined to be invisible neighbors to one another. He opened the door and kindly invited her in. Jack offered her coffee and a slice of peach pie he had bought at the grocery that morning.

"I'm so sorry for our last conversation on the trail. I was completely out of place. I truly can't tell you how disappointed I was with myself," she said.

"There is no need to apologize. God only knows what you were going through on that day. If anything, I would say you were entitled to take it all out on me."

"It was disrespectful and totally unnecessary. That is not who I am. I owe you a big apology."

"Well, in that case, consider your apology fully accepted," he said, smiling at her. Jack was genuinely surprised that Lynn Harris had come forward to discuss the matter.

"In all honesty, although I don't think you owe me any kind of apology, I wanted to ask you a question about that conversation, if you don't mind. Something that has been bugging me a great deal."

"Of course. What is it?" Lynn asked.

"How did you know about the Derringer boy?"

"Who's the Derringer boy?"

"You don't remember mentioning the Derringer boy to me?"

Jack asked.

"This is no justification, but I was in a terrible place. I don't even remember what I said to you. I just knew afterward that the conversation wasn't my proudest moment."

Jack didn't say anything, even though he wasn't satisfied with the answer. He could tell Lynn looked genuinely unaware of anyone named Derringer. He decided to let it go for now.

"How are you holding up?" Jack asked.

"I don't know," she shrugged as Jack noticed her eyes gleaming from the tears collecting in them. "I had a few good days during and after my trip out west with Jane and Bill. I think Frank is doing better, but these past few days, including when we met on the trail, were really hard." She continued, and Jack noticed she had been playing with a necklace she was wearing. He nodded. The woman was in the mood to talk, and he didn't want her to stop. There was something about her that was radically different compared to how she was on the trail. Even in the struggle of grief, there was a calm and peace to her that he wanted to know more about.

She talked about her hiking in the national parks, the stunning landscapes, and how being away from home had given her the chance to think. She also mentioned how close she had felt to her son, Will, lately.

She played with the silver plate of her necklace the whole time as she talked to Jack. She grabbed it and turned it, unwilling to separate from it.

When she was about to leave, she stood up and grabbed the phone from her purse. That allowed Jack to glance at the necklace she was so jealously hiding in her hands.

It was a circular pendant, maybe one inch in diameter.

On the face of the medal were two archaic symbols of a man and a woman. They were depicted upside down. The symbols were simple and looked as if children drew them. Jack had only a few seconds to look at it before it disappeared again in the hands of the woman who seemed obsessed with it. Blurred thoughts started taking shape in his subconscious, things that he wasn't ready to accept. But an alarm was triggered at that moment. Jack was sure he had seen that symbol before. He just couldn't put it in focus in his mind.

When the woman left, he kept watching her from behind the window's blinds, observing with attention the way she walked. He couldn't notice anything unusual besides her continuous fiddling with her necklace.

When she was out of sight, Jack went to the small table he had set up in the far corner of the room, near one of the bookshelves, grabbed a pen, and drew the engraving he had seen on the metal plate hanging from Lynn's necklace.

When finished, he looked at his drawing on the yellow post-it note, then flipped it upside down. The two childishly drawn figures were now standing on their feet. They looked just like a man and woman in very simplified geometrical shapes—a circle for the head, a triangle for the core, and lines for the arms and legs. The woman's body had an additional triangle that was clearly the dress that differentiated her from the man. He kept flipping the note in his hand up and down, flexing his old and rusted photographic memory. If the picture of the man and woman was straight, with them standing on their feet, maybe it was just a gift from a young kid. There could have been so many completely legitimate explanations for it. But Jack could have sworn he saw the figures upside down.

And then it came to him suddenly, and he knew exactly where that symbol came from. He gently patted his forehead, almost as if congratulating his brain for remembering. But then the realization of what the symbol meant came, and he felt a wave of discomfort and dread assailing him. He shook his head as if he could kick his thoughts away or reject them just like that. But he couldn't. The symbol engraved on the necklace Lynn Harris was wearing and playing with was Native American. He couldn't remember if it had been specific to a certain tribe, but part of him believed it was quite universal in the indigenous culture and tradition. But that was just a detail. The meaning of it was what put him in such discomfort.

The upside-down signified a contrary meaning, the antithesis of the specular symbol. If the symbol of the man and the woman standing on their feet meant 'people,' then the upside-down of that meant the opposite of people.

It meant 'dead people'.

# 4

Jack Sullivan knew there weren't many easy ways to research information about Native American traditions and folklore. The tradition was passed from generation to generation orally in most cases. All that was available online was relatively superficial and quite in contrast with what he had learned about those civilizations in the past.

All he knew about it was from an old friend of his named Joel Kopernick. Joel was a fourth-generation Native American from the tribes that once populated the Dakota lands in the northern cold prairies. Jack had met him long ago when they were both on a discussion panel about the inclusivity of religion. That was only the beginning of a beautiful friendship between the two, nourished by respect and deep admiration for their respective knowledge. After their first encounter, they visited each other throughout the years, met each other's families, and stayed in touch as best as they could, given their geographical distance. Joel was among the very few people that Jack knew he could count on. He also happened to be one of the most prominent experts in Native American folklore.

He reached for his phone and scrolled in the contacts until he found Joel's number and dialed it. It took Joel four rings before he picked up.

"Jack. Is this really you?" the man on the other side of the line asked rhetorically. His voice didn't show any sign of age. He sounded just as Jack remembered him, always cordial and unable to hide the emotions that made it out through his tone. Jack could tell he was smiling on the other side.

"In the flesh. At least what remains of me."

"Is it Christmas already? That's usually when I get your calls these days."

"You know, you always tell me I need to call more, that we should catch up more often, so here you go. I told you to be careful of what you wish for."

Jack and Joel kept laughing, giving each other the usual hard time that always preceded serious conversations. It had always been like that. It was their preparation time, much needed before facing the weight of some of their conversations, which were always very difficult and delicate topics.

Listening to Joel's stories and realizing the extent of his knowledge had always humbled Jack on the limited perspective that inevitably came with being a part of the Western world, with the extreme capitalism and the way it had shaped society. Among the most eye-opening conversations they had, one stuck out about their different approach to divinity. The Native American God wasn't a superhuman or a supernatural entity in the shoes of a prophet. God was the water that flowed in the small creek near the village, the fire that kept the tribe warm during the rough winters, the rain that made the soil fertile, the harvest season, the hunt, and the promise of another year.

God was the land.

Every time Jack Sullivan thought about Joel Kopernick, it occurred to him that there couldn't have been a crueler thing that the Western civilizations had done in their obsession with colonization than to take away God from the indigenous. Many other civilizations and religions in the world have been able to establish communities around the world, keep their traditions and beliefs going, and carry their message forward. But that just wasn't possible for the Native Americans because all they had always known about and believed in was the land. That was taken away from them, and they were called heathens for fighting against that with all they had.

After a few minutes of catching up on the latest events that had unfolded in their respective lives, silence had fallen in the conversation. Jack knew the moment for his question had come.

"I need a little grain of your wisdom, my friend. I have tried to research online, but you know how it is," Jack said. He omitted to mention that the matter he was going to ask about had already started to trouble him way more than he would have liked.

"I will do my best. I'm all ears."

Jack told him about the necklace, the material it was made of, and the engraving that was on it. He told Joel that he found out the meaning of the symbol on it and that it meant 'dead people.' He asked if he could provide a little more context on the symbol itself.

After a few moments of silence on the other side of the phone, Joel sighed and began to speak.

"Ok. You are certainly right about the symbol and the meaning. While there isn't a simple answer to your question, I will try to do my best to summarize the concept.

"The symbols of life and death are very common, as you can imagine, and universally used in all the tribes. People are born every day; they die every day. So, it is common to make a silver or a copper plate as a welcome gift for a newborn, just as it is common to make those that say goodbye to this world. Depending on the tribe and their traditions, there are a few more contexts where the symbolism of dead people is used. It really depends on the tribe."

Jack stopped to think about that for a second, then asked: "What can you tell me about the tribes in Utah or the southwest region?"

"That narrows it down quite a lot. Ute and Paiute from the Great Basin, but also Navajo and Hopi from the southwestern region, share many traditions. There are many stories from some of those tribes about indigenous people being sent into exile for using their medicine for things that weren't allowed or positively seen in the communities. I can't share the stories in detail, but I think you know where I'm trying to go."

"Witchcraft," Jack said without hesitation. This was a common element in every religion or system of beliefs managed by human beings.

"Exactly. Death has always been processed and accepted as the beginning of our return to the land. Remember, the land is God, and we came from it. Returning to it has always been a great achievement amongst our people—an indispensable step in our reconciliation with the Great Spirit.

"For this reason, the loss of a loved one is processed differently than most Western civilizations do. And that makes perfect sense if you think about death as the end. With that being said, there are always exceptions to the rule. Sometimes, it happens that the grieving process is more difficult, and it takes longer to process. And that's exactly where the dark spirits lure in the darkness. Some people who were pushed away from their communities used their medicine to create a bridge with the dark spirits. That's when the symbol of dead people started to be associated with the heretics and the dark spirits they allied with."

"Are those dark spirits related to the Wendigos?"

"Not exactly. Wendigos belong to the stories and folklore of the tribes in the Great Plains and Great Lakes. The legends say that a human can become a Wendigo when greed and hunger become insatiable. The spirits I'm referring to are somewhat different, even though just as evil.

"In some stories, they are known as Yee Naaldlooshi. You might have heard of them as Skinwalkers. In some legends, they are called Shapeshifters. In some others, they are called just the Hollow spirits. What they all have in common is their hunger for negative human feelings or emotions. Greed, rage, jealousy, envy, and of course..."

"Grief." Jack Sullivan finished Joel's sentence without even wanting it. Everything Joel had said had turned on the lights in the dark warehouse of his subconscious.

"Yes. Especially grief. That is the main course, Jack."

## 5

Jack arrived at the barbecue organized by Jane Hanson two minutes before six and went straight to the backyard gate. He couldn't help but think about the conversation he had with Joel a few days before, after the unexpected visit of Lynn Harris at his place. During his life, because of his job and the things he had seen, there had been times when he thought he could get used to evil, that it would get easier every time he realized that he was in front of something malevolent. But the reality was that it never got easier. The knot that punctually formed in his stomach, the feeling of dread, the tensing of the body, and the unraveling of the mind were always there. Jack dug deep inside himself to find out he wasn't entirely sure what Joel Kopernick had revealed to him was connected in any way with Lynn Harris. The annoying part for him was the incapacity of deciding if he was just trying to make connections that weren't there or if something was going on. His gut and experience told him something was not right; something was off, but he hadn't yet been able to prove it.  He always did that before deciding if a case of possession needed his intervention. He went through the files, the tapes, the recordings, and the interview transcripts. At some level, his job was no different than the one of a detective. He needed to get some evidence to support his suppositions, which was why he had accepted the invitation from Jane Hanson.

She had invited many families from the neighborhood, and Jack thought it was the perfect opportunity to observe Lynn more closely. For now, the strongest evidence to support the case of an evil presence was Lynn Harris mentioning Joshua Dillinger and sharing her knowledge of a nickname that was practically impossible to know. This wasn't a conclusive piece of evidence, but it was something that a demonic possession could have explained very well. The knowledge of very personal things, or ancient languages, were characteristic elements of demonic possessions.

Bill Hanson welcomed him and took the box Jack was carrying.

"That should be freshly baked," Jack said, pointing his finger at the peach pie.

"Thanks. We are happy you could join us. Please come in. Meat is on the grill, and the drinks are in the cooler. Would you like a beer?"

"I could use a cold one. The heat has been relentless this week," Jack said as he looked beyond Bill at the other guests in the backyard.

Camilla Meyers and Ruth Howard, who lived three and four houses south down the road, were helping Jane set up the table outside; there was no trace of Lynn Harris.

He followed Bill to the cooler, and the man offered him a can of

Miller Lite, still dripping cold water from the cooler. It felt good at the touch, and Jack placed the can on his nape and wrists before opening it.

The women saw him and immediately came down from the patio to greet him.

"Welcome to the most exclusive summer party in Indiana, and also probably the only one," Jane said, laughing. "And thank you for the pie. I was actually missing a dessert for tonight."

He spent the next twenty minutes catching up with the neighbors. In the men's corner by the grill, the conversation was already quite deep into baseball, which he never had had a genuine interest in. He listened to the conversation distractedly and without actively participating.

So he had moved to the women's corner, where more interesting topics were being discussed. His mind was entirely focused on Lynn Harris, or, more precisely, the absence of Lynn Harris at the party. He kept gazing at her house. He was about to ask Jane if they were coming when he saw them walking in. Frank led the way, carrying two bottles of wine in his hands, and Lynn followed him behind.

The difference in their facial expressions couldn't have been more different and odd. Frank was the picture of silent pain. Jack had seen that so many times in so many different people. His eyes were red as if he had recently cried. They were also absent at the same time. He carried himself lazily, by inertia, head down, clearly trying his best to avoid eye contact with the guests.

On the contrary, his wife was smiling and walking at a vigorous pace. She wore her hair in a ponytail, and Jack noticed she had put some make-up on. Her right hand was near her neck. From a distance, it might have looked like she was massaging it, but Jack knew what she was doing. She was holding her necklace, just like the last time he saw her at his house. He also noticed something unusual with her right eye. It was as if she had a tic or a nervous spasm within her eyelid, randomly vibrating without notice.

*It could be just a nervous reaction of her body to the high stress she is going through.* Of course, that was a perfectly normal explanation, but she didn't seem stressed at all. She looked like someone who didn't have any worries in life.

Jack was listening to the conversations in the women's group. Camilla and Ruth were talking about the parish and the new priest. They were the only two discussing how they weren't particularly impressed by the last sermon he delivered the previous Sunday. Jane and Lynn, clearly not interested in the religious topic, were discussing their trip to Utah. Jack took that chance to get into the conversation, telling them about his experience and memories from when he had been there.

"You know, it was so many years ago, but there is a road that goes from Moab all the way up through the canyons, twisting around the Colorado River. It was one of the most amazing drives I remember to this day."

"Yes! That was Route 128. Oh my gosh! I totally forgot about that. Remember we had dinner at the Red Cliff Lodge? That's the place where movie stars like John Wayne used to stay when they filmed the westerns. It's such a cool place. Do you remember Lynn?"

"Of course I do," she said, smiling, then looked at Jack Sullivan. Her eyes were gleaming with a strange light in them. She bit her bottom lip, which was red and full. Her body language, the way she touched her hair, couldn't be more eloquent than that. Jack felt a wave of terror invading him, not because he was tempted by it— Lynn Harris was an extraordinarily good-looking woman— but because that was the confirmation he was waiting for.

The person in front of him wasn't Lynn Harris. It was someone else, or something else, that was trying to seduce him. She was sexually aroused by a seventy-year-old man she knew was a priest. And she was flirting with him in front of her neighbors and her husband.

Jack Sullivan wasn't a judgmental person. He knew sometimes people reacted to grief in mysterious ways. But all of it was too bizarre and wrong to be just that. He was now concerned his cover was ruined. If a Hollow spirit, the kind that Joel had talked about, took control of Lynn Harris, then she was likely flirting with him because the entity wanted Jack to be on the same side.

Jack excused himself and asked Jane if he could use the restroom.

When he closed the door behind him, he leaned on the sink and put some cold water on his face, trying to calm his breathing.

Everything checked out in a concerning way. Lynn Harris was oddly and unusually relaxed; the Faustian bargain was the entry of any kind of evil he had ever dealt with. Her body was reacting to it, showing slight signs of spasms, and she was sexually aroused by him. The whole situation looked less and less like a coincidence to him and more and more like a case of possession.

He let the cold water run and wet his face again. When he opened his eyes, his heart sank in his chest, and he remained paralyzed, unable to scream or close his eyes. In the mirror in front of him was the shape of a young man, who he recognized as Will Harris.

The reflection in the mirror showed a tall guy with dark and long curly hair. He wore a leather jacket and a red t-shirt underneath. His cheekbones were high, and his face was lean, exposing a very defined jawline. The entity that carried Will's features grinned sinisterly at Jack. His lips looked fake as if they were made of play-dough. With furious strength, he felt the Hollow getting into his head, and images started to run in front of Jack's eyes. He was a powerless spectator of his own nightmares as the slideshow continued in front of his eyes. Jack felt the Hollow's pleasure as he experienced fear, regret, and guilt. It ate, drank, and inhaled them, snarling like a wild beast.

Jack and the Hollow were not in the bathroom anymore but in a room that was familiar to Jack. It was Joshua Derringer's bedroom.

He heard a deafening buzz of bugs and flies as if they were in his head. He tried to scream, but no sounds came out of his mouth. He watched his body on the floor as if witnessing the whole scene from above. He saw Josh breaking the chains that restrained him to his bed and moving around the room with incredible speed. He watched him devouring his mother by the neck, then killing the local minister and running on all fours toward the hallway where his dad sat. Mr. Derringer's eyes were filled with tears, madness, and astonishment. Before the beast could reach him, he had already put the barrel of his shotgun in his mouth and pulled the trigger. The beast that possessed Joshua growled and screamed, a hideous sound that didn't have anything human in it, with disappointment because the man had denied it the pleasure of killing.

*"You let them die, priest!"* The voice of the Hollow was guttural in Jack's head, resonating with violence against his skull.

*"You are weak, priest. Stay away from her. Last warning."*

Then, suddenly, the slideshow stopped, and Jack Sullivan was back in the bathroom, gasping for air.

The Hollow was gone, and he could move again. He stood up and waited for his breath to return to normal.

One thing was now pretty clear: Lynn Harris was the vessel, and the Hollow already knew everything about Jack. All it took was a quick stroll in his mind to check his darkest moments. And while he thought the demon possessing the Derringer boy was extremely dangerous, this one was something different. Something ancestral.

He was dealing with an extremely powerful evil.

This time, Jack wasn't quite sure it could be stopped.

# 6

During the following week, Jack Sullivan kept researching every possible information about the Hollow. He had spoken with Joel Kopernick another two times. His Native American friend had mailed him his personal notes on the topic, and Jack Sullivan had found the black leathered notebook a priceless source of information.

Learning about the enemy was the first step to winning the battle, but the Hollow had done the same when he was in Jane Hanson's restroom. Jack had thought a great deal about its unfinished features. Even though he had never met the young Will Harris in person, he knew that the Hollow's self-representation of him was inaccurate. Several areas of its face looked as if they were made of Play-Doh. They were smooth and perfectly in sync with the color of the skin, but they were missing detail, depth, and realism. He also remembered the grin painted on the Hollow's face, a monstrously wide grin extending all the way to its ears. In Joel's notebook, Jack found several sketches of Skinwalkers or Shapeshifters. These drawings were not so dissimilar to what he had been able to find online on his own. Of course, the shapes they could use were various because of their own names, Shapeshifters.

Four days after his first and latest encounter with the Hollow, Jack was shopping for groceries at the local store when he saw Lynn Harris. He didn't intend to get too close to her and observed from a distance. She pushed her cart through the center aisles for a while but didn't pick many things up to place in her cart. She kept looking around as if she was searching for someone. *Maybe she was supposed to meet a friend at the store, and she was having a hard time since the store was packed with people*, Jack thought. By then, Jack Sullivan was actively following her and checking from a distance, being careful not to be seen, putting on his hat to blend in with the crowd more easily.

Lynn looked nervous and anxious; her body movements were sudden and downright clumsy. She kept turning around jerkily, seeking something or someone she wasn't finding. Then, after a few minutes, Jack noticed she wasn't looking anymore. Her focus was fixed and steady in front of her. She had clearly either given up or she had found it.

Jack left his cart, with the groceries he had filled it with, in the canned food aisle and left the store. He moved his car to a different parking spot, one from which he would have a clear view of the people leaving the store. He stayed there for a good fifteen minutes before he spotted Lynn Harris carrying one half-full brown paper bag in her arms. She put it in the trunk of her car and rushed to the driver's seat.

Jack Sullivan turned the engine on and followed her out of the parking lot, keeping his distance by always having at least two cars between them so she wouldn't feel like she was being followed. She got off the US-36 and drove into a cookie-cutter residential neighborhood where the one-story houses were barely distinguishable with their light gray vinyl siding. When Jack saw her slowing down and bringing her car to a halt, he cruised at a very low speed until he had a clear visual, still conserving a good, safe distance. A man wearing a baseball cap and comfy clothes was carrying groceries inside his house. That's when it first occurred to Jack that Lynn Harris was following this guy from the grocery store. He couldn't find any other plausible explanations.

A few moments after the man closed the trunk of his car and disappeared behind his front door, Lynn turned the engine back on and did a U-turn in a speedy maneuver. She drove at full speed away from the neighborhood. Jack laid low, hoping that she didn't see him.

Then he returned home with a million questions in his mind.

And all his questions were answered at once two mornings after, when he was coming back from one of his walks. Jack Sullivan did not own a television. He never had any use for one during his life, and he didn't intend to own one in the days of his retirement. But he always liked to read the local newspapers. That's why he had subscribed to the Indy Star.

He grabbed it from his driveway, unwrapped it from the red plastic bag it had been packaged in, unrolled it to the front page, and almost fainted at what he saw.

Man found dead in Avon, Hendricks County Sheriff Office investigating, the title on the front page read. At the bottom of the page was a picture of the house and the neighborhood. It was the house of the man Lynn Harris had followed from the grocery store. It didn't take long before the death of Oliver Curry became the most discussed topic, not only in newspapers and local TV news but also in the neighborhood.

Sitting on one of the very comfortable chairs that Jane Hanson had bought for the backyard -the wide wicker frame hosted a very thick and firm cushion, offering an incredible feeling of floating- Jack Sullivan pretended to listen to the chitchat that was going on in the background.

But he was not listening.

He wasn't listening because Camilla and Ruth repeated the same concepts over and over and over: "This is shocking for a neighborhood like that," or "This will definitely drive the price of the other houses down," and other completely irrelevant comments that he couldn't care less about.

Jack Sullivan was thinking. He was thinking about the shift that had just happened and how quickly it had happened. He had a particular experience in the timing of possessions in a very clinical way. Most of the entities hosted in a human body typically took several weeks before having some kind of control over the vessel.

He remembered when he was in his late thirties, and he was in Maine. He was shadowing and learning from his mentor, Father Cantoni, an Italian minister from Naples. Father Cantoni was a very rigid and severe man with an endless sea of knowledge in theology and religion, especially regarding the occult. This mission in Maine was Jack Sullivan's third one, but it felt much different than the previous ones, in a challenging way.

Mrs. Calloway, a forty-eight-year-old woman who lived in the suburbs of Bangor and a very devoted Catholic, had expressed her concerns to the priest about her husband and the abnormal shift that she had noticed in his behavior for a couple of weeks. Hugh Calloway, a man who had always been fiercely against alcohol, was suddenly coming home reeking of booze every night of the week and would lock himself in his studio for the whole weekend, probably drinking himself to sleep. He had started skipping church on Sundays, and supposedly, he talked a lot in his sleep, in a language she didn't recognize.

The woman was asked to record his sleep talking, and the tape eventually made its way onto Father Cantoni's desk. He and Jack Sullivan were immediately dispatched to Bangor, Maine, for an exorcism. The unknown language had turned out to be Aramaic.

Jack remembered how obsessed Father Cantoni was trying to find out exactly when the possession had started, within a twenty-four-hour margin. According to him, there was a recurring unfolding of events in possession cases. If they knew when the possession had started, they could plan and predict what would happen to Mr. Calloway's body before evil took control.

That particular possession had been imprinted in Jack's brain profoundly, because they had misjudged the start. Before Father

Cantoni could do anything about it, Mr. Calloway ended up slaughtering his whole family with a sledgehammer.

That's what Jack Sullivan was thinking about in the shade of the umbrella that Jane Hanson had set up on the freshly cut grass of the backyard. Jane had been inviting him to the house often, and he could feel a genuine friendship was blossoming between them. She had started opening up with him about quite personal topics, especially related to her spirituality. While she didn't classify herself as a Christian, she showed a deep curiosity about aspects connected to the spiritual world that her pragmatism and rational thinking couldn't stop.

"Are you ok, Jack?" A voice brought him back to reality. He looked around as if he had just awakened from a dream and saw Jane staring at him. From the look on her face, she must have been watching him for a while as he was lost in his thoughts.

"Oh. I'm sorry; I spaced out. Yes, I am terrific. Enjoying the beautiful weather and your hospitality," Jack said, raising his can of Michelob Ultra in the air for a toast.

"I need to talk to you about something in private." She lowered her tone as she pronounced those last two words, which came out almost in a whisper.

"Of course, of course."

Jane led him inside the kitchen and closed the sliding glass door behind her. Jack looked outside, Camilla and Ruth still busy talking over each other and Bill Hanson napping on the hammock in the shade of the weeping willow.

"What's going on?" Jack asked, studying the concerned expression on Jane's face with curiosity.

"I don't even know where to start, to be honest with you. You might think that I'm going crazy or something."

"Start wherever you feel comfortable; if it isn't clear enough, this is a safe space," he said, smiling.

That seemed to tranquilize her a bit. She sat on one of the bar stools in front of the kitchen island, looked outside, and sighed.

"It's about Lynn. I'm really concerned about her."

Jack hadn't seen that one coming. He hoped his expression didn't look too surprised, but he couldn't hide a little bit of relief that came with the awareness that he wasn't the only one who had noticed concerning aspects of Mrs. Harris's behavior.

"What about Lynn?"

"We have always been very close, even after Will passed. She has gone through the most terrible times, and I almost feel ashamed of myself for telling you this, but she hasn't been herself in a few weeks. Since we came back from our trip, she has seemed off. I cannot even imagine what grieving my son would do to me, so I cannot judge the situation, but her behavior lately is just concerning."

Jack nodded and gestured with his hand to keep going. He needed to buy some time. He never thought about sharing what he knew with Jane Hanson. While the option was attractive because teaming up with Jane would make it easier for them to monitor Lynn Harris and act at the right time, Jack wasn't sure he was ready to share. The latest threat from the demon still resounded in his head.

*Stay away from her. Last warning.*

The last thing Jack Sullivan wanted was to bring this thing onto Lynn Harris and her family.

"Again, I don't want to sound like I'm judging, but she has been entirely different since we returned from the trip. Trust me when I tell you I am the first person in the world who wants to see her happy, but this feels weird. She is always in control of her emotions, and now she almost seems... happy and serene again. I feel horrible for saying this, but if Peter had passed away just six or maybe seven months ago, I don't know anything about grief, but I cannot imagine myself being that composed and joyful if my son died that recently. And I am sure she didn't even scratch the surface of her own hell.

"All this rant to say, I'm deeply concerned that she is developing a bipolar disorder or some other mental health issue, or even worse, maybe she started using."

"Do you mean drugs?" Jack asked.

Jane nodded and then started crying.

"She doesn't show up anymore when I invite her over." Jane stretched her hand toward the glass door to show him her absence. "She doesn't want to go on walks or hikes with me anymore, but, most importantly, she doesn't speak with me anymore. It's like something in her head just shut down, and something new is coming out of it. Something I don't like at all."

"The other day at the solstice party, after you left, she started getting flirty with Bill. Normally, I don't mind because I know she is joking, but she hadn't done that in a long time. And I felt terrible for Frank. I also couldn't help but notice the look she was giving you. Now please tell me that you noticed the same. I mean, have you seen Frank lately? He looks like a train wreck, and rightfully so. He lost his son, for Christ's sake. You think I'm out of my mind, don't you?"

"No, I don't. I think what you have described is very similar to what I have noticed. Of course, I'm not as close to Lynn and Frank as you, but the contrast you are talking about is very evident."

"Oh, thank God! It's not just my impression." She exhaled in relief. Tears were still filling her eyes."

"You see, grief is a tricky beast to tame. Some people never really process or accept that the person they have lost is gone forever. And so, they escape in a safe bubble. They build the bubble and try to establish a new order for everything, because outside of the bubble, the ground is still shaking.

"So, my first theory is that you are correct. Lynn might have built a bubble of delusion in her mind. She might be trying to convince herself that everything is back as it was. But that theory doesn't quite convince me in the sense that it doesn't add up fully. You see, when people develop mental illness as they try to escape grief without facing it, the bubble explodes quite immediately in most cases. Which brings me to my second theory."

Jane Hanson looked at him, craving for him to finish his sentence.

"What? What's the second theory?"

And so, Jack Sullivan had ultimately decided that he had to share his discoveries with Jane Hanson. He never spoke easily with people about the supernatural, despite his life having been devoted to it, in one way or the other, and that's where his initial hesitance had come from. But as he had gotten to know Jane better since he arrived in town, he could tell she was extremely intelligent and open-minded. If he had one shot to share this madness with someone who could listen, that would be with Jane Hanson.

"My second theory is a long one. Please come to my place tomorrow morning, and I will tell you everything I know."

# 7

The following morning, twenty minutes before the appointment scheduled for 8 a.m., Jack Sullivan frowned when someone knocked on his front door.

When he opened it, Jane rushed in and stood before him with her arms crossed. She didn't look very relaxed.

"I didn't close my eyes for one minute last night." She said, sending him a blaming glimpse.

"In that case, I'm not going to ask you if you need one of these," Jack said, raising a coffee mug he had bought in a souvenir shop in

Jackson, Wyoming. "Milk, no sugar?" he asked rhetorically.

They sat around the coffee table between Jack's recliner and the loveseat, where Jane took her place.

"I've been trying to guess what the second theory number is. Please tell me it's not drugs. Tell me Lynn is not on drugs."

Jack sighed and took a sip of coffee, then put the mug on one of the coasters on the table.

"My dear, I wish the answer was as simple as that. As bad as drug addiction sounds, I'm afraid the second theory is a problem with a much more complex solution.

"What I am about to tell you requires you to have the most open mind you can bring," Jack continued. "Without an open mind, it will be a loss of time. I know you are not a religious person, let alone a superstitious one. You might find what I'm about to say very difficult to accept, and trust me; I speak from experience when I tell you that you might be tempted to discard it all as just another story of insanity. I need you to promise me that you will keep an open mind. All I am about to say is the truth, and I trust you to be able to carry that truth. It won't be an easy one. Can you promise me you'll keep an open mind?"

"Yes, I can," Jane said with no hesitation, though with more of a note of concern in her voice.

And so, Jack Sullivan filled his neighbor in on everything he knew. He went systematically from their first encounter on the trail, to her visit when he had first noticed her obsession with the necklace, the complete shift in her behavior, the first encounter with the Hollow and finally, Lynn Harris driving in front of Oliver Curry's home, the day before he was found dead. Jack also filled Jane in on everything he had learned from Joel Kopernick.

Jane listened in religious silence and never interrupted. She remained silent even after Jack was done with the story.

She walked around the room, chewing nervously on her nails, looking down as she tried to evaluate all she had just heard.

"You are right," she finally said. "I'm not sure I can say I believe a word of what you just told me. I mean, this whole thing challenges the very foundations of everything I believe in. I...I don't know. I think I better get home now."

She stormed through the room and walked through the front door, leaving it open behind her.

Jack called for her, moving quickly through the room and to the front door, where he stopped. She kept walking when she crossed the street without looking for oncoming cars.

Jack Sullivan watched her struggling to find the keys, unlocking the front door of her house, and disappearing through it. He knew it was a long shot, but he couldn't hide a slight disappointment from how the conversation had gone. For a moment, he thought that he could share his latest experiences, that they could team up, and he would not be alone in fighting this thing. He found himself ashamed of his foolishness.

He didn't blame her for going away. To embrace certain truths meant sometimes losing a great deal of one's old self. Once certain gates were open, there was no turning back. The human brain, by design, is programmed to keep people alive. When a threat is perceived, the brain chooses not to engage, to fulfill its self-preservation. And looking into the dark well of what is beyond human logic and comprehension changed people profoundly, irreversibly. It had changed him forever. And Jane Hanson had just resisted everything he told her as a threat. And rightly so. Nothing wrong with it. Some things are better not to be shared. And Jack just had a powerful reminder of that.

He went to bed around ten that night. He never slept more than five, six hours at the most. He always read for about half an hour before turning the lamp off and initiating the process that would bring him to sleep - it wasn't an easy one because his brain just refused to slow down, to coast to a slower rhythm- in that respect meditation had helped him a lot. He wished he had discovered it a lot earlier in his life.

But that night, his brain refused to give up and slow down. Jack wondered where the Hollow originated from -he was obsessed with unanswerable questions. He also wondered how it anchored to the vessels. Most evil spirits had to be somehow invited. The vessel had to agree to carry the evil to a certain level. There was a profound difference between a host and a vessel regarding possession. While being a host meant that the demon would physically enter the body and assume control of it, a vessel could even carry the evil for a while without physical implications. The more he thought about it, the more it appeared to him that Lynn Harris was a vessel. This made sense to Jack, given the timeline. If Lynn Harris had been possessed during her trip to Utah, by this time, there would be far greater signs on her body that would prove it.

He wondered what that transaction between Lynn Harris and the vile creature had looked like. *What had she bargained with? Was the Hollow providing her the relief that a mourning mother needs more than air in exchange for her being a vessel? When did that happen? It must have been in Utah,* Jack thought. Everything made sense with the timing: Lynn had started to manifest shifts in her behavior after the trip, the necklace artifact was clearly Native American, and Joel Kopernick had confirmed the symbol engraved on it. These were the details he had hoped Jane would confirm.

*These are just more unanswered questions.*

He put the book on the humble nightstand -which wasn't even with the floor, and so it rocked, able to only touch on three of the four legs - and switched the light off, letting the darkness swallow him entirely.

That was the part where he would typically meditate to doze off. But that night, he didn't feel comfortable. As his eyes got used to the darkness and the objects in the room started to take shape, he noticed his breathing was irregular and unsteady. He couldn't tell why at a deep level, but he was getting anxious. A panic attack?

He felt observed: something in the darkness lured, gloomy, and perched onto the shadows around the room. Jack's mind went back many years to when he was just a kid, and like every kid, he was scared in the absence of light. As he fought his heartbeat, clearly still climbing, he thought about human fears taking shape in our very young minds as children, in the dark of an empty room, and surviving after all these years.

He knew he was being observed; he had been his entire life. And despite him being used to that feeling, it didn't mean it got any easier to face. On the contrary, he felt increasingly scared as the years passed.

Suddenly, there was a change of pressure in the air; it felt like when an airplane goes up or down too quickly, making ears feel clogged. The sound of buzzing flies and bugs was back, and even before he recognized the stench of rot, he knew the Hollow was there with him.

Jack couldn't tell if it was physically there or just projecting. But it felt incredibly close to him.

*Jack.*

The voice that he heard in his head was the voice of his father.

It all seemed like a dream.

He closed his eyes, and when he opened them back, he was in the kitchen of his hometown house. Sitting at the kitchen table was himself, his mom and his dad.

*Jack.*

His father's voice came again at him, but his father's lips didn't move. As a matter of fact, both parents were utterly still, like wax sculptures sitting in a Madame Tussaud Museum.

*Jack, why would you do this?* his dad asked. Jack remembered the conversation he had had at that kitchen table on that day long ago. It was the day he told his parents he wanted to take the vows and become a Catholic church minister. His dad wasn't happy with his decision because Jack wouldn't be able to marry and have kids, so the Sullivan name would end with Jack.

Jack looked at his dad across the table. There was a grin on his face that didn't belong to him. Jack had never seen his father smile.

Then the kitchen disappeared with all its furniture, and he sat in a hospital room on a chair. He looked at his sister Clara, intubated and hooked to the machines that monitored her vitals. On the other side of the room was his other sister, Andrea, who wouldn't die that day. The one that was still alive to the present day.

*Jack! Oh, Jack. It's so good to see you. I haven't seen you in such a long time.*

The voice was Clara's now. She didn't move her lips either; she had her eyes closed, and despite being intubated, she was grinning. At that moment, Jack knew what the Hollow was trying to do. The Hollow wanted Jack to feel so that it could feed from those feelings. It wanted Jack to feel shame for the judgment and disapproval that came from his father for his life choices. It wanted him to feel guilty for not visiting his sisters and not having the chance to say goodbye to one of them.

And, sure enough, as Jack re-lived those days of his life, tears were collecting in his eyes, dripping on his wrinkled cheekbones and rolling down to his white beard.

Jack felt the demon's infinite cold and void, sensing the feelings leaving his body and getting devoured by it. He felt naked and inhuman, and he guessed that's how the Hollow must have felt all the time. It was a horrible feeling of loneliness and hopelessness, and Jack was almost to the point of thinking that he should end his own life.

Then, the hospital bed and chair disappeared with his sisters, and he was floating in utter darkness.

Jack could still see an even darker shape in front of him in the darkness. And he knew that he was looking at the natural form of the Hollow, or at least at one of his primordial shapes.

The Hollow was about twelve feet tall with very long limbs and a compact core that almost made it look like a spider but had only four legs. The body was curved, but the hollow could stand on two legs like a human.

Jack knew the Hollow wanted him to listen.

*Stop! Stop or die!*

The voice was deep and coarse and had a raspy note. It sounded like a beast growling and a man wheezing with emphysema.

*Stop Jack! Stop or die!*

# 8

In the following months, Jack laid low, barely having any contact with his neighbors. It wasn't him who tried to avoid them but rather the opposite. Jane Hanson, who would typically be on the front porch reading during the hot afternoons, was nowhere to be seen. Her car was parked in the driveway as usual, but there was no trace of her outside. Jack had seen Bill several times on Main Street in town and around his yard. He always waved at him respectfully, but Jack was quite sure he wasn't aware of what he had spoken about with his wife, and he doubted Jane had opened up with him about her concerns for Lynn. So, there were no changes in the relationship with him.

Jack thought once more about Jane's reaction after their latest conversation. Had she fled because she believed he was completely insane? Or maybe it was possible that she couldn't process all of that at once, that deep inside her, she believed him and was now dealing with the fallout of that discovery. Jack knew the feeling or learning about the existence of the supernatural. Despite his faith, which was cast in believing in the supernatural by definition, he recognized a huge difference between having faith and realizing that there was another invisible layer of reality to most people. Jack had always believed that society shaped people to believe in Christ without knowing exactly what Jesus Christ's message was about. The message had been shaped, especially in America, in a way that wouldn't raise questions. An unquestioning belief. This belief was founded on the binary concept of good and evil, black and white, God and Devil, because it was easier for the masses to accept it like that. But the reality of the layer he had dealt with throughout his life was very different. The adjacent world was so deep and complex that humans could not comprehend it fully. In that parallel layer of reality lived powerful forces. They were designed to live in their neck of the woods. Still, sometimes, in the chaotic revolution of the universe, the layers collided, rubbed against one another, stretched thin, weakening the fabric of reality and opening opportunities to cross-contaminate each other. There was no way to stop it or control it.

Lynn Harris and her husband Frank had also gone MIA.

Jack didn't intend to yield to the threats of the beast that manifested to him in the bathroom of the Hanson's house or in his dreams.

*Stop! Stop or die!*

Those words that reached him in the ominous voice of the Hollow were still echoing loud in his mind. The Hollow was aware of what Jack Sullivan was trying to do. It knew not only him and what he had done in his life but also all Jack's fears, all his regrets, the guilt. It had fed on it like a hungry beast fighting for survival.

Jack had fought powerful creatures during his life but never had one of these things gotten so close and intimate inside his head, not even the one that killed the Derringer family. This entity needed the knowledge to be able to attack and strategize.

That was why he hadn't tried to go after Lynn anymore; if he wanted to fight this thing, he had to do it from a distance without giving it the advantage of sneaking into his mind.

That was also the reason why he was concerned about Jane Hanson. Jack felt guilty because by telling her what he had discovered, he might have exposed her to the Hollow, in a way he never meant to do. To limit the damage that was also required to isolate himself from Jane, Jack Sullivan spent the rest of the summer just doing that, isolating himself from the rest of the world, deep in his research and reading.

And before he realized it, September had arrived, and the promise of the fall with it. It was his favorite time of the year, the season of harvesting.

On one occasion, as he raked crunchy fallen leaves in his front yard, he saw Bill and Jane Hanson walking out of the front door and getting into their SUV.

Jack waved at them, giving them a smile soaked with nostalgia and unspoken apologies. He saw Bill waving back at him from behind the windshield and then looked at Jane, standing near the open door on the passenger side, staring at him. Her eyes were filled with pain, fear and absolution simultaneously. There was forgiveness in her eyes. He knew right then that she didn't have any bad blood with him, but he also saw how it would be between them going forward. She had to hold back just as Jack had to.

Jane pressed her lips together as if she was trying to hold a cry and then got in the car.

The white SUV drove away going north, and Jack felt the need to wave at them again.

That was the last time he saw Jane and Bill Hanson alive.

# Part Four:

# The Hollow

# 1

Peter didn't know if he had screamed when he woke up, but he was confident he had, considering the nightmare he just had. His heart galloped in his chest, his lungs desperately looking to be filled with air. He felt as if he had been underwater in his sleep. He took a sip of water from the bottle on the side table and got up, covered in sweat.

Luna sat comfortably on the soft rug in the hallway, waiting for him to let her outside so she could take care of her business. Peter looked at her from the bathroom as he urinated, her composure betrayed by the uncontrollable wagging of her tail. She was sitting right in front of his parent's bedroom door as if she was guarding it or waiting for them. The thought of that gave him a physical pain in his chest, like a cramp.

She sprung up as he came towards her and led the way downstairs, randomly turning to check that he was following along, then stopped in front of the door and gently scratched twice at the glass of the kitchen glass door that opened to the back patio and yard. She sprinted down the steps and chased a rabbit that, up to a moment before, was quietly snacking on the tall, dark green grass he needed to mow.

He poured himself a cup of coffee from the pot he had prepared the night before; he had set the timer to start brewing at 9 a.m., and even though it was almost eleven 'o'clock, the machine had kept it hot for him. He didn't remember much from the previous night, no waking up in the middle of the night, no memories of dreams or nightmares, but he felt tired, as if he hadn't rested.

He watched Luna chasing the rabbit. She went about her business, started sniffing around and walked towards the woods.

When Peter called her, she turned towards him and then kept following the trail her nose had set for her. She stopped near the fence that Peter's dad had installed around the perimeter of their property. He remembered helping him with that a few years back, digging deep to set up the metal posts, then pouring the concrete and trying to eyeball from a few feet how to hold them in place so they would be straight.

He remembered how hard they laughed when they looked at the finished result from the back patio. The green iron posts were as crooked as the Tower of Pisa. They tried to blame it on one another, laughing their asses off in the process.

That was his dad, a man with thousands of ideas but, by his own admission, not enough skills to make things as perfect as he would have liked or envisioned. He strived for perfection, but he was not a perfectionist. He didn't care about the final result as long as he had fun.

Peter was quite different in the sense that he would care way too much about the perfect final product—an aspect he had unconsciously brought into his writing.

And that thought brought another memory of his dad, this time telling him that art is messy, not perfect. Perfection and creativity were at the antipodes.

Peter felt a rush of anger coming from his stomach, and he tightened his fingers around the coffee cup's handle to the point of hurting himself. His heart accelerated again, and a single tear came down from the small pool that had gathered in his eyes. He clenched his teeth and stiffened his jaw. The detective's words, reading the police report to him, stormed into his mind like a fury.

*Suicide.*

*Depression.*

*Suicide.*

The pictures of these words from the report flashed in his mind like a stroboscopic light, sending pressure waves at every beat, diffusing a mix of pain and pure rage in sync with his heartbeat. And then the hate came. He could feel it like a poison in his bloodstream. He could feel its power and its darkness flowing in his veins.

He hated his dad and himself for hating him at the same time. He hated that he wasn't there with him anymore and would never be again. *If the suicide theory was true, had he had the guts to take his mom with him, too? How could he possibly be such a coward? How could he do something like that to his family? Or what was left of it anyway.*

*Was his mom aware? How could she possibly be okay with something like that? She couldn't have known. And how the fuck am I ever going to know if that was the case?*

He was short of breath and had begun to hyperventilate, his strength leaving him after the rush, and he felt like fainting. The world became blurrier. He looked down at his feet and saw the coffee mug shattered on the deck; the hot liquid that had poured on his foot left a burning red mark. Luna was now a few feet away, barking in his direction. He couldn't hear anything. The world had stopped making sounds, or maybe he had gone deaf.

When he raised his eyes, he saw the dark stain again, but it wasn't near the Harris attic window this time. It was on his house's exterior, near his parent's bedroom. The stain was moving, forming a cloud of black powder that migrated toward him. It was like a dense dark smoke, changing shape, following beautiful and intricate patterns as it twisted and turned. It swirled and expanded, only to collapse on itself again. He slowly reached with his hand to touch it but couldn't. The volatile matter that looked like mold adjusted its shape as it wrapped around his finger without touching his skin. He felt a vibration, a buzzing feeling of static electricity around it.

And then the voices screamed in his head all at once, and they deafened him. The moans became shouts of pain, then excruciating cries of loss and grief. The sounds mutated until they became buzzes of insects.

He felt a terrible taste in his mouth, like rotten meat infested with maggots.

Rot and decay.

Death.

Peter felt his anger leaving his body like it was being extracted by him, sucked out with a straw. The cloud fed from it, craving for more. He found himself with his eyes closed. He wouldn't dare open them. Beyond the darkness of his eyelids, it was as if he stared at a bottomless well of horror and pain. And his body and mind decided they couldn't take any more of it, and the world went dark around him.

When he came back to his senses, he felt the warm and wet tongue of Luna all over his face.

"Alright, alright, sweet girl. I love you, too," he said as he lifted himself up and scratched her behind her ears. Peter looked around and couldn't tell how long he had been out. He remembered the convulsed darkness, the sounds and the cloud of powdery mold that he had seen right in front of his face.

"What is happening to me?" he said aloud, his voice trembling. He couldn't imagine himself going insane, even if he wanted to. The thought of losing his mental capacities, and being delusional, had always been his greatest fear. To end up in an asylum, filled with tranquilizers and several other drugs, with other people screaming and banging their heads on the walls, not being able to have a pen or a pencil to write ever again.

He grabbed the empty mug that had fallen from his hands in the grass. He called Luna and went inside the house, closing the sliding glass door behind him. He didn't know what to do with his day. He had thought about going for a run but felt light-headed after passing out in the backyard, so he grabbed his laptop and went into the den, sitting on the sofa. Perhaps out of all that madness, he could write a bit, just as he was doing before his phone rang on that goddamn day. That made him think about the soothing voice of Detective Cooper. There was something about that man. The detective looked like he cared about the tragedy that had hit him so hard. He left his laptop on the couch and got up, looking for his wind jacket, the same one he wore on the day he went to the police station and the morgue.

He found it hanging from the back of one of the chairs around the dining table.

He looked in all the pockets until he found what he was looking for. He fished for a rectangular piece of thick paper. It read: Det. Robert Cooper, Homicide Division, IMPD. The mobile phone number at the bottom of the card was highlighted in yellow.

A wave of sadness hit him hard, and tears flowed abundantly.

He missed them so much. The people who had always offered him a shoulder to cry on were now why he was crying. And he realized just how lonely he was now and what an unfillable void he was left to deal with.

He called Melissa, the girl he was dating in New Orleans. They had known each other only for a month or so, but she was the only person he could talk to that came to his mind. They spoke for over half an hour. Peter explained to her what had happened and apologized for being MIA. Melissa was shocked to hear his story and promised to jump on a plane to Indianapolis the following Friday. He told her it wasn't necessary and appreciated her offer, and then hung up.

The outburst had felt good in the moment, but now the sense of dread and loneliness was creeping back in. He could see no light at the end of the tunnel. He hadn't felt so desperate in the days immediately following the news of his parent's death. But he did now, the numbing feeling of his nervous system trying to shut him off to preserve himself and keep him away from the threat and the unbearable pain and anger that kept his heart beat high and strong, pumping blood furiously in and out.

*Is this what grief is like? Is this the worst of it?*

*If it is going to get worse, I'm not sure I'm strong enough to deal with it*, he thought. And that thought led to doubts, questions and anger again. He wondered if this eternal loop would ever end.

He crashed on the sofa again and let himself doze off into sleep.

It wasn't a restful one, though. He kept drifting in and out of it, stuck in a limbo between the madness of his interrupted dreams and the intolerable pain of reality.

# 2

He knew he was in a dream but in a very subtle way, the way one knows only at a very deep subconscious level. Peter found himself in a room of an old house. A lady stood in front of a tall window. The room was dark, and the only light came from an oil lantern placed on a high dresser made of wood. The light struggled to find its way in the room's darkness but was enough to show Peter the woman's features and her reflection in the spotless glass of the window. She wore round and thick glasses that glared in the window. Behind them were staring eyes, still dark and lifeless. The furniture, the drapes, and the dress she wore didn't belong in Peter's time.

He approached the window to see what drew the woman's interest.

The window was on the second floor and faced a road immersed in the darkness of the night. There was a full moon that shed light on a wagon passing by. The clopping of the horses on the stone-paved road echoed in the silence of the night. Victorian-style houses stood silently on the other side of the street, reminding Peter of Savannah or New Orleans. Feeble lights glared in the darkness on the left side, which was what the woman was staring at.

Peter squinted, trying to put the lights on focus. The lights came from candles, their flames fluttering in the night. Around the candles stood crooked stones in a modest graveyard. The woman didn't seem interested in the cemetery, the candles, or the few people kneeling in front of the headstones, intoning a slow, whining chant soaked with sorrow. What the woman stared at was the little girl who stood at the entrance of the cemetery. Her golden, thin hair rested on her white dress, moving in the night breeze. Peter could sense the woman's anger as she looked down at the little girl. He felt it like a vibration invading the room, resonating, giving him goosebumps and fear. That dark energy contrasted greatly with the unnatural stillness of her body. From what Peter could tell, she wasn't even breathing.

The girl seemed to sense the same energy and turned around, looking at the window the woman spectated from, so she started walking towards the house with her head down, like a girl who knew she was in trouble. A girl that is going to be punished. Peter wondered if the woman was her grandmother. Her silver straight hair was gathered in a long, heavy braid, almost touching her waist.

She suddenly turned towards him, aware of his presence. The glasses glared, masking her eyes, but could hide her dark complexion, wrinkled skin and a headband with Native American symbols. He drew a deep breath of relief when she made it to the door, ignoring him. She grabbed the oil lamp on the dresser and descended a long set of stairs curling in a spiral. He followed her, keeping the necessary distance. He knew he was dreaming, but that didn't change the fact he didn't want to be there. A strange sense of still silence, heavy air and dust pervaded the house. He desperately wanted out of this dream and to wake up but couldn't. All he could do was follow the lady down the stairs, her head lolling forward at each step. The stairs ended in front of the main entrance, a majestically large door made of thick wood and giant circular handles.

The old woman opened the door.

The little girl stood outside, her blue eyes and freckles illuminated by the lamp.

The woman looked at her and smiled as if she wanted to reassure the little girl that everything was fine, and she beckoned her with a long, gnarly finger.

The little girl instinctively recoiled, but both she and Peter knew she had no choice. She had to go into the house. The woman stared at her with dead eyes and muttered something Peter couldn't understand in a lifeless voice. Her eyes stared vacantly, a dark well of sorrow and a stark grin painted on her face. The little girl took a few steps forward; her head was down, but Peter could still sense her terror and resistance. She didn't have a choice. When she was at the doorstep, she raised her head and looked at the woman with imploring eyes. The woman stepped aside to let her in and closed the door behind her.

As she slid the heavy iron bar into place to lock the door, something in the woman shifted. She stood there, looking at the door, turning her back to Peter and the little girl. She began to shake as if having a seizure; her body moved jerkily. When she turned, Peter tried to scream at the top of his lungs, but his voice died in his throat, and all he could produce was a rasping, choking sound.

The woman was not a woman anymore. It was something that never belonged to this world. The white in the eyeballs had disappeared entirely, leaving room for utter blackness. The grin had grown broad, way beyond a human smile. Her fingers had grown longer, and sharp claws stuck out at their ends. The girl began to scream, but the woman hit her in the face with a swinging slap. The claws dived into the soft skin, sending spurts of thick blood on the wall. The monster kept going and going until the little girl fell onto the ground, blood gushing from the wounds on her throat.

Then it stopped and turned to Peter. He thought he would be next momentarily, but the creature just wanted to ensure he was watching.

He didn't have a choice.

And so, he watched the evil tearing the little girl apart, even if she was already dead.

At last, it raised a foot above her mangled face and stomped on it.

And Peter woke up at the sound of the hit, still paralyzed, feeling the horrid wave of vibrations deep down his spine.

Panting in the solitude of the house, unable to get up, lying on the sofa, Peter understood with an utter sense of horror and despair that whatever was going on inside his head when he was awake was following him in his sleep.

# 3

In the afternoon of that same day, Peter was upstairs in the room that his parents had always called the office -it was technically a room surrounded by bookshelves with a large desk. He looked at the family portrait where he and his parents stared at him with joyful eyes that clashed intensely with his state of mind. He was jumpy and seriously sleep-deprived. After the nightmares that oppressed him, he wasn't quite ready to admit that he simply didn't want to be asleep.

While he looked distractedly at the hundreds and hundreds of volumes, passing his finger through the dusty spines, he thought about the last time he was in the room with Rosa, looking for the paperwork to make arrangements for the funeral. It suddenly came to him that an envelope with his name on it was waiting for him in the safe. He remembered refusing to open it when he first saw it, too fragile to read whatever his mother wanted to tell him. With that came the realization that he wasn't any better than when he arrived at the house; if anything, he had never been as miserable as he was right now. A question lingered in his mind as he reflected on the deterioration he was experiencing: *When will I touch rock bottom? How long will it be before I feel that today was slightly better than the day before?*

He doubted that opening that envelope would make him feel any better, but he hoped perhaps his mother's thoughts would help answer some of the questions that tormented his mind. He entered the code, which also happened to be his birth date, and smiled. His mother's safety standards for any device that required a code or a password had never been particularly high. He found the envelope inside the safe with his name written on it. He recognized the sharp-cornered handwriting of his mom. That made him think about the book of family recipes she had written by hand. That had been a Christmas gift for him, the last he would ever receive from her.

The envelope opened easily and without tearing; the glue was weak around the edges. Inside the envelope were two sheets that were folded around a picture. The pictures showed him and his parents at his first book signing event at a local bookstore, where Peter promoted his debut novel. His parents were barely able to contain their pride and joy. With a heavy heart, he put the picture aside and began reading the letter his mom wrote for him. It was written the day before their death. He looked at a line where something had smeared the ink. The area around that was wrinkled and slightly uneven. Peter knew it had been caused by one of her tears.

*Dear Peter,*

*I was looking at this picture and couldn't help but think how proud I am of you. I guess you should know that by now, but your father and I never tire of reminding ourselves how true that statement is. We both hope you know that. I've not felt much like myself in the past weeks. I feel like something is weighing on me, an unsettling anxiety, maybe a sense of dread which I've never experienced before. It's like an omen, a feeling that something is about to happen. Putting my thoughts in words, just like you taught me, helps a little. I'm not sleeping much, and I wake up with a sense of unease when I do. I guess the nightmares make it worse, and you probably have noticed I've been calling you more frequently these days. A couple of days ago, I came really close to talking to you about it, but I never could bring myself to do it. I don't want to worry you, and I hope you'll never read this letter and that I'm just overthinking this whole situation.*

*Writing this is so much easier than telling you over the phone.*

*I've never been a superstitious person, you know that. Your father has always found my logic annoying and utterly unromantic, but I have to admit that my logical and rational thinking is shaking right now. Something is watching me; I sense it and feel it on my skin. Something is causing my anxiety, my bad dreams, and my sleepless nights. Something is feeding off it, and I'm growing more and more wary of it.*

*I can't be sure, but I think Lynn is part of it. She is not talking to me anymore. She avoids me.*

*It eats Peter. It eats.*

*It is eating me alive. I think I see it in the streets, at the grocery store, at the movies, on my hikes. It's never the same person or doesn't look the same, but there is always something off. I feel it on my skin like somebody is constantly watching me. I shiver when I feel it.*

Peter realized he was holding his breath; his heart stomped in his chest. He felt his pulse in his fingertips. A wave of terror assailed him as he put down the first page and moved on to the second one. He watched the handwriting change, become irregular, less familiar as if someone else had taken over to finish the letter. More signs of tears were present on the second page.

*I hope you never find this. Don't. I hope you never read this. If you do, talk to Jack Suuuullivaan. Talk, Peter. Talk to him. He's got the aaanswers. He knows.*

*I love you with all my heart.*
*Gigaa udanvliyea, janhuwvi, gigaa.*
*Anijalagi gohusd agisdi.*
*Nalisquadisgvna uyoayeldvi.*
*Adahisdi.*
*Adahisdiii.*

At the end of the letter was an upside-down drawing of a man and a woman.

Peter folded the letter back in the envelope and placed it on the desk. He felt lightheaded, and a cold drop of sweat had appeared on his neck. He leaned forward and pulled the trash can underneath the desk just in time to vomit inside it. He retched twice with spasms so violent it hurt his head. What in the world had he just read? The smothering weight of his mother's words hit him harder than anything he had ever experienced.

His mother was the most rational and yet positive person he knew. Reading her words and realizing the state of mind she was in hurt in ways he didn't think were possible.

*It eats Peter, it eats.*

He thought about all the strange episodes that had happened to him since the funeral.

*Something is watching me.*

He thought of Will Harris, watching him at the funeral parlor.

*The nightmares make it worse.*

The image of the old woman with glaring glasses returned to his mind, the same grin of Will Harris. His mom had mentioned Lynn Harris's change of behavior towards her. Was she involved in his parents' death? And if she was, how was she connected to all this?

His mom wrote about Jack Sullivan, too.

*He knows. He's got the answers.*

He grabbed the envelope and rushed down the stairs to the front door. He put his shoes on and turned the doorknob, ready to pay his second visit to Jack Sullivan.

He froze on the doorstep.

Someone was there in the room with him.

*Someone is watching me, Peter. I feel it on my skin.*

His mother's words were starting to make too much sense.

He knew whoever was there with him in the room was behind him. He didn't only feel it on his skin but in the air. The air had that way of getting heavy when evil things were around. He was sure of it but couldn't make himself turn around and look.  It wasn't only the feeling of being observed; the temperature had dropped considerably in the room, and no, the cold wasn't coming from the door he had just opened. This was a different kind of cold that pierced through the bones and hit deep in the soul. He could hear the flies buzzing again, not as loudly as he had heard them a few hours before. They set the background noise, a high-frequency sound that reminded him of the static of an old TV with a broken antenna.

He didn't know how far it was behind him, but it was there. It smelled like damp wood and sweet decay. Peter stood still at the doorstep, his hand clutching the doorknob as hard as possible. He considered his options. He could have run outside, but that didn't sound like a great idea. Peter had the feeling that whoever or whatever was behind him would be much quicker than him, just as fast as it had materialized behind him.

He looked up at the mirror, and that's when he saw him. A tall and dark figure stood behind him. He had his father's face, but he clearly wasn't him. Not only was he cremated and now in an urn in the living room, but also because he was so much taller than his dad.

And something was wrong with the features of his face. It looked as if he wore a mask of his dad, the skin not adhering correctly to the flesh; it looked deformed as if it was melted.

It knocked the wind out of Peter.

As he lowered his head to avoid the horrific reflection in the mirror, the glare of a metallic object resting on the shelf next to the door caught his attention. The silver pendant dangled from the shelf, moved by an invisible force like it was swinging in the wind—a paperweight lying on the lace, keeping it from falling.

He recognized the symbol on it. It was the same one he had seen on his mother's letter. It was the relic Lynn Harris had given him. It seemed so foggy in his mind.

*"It helped me a lot after Will passed,"* she had said.

How in the hell did the pendant end up there? He surely hadn't put it there, and nobody had been in the house in the past week. The pendant claimed his attention. Something in his mind wanted him to grab, hold, worship and wear it. Peter could feel the impossible cold of the metal on his skin. The circular metal plate had the same symbol he had seen on his mother's letter, the upside-down man and woman lolling in the air. He looked back to the mirror, expecting to see the grotesque reproduction of his father, but it was gone. It had vanished without making a noise. The temptation to touch the shining metal was strong. Even from that distance, Peter seemed to perceive the vibrations of its cold surface.

The relic was the promise of comfort, relief and warmth.

*It helped me a lot after Will passed.*

Lynn Harris's words returned to him once more, and he believed them now. He knew there was something about that simple yet powerful artifact. The house was unsettlingly silent as if it had fallen into a vacuumed dimension of existence. The only sound Peter could hear was his heartbeat and the whispers that seemed to come out of the pendant. The words he heard were not in a language he understood. *Like those meaningless words on the letter,* he thought.

*Did his mother write those words? Was she forced to write them by someone else? But who? That didn't seem like a plausible option. Did something snap in her mind? Had she gone insane just like he was now?*

Those questions distracted him from the irresistible attraction to the pendant. Every part of him wanted it.

He forced himself to walk out of the house.

When he shut the door, the sounds of the world were back, and so were his anxiety, dread, and unease. He needed answers to shed light on this strange sequence of events that kept piling one on top of the other. And according to his mother, the person she trusted the most, Jack Sullivan, could help him get those answers.

# 4

Jack Sullivan woke up abruptly from a peaceful nap. Despite having a lot of free time during his days, he was not a napper by habit. He preferred to spend that time reading or being outside when the weather was pleasant enough. He looked around, confused. Something woke him, but he couldn't tell what it was. He placed the bookmark on the page of the book that rested open and face down on his chest and pulled himself up with a light groan. He looked up, then to the side. And froze.

There was a sound, a scraping sound followed by a thud and more scratching.

Squirrels, he thought. One of them, a heavy one, must have landed on his roof. The streets were full of them. They rummaged and scavenged the yards for acorns, and, in the process, Jack had seen plenty of fights among them. They could get feisty. He got up and almost reached the kitchen when the sound came back. This time, it was stronger than before. It sounded like it came from inside the house this time, from the end of the hallway where the bedroom was.

He walked slowly; the house was quiet now, and the sounds from the outside world were minimal. Jack held his breath, waiting for the sound to come back to understand the source of it. He looked back several times as he walked the hallway, an omen that something might surprise him from behind, his heart racing in his chest. He looked inside the guest bedroom. With the blinds shut and the daylight making it through in narrow slits, the room was filled with shadows. They made the piles of boxes look taller than they were. Jack scanned the room, looking for movements.

Maybe something had sneaked in from the back door. He had the habit of leaving it completely open when he spent his time reading outside in the backyard. A mouse, maybe?

Then the sound was back; this time, it was so strong and close that it made him flinch.

No, not a mouse. He thought. That one was something bigger.

He went into his bedroom. Nothing was out of the ordinary. He opened the closet and pulled the cord hanging from the bulb. The light blinded him. Everything was clear.

Then the scratching again.

This time, it seemed to come from below his feet. He felt the movement, the vibration coming from underneath him.

The basement.

He hadn't been there much since moving into the house. He planned to move most of his stuff down there after a deep cleaning, but those sounded like winter activities. He didn't want to waste any beautiful days offered to him to be inside. That much he had learned since moving to Indiana.

A single thump right under his feet.

He kneeled, put his hand on the hardwood, and recoiled immediately as his brows arched with surprise. The floor was cold. A cold that didn't make any sense. He looked at the thermostat in his bedroom, which read sixty-seven degrees. That floor felt like the wall of a freezer. He returned to the living room, passed the kitchen and opened the door to the basement. He flicked the switch on the wall, but nothing happened. He took a few steps down and looked on the shelves right below the rickety banister. He had placed a couple of flashlights there. When his hands blindly patted and found one, he shook it, feeling the weight of the Duracell batteries, and then searched for the power button.

When he found it, a beam of light pierced the darkness, and Jack Sullivan shrieked.

He saw it for a brief moment. Something was gliding spider-like, quickly getting away from the light spot on the unfinished concrete pavement of the basement. *What was that?* Jack thought, and suddenly, the idea of going down there to check the noise didn't sound wise anymore.

He went down all the way, the light beam trembling ahead of him, showing dancing twirls of dust and unfinished walls made of concrete blocks and bricks. He looked up at the wood beams, electrical cables, and plumbing pipes tidily running along them. To his great surprise, the basement didn't feel cold at all. *Where was that cold coming from?* He wondered once more. He moved the flashlight back and forth, checking every corner of the large open space he was in. He smelled the dust and a faint odor of smoke. It was like something burning, but he couldn't see where it could come from.

The wall on the far end of the room had an opening in it. The door was missing, and someone, the old owner most likely, had placed a dark-colored curtain hanging from two thick studs from one of the concrete blocks.

Jack paused for a moment to think about the topology of the house. He drew a blueprint sketch of the house in his mind, looking at the opened door behind him at the top of the stairs. Yes, the room behind the black curtain would be right underneath his bedroom, where the cold came from.

He pointed the flashlight in that direction, the beam hitting the curtain. There was a small gap at the bottom as the curtain wasn't long enough to reach the ground.

The scratching resumed, this time more insistent. Something was trapped down there and was trying to escape, and Jack couldn't blame it, whatever it was. He felt the urge to run away, too. A sense of disturbance and unease invaded him, sending cold chills down his spine. His mouth was dry; the dust looked thicker in that part of the basement. He walked forward, and his slippers produced a scraping sound on the rough floor. He took a deep breath and placed his left hand on the right edge of the curtain, getting ready to point the light inside the room.

The sound suddenly ceased. The animal that was trapped there must have heard him coming. The smell of smoke increased considerably and was mixed with a faint urine smell.

Three...

He started counting with a heavy feeling in his heart. A familiar feeling had started to creep in.

Two..

It was the feeling of pressure, like something weighing on the air: a presence, a dark force taking up the space, diffusing everywhere.

One...

He moved the curtain to the side and stepped in.

It felt like stepping into a different world, like a forest of charred black trees in winter. He could see his breath mixing with the dust and smoke. The light bounced back on what seemed to be a thick mist. He pointed the light upward, and Jack felt his legs trembling, getting soft. The ceiling was so tall that the light couldn't reach it. The beam died, swallowed by the darkness.

*What is going on?* Jack thought.

He turned back toward the curtain, but it was gone. He panted, moving the flashlight from left to right, trying to find a way out of that place. The fog was too thick, and he could barely see anything six feet away.

Something moved around him.

He could feel the shift in the air. The pressure kept growing, and he felt his ears popping slightly, like an airplane descending too fast. Then, the mist started to fade, drawing a path in front of him. He walked the course for what he believed was an eternity. Flies buzzed in the thick mist; something moved again at his feet. He eventually reached another opening, covered by another curtain, a bright crimson one.

He opened it and found himself in what looked like a large tent.

It was winter, and the fire that had been set in the ground, delimited by sharp-edged rocks, was reduced to a pile of smoking embers. A Navajo woman delivers a stillbirth baby at the far end of the tent. Two men wearing cassocks that Jack Sullivan was familiar with -thirty-three buttons, one for each year lived by Christ, and a wooden cross pendant sticking out on the black fabric- were handed the dead fetus and walked out of the tent, unconcerned by the agonizing screams of the mother.

Jack Sullivan followed them out of the tent. One priest held the baby by a foot, head down, while the other recited prayers in Latin, one holding the book and the other extending to the dead baby. Jack watched with unspeakable horror the two priests throwing the baby into a big fire set in the village's center. He didn't know much about Native American traditions, but that fire pit, strategically built in that position, must have been sacred for the village. He could picture people sitting in front of it, attending ceremonies, passing the tradition on.

The fire was now a pit of death.

Another child was born in a tent on the other side of the fire, this time alive. The piercing first cry of the newborn signaled that a new and separate life had begun. The cry had fit well with the world he had come into. The smell of smoke and burned meat invaded the village and the tents.

Another priest took the baby and cleaned him. It was a boy. The mom, still out of breath from the effort to deliver, sat in bed with her arms stretched out. Her only desire was to hold her baby. She knew they would be taking him away. That's what they did. They took the babies away from their families to educate them in their residential schools, to erase what they claimed to be evil from them, to show them their God, the only and one.

But yet, she extended her arms and started sobbing desperately as they took her baby out of the tent. She would never see him again. In another tent, Jack saw a young woman raped by so-called Sheriff Department members.

Just outside the village, all the men of the tribe had been put to work, chained to one another. They were now contributing to society by building a new school just on top of their sacred place since the beginning of their life, of their tribe. The place that was no one's, yet many claimed to be theirs. The unclaimable had been claimed. The school would show the superiority of Christianity over any aborigine's cult. The men worked heads down, crying as they desecrated their God. The Land. There was another fire going, smaller than the one in the village. It burned the remains of the few who tried to fight back. The ones that couldn't take it would have preferred to die than to be part of it.

Suddenly, the world seemed to shake violently—a quake. The men and the priests guarding them didn't seem bothered by it. Jack Sullivan stumbled, trying to keep his balance. Then the quake stopped. Then re-started. Three massive rhythmic hits in sequence.

He woke up in his chair, with the book resting on his chest, gasping for air. His heart was racing fast.

Someone was knocking at the door.

# 5

He opened the door without looking into the peephole, as he typically did, still shaken by the dream. Peter Hanson looked pale and upset, standing on the doorway mat with his thick-framed glasses hanging low on his nose and his curly black hair untidy, pointing outward in every direction. He wore sweatpants and a white shirt, which was a little too light for the crisp air outside. He looked as though he had just woken up.

"Peter, are you alright?"

"I'm not sure, Mr. Sullivan. Do you mind if I come in for a moment?"

"Of course, of course. Come on in."

Jack looked at the man in distress, moving nervously in the foyer, unable to stay still.

"What's going on? You seem upset," Jack Sullivan said, inviting him to sit in the living room. Peter followed him but remained standing.

"Things are happening to me that I cannot explain. I think I might be going insane."

"Can you be a little more specific? What kind of things?"

Peter sat down and covered his face in his hands, slightly shaking his head as if he couldn't believe what he was about to say.

"I'm seeing things, people. I'm feeling this constant dread like someone is watching me, someone close. I'm having horrible nightmares, and I feel... I feel..."

"Haunted," Jack Sullivan said.

Peter looked at him with an expression that was a mixture of relief and disbelief, then nodded.

"Do you think what you are experiencing might be connected somehow to the loss of your parents?"

Jack saw the darkness in Peter's eyes. It came with the ache of remembrance, the sense of cold that comes with feeling death hitting so near. It came with the void, unspeakable loneliness, sadness, unbearable silence and stillness. No movement, no breathing.

"I don't know. To be honest that's what I thought initially. I never knew anything about grief up until now. I still don't know anything about it. It comes and goes in waves, but the hallucinations and dreams make me question everything."

Jack Sullivan remained silent for a long time, looking down and brooding over the situation.

"Grief is a dark place, my son. I've seen enough of it for several lifetimes. It is different for everyone, as we are all very different. But it ultimately comes down to acceptance. Acceptance is the most challenging part. To realize that the people that we loved have moved forward, that we have been left behind. To come to realize that entirely takes time.

"The Western world, our society, so deeply swallowed by capitalism, doesn't give us the time to process that. They give you a few days to bury your people, then back to work, to produce, to consume, to make money.

"There is a village in the mountains of Indonesia, the Toraja tribe. They mummify the bodies of their beloved that have departed and care for the bodies as if they were still alive. They believe the soul remains in the house after death. The families keep feeding the mummies; they sit them at the dinner table and even give them cigarettes. Some might find this shocking or disturbing, maybe a way to delay the inevitable closure. But I believe it helps them process; it gives them the time, especially when the death occurred in violent and sudden circumstances."

Peter sat there, listening with interest. He seemed slightly more relaxed. Jack knew he needed to talk to someone desperately. For all he knew, he hadn't seen anyone after the tragedy that hit his family.

"I didn't know that. So, you think this is all happening because I'm in shock?" Peter uttered, his voice broken by emotions.

"Well, I'm no doctor or psychologist, but I think it would be a good assumption to explain what you are going through partly."

"Did you know my mother? I mean, did you know her well?" Peter asked.

The question didn't come entirely unexpectedly to Jack, although he had hoped they wouldn't go there just yet.

"I did know her indeed. She was the kindest soul I've met since I moved here. She introduced me to everyone in the neighborhood."

Peter took another hit of ache. The remembrance. The death. There was a moment of silence, then he continued. "Were you aware of a change of behavior that was going on with Mrs. Harris? My mom and her were really good friends. It seems like their relationship had declined quite a bit in the last month or so." Peter fished a piece of paper and handed it to Jack.

"That's what I came to talk to you about. My mom sounded anxious, something I rarely saw in her; she told me to look for you. That you have answers to my questions."

Jack read the letter. When he was toward the end, the paper trembled in his hand. He let his glasses fall on his chest, held by a cord around his neck, and looked at Peter.

Regret was what he felt at that moment, guilt for dragging Jane Hanson into his discoveries about Lynn Harris. He might have been the ultimate cause of her death. But the letter he had just read changed everything. He couldn't just ignore that anymore.

"Yes. I did notice the change in Lynn that your mother talks about in her letter."

"What is it then? What's going on, Mr. Sullivan? I mean, did you read what she wrote? Was she speaking another language? Was she on drugs? What in the world do those words mean? I feel like I'm going insane here. Why aren't you shocked by what you just read?"

"I understand how you feel and how confusing this might seem. And I will do my best to answer your questions; well, at least the ones I think I can answer. Would you like a cup of coffee?"

"Yes, please."

Jack Sullivan returned with the coffee and sat back in his chair. He collected his thoughts. He wasn't sure where to start, so after a few moments of hesitation, he went straight to the point.

"What I am about to tell you will make you think I've gone mad, but I guarantee I'm not. I am a man of faith. I used to be an exorcist for the Vatican. Although I'm not representing the institution anymore, I would be a fool in not believing in the supernatural and the occult, not after what I saw and experienced with these very eyes.

"There is evil at play in this world. I'm talking about evil that you don't experience every day, invisible things, monstrous things. These entities have no religion or any of the social bullshit we humans impose on ourselves. I believe Lynn Harris, your mom, myself, and now you have been exposed to one of these entities. This evil is one that I normally classify as belonging to the parasitic kind. It feeds off human emotions such as grief, anger, revenge, anxiety and fear. Once these emotions or feelings are exposed to this entity, the process of possession will start, and, just like any other parasite, it will feed itself until the host is not desirable to it anymore and will move on to the next one.

Lynn Harris was the first to be exposed to it. She was going through the terrible mourning of her son, Will. It must have happened during her trip to Utah with your parents. Your mother seemed to confirm that the change in her behavior started right around that time. Are you with me so far?"

Peter was still, eyes wide open as he processed the information. He invited Jack to continue with a slight nod.

"Your mother saw Lynn acting in an utterly different way after they returned from that trip. Before then, she was lost, isolated, and scattered in pieces, but when she returned from that trip, she seemed serene, relieved, and on her way to complete healing. Only I've never seen this happen to anyone that quickly. Like I said before, grief hits us differently, and at first, I thought she was having a good day. The grief comes in waves, so why not? But there is more. Her behavior was incredibly volatile. For example, on one occasion, she openly flirted with me, a seventy-year-old man, while she was in front of her husband. Something was just off with her, to the point that it started concerning your mother, too. Lynn Harris, according to Jane, had always been a shy woman, very reserved and introverted, but none of that was in the Lynn Harris that we both had seen after that.

When your mother expressed all her concerns to me, I told her my theory, and she didn't react well. Your mother wasn't a religious person; on the contrary, she was extremely rational and logical, so she rejected my theories altogether and kept her distance from me. She must have thought that I was a lunatic, so we didn't talk much after that.

"For the record, Peter, I don't believe your parent's death was an accident or a suicide. I know this is very hard to hear for you, but that is my opinion."

Silent tears dripped down Peter's cheeks as he blinked. He brought a hand to his face to dry them. He got up and gestured to Jack Sullivan to keep going.

"Now, a very good friend helped me research this entity. It is his opinion, which I trust very much, that these kinds of spirits are present in the Navajo folklore and tradition and are known to us as Skinwalkers. There are a great deal of stories, passed through oral tradition among several Navajos tribes, about these spirits; they are all different. However, a branch of these traditions seems to converge to a single kind of entity. These parasitic entities I told you about are known as The Hollow."

"They seem to be able to assume different shapes; indeed, they are called Shapeshifters, among other names," Jack said as he grabbed a brown envelope that rested on the coffee table and handed it to Peter. "Now, I'm trying to focus on the *vessel*. These entities cannot always pass from one host to another unless the new host welcomes them. In other words, they need some form of indirect permission to take control of a new host. I observed Lynn Harris play with a necklace she was wearing all the time; the pendant had a small metal plate with a symbol engraved in it. If you open the envelope, you will see the symbol I'm talking about. I believe she is the vessel the Hollow uses to pass from one host to the next."

Peter opened the envelope, and his eyes grew wider with disbelief. He put the envelope down, holding onto the first document Jack had put together. He slowly turned the sheet toward Jack, and his finger pointed to the symbol of the upside-down couple.

"Where did you see this?" Peter asked.

"It was on the necklace that Lynn Harris was so obsessed with. The one I just told you ab..."

"I have it," Peter said, not waiting for Jack to finish.

"You have...wait. Do you have the necklace?"

"She gave it to me after the funeral. She told me it helped her after Will passed." Peter stood up, pacing the living room back and forth, his right hand pushing his hair off his forehead. "I just literally saw it at my house, in the foyer. I had no idea how it had gotten there. I didn't pay any attention to it after she gave it to me. I could swear I just forgot it in my jacket."

Jack stood up as well and grabbed Peter by both arms.

"Listen to me, son. Slow down a bit, would you? Tell me more about it. Did you touch it? Were you in contact with it at all after she gave it to you?"

"No... I guess I touched it once. On the day she gave it to me. It was cold, incredibly cold. It looked like silver, but it felt as if it was made of some strange material. I don't know Mr. Sullivan. I need to get back home."

Peter stormed through the room to get leave. He seemed to be in distress.

"Peter, wait a second. Please. Peter."

He stopped at the door but didn't turn.

"Peter. I understand what we talked about is a lot to take in, and I don't blame you for your reaction. Everything seems absurd and surreal, but let me tell you something. Your mother rejected all I told her, and she left my house exactly like you are about to do. I never had another chance to speak to her. I know this is hard to accept, but I'm not lying to you. I'm sure of it. I'm not crazy."

Peter turned slowly, revealing eyes that were red and small from crying. He turned but couldn't face him, resting his brows on quivering fingertips.

"I trust you, Mr. Sullivan. I do. But I just need to think this through. Like you said, it's a lot to process right now," Peter said, his voice broken between sobs.

"I get it. I get it. And you should take that time," Jack uttered, attempting to sound comforting and hide the disturbing thought of Peter returning to that house where the pendant was.

"But let me warn you, son." Jack admonished him, and this time, the comfort in his voice was gone, exposing awareness and fear. "Do not take this lightly. This Hollow entity is not in your imagination. It is real and not to be underestimated. It lives in the darkness of your thoughts. And you're going through a storm that will try to take advantage of. And that's why I believe you will be better here, with me as we work this out. Will you please listen to me?"

Peter let himself crash to the ground, hiding his face between his legs, rocking back and forth as if sitting on the wooden chair on his patio. He let go of an excruciating scream.

The ache of remembrance. The death and the void. The unbearable loneliness.

Jack kneeled next to him, gently patting his shoulder. He wished he could do more for him, and maybe he would.

But not now.

Now was the time for him to wake up and react, to acknowledge the imminent threat upon them both.

"Look at me, Peter. Look at me."

"Please listen to me. Stay here for a few days. You can make me a list of what you need, and I will get it myself, but you shouldn't be in that house, not now. Do you trust me?"

"I do." He said with no hesitation, drying up the tears from his eyes, digging deep for a handful of strength.

"Good. That's good," Jack said.

"Are we dealing with a supernatural creature here? One of those I write about in my books? This is unbelievable. I cannot believe it," Peter uttered. He had recomposed himself but was still clearly in shock.

"I told you I was a priest, a minister, an exorcist, right?"

"You did."

"When I quit, many people asked me if I had lost my faith."

"Did you lose your faith?"

"In the institution? I certainly did. But I never lost my faith in God. And you know why that is?"

Peter shook his head.

"Because of evil."

"I'm not sure I follow," Peter said, looking at Jack straight in his eyes.

"You know...Evil is everywhere: in the school mass shootings, in the desperation of people at the margins of society, in the people who are determined to prevail on the ones left behind, in their willingness to humiliate them. Evil is in war and the thirst for power of those who cannot let it go."

"But you see, son, the silence of God is terrifying. Because it instills doubt and it makes our faith blind. The ultimate test. And evil thrives in the silence of God, where we believe it does not exist."

"My faith, my reminder of God, is in the evil that surrounds us."

# 6

Robert Cooper sat in the silence of his car, with the driver's window not fully closed, allowing the crisp air of the fall to pass through the small crack. He wasn't in his service car, the IMPD Ford Taurus. That would draw too much attention, which he didn't need right now. He was in his car, the one Caroline used daily, a Chevy Suburban that was starting to show signs of age. He didn't know exactly what he was looking for, but his gut tried repeatedly to tell him something. Something his logic couldn't quite take. Caroline's words kept coming back at him.

*When logic and rationality fail you, all you are left with is the supernatural.*

As he flicked through the pages of the Hanson's case, his eyes fell on the pictures of the bodies on their literal death bed. Their features contorted in a hideous grimace. Were they screaming in pain? Cooper wondered from that angle, trying to put himself in their shoes. No, it wasn't the pain that they went through; it was something else.

It was fear.

*What did you see?* he asked, whispering to himself in the car. What could you have seen that scared you to the point of having a heart attack? He had heard stories from some acquaintances at the DEA about potent synthetic hallucinogens that could cause vivid dreams or nightmares, depending on the case. However, the toxicological report from the pathologist didn't show any trace of drugs or narcotics that could explain that. And that, in Cooper's mind, could only mean one thing: they were staring at someone in the house, someone in front of their bed and scared them to death. At the same time, there was no evidence that someone entered the house, at least not from the security cameras on both entrances. All his angles and theories were weak; they wouldn't stand a chance in a trial, not even if the prosecutor were a kid in kindergarten. He kept flicking through the pages and landed for the hundredth time on the prints found on the scene. They all belonged to the Hansons. If someone got inside the house somehow, he didn't leave any traces behind him.

He traced back all the ends of the case, going around in the same circles he had already gone through. Then he put the sheets he had rested on the passenger's seat back into the folder and threw them inside the glove compartment, slamming it shut in frustration. He gave the neighborhood a brooding glimpse—nothing out of the ordinary. Life flowed in its unstoppable routine. The Halloween decorations were up, a couple walked their French bulldog, who stopped to smell around the hydrant in the Hanson's front yard, then peed on it. Cooper flinched when his phone buzzed loudly on the dashboard.

It was Davis.

His first instinct was to reject the call. He hadn't talked to him for a few days when he stormed out of his office, slamming the door. They hadn't left that conversation on good terms. He exhaled a frustrated sigh and put his boss on speaker.

"Cooper."

"We have a situation on the westside. I don't want to send anyone else. You need to take care of this. Tibbs is waiting for you at the scene. How far are you?" Davis thundered on the phone like he did when his blood pressure was hitting the roof. Cooper didn't want to tell him he was already on the westside.

"I'm not far. Send me the location, and I'll be on my way."

"Coop, this is not good. Please report to me only about this. And tell the fucking patrols to keep the vultures away."

"Copy that, sir."

# 7

He arrived at the scene a few minutes later. The perimeter had been established, and a few agents were trying to screen against the Channel 13 camera, telling the reporter and the cameraman to step back. The reporter was Judy Garrett. Cooper recognized her immediately, even before seeing her face. Her vivid pink two-piece suit, white shirt and matching heels left no doubt. She was also one of the most experienced reporters, covering the biggest stories, usually those destined to make it to the national news. Cooper didn't know what to expect beyond the perimeter, on the scene, delimited by the yellow ribbon, but it couldn't be good if they sent her.

When he passed by her, a whiff of Chanel No. 5 perfume hit him in the face. She turned and saw him; then she launched at him like a vulture on a fresh carcass.

"Detective Cooper," she cried in her usual high-pitched tone that she tried to mask when she spoke to the camera. "A word, please."

Cooper stopped sighing. If he had learned something in his career, promising to throw a bone to the media was the only effective way to calm them down, to convince them to let go a little so that the agents could do their job without worrying about them.

Cooper looked at her without bothering to show how annoyed he was. Not that she cared anyway. He could see the thick layer of make-up on her cheeks, a bronze cloud on top of a foundation that was a couple of tones too light compared to her skin. The blue eye shadow on her eyes was as heavy as the eyeliner. She looked as though she was wearing a mask.

"Detective. Can you share any details?" she asked with begging eyes that might have worked with a much younger and less experienced version of himself.

"I'm not briefed. I'll be back in a few minutes.  After examining the scene, I promise you will be the first one I come to. Please let my guys do their job in the meantime, would you?"

She looked disappointed. Her smile disappeared instantly like an actress would do right after cutting an overly boring scene; then she told her cameraman to put the equipment down and took a few steps back.

He stepped inside the perimeter and wore white latex gloves, and disposable shoe covers that he found on one side of the fence that separated the railroad tracks from the small station. It wasn't an active station anymore or even a stop these days. Judging from the degraded roof, the broken windows, and the vegetation that had grown inside the cabin, that stop must have ceased to function decades ago. On the back wall, facing the tracks, a swastika had been drawn with a white spray bottle, followed by a Sieg Hail.

The back of the station looked like a movie set from a dystopian novel. Once fertile and filled with tall grass, the soil was now smothered by dark stains from a recent fire. Three discolored blue trash cans were filled with junk and emanated a nauseating smell. Further ahead, what was once a crop field was now a wasteland of dark soil as black as tar. Plastic bags and debris were scattered across it, giving Cooper a feeling of neglect and desperation.

Not the best place to die, he thought.

There was a small barrier of patrol agents talking with Detective Tibbs around what he presumed was the body. The forensic team was in action, bent over the body and collecting evidence.

Tibbs saw him and rushed towards him.

"You made it, Coop," he said, panting. "I've never seen anything like this before." He trailed Tibbs to the other police officers. They stood in a semi-circle, hiding the body from the cameras and the small group of residents that had gathered outside the perimeter. They were all facing away from the body. Their eyes were low and frightened—the eyes of kids who had just seen something haunting that could not be unseen.

Cooper looked at them frowning, then went around them and saw it.

His first instinct was to retch. He was just able to avoid that, but he turned around instinctively. He had seen all sorts of corpses, wounds, and mutilations, but Tibbs was right. He had never seen anything like that.

The body of a man lay naked on his stomach. He only wore a pair of cotton socks, the kind one wears under a suit at a wedding, high to his knees. The body was so severely mutilated that he could already imagine the length of the coroner's report about the possible causes of death. One of the legs had been cut at hip level, severed by the train that had passed by and that had now been moved forward to clear the scene. The back was a triumph of blood in different shades of red. Scratches were scattered everywhere, and a deep and precise cut crossed his whole body along the spine.

But that wasn't what had forced him to turn the other way. Robert Cooper was no stranger to mangled bodies. He was never a fan of the sight, but it took something special for a dead body to disturb him.

He turned back to the body, forcing himself to do it, and he now understood the agents facing away from the body.

The head of the man had been turned one hundred and eighty degrees and faced backward. The internal bleeding and the neck fracture had created a dark band around the neck. A sharp bone stuck up from his Adam's apple. The eyes of the man were white and shady, wide open.

His features were stretched with fear in a horrible scream.

Just like the Hansons.

# 8

"Is that all you need from your place?" Jack asked, reading from the list of things Peter had written. He didn't understand why Jack was so keen that he stayed away from his house. Peter offered to go and be back in ten minutes since he knew where his things were, but Jack had firmly opposed the idea. The same thing had happened when he offered to go together, escorted by Jack, but that offer was also rejected. So Peter wrote down what he needed from his house: his dog, a few changes of clothes -still mainly gathered in one of his suitcases- his laptop, in the unlikely event he could get some writing done, and his basic bathroom supplies. He made sure to specify where those things he needed were since Jack Sullivan wasn't familiar with the house.

"Yes, sir. It's all in there. I'm pretty sure it would take us two minutes to get in and out of there if I was with you," Peter tried once more.

Jack threw him an annoyed glimpse, the one of a man who wasn't going to repeat himself. Then he closed the door behind him.

And Peter was alone.

He paced the room, still trying to gather his thoughts, establish an order in his mind, and come to peace with the impossibility and irrationality of everything happening around him. He looked at the hundreds and hundreds of books that Jack Sullivan kept on the shelves. They didn't seem to be sorted by author's name but by genre. It gave the shelves a sense of scattered, colorful chaos. Peter walked by the row of the classics, passing a finger on the dusty spines of Joyce, Tolstoy and Shakespeare.

His eyes were captured by a section that seemed to be populated by non-fiction books. Phenomenology of Demonic Possession, Archeology of Evil, and The Salem's Witch Trial were only a few of the dozens and dozens of titles that seemed to be focused on evil entities and creatures.

These were all topics that Peter Hanson would have usually loved to discuss and explore with Jack Sullivan -just recently, he had started thinking about steering a little his writing, which would typically be true crime and psychological thrillers more into the supernatural- but now that he was dealing with that on the front line, he wished to run away from it, as far as it was humanly possible. He guessed if there was someone to have on your side in a situation like this, that person would be one like Jack Sullivan. His knowledge on the topic should have reassured him or at least made him feel a little better -and in fairness, he was feeling better- but the reality was that Peter still hoped he would wake up from this wild nightmare and that the world would have made sense again.

Only then did Peter realize how surreal the silence in the house was as he listened to his steps echoing in the living room as if it were a deep cave. Just like when he was in his house, silence triggered his mind to start spinning. The silence was a deafening source of desperation and a constant reminder of his loneliness.

He thought of Melissa again. He tried to focus on the only person he could think of who warmed his heart. He thought about a future with her. Maybe kids one day.

Kids that would never meet their grandparents.

Because they died in their bed, he would never see them again.

In the silence of the room, a soft singing voice raised. It came from the hallway or the bedrooms on the other side of the house. At first, he didn't recognize the song, but as he got closer, the words and the melody became more familiar. The volume went up a notch, and it suddenly came to him.

The song was a lullaby, a melody he didn't have a conscious memory of but that reminded him of his mother. It reminded him of her, and the song was her in a way he couldn't quite explain. He felt the warmth of the blanket of his old bedroom wrapping around him as he was being tucked at bedtime. He felt the smell of his mother, her smooth hands lifting his hair from the forehead. He felt the fear go away and be replaced by the safety of her sweet voice. He was a kid again; his mom was with him, and the world was safe as long as she kept singing that song.

Peter turned the corner of the living room and entered the hallway, following the song that loomed at the edge of his dreams.

His eyes stared vacantly, and meaningless mumbles came out of his mouth.

When he was halfway through the hallway, the song seemed to come from above him. He raised his head and saw the attic hatch and the regular gap that the opening formed with the ceiling. Without looking, his arm stretched to the right and padded the coarse plaster wall until his hand found the metallic hook. He raised it to the ceiling, always staring at the hatch as it opened, sending dust and small debris to the hardwood floor.

A squeaky ladder came down, unfolding around its hinges until it touched the floor and locked itself in a clicking sound.

He stepped on it and went up into the attic.

Peter stood in the darkness of the unexplored room, and yet his hand knew exactly where the light switch was. He flicked it, and the darkness died, revealing his old bedroom with the Power Rangers and Jurassic Park posters illuminated by his blue lava lamp. He looked at the shapeless, dense fluid floating inside the glass cylinder. All his Goosebumps books were neatly arranged on the shelves, from the first to the last, in their slime-green spines. When he turned to his bed, he saw his mother kneeling beside the bed. Her long hazel hair was arranged in a ponytail and moved to her right shoulder.

She sang to the empty bed, waiting for her son to join her. That was the safest place in the world. Peter walked to the bed automatically, propelled by an invisible force. When his mother looked at him, tears flowed from his eyes. She was beautiful, and he wanted to hug her.

To hug her was the only thing he wanted in the world—one more time.

He smiled back at her with genuine sadness, thinking he'd never seen her again, let alone hug her, listening to her song. Peter got in bed, and his mother tucked him in. The notes of the lullaby surrounded him, sending warm feelings through his whole body. She moved the hair off his forehead and kissed it.

"My baby. Oh! My baby," she said, still singing.

"Mom," Peter said, his voice broken in sobs. "I miss you, mom."

"I'm here, my baby."

"Is this a dream?"

"Shhh, sleep my love. You are safe."

She kept singing the song. She lifted her hand from his face and reached behind her back, undoing her necklace. Then she smiled at him and put it around his neck. He felt the cold metal of the plate and the lace against his bare skin. It was cold, but it burned at the same time. The voice of his mother changed a bit. It was as if she sang a little out of tune.

"Mom, what is this?" Peter said as she joined the two ends of the necklace.

"Don't worry. My love. Sleep. You are safe now." Her voice had definitely changed now, to the point he didn't recognize it anymore.

Her sweet smile became a stark grin, and her eyes darkened as the pupils became larger, devouring the white around them. Her gentle sighing grew irregular and became guttural. Dark veins began to emerge from her skin. Peter could see the pulse in them as a strong smell of urine and ammonia invaded his nostrils. Her neck grew longer and blacker. The veins looked like dark sap running inside an old tree. She shifted her shape and snarled at him; the grin had grown wider, and the white, perfectly aligned teeth had now become sharp fangs. Her hair started to fall on his body like hay straw.

The Hollow pushed its claws to his neck, pressing the metal plate on his skin with a hissing sound. The cold spread in his body as he tried to recoil and push the hand back. When his hand landed on the creature's arm, it felt like he had just touched the mossy bark of a damp tree. The creature was strong, much stronger than he could have ever been, and with that came the realization that he couldn't do anything to escape it. Peter gasped for hair, feeling his lungs burning and the blood pumping hard in his head.

"It's your fault, Peter." The creature bellowed in a coarsened voice, followed by a yelping laugh that gushed out of its throat. "They are all dead because of you."

Peter felt his strength abandoning him as he struggled to free himself. But the grip of the creature was strong and firm. The Hollow blotted out a sudden and loud noise, and his grip loosened a bit, giving Peter a few more seconds of air. It snarled furiously like a beast being bothered as it prepared to maul its prey.

"*Nah-luss-ah fah-lah-yah,*" it bellowed in a guttural sound that seemed to come from the depths of hell itself. Then the creature recoiled, and Peter's neck was free from the impossible pressure.

He felt as if the bed he was lying on opened like a hatch that sent him into an endless fall of darkness. He landed on his back, violently thumping on the hardwood floor of the hallway. He couldn't breathe for a few seconds and struggled with his limbs hitting the floor.

Jack Sullivan's face was blurry, and his voice was distant. The world went on and off like a faulty flashlight.

"It's ok, son. It's ok. Breathe, breathe. Goddamnit." His voice seemed to come from another world.

Then his lungs recovered from the shock, and could breathe again. He gasped for air and coughed. His throat and lungs were burning.

"Thank God. You are okay, son. You are safe. Keep breathing."

And Peter kept breathing, lying down on the floor. As his vision became less blurry, he saw the dark opening of the attic and a piece of rope dangling from its darkness. He turned on his side and saw the other part of the rope that Jack Sullivan had likely cut.

It stood lifeless on his side, in the shape of a noose.

# 9

Down at the police station, just outside the main entrance, was a small courtyard with a few concrete benches and a mat of synthetic grass to give it a resemblance of green. Tibbs sat in front of Cooper at one of the benches, sinking his crooked teeth in one half of his foot-long Subway sandwich. Several pieces of lettuce fell as he bit into it with commitment. A piece of pepperoni, smeared with mustard on top, landed just outside of the sandwich wrap, right on the concrete table.

Cooper stared at it as he smoked his cigarette.

His body was there, but his mind was still at the crime scene, playing and rewinding over and over again what he had seen. The wound on the victim a homeless person that went by the name of Adam Kroger, at least that was what the officers had found in a wallet near a pile of clothes inside the shack that once was a small train station- was so deep that he could see the white of his spine, pearled with blood, freed up from the tissue that surrounded it. He wondered what kind of weapon could inflict such a level of damage.

A machete, maybe? An axe? It looked like someone had planted a sharp blade deep inside his flesh, stopping just before hitting the spine and pulling it down until just above his butt crack. He would have to wait for the autopsy from the coroner, but he had never seen such a clean wound in his whole career. The body looked like a giant tuna that had just been gutted on a fisherman's boat—a long and neat cut.

The train was not the weapon; it would have mangled the body, maybe dragging it for several hundred feet before stopping completely, and there were no traces of any dragging on the rail tracks. The forensic had quickly run him through a reconstruction of the scene. Once the train was moved, the train had severed one of the victim's legs, which was found on the tracks. Had his back been wounded before or after the train? And what about the head of the victim facing backward?

The pathologists down at the coroner would have to answer those questions, but he couldn't see how a train could provoke such damage. Whatever happened to the man, the scene was clean, which suggested that the man was killed somewhere else. The killer had broken his neck, twisting it to the point of having it face backward and cutting his back -not necessarily in this sequence- then dumped the body near the tracks, presumably to make it look like a suicide.

Just a man throwing himself under a train.

The killer must have hoped for a different result. If the intent was to have the train cause the most damage to the body, to mangle it so that the previously inflicted wounds would blend with the aftermath of the impact, then the killer failed miserably. Cooper didn't believe that was a solid theory. No matter how much in a rush the killer was, why go through the trouble of carrying the body only to leave one leg on the tracks? Why not lay the whole body down to maximize the damage?

"Do you want the other half?" Tibbs asked as he talked with his mouth full, chewing avidly into the whole wheat bread.

"How long do you think before the goddamn IT uploads the security footage from the street cameras?" Cooper asked, ignoring Tibbs' offer and putting the cigarette out on the bottom side of the concrete table.

"Don't know. The footage is not going anywhere. Take it easy, Coop. You look jumpy. Are you sure you don't want a bite?"

Cooper gave him a glimpse that was a mix of disgust and annoyance, releasing the rest of the smoke from his nostrils.

His phone buzzed in the pocket of his jacket.

"Cooper."

"Where are you?" Davis was on the other side.

"Just underneath your big ass window." He looked up, squinting as the sun hit him straight in his face.

"Oh really! Come up here! I've got ten minutes before my next meeting," Davis said frantically.

"You know Harry, I remember when you used to be fun. When you had the time to talk about cases outside of that office instead of spending your days kissing politicians' asses."

"Very funny," Davis uttered unamused.

"I'm serious. It's a beautiful day. Get out of that office. I'll be down here." He hung up before Davis could object.

He didn't think he would come down, but a few minutes later, he saw the man coming out of the door, agents stopping to cheer and salute him. He looked like a fish out of its bowl, making Cooper sad. The man was the best detective in town. He solved hundreds of cases, even a few cold ones that nobody else would have picked out from the archives: nobody but him. There was a sense of duty and determination in him that Cooper had never seen in any other policemen he had worked with. It flowed in his veins like a poison, like an addictive drug. It kept him awake at night, working in the low light of his desk lamp, putting pictures on the walls, just like in the movies. One case after another, the scene, the brainstorming, the stopping point, the discovery, the revelation and the solution. Until the next dose. One more. One last time, until the last time came, and nothing was left of him. His total, unbiased commitment to the job, which many confused for obsession, brought him close to death after a terrible heart attack that the cardiologists at IU Methodist Hospital called a miracle.

That's when everything changed for him. And Cooper couldn't really blame him for that. The thought of leaving Caroline and Tyrese paralyzed him, making him more careful and aware, especially after Harry's episode. The man was transferred to an office job, and just like he had done when he was on the streets in action, he had carved his way up the chain of command. He was now the Lieutenant head of the Homicide Division, one step away from being head of Indianapolis Metro Police; so much for reducing the stress level only to end up in the most stressful desk in town.

He looked left and right, then spotted Cooper and waved at him. On his face was a hint of a smile.

"Was it that bad after all?" Cooper said as he approached him, putting on his sunglasses. "Look at this weather. And they say that Indianapolis weather sucks."

"I'm not sure if one week can make up for a year of shitty weather," Davis chuckled.

"Who is your meeting with?"

"Ah! Fucking guy from the Chamber of Commerce. He's an asshole, but I guess I need his endorsement if I want to have any chance for the next round," Davis uttered as he massaged his temples.

"Can you tell him to fuck off and reschedule the meeting? I mean, you are the Lieutenant, after all."

"I guess I could if a very urgent matter made me temporarily unavailable. That would be possible."

"Well, I've got an urgent matter that I'm about to check in the evidence room. If you want to join."

"Very tempting. Is that the Kroger case?" Davis said, nodding at Cooper's manila envelope in his left hand.

"Indeed."

"Ah! I'm not sure, Cooper. I've got to meet this guy. I hate to do it, don't get me wrong, but I'm not sure I can skip it."

"Just give yourself a break. Do it for the old time's sake."

"For the old time's sake, huh?" He smiled, looking down as a veil of nostalgic tears appeared in his eyes. The spark that he was forced to suppress, but that really never went away."

He grabbed his phone, tapped it a couple of times on the screen, then put it next to his ear.

"Gill, cancel the meeting with the Chamber. I am requested for an emergency. Reschedule for next week, please. Thanks."

Cooper nodded at him with a smile.

"For the old time's sake."

# 10

Jack Sullivan entered the guest bedroom where, with great effort, he had dragged the unconscious body of Peter Hanson while at the same time trying to calm down the poodle that he had brought along. It took some convincing before Luna, that's what the tag on her collar read, realized Jack was a friend and was trying to help her owner.

Peter had been in and out several times, like waking up from a terrible nightmare and immediately dozing back into it. He didn't consider himself a medical expert, but he knew enough to keep calm and assess Peter's vitals. The heartbeat was high but regular; the blood pressure was normal despite his irregular breathing. Under normal circumstances, he would have called 911 and had Peter hospitalized, just like everyone else would have done after an attempted suicide that was only seconds away from being successful. But there was very little normality in the circumstances. The attempted suicide was the result of a direct attack from a supernatural entity. It had nothing to do with Peter's mental health. At least, that was what Jack talked himself into. The doubt still lingered in his mind. It didn't matter how much evidence or proof he had had so far. Dealing with evil always comes with the utmost precautions. There were a few reasons for him to doubt: the first was nothing more than the force of habit. Even though he specialized in exorcisms, his training and experience had taught him that only a small percentage of alleged possession cases were due to supernatural reasons. The Catholic Church was the only religious institution that still resorted to exorcisms but kept it in a hidden drawer. Every other religion had accepted the progress of science and the quantum leaps done in psychoanalysis, mental health, and dissociative identity disorders. Psychiatry offered a much more convincing explanation in the majority of the cases. To this day, exorcisms performed by priests were considered a last hope to stop a borderline personality disorder from advancing, always inside the medical realm rather than the spiritual one.

The other reason for his caution was the paradoxical inexperience. Knowing how to perform an exorcism didn't necessarily lead to being an expert. In fact, because of the small percentage of confirmed cases of demonic possessions, he had investigated hundreds but only performed one twice. And given how it went with the Derringer boy, his success rate was only fifty percent.

In both cases, Jack had learned that when evil used a human being as a vessel, there was always more risk of creating further damage than healing the one it had already caused.

For these reasons, there was still a possibility that Peter Hanson had fallen into a deep depression. Since the day he had met him, he looked as if he was walking on a flimsy bridge overhanging an abyss. As he sat on the chair next to the bed, Jack pet Luna, sadly perched near her dad, anxiously waiting for him to wake up. The old man watched Peter breathing more calmly and rechecked his heart rate before putting his reading glasses on and opening the book where he had left it.

Luna became more agitated and got up on the bed, tail down and ears up on high alert. Her head slightly tilted to the side as a low growl and a whining noise grew louder inside her chest.

She looked in the direction of the door.

Jack put the book down, stared through the open door in the hallway, and held his breath, trying to catch any noises Luna might have heard. The silence of the house was unsettling and surreal. Outside, the world seemed to have stopped: no squirrels running through the dry leaves, no birds chirping in the sky, no airplanes, no cars on the street, no kids playing outside.

Uneasiness hung in the still air of the room.

Then Jack felt it.

A sudden cloud of cold air entered the room. He turned his worried gaze to the window. It was closed shut, just like he was sure every other window or door in the house was. He felt the cold hitting him in his bones and veins, like thin ice traveling in his blood, scratching at the walls of the vessels. Jack shivered and watched the moisture in his breath condensing before his eyes. Luna barked once. Her body was tense, ready to attack. Her growling intensified. Jack squinted at the darkness that fell in the house, and instinctively, his whole body and mind got ready.

Something gleamed in the room on the other side of the hallway.

Luna's growl had turned into a scared whine. She moved, sitting on the pillow next to Peter.

Then Jack saw it.

Jack's gaze met a shadow among the piles of boxes sitting in the darkness of the room. It was as tall as the ceiling, like a giant that had to duck his head to fit. Two long, narrow shadows elongated, running in the walls like gnarly tree branches.

Jack saw the shadows moving, changing shape, twisting, and turning in darkness. Thousands of flies buzzing, clashing with one another with madness. Only one part of the shadow was still. A pair of black eyes gleamed in the corner where the ceiling met the wall. Broad, dark, unblinking eyes stood in hollow sockets: a mask of empty and unthinkable malevolence.

Hair pricked on the back of his neck at the sound of a guttural and deep voice thick with menace and power. Jack turned toward Peter and recoiled, flinching.

Peter sat up straight on the bed, eyes wide open as dark as the creature in the other room. His chest was still. He stared right at him and talked in an alien language.

*Alewisdodi alisdelvdi.*

*Ayoosga.*

*Alewisdodi.*

*Ayohuhisdi.*

Jack grabbed the book, opened it on the first page, then -as he fought his instinct to scream- grabbed a pen from the inside pocket of his jacket with a trembling hand. And he wrote the sounds that came out of Peter Hanson's mouth. He didn't know that language, so he tried his best to do a transcript of the guttural, monstrous voice that came out of him. Peter sat still, bellowing incomprehensible words like a marionette operated by an invisible master who wanted to make it clear that he had entered the vessel, an empty shell with no power over the monster that now lived inside him. He kept repeating the same words, like a broken record playing at a tenth of its nominal speed.

When Jack turned to the hallway, the shadow was gone, the dark eyes were gone, and the room looked just like he expected it to be: filled with boxes filled with books.

Peter's ranting slowed, and the bellowing changed, transitioning back to his voice. Then he exhaled and collapsed on the pillow while Luna looked at him skeptically.

In a loud and neat thump, the book fell on the hardwood floor on its spine when Jack sprung forward from his chair to check on Peter's pulse. The man's features, an ominous mask until a few moments before, had returned to normal. The large black eyes were now hidden by peacefully laid eyelids, caught randomly in minor spasms. The raspy animal-like breathing was barely audible, and the still chest regularly rose and fell.

Jack pushed two fingers on the side of Peter's neck to assess the pulse when he noticed something just below the collar of his shirt. He tucked the fingers underneath and pushed the shirt down about one inch, revealing a large bruise, which he initially assumed had been caused by the noose around his neck.

When he looked closely, Jack Sullivan's heart jumped in his chest. The bruised and reddened area blended with a more extensive and black burned band of skin. On top of it, a complex net of blood vessels protruded as if they were exposed, pumping blood to and from Peter's neck. Like a tumor, a parasite.

Jack grabbed a pair of scissors from the small desk on the far hand of the room and cut Peter's t-shirt from the neck's opening down to the waist. And that was when even the last one of his doubts disappeared, like the last leaf of fall in a tornado. The Native American symbol with the upside-down man and woman Joel Kopernick claimed meant 'dead people' was marked on Peter's chest. The burned areas around his neck with the protruding veins completed the picture of a necklace; only this one was kept on his skin. A terrible burn that would stay with him forever.

Jack Sullivan learned about evil, fought it, lost against it, and escaped from it, only to walk into a different one, a kind he had never seen before.

Goosebumps popped on his flesh as the image of the Hollow stared at him from the darkness of the spare room. And suddenly, it was clear to him why the creature had been known by such a name. In those black and spherical eyes was an ancient, morbid resolution. An unquenchable thirst to devour and tear apart, to provoke dread and binge on it simultaneously, but to never be satiated. An eternal curse that it carried through the centuries. An evil that could have only been born from a bigger one. Jack knew the quest would be very hard this time, much harder than ever.

Inevitably, the memories from Joshua Derringer's case emerged. Would Jack be able to do better this time? The guilt that he had buried through the years came like a wind, carrying the mental images of Joshua, of the smile long gone, the dead eyes in the hollow sockets, and of all Jack's failure on that doomed day when he had let the evil in when he left the gates open in an act of overconfidence. Every case was different, and every exorcism was different. There was no such thing as a rulebook for situations like these. There was only his faith and the knowledge of the enemy. He looked at Peter, sleeping peacefully in the bed, not fooling himself even for a second, that the quiet would last. A storm was coming, and Peter Hanson had invited a difficult guest into Jack's home.

Peter Hanson was in the *well*.

# Part Five:

# Lynn

# 1

On a cold day in March, six months before the discovery of the bodies of Mr. and Mrs. Hanson, Lynn Harris received her daily phone call from Jane Hanson.

"Hello, dear."

"You are not going to believe this," the voice on the other side of the phone, and as a matter of fact on the other side of the fence, said.

"I am all ears. What is going on?"

"Bill and I have just booked a trip to Utah, and you are coming with us."

Lynn blushed, even though she was sitting alone on the couch in the living room; a picture of her son, Will, seemed to stare at her from the TV stand. She hated to be put in situations where she had to refuse. She had always been a pleaser, a yes woman, even in circumstances when her instinct wanted to scream no. She would kindly smile, only to end up agreeing.

But this time was different. She had to decline.

"Oh my gosh, Jane. How exciting for you. I'm not sure I'm going to be able to come." Lynn clenched her teeth as she waited for Jane Hanson to start listing all the reasons why she should go. She knew Jane so well that she could be annoyingly insistent when she put her mind to something. Lynn was aware that this would be a tough one for her to give up on. She had been mentioning making a trip together for months, even before Will died.

"Oh no, no, no. Lynn, you had promised you would consider it. You need to get out of the house, and I know Frank has made it clear that he won't go anywhere. That doesn't mean you have to stay home all the time, too."

She wasn't making that up. Frank was still in deep mourning, just as she was, but he was really struggling. He had lost a lot of weight and spent most of his day in the garage. At first, she thought that could be a good valve to release his emotions, but he had also started isolating himself from her. He started drinking more than usual. Lynn had tried to convince him to see a grief counselor, but he had refused. There was no way he would go on a trip to Utah.

Jane wasn't lying about her promise either. Lynn had told her she would seriously consider the possibility of a trip with her friend. After one of her worst episodes, Jane had calmed her down, and they started talking about going on a trip together. The idea had excited Lynn at that time. The house had become her personal prison, and the walls felt like they were closing in on her. Every inch of the house reminded her of Will. She knew she would eventually have to move on, but she wasn't ready yet. A change of scenery had sounded like a fine idea.

"I know," she said, ashamed. "We were only talking about it. I didn't know you were going to book so early, and I would hate to ruin the trip for you and Bill. I mean, why not use this chance for a romantic getaway?"

"Don't be silly, Lynn. He is on board with the idea. It will be fun. You'll see when I show you the itinerary I'm working on."

"I can't commit to this plan just yet. I need to talk to Frank about it. I'm unsure if leaving him alone is a good idea. He's not doing so well, Jane."

"Listen, I wouldn't insist so much if I really didn't think that it would be good for you. Healing has to start somewhere. Think about the walks and the hikes we could have together. And I'm not talking about just taking our weekly stroll at Eagle Creek. I'm talking about some of the most scenic hikes in the country."

Jane was selling it well. They hiked together every week. It had helped her a great deal. She wished she hadn't told Jane about how she had always wanted to go to Utah. It was so evident that she had booked this trip for her. Jane and Bill had already visited Utah and most of the national parks.

"I need to think about it. I will mention the idea to Frank and will let you know."

She said goodbye and then hung up the phone.

Lynn knew Jane Hanson would not give up easily on this idea, and deep inside, she was excited at the thought of going. But it was one thing to dream about it; bringing herself to do it was a completely different task.

After Will passed, she stayed isolated in her room for almost two weeks. Frank was worried and tried to care for her—as much as a wholly destroyed man who had never cooked a meal could. She didn't even allow Jane to come into her room. She spent most of her time sleeping, crying into her pillow and staring at the ceiling in the utter silence of her bedroom, wondering what she had done wrong along the way as a mother. All she had done for those two weeks after his death was blame herself for the dumbest things, as if it had been her fault Will had gotten into drugs. She questioned if she had been too restrictive as a mother or not enough. Lynn blamed herself for not being able to recognize the latest signs. Will didn't show up for lunch on Sundays. When he did show up unannounced, the only conversation they had was how he was short on money, how he was going through a rough period at work, or any other excuse to get some cash. Will had stopped returning her calls, and after a few weeks, Lynn had called his workplace and found out he hadn't been fired. His boss had told Lynn that he was showing up late for work and never in a state of sobriety.

She had talked to Jane about it. They had researched meetings for drug addicts organized by the church. She asked Jane if Peter could get in contact with Will. They had been inseparable their whole life, and even though they had taken different paths, Lynn had thought his old friend could have talked some sense into him. She thought there could be a glimmer of hope.

But nothing seemed to work. At his friend's suggestion, Lynn and Frank had organized a meeting with all the people who loved Will to express their concerns about his drug use. They had put together old family photos, and they all had written letters in an effort to make him realize that his family and friends were there for him. They wanted him back.

Lynn had the feeling Will would not take the meeting well, that he would see it as an ambush, and that he would misinterpret their intentions.

And she was right. Will was furious and left as soon he realized it was an intervention.

He disappeared for a week: no contact, phone calls, or visits. Lynn was on the verge of calling the police and reporting him as a missing person, but Frank had talked her out of that idea.

The following week, she came home from the store, and while putting away the groceries, she heard a noise coming from upstairs. She walked up the stairs to check if Frank had come home early from the golf course but found Will instead. He was filling up a box with some of his stuff from his bedroom. He saw her and stopped, looking at her for a long time. They didn't speak. When Will noticed his mom was crying, he hugged her. She sobbed on his chest as he held her tight and caressed her hair. She felt the bones of his rib cage and the cold of his hands.

Lynn didn't ask him any questions. She was just happy to see him and didn't want to ruin this moment by saying anything that could upset him.

She watched him as he kissed her on the cheek and walked away.

"I love you, Mom," he said, stopping at the doorstep and smiling at her.

"I love you more," she said as tears filled her eyes and smiled back.

Her heart filled with warmth. That was her son. She recognized him in his eyes, in his smile, and in his voice, the one that was cordial and kind, the one she had known before the drugs. She had felt hope that not everything was lost.

That was the last time she had seen him alive.

She remembered that horrific day in November when she and Frank had to go to the morgue to identify their dead son. The officers in charge of the investigation were talking to her, but their words were muffled as if they were speaking from behind a thick glass. She didn't listen to a word they were saying. She kept staring at the abyss that had just opened before her and threatened to swallow her whole.

They were led to a room where other dead people waited for autopsies, resting in refrigerated drawers.

When they pulled the zipper of the black bag that contained him and showed his wan face, she turned to her right and vomited on the floor. She didn't apologize but just turned around and left the room. Frank did the formal recognition. One of the detectives gave them a box with Will's personal belongings. It was the same box he carried the last time she had seen him. Frank signed on a piece of paper, and that was it. They got into the car and drove to their unsustainably empty home.

Lynn put the box on Will's bed and sat next to it. Her heart raced fast, trying to tell her perhaps it was too early to go through his things, but she did it anyway. Beams of light passed through the openings of the blinds, and suddenly, her mind went back to when that room was all colored in light blue, and Will was crying in his crib. She witnessed that same light now and wondered if it was Will, just trying to tell her that he was okay, that he was at peace.

In the box was a keychain holding both the car and apartment keys, a pack of cigarettes, a short glass pipe that was brown at both ends—Lynn assumed that's what he used when he smoked meth—fifteen dollars, two five dollar bills and five ones. And then, at the bottom of it was a white envelope. It had been sealed, and judging by the two stamps on the top right corner, it was ready to be mailed.

She flipped the envelope in her hands.

It was addressed to Peter Hanson.

# 2

On that same terrible night of November, she and Frank sat silently at the dining room table, looking at the food on their plate. So much food had been prepped and handed to them as a sign of comfort to their family. Even in such a dark moment in her life, Lynn didn't fail to acknowledge how grateful she was to be a part of such an incredible community.

As she watched Frank getting up several times and letting himself release agonizing sobs, her mind was all about the envelope she had found in the box. She had left it there, resisting the temptation to open it.

It made her upset that the last person he decided to write to was Peter. She felt jealous of that attention and commitment. Whatever Will put in that envelope, he wanted to send it on the day he died. That could be the only reason why he had it on him.

Lynn's fists tightened at the thought of Peter Hanson. He was her best friend's son and her deceased son's best friend. He had been a constant presence in Will's life and perhaps the curse that led him to his end. In the storm of the intolerable grief living in her heart, it felt effortless to surrender to easy blame. She had always had this hunch about Peter, about how Will had been changing as they grew up together. When Lynn had caught them smoking in the attic, Will was grounded for two weeks, even though she did not doubt that it had been Peter's idea. She knew her son better than anyone else; she knew the boundaries he had built for himself and within which he felt safe. She could never gather evidence to support her gut feeling, but a mother knows better. And she knew that Peter Hanson, the popular guy in high school who was invited to the parties, had dragged Will into a dimension that never belonged to him in the first place. Lynn didn't think Peter had wanted to involve Will with malicious intentions or in bad faith, but even good intentions could cause irreversible damage. Peter didn't even show up at Will's funeral. Jane had tried to cover for him, to explain his reasons, but that never helped to reduce the grudge, that sense of blind rage that occasionally caught Lynn when thinking of Peter Hanson.

She knew it wasn't her right to open it. The right thing to do would be to give it to Peter the next time he visits. On the other hand, she was a mother who had just lost her only son, and she wanted to know what Will had to say. She had the right to know and wanted to feel close to him again, even just once more.

When she made up her mind, she left her food untouched on the table and, without saying a word to Frank—who had started to drown his pain with bourbon— she went back upstairs, grabbed the envelope, and brought it to the bathroom.

She locked the door and sat on the toilet's lid, tearing the envelope's opening and feeling the glue on her fingertips. Lynn recognized Will's handwriting on both sides of the letter. Tears came immediately, this time uncontrollably, as she let out a horrible whining sound. Her baby was gone. He was just gone, and she held in her hands some of the last thoughts of his life.

She attempted to recompose herself and began to read.


*Hey Hanson,*

*Yeah, I know! Hanson. Peter just doesn't come out anymore. Not like it used to be. There is so much I want to tell you, but I don't know where to start. I miss the old days. I miss our summers, all of them. Remember that time we went to the abandoned warehouse? How long had we worked out our plan? And how cool was it when we finally broke the chain and went in? Looking around at piles and piles of sodas on the pallets, still wrapped in plastic. Of course, I'm not particularly proud of that moment. I mean, we broke the law when we took our two bottles and ran away to hide them in our tree house. But I'm not ashamed of it either. It was one of the best feelings ever. I still find myself smiling when I think about it. I'm sure you think about it too.*

*I drove by that place the other day, as I always do when I have a bad day. I parked in front of the abandoned lot. It is really abandoned, not like when we were kids, and we liked to think that it was, just to spook ourselves a little more. The place is empty now, but I still like to sit on the hood of my car, smoking a cigarette and looking through its open gate. I like to think the gate has never been closed since we opened it together. I like to think the place had surrendered to us because we were a force of nature together. And now I look at it, at the place, and I see its weakness, and it makes me sad because that's kind of like our friendship. It was also incredible but fragile, like a beautiful ice sculpture, ready to break at the first impact or melt at the first sun, but still so beautiful to admire.*

*I don't blame you just as I don't blame myself. Some things just go that way. They burn and burn until there's nothing left to burn, and they die.*

*I'm in a difficult spot, Peter. Yeah, it finally came out. You see? It still doesn't take that much to forgive you if there is anything that needs forgiveness. I got myself in a bad situation. There's no one I can talk to. I meant to call you so many times, but I never did. I felt so silly and childish.*

*I got fired, I'm doing drugs. They keep my mind distracted. They help me escape from my failures, but they are also killing me. And I'm trapped now.*

*I hope you get this letter.*

*I wish you were here now, and that gate was still closed with its chain. That would be cool. That would give me a reason.*

*There are not many reasons right now.*

*Take care, Peter.*


*Will*

*P.S. Congrats on your book. I always knew you would do it one day. I loved it. It spooked the hell out of me.*


# 3


"He will be alright," Jane Hanson said as they saw the one-mile sign approaching. They were on their way back from a hike in Bryce Canyon National Park. The April air was cool and crisp. The trail was marked by crushed rocks which had turned almost into dust. All around them were stunning sculptures of red and white canyons with bright green bushes scattered everywhere. Lynn had wondered, as they hiked, how the bushes could be so green and fertile in a place that was so rocky and sandy.

"I hope you're right," she said, trying not to think about Frank. It had been impossible for her not to worry about him.

When the time of the trip to Utah had come, Lynn had talked to Frank about going. He had declined, of course. When she first mentioned the trip, he stopped what he was doing in the garage and looked at her without saying a word. She realized how old he had become. He had stopped shaving and had lost so much weight. His clothes were baggy on him, and the wrinkles on his forehead had carved their way down into the skin like slow dripping water shaping the rocks and marking an inexorable path. He had stopped taking care of himself and indulged himself in drinking. Frank was never violent, and he hardly raised his voice with her. Quite the opposite, he was just off, slowed down. He had lost his spark when Will had left them. He had lost his compass and his desire to live and move on. He was the ghost of who Frank Harris used to be. It was as if he was waiting for the end to come.  They looked at each other without saying a word. She waited for him to get upset, to give her a sign of life, but he didn't. There was still a little bit of him somewhere deep inside. A tiny bit that wasn't gone with all the rest.

"I think you should go, love. It will be good for you. I'm sorry, but I can't come," he had eventually said before leaving in a rush, avoiding a conversation he couldn't bear at all costs.

She was determined to enjoy Utah's majestic scenery fully, but she still laid in bed at night and pictured herself coming home and finding Frank dead. The idea he could kill himself was obscene and remote but not completely out of the realm of possibilities. She called him three times a day to make sure he was still breathing. That gave her enough peace to enjoy the nature surrounding her.

"I have a surprise for you," Jane said, panting, as they stopped for a water break.

"Oh boy! Should I be worried?" she answered with a smirk.

"One of my coworkers, Sandra, texted me the contact of a Native Navajo woman who lives near Moab. She is a medium and, apparently, from what Sandra had told me, a legit one. We will be there in a couple of days, and I thought you would have liked the idea. What do you say?"

Lynn smiled at her as she did every time she was paralyzed with fear. Of course, her mind went to Will. She was skeptical about the alleged skills mediums claimed to have, but the idea that she could be in contact with Will made her legs shake and her heart run fast.

"What's her name?" Lynn asked.

"Sandra didn't say. Apparently, she works in the back of this souvenir store in Moab. She doesn't have a phone, and there is no reservation process. Sandra told me to go to this store, talk to Monica, the owner, and ask to talk to the medium. Isn't that super exciting?"

Lynn thought it was kind of scary, but she couldn't lie to herself: she was interested. She was a private person, so she was always nervous about showing her emotions in public. Her first thought was how she would react if the medium woman mentioned Will or even something remotely connected to him. Lynn had never believed in the world of the spirits, but she would have given everything to feel his presence for one second.

"I want to do it," she said as a single tear rolled down her cheek.

# 4

Two days after the Bryce Canyon National Park hike, Lynn Harris walked the crowded Main St. of Moab, Utah. The trip had been incredible so far, and Lynn was happy she had ultimately decided to go with the Hansons. They had flown into Las Vegas, rented a Jeep—one of those with the removable top—and drove to Grand Canyon National Park. As she had walked from the car to the viewing spot, she had almost fainted witnessing the immensity of it. They had slept in Flagstaff for the night and drove to Monument Valley National Park, at the border between Arizona and Utah. They had spent the night in teepee tents in the middle of the valley, building a campfire and looking up at the most beautiful sky she had ever seen. There was a full moon that night, and despite shining its powerful and magical light into the valley, it didn't deprive them of the spectacle of thousands of stars. When they left Monument Valley, they drove to Antelope Canyon, where she had been stunned once more by the shapes of the rocks that water had worked for so long to sculpt. Afterward, they headed towards Zion National Park, then to Bryce Canyon, and finally to Moab, where she had decided to visit a Native Navajo medium.

And here she was, walking nervously on the sidewalk. Bill and Jane Hanson walked closely in front of her. Bill wrapped his arm around Jane, keeping her close to him. They still looked as in love as they were in high school. The same happily distracted expression on their faces, almost the same innocence and naiveness. She remembered when the four of them went out together to dance on Saturday nights. Frank was always the life of the party. He made everyone laugh. It broke her heart to picture him in the garage, probably drunk and asleep on his working bench.

Jane brought Lynn back to reality when she stopped in front of a souvenir store. The sign on top of it read: Authentic Navajo Artifacts.

"This is it! I think this is the one," Jane said, looking at her phone to double-check the address. "If you are having second thoughts, it's not a problem," Bill said in his kind voice. "We can do whatever we want. There is no pressure."

"I really want to do it. I will be alright," Lynn said, trying to appear calm and relaxed, but her heart was galloping in her chest.

Jane took her hand, and they went inside the store.

The place was dark inside, illuminated only by a few candles, and smelled of incense and cedar wood. Lynn was expecting it to be quite crowded, given the traffic outside walking the streets, filling the bars and restaurants on this beautiful summer day, but there must have been five or six people, including them. Two of the tourists were loud and ruined the atmosphere of the place, which emanated relaxing vibrations.

They looked around through the shelves. There were several necklaces, earrings, and rings with colored stones nested into them. Each stone had a description of its healing properties when in contact with the skin for a prolonged amount of time. An entire section displayed only dreamcatchers varied in size from five feet to a few inches. Pocket knives and hand-sized tomahawks were underneath a glass counter at the far end of the shop.

There were books about Moab and its history, rugs, and handmade blankets with beautifully sewn patterns. They were pretty pricey. One interesting thing she had noticed—and with all frankness that she loved—was the total absence of souvenirs. There weren't t-shirts, mugs, ashtrays, or shot glasses reading 'I love Moab' or any other crap like that. That would explain why the store was almost deserted, she thought with a hint of hatred towards humanity.

Jane had already picked two matching blankets, and when Lynn was ready, they both walked toward the register.

The woman at the front desk smiled at them and asked if they had found everything alright. Jane introduced herself and Lynn, mentioning they were friends of Sandra and asking to speak with Monica.

"Give me one second. I'll go fetch Monica for you," she said, then disappeared behind a curtain made of crystal beads. Lynn heard them clinking as they clashed.

A few moments later, a woman in jeans and a cowboy shirt came through the curtain. Her dark and thick hair was arranged in one single braid that rested on her chest, tied up at the bottom with a red ribbon. She wore a thin leather headband, which matched perfectly with her golden and smooth skin. Lynn thought she looked so young, even though she was probably in her forties. She was beautiful.

"Hello," she greeted them. "You must be Sandra's friend. I'm Monica. How can I help you?"

Jane explained why they were there and if it was possible to meet with the woman Sandra had told her about.  Lynn couldn't help thinking they must have looked just like the tourist-kind she despised.

Monica looked around, almost to make sure other customers didn't see them, then gestured to Jane and Lynn to follow her through the curtain. Jane went around the counter first, and Lynn followed.

Monica led them through a tight, dark hallway into a small storage room filled with piled boxes.

"You're here to see Komeha'e. She is very old and does not speak English, so I will have to translate."

Jane and Lynn both nodded.

"Please do not share this with other people. This is not part of our business; we don't want this place to become a circus. Komeha'e just likes to come here and play cards sometimes. She talks to people occasionally, but you have to understand that she is very skeptical and doesn't trust tourists. She thinks they treat this place as if they were at the fair. It will take me a few minutes to convince her. Which one of you wants to talk to her?"

Jane and Lynn looked at each other.

"I think you should go," Jane said, looking at Lynn.

"Only one. It won't be more than ten minutes."

"Are you ok with it, dear?" Jane asked Lynn, holding her hand.

Lynn nodded.

"One more thing. Komeha'e doesn't do this for money. Please do not try to offer her any. She hates that. If you'd like to make a donation to the store, it's ok, but do not offer her cash. Understood?"

Lynn said she understood.

After five minutes, Monica returned to the storage room and told Lynn to follow her.

They walked to the room at the end of the hallway, which had been left ajar; an orange faint light came out of the opening.

"You ready?" Monica asked.

"Yes. I'm ready," Lynn replied.

It couldn't have been further from the truth.

# 5

As she walked into the room, her eyes needed a few seconds to get familiar with the strange light. Five candles stood on a small round table, the flames fluttering in the air despite the stillness of it. The room was not air-conditioned. Lynn felt beads of sweat starting to form on her forehead.

Behind the table, an old and incredibly thin woman sat on her chair as she fished cards from an old deck and placed them in front of the candles. She suddenly turned toward the door, almost jerkily, as soon as Lynn and Monica entered.

Her hair was long, gray, and as thin as cotton candy. She wore it loose and messy, framing a deeply wrinkled face. Her eyes were the color of oak, showing a pretty advanced stage of cataracts, giving them a layer of satin white in the middle. By the look of it, Lynn would have guessed she was already blind. But she stared in her direction, straight into Lynn's eyes, as if she had the sight of an eagle, as if she could look at her and through her. She had tremors, and her hand shook visibly as she held the card she was about to put down.

Monica gestured to Lynn to sit in front of the old woman—Lynn wondered the meaning of her name. She didn't know much about

Native American culture, but she had learned that their names always had a meaning.

She sat before her, keeping her eyes down, afraid to look straight at her. There was an energy in the room and no doubt it came from the woman. Lynn couldn't quite explain why she felt that way, but she was certain the woman was not ordinary. Monica gently put her hand on hers and bent down to whisper in her ear. Whatever she said to her seemed to calm her down a bit. She slowly collected the cards and put them aside on the table.

Lynn's heart was beating so fast that, for a moment, she thought she would probably have to get up and run away.

Komeha'e said something incomprehensible to her, revealing a hoarse voice. Lynn had the feeling that it was the voice of a woman who had cried, yelled and screamed. She had suffered a great deal during the journey of her life.

"What is your name?" Monica translated.

"Ehm...Lynn. Lynn Harris," she answered in a trembling voice.

The woman nodded; no translation was needed. She moved one of the candles to the side. Then she stretched her arm through the space she had created as if she wanted to grab Lynn's hand. Lynn offered hesitantly her hand to the old woman, who grabbed it firmly. She could feel the deeply wrinkled and hard skin as the woman kept looking at her. The tremors seemed to have passed. She was incredibly still.

Lynn felt a low vibration coming from Komeha'e's hand. It felt a little bit like she had her hand on the belly of a purring cat. The woman's expression changed, and she slightly moved her attention from Lynn's eyes to the right. It was as if she was looking at someone else in the room.

"*It's ok, Mom.*"

Lynn's heart sank in her chest, and she almost collapsed. The voice came from the old woman's mouth, but it wasn't her voice. It was Will's.

The woman was just a vessel now. Her son was talking to her.

*"It's okay, Mom. It was not your fault. You have to let it go now,"* Komeha'e said in Will's voice again. She was perfectly still, and her grip on Lynn's hand was firm, the energy flowing to and from her.

"Will... Will," Lynn said as she started crying. "My boy. My love. Are you ok?"

At first, the woman didn't respond, and Lynn thought she had ruined everything. Then Will responded through her.

*"I'm ok. Dad is not well. You have to take care of him. There is a woman here with me. She is kind. She has your voice. I have to go, Mom. I love you."*

"Will, Will, please don't go. Please," Lynn sobbed, letting herself fall on the table. "I love you. I love you more."

Then the woman retracted her hand, filling the room with Lynn's heart-wrenching whines.

The woman looked at her and then said something. Her voice was back, and Will's was gone.

"I know what you are feeling," Monica said, and it took Lynn a moment to realize that she was translating again. "I have something I want to give you. It will help you to feel close to your son."

The old Navajo woman raised her eyes to the ceiling. The candle's light glared on her cataracts, and she stared off as she started undoing the necklace she wore from the back of her nape.

She reached out to her again and grabbed Lynn's hand. The necklace was cold to the touch as Komeha'e pressed it into her palm with strength. She pressed harder, to the point where she felt the stinging pressure of the edge of the necklace cutting into her skin.

Lynn instinctively tried to retract her hand, but the woman held it firmly. She was much stronger than she looked.

She realized the psychic was now very close to her, looking her straight in the eyes. Their faces were so close that Lynn could smell booze on her breath.

She was scared but, at the same time, couldn't divert her gaze from the woman's eyes. They were like dark holes with a faint light in them. It was like looking at galaxies dancing in the cold darkness of outer space, at the sheer helplessness of human existence in a universe full of dead stars.

And then, all of a sudden, she understood what was happening.

Komeha'e was trying to share something with her—something intimate, a secret place where the deepest fears resided. Only mothers knew and were allowed to access the sacred place, the battlefield where the pure expression of love fought with fear.

Lynn recognized that place and understood that Komeha's pain was *her* pain.

She saw a much younger version of the woman who spoke with the voice of Will. She must have been sixteen years old and laid on a pile of blankets and wool in the middle of a tent.

Around her were other Native American women, chanting and singing to support her, to give her strength.

Young Komeha'e took deep breaths between the contractions that had begun to shake her whole body. She moaned in pain while another woman put a wet towel on her forehead. The oldest woman in the room kneeled in front of her spread legs, ready to grab the baby.

A prolonged, agonizing, final scream was followed by the first cry of the newborn. The older woman wrapped him in a blanket, recited something in her language, and immediately gave him to his mom.

Komeha'e looked at him and cried. Lynn felt the love filling the tent. That love that changes a woman forever that makes her whole with the universe. But Lynn felt something else, too. Komeha'e was afraid to lose her baby. In fact, she knew she was going to lose him.

Moments later, three armed white men entered the tent and ordered all the other women to leave. The leader drew his weapon and pointed it at Komeha'e and her baby.

His voice was muffled, but Lynn could hear him ordering Komeha'e to hand the baby over.

Komeha'e cried. They had waited for him to be born to take him away from her, to torture the mother, to make her suffering unbearable.

She spoke a few words to her newborn and kissed him on his cheek before they took him out of her hands and out of the tent.

She knew she wouldn't see him again, and she would never know what happened to him. That's what the white men did to the women of her tribe: to take the babies away from the devil so they could try to convert them to their religion, to purify them when the baby's only sin was to come from the womb of a devil.

She screamed and cursed them as they took the baby away.

Komeha'e let Lynn's hand go, and she could see no more. The tent disappeared, and the desperate scream faded away. She was back in the storage room. Monica and Komeha'e sat in front of her.

Lynn opened her hand and looked at the silver medal and the metallic lace that held it. Mixed with her blood, the medal portrayed the symbol of two people upside down.

She realized the power of the relic she was holding. It gave her an instant sense of relief. She felt Will was in it. She didn't know how, but she was sure of his presence. He would be close to her as long as she had the relic.

And there was nothing in the world that could ever separate Lynn Harris from it.

# 6

One week later, Lynn was back home and relieved to see that Frank was still alive. She hugged him as she remembered the words that came out of the old woman's mouth, with the voice of Will.

*Take care of dad. He is not doing well.*

And from that moment, she had been more than determined to see that he was cared for.

Despite Frank's evident desire to return to the garage, they talked. She told him everything about the trip, almost everything. There would have been a time to tell him about the meeting with Komeha'e and how that had changed everything for her.

After some time, she got Frank to open up a little bit. He cried his desperation to her and the guilt that threatened to eat him alive. Lynn offered to go to see a grief counselor together. It took some real convincing, but she eventually got him to agree.

She didn't need grief counseling, not anymore, she thought as she grabbed the necklace and felt the ribs of its design in her palm. Every time she touched it, she felt a warm feeling of comfort starting from her hand and invading her body. And she felt Will's presence next to her and just couldn't get enough of it. Her mood was improving, and, for the first time since Will passed, she could see the light at the end of the tunnel. Her mission was now to bring Frank on the same healing path.

They cooked dinner, drank a bottle of wine, washed the dishes together, then went to bed and made love.

She fell asleep and woke up next to him the morning after.

Life had restarted on a different path where hope wasn't just a word but a tangible prize. She didn't feel guilty anymore because Will had told her that it was okay and to let it go. He had told her that it was time to move on.

When she went to the bathroom to shower, she untied the necklace and gently placed it in a piece of cloth she had bought from Monica's store in Moab.

A few minutes later, as she rinsed her hair from the shampoo, unease began to sneak upon her. She shivered under the hot water, and the light coming through the window suddenly dimmed down.

A familiar sense of heaviness was back; dark memories carried the terrible feeling of guilt that she had fought so hard to get rid of. Everything was back to how it was before. She panicked and, with the water still running, got out of the shower and stretched out to reach the necklace. She sat back down in the bathtub as the water hit her on the face while she held the pendant tight against her chest. She was almost to the point of screaming out all her frustrations— for she had ruined the greatest gift given to her—when the light shone again outside and flooded the room through the window. The warmth returned to her body and soul, thawing her from the gelid hug of desperation, wiping out the guilt.

She kissed the medal and put it back on her neck, promising herself she would never take it off again.

Later on, she went downstairs and sat comfortably on her couch in the den, planning to read Stephen King's novel *The Outsider,* with the company of a hot cup of coffee. She played with the medal in her hand as she read. It was so cold to the touch, but when it was in contact with her skin, it gave her a sense of warmth, as if she was wrapped in an invisible blanket.

Lynn flinched when the doorbell rang and almost spilled her coffee. She got up and wondered who it could have been. Lynn opened the door; but no one was there. She checked her front porch to see if a package had been delivered, but nothing was there.

When she closed the door and turned, she saw Will standing in the middle of the den.

Her first reaction was to scream, but nothing came out of her mouth. She stood there, unable to process what was happening in front of her eyes. Lynn Harris had always been an extremely rational person. She wasn't religious, despite growing up in a family where religion was everything that mattered. She had worked as a lab technician for a pharmaceutical company for almost twenty years before her early retirement. She didn't believe in ghosts, spirits, or the paranormal world. But these days, everything she thought she knew or believed in seemed to have flipped. The foundation of her logical thought process had been violently shaken since she met Komeha'e.

The disbelief and fear disappeared after a few moments, and she smiled at Will.

He didn't smile back. He just stood there and stared at her. He looked so real except for his eyes. His eyes were off in a way she couldn't quite explain. His pupils had expanded, and his eyes were almost entirely dark. She was afraid but couldn't quite bring herself to admit it.

*Mom.*

The voice was almost the same as Will's. It sounded metallic and altered.

"My boy!" she whispered as tears started to fill her eyes. "Is that you, Will?"

*Come over here, mom.*

And that was when she realized his voice was not coming from his mouth but from inside her own head. Will's mouth hadn't opened. His lips were frozen the whole time. He was there, in front of her in the flesh, but he was also in her head.

She obeyed, though hesitantly, and slowly went toward him. The closer she got, the more off he looked. It was almost as if he was incomplete, an unfinished painting. She noticed his mouth was different, and the dimple that had always been on his chin wasn't there at all.

When she got closer, he stepped forward with preternatural quickness inches from Lynn. She stared into those dark eyes, a dim light in the middle of them, the same presence she had felt in Komeha'e's when she had forcefully shared her story with Lynn.

From that distance, she noticed he wasn't breathing. His chest was still, and no air was coming from his nose. His lips were shut, but she could hear a low growling noise coming from his depths. He carried a smell she had never experienced. It reminded her of ammonia and damp wood after a night of rain.

Then he leaned closer to her, reaching for her neck. She couldn't move. She wasn't in control, not anymore.

He smelled her neck and hair while he made a clicking sound with his teeth.

*I need you to do something for me.* Will said without speaking.

Lynn Harris nodded as she listened to his instructions.

# 7

The Super Target store on the westside was extremely crowded that Saturday morning. Lynn placed her three reusable grocery bags in the red plastic cart and began to push it. She scanned the people standing in line at Starbucks and those browsing the baked goods section in front of it.

She was worried she would not be able to find the person she was looking for. How was she supposed to know who was a good fit? After all, Will—or whatever was carrying his features earlier in the living room—hadn't been clear or specific about his needs. As a matter of fact, he hadn't spoken at all. She just knew she had to find the right person. She couldn't deny the fear that she felt. For a moment, she had hoped that she could find comfort, albeit ephemeral, to be close to her son again, but that hope was short-lived. It was wiped away like a rickety barn in the middle of a storm when the awareness came that what stood before her was something different, something evil. And the hope was replaced quickly with fear and dread. It wasn't really that she was scared of the thing that wore Will's features. She wasn't frightened or physically threatened by it. Her fear was to lose the effect of the Navajo relic, the terror of falling back into her abyss of grief. Nothing was scarier than that. If this *thing* wanted her help, which meant to keep healing, that was enough for her. She couldn't be sure, but somehow, she knew there was something in return she had to give to get that sense of relief, a Faustian bargain she had just signed with the entity.

She went through the aisles, back and forth, multiple times, grabbing stuff she didn't need from the shelves. She tried to blend in with the crowd and not raise suspicions or attention to herself.

She was almost about to give up when a buzzing feeling, almost a small electric shock, directed her focus to a big man in the dairy section. And with no apparent explanation, she was sure he was the one. The voice inside her head, the presence that now controlled her actions, had chosen. The big guy with the Red Sox hat was the one she was looking for.

She had no idea why, just like she didn't have the faintest clue of what the intentions of the creature inside her mind were.

And she wasn't sure she wanted to know.

Lynn felt like she was a puppet, driven by an invisible force. Unable to resist, her only option was to execute. Her thoughts weren't hers anymore. The power of the relic, still hanging from her neck, had sealed a pact between her and the entity. She had no idea what the terms of that pact were or to what extent its requests would stretch. She knew that whatever the entity wanted from this man couldn't be good.

She left the store when the man did. She jumped in her car and followed him without even thinking about it.

A few minutes later, she turned off US 36 to take a right into a neighborhood. She parked on the side of the street and drew a huge sigh of relief. She had the instinct during her drive—or was it rather an order? —of maintaining a certain distance from the white Buick she was following. On the other hand, she had the challenge not to get too far behind. Otherwise, she could have lost the man. She was pretty confident, at that point, that would have meant an immense disappointment for her puppeteer and trouble for her.

The man hopped out of the car in front of his modest ranch-style house. It was quite old and looked like it needed some remodeling. The grass had not been mowed in a while. The roof had some shingles in pretty bad shape, and one of the steps leading to the front porch was broken.

He went around his car and popped his trunk open using the remote button on his car key. He grabbed the plastic bags and went inside the house. A second trip was needed to get the twenty-four-pack of bottled spring water and lock his car.

Lynn realized the creature that looked almost like Will was in the backseat of her car as she heard the low growling sound. When she looked in the rearview mirror, she saw the black eyes looking at her.

The entity exited the car and mentally told her she could go. Immediately, she felt its grip loosening, her mind clearer, and the fear ramping up again. The creature wasn't in control anymore. With her heart thumping in her chest, she started the car and pulled into the street. She looked at the mirror on the passenger's side, watching the figure of her son standing on the sidewalk and becoming smaller and smaller as she drove away. She wondered if she had just completely lost her mind. After all, it wasn't uncommon for grieving people to be completely unable to accept the loss. She wouldn't be the first, or the last, to have hallucinations. They clung to their refusal to the point of being delusional. Part of her wished that was the case.

She revved the engine, wanting to be home as soon as possible.

# 8

On the following morning, Lynn was in the kitchen fixing breakfast for Frank and nervously tapping her hand on the quartz countertop of the kitchen island. She kept glancing at the TV in the living room, waiting for the local news on Channel 13. At first, she hadn't realized why she was so keen to watch the news—she hardly watched TV at all, let alone the news exclusively related to the ongoing pandemic that was putting the world on its knees for the second year.

Then she thought about the previous day and the request the entity had expressed to her. She felt the need to turn the TV on and check if something unusual would be reported.

The rational part of her kept trying to keep calm, but her instincts told her otherwise.

Frank came down the stairs and smiled at her as he swung by the coffee machine and poured himself a cup.

"Morning! How do you feel about today?" she asked him, referring to their third appointment with the grief counselor. Frank shrugged as he sipped his coffee. "I don't know. How are you feeling about it?"

"I think it's been such a positive change. I'm always nervous before going, though, you know?" she said distractedly, sending a quick gaze to the TV.

Frank turned to see what she was looking at. "Waiting for something?" he asked.

"Just the weather. I'm trying to decide if I should go for a walk before our appointment."

She took the sizzling bacon and scrambled eggs off the stove and served them to Frank.

She was glad to see him regaining some of his appetite. It wasn't nearly as strong as it used to be, but she tried to take in every small victory. That was the way it was now. One day at a time. She said she would get ready and stopped at the bottom of the staircase, where Frank couldn't see her while she had a clear view of the TV.

The hosts of the local morning news were a blonde woman in her late thirties and a bald man wearing a jacket that looked way too tight around his broad shoulders. The female anchor started to talk, but Lynn was not listening anymore. She instinctively brought a hand to her mouth as she read the crawler at the bottom of the screen.

The town of Avon is in shock after a fifty-six-year-old man is found dead in his house.

Lynn's heart sunk in her chest, and a sense of heaviness started to invade her. She looked at the reporter on the scene, standing in front of the house where her car had sat on the side of the road the day before. *Oh my God! What have I done?* She thought as she sat on the couch, afraid she would faint. Even if she didn't have direct contact with the man from the Super Target store, she felt as responsible for his death as if she had slayed him with her bare hands. A sense of imminent danger assailed her. *What have I gotten myself into?* Lynn thought of Komeha'e and the vision that she had shared. Something came out of that pendant. Something that had been put there for a reason and wasn't supposed to come out. When she was in the car, maneuvered by the creature, she sensed its hunger.

She instinctively reached for the necklace and held it tight in her hand.

But no comfort came from it. The magic had vanished, and the horror was the only thing that remained.

Lynn spent the majority of the following days on her laptop, researching about the death of Oliver Curry on the internet. She had found several videos where his neighbor and friends talked to the reporters about how good of a guy he was. He had worked as a janitor at the local high school, and all the teachers and colleagues described him as a cordial and kind man who never missed a day on the job.

Local media had released the salient parts of the police report, claiming that the investigators were still exploring different paths, but there were no conclusive leads at the moment. The police had now seized the victim's laptop and were going to conduct a thorough check of his social media account, searching for clues. There was no information about the cause of death, despite the media having posed that question several times. The investigators refused to answer any questions, reminding the reporters about their inability to share details in an ongoing, wide-open case. A local resident, interviewed by Channel 13, had stated that something really messed up must have happened at the Curry's residence, given that the police were keeping their mouths shut. One of Curry's neighbors, Charlize Reinbach, who worked for Indy Star, had leaked a few photos on her social media showing a massive police presence at Curry's residence. According to the caption of her post, several forensic teams had worked on the crime scene for over six hours. Lynn found videos of some concerned residents claiming a serial killer was on the loose, and the cops were hiding it to avoid spreading panic. The police had to release an immediate statement to reassure that the residents would be informed as soon as the investigation made substantial progress. The sheriff of Hendricks County invited everyone to maintain calm and not spread false rumors.

Lynn closed her laptop and looked out of the window, peeking between the blinds of the living room window. It was still cold outside despite the late May sun. Days had started to get longer again, and daylight was still out past dinner time.

The sense of guilt was eating her alive. She wanted to talk to someone about this, but she couldn't. They were going to think she had completely lost her mind. Or maybe she could just shut up and go on with her life. She had been in the depths of grief, and she honestly didn't know if she and Frank, especially Frank, would have gotten out of that situation sane, still together, or even alive. Then, the miracle came. She had been able to not only communicate with Will, but she had seen him and touched him. What was the point of throwing all that away? And for what? At that point, she wasn't even sure she could throw it away. It might have been too late for that already.

She reached for the necklace, and this time, a warmth was back as if it had recharged its batteries with fresh energy. Along with it came the subtle grip she now associated with the entity. Her thoughts were now shared again, a mix of hers and the creature's. Her fear and guilt were replaced by confidence and ruthlessness. They didn't belong to her. She never had them in the first place, even before the pendant.

The creature living inside her head wanted her to know that the renewed energy came from Oliver Curry's death. It invigorated it, another step towards its full shaping. It would take time, victims, and all the help she could give. The thought of it made her shiver. She was slowly becoming aware that her happiness and future depended on whatever was living inside the pendant. She was addicted and couldn't live without it anymore. She also realized that the thing inside the relic had to be fed from time to time. She knew it materialized when it needed her to do something, when it was hungry.

She had never thought—not after Will had grown up and left the house anyway—that she would have been involved with the maternal duties of feeding a child to look after his necessities. And here she was, under quite different circumstances, ready to do anything she must to feed this creature.

It didn't matter what the diet looked like now.

# 9

One week passed, but the police made no significant progress on Oliver Curry's case. The coroner's office finally released the body to the family for the funeral arrangements. According to the recollection of the events, Mr. Curry went about his day on May 16. He went to the grocery store and came home immediately after. Around seven o'clock in the evening, a friend of Mr. Curry knocked on his door, waiting for a few minutes before peeking through the living room window and calling 911. Even though the Sheriff's office believed that suicide was the most likely outcome of the investigation, they didn't find any conclusive evidence supporting that lead. No other information was disclosed as the case remained open. The newspapers, Channel 13, and online articles never mentioned anything about the cause of death. All this uncertainty led to more questions and drew even more attention from the media.

*It makes perfect sense, right?* Lynn thought. *A man wakes up, goes to the store to buy eggs and milk, and returns home immediately to kill himself.*

The necklace began to emanate a faint vibration as if it wanted to be touched.

Lynn grabbed it, and she was in a different place in the blink of an eye as if she had traveled through time and space into another home, a kitchen.

The room was unfamiliar, but she somehow knew who it belonged to. She stood in Oliver Curry's kitchen right before the window, looking at a small round table with three chairs around it. The place was dirty and smelled terrible. There was a pile of dirty dishes in the sink. The trash can was overflowing, and the lid rested on the garbage, unable to fully close. Judging by the conditions of the house, she guessed the man lived alone, with no wife, no kids, no grandkids.

The front door opened, and she panicked instinctively when the man she had followed around the store and to his own house came in. She calmed down when she realized she was invisible to him. She knew Will wanted her to know what had happened. He was showing her exactly how it went. Curry was a big man in his late fifties. He had a bit of a belly, but overall, he was in good shape. He wore a baseball hat, a baggy hoodie, sweatpants and sneakers. He put the plastic bags with his groceries down near the front door, went back out, and returned with a case of plastic water bottles.

He walked to the kitchen, looked right where she stood, opened the fridge, and grabbed a beer. He went into the small living room where an old leather recliner chair had been placed in front of a TV that seemed to belong to the nineties, the kind with the old cathodic tube. He turned it to a basketball game and sat down, making noises of relief for his back.

A few seconds later, someone knocked at the door. Lynn knew who it was. She observed the surprised look on Oliver's face as he got up. He clearly wasn't expecting any visitors.

When he opened the door, no one was there. It reminded Lynn of her first encounter with the entity a few days earlier. Oliver shut the door and returned to his chair, shaking his head. Something had entered the house. Lynn felt the shift in the air, goosebumps on her skin, an evil energy spreading across the room. Oliver must've felt the same because he looked around, ensuring he was still alone.

He sat back on his chair and reclined all the way.

Lynn flinched when she saw Will observing Curry from behind his chair. A disturbing grin painted on his face. Its features had shifted: the opening of his mouth extended to its ears, exposing long and sharp fangs that looked like icicles. They were dirty and bloody. His eyes were completely black and showed a hunger and a fury that didn't belong to this world.

The creature sank its fangs into Oliver Curry's face from behind. Lynn wanted to close her eyes, but she couldn't. The entity wanted her to watch. And so she watched the man screaming in a mix of pain and surprise, unable to process what was happening to him. The fangs tore into the flesh and the skull with incredible ease as the entity mauled the struggling Curry; blood squirted and dripped on the leather chair. Curry's body struggled briefly, then went still, and a bleak silence fell in the room. The only noise she could hear was the squelching sounds of the beast feeding itself.

Then it went down and walked on all fours around the room at an inhuman speed. Its spine was curved, and its head was down, licking the blood from the ground. The body of Oliver Curry laid on the chair with the top part of his head missing. His jaw, mouth, and chin were still intact, completely covered in blood, brain, and pieces of skull.

The abhorrent creature was now still and quiet, looking at her with those unspeakable dark eyes and panting as the hunger was satisfied and his thirst quenched. It occurred to Lynn that the creature had fed its body and was now feeding its soul. As it looked at her, it absorbed her terror, her fear, a precious dessert after its main course. She felt those feelings and emotions leaving her body and migrating into the creature. As this happened, its features returned to the ones of her son.

The demon might have liked to eat human beings alive, just as any wild animal, but she could tell its craving for negative emotions was way greater than the physical need. That was the primary fuel of its existence.

It suddenly made sense to Lynn why the police hadn't disclosed the cause of death to the public. The level of damage on Curry's head and part of his back was extensive. She could almost see the looks on the investigators' faces, lost in confusion and chaos over something they would never really be able to explain, not with the rational tools their job required them to use. A necessary step into madness was required to understand the beast and its doing. A step she had already taken, not really by choice but by coincidence. *Was there such a thing as a coincidence?* Her mind flashed back to Komeha'e. *Why had she given her the pendant? Was it to curse her? Was it to help her? Or was it perhaps to get rid of it? How had she been able to live with it for so long? Had it been her own decision to give it to her? Or had it been the entity commanding her to do it?* After all, it could have used Komeha'e just as it used her now. Lynn felt the old Navajo woman's hate, grief, and revenge that accompanied the vision of her own past experience. A grieving mother. Just like her.

The questions kept coming as she watched, an unwilling spectator, the triumph of blood, flesh, and bones in front of her. She looked at the monster, feasting as it looked at her, and snarled while little tears of blood ran down the corner of its mouth.

# 10

She attended the funeral service that was organized for Oliver Curry at the Taylor & Barnes Funeral Parlor. It was on the westside of town, a few blocks away from the home where he was brutally killed.

She had no desire to attend. She didn't know the man—though she felt greatly responsible for his death, as she should. After all, she had delivered him to the beast on a silver platter. The guilt she felt was terrible, and the side effects of the necklace were starting to overcome its benefits. Her sleep had worsened, and so had her positivity, mood, and strength to be there for Frank. After a few days of sun, dark clouds were in the sky again. She never meant to go to Oliver Curry's funeral. What would she say to the man's family members had she been asked how she knew him? *My most sincere condolences. By the way, I'm the one who hunted Oliver from the grocery store to his house, and I drove the creature that took his life right to his front door. I'm so very sorry for your loss.* But her decisions, actions, and willpower didn't matter much these days. The beast had wanted to go, and so she went. She was merely a vessel; she was its eyes and ears. Through her, it could hunt, feel the pain, the anxiety, and the fear, and feed from it.

One gentleman welcomed her at the front door. He was a handsome young man around Will's age. The man offered her his condolences and asked which service she was here to attend. He explained two services were going on simultaneously in two different areas of the parlor. When the thing living inside her became aware of that, Lynn could almost feel its excitement grow; she could hear its growling increasing in intensity.

She said she was there for Oliver Curry's service, and the man pointed her to the room on the left at the end of the hallway. She noticed other people turning to the right to attend the other service. She knew the beast would demand to go in the other room, too, at some point, and she knew that refusing wouldn't matter. It would have made her do it, even if that meant making her crawl.

The room prepared for Curry showed six rows of white chairs, ten per row, five per side of the aisle. She was surprised by how few seats had been prepared but even more surprised that there were no more than ten people in total in the room. That made her incredibly sad. She remembered hundreds of people at Will's funeral. She hadn't really cared on that terrible day, but she couldn't imagine how Oliver's family must have felt, not having all the support people needed in moments like that.

A woman in her fifties sat in the front row. She wore sunglasses, but Lynn could see she had been crying. She sat beside her and learned she was Oliver's younger sister, Tara. Lynn introduced herself as a friend who knew him from the high school he worked at. She was a talker, so after a while, Lynn learned about the man's family situation.

Oliver had never been married and had no kids. Tara Curry was his younger and only sister. She was married and lived in Ohio with her husband and her two kids. She didn't feel like bringing them to the funeral, so she had come alone. She mentioned she still had to figure out how to tell the kids that their uncle was gone. She said the kids were in awe of him, always treating them with presents and surprise visits.

"What am I supposed to tell them, huh?" she sobbed, grabbing a Kleenex from her purse to dry her tears and blow her nose. Lynn felt the monster grunting in pleasure. The woman's grief, anger, and confusion fed and satiated it with incredible power. The woman excused herself and rushed to the bathroom, where she would probably cry and let herself go for a bit. Lynn prayed that the beast wouldn't ask her to follow her there and was relieved when it didn't.

Instead, it ordered her to check the other room, which, judging by the number of people she had seen entering it, must have been way more crowded. She sneaked out of the room and crossed the hallway, making sure she was not seen by the parlor's employees who were patrolling.

She entered a much wider and more crowded room where all the seats were already occupied. She stood at the back of the room where other people stood with their heads down in prayer.

Lynn's heart stopped when she looked up at the room's far end and saw a miniature white casket lifted on stands. On the side of it was the picture of a girl who must have been five years old at the most. A banner with a gold ribbon stood in front of the stand that held the casket. It was the symbol of the fight against childhood cancer.

The blood literally froze in Lynn's veins. The pain filling the room was so intense that she could almost touch it in the air, and so could the monster feeding off it.

She reached for the door immediately, but her muscles wouldn't obey her. She tried again but felt paralyzed. She was just a shell for the entity that controlled her body, leaving her mind open to experience the fullness and dread of the moment.

Unable to move, she started crying silently and stood there as if she were a mere camera, offering the horrifying spectacle to the demon that had conquered her. She was forced to witness the full horror of the monster celebrating the tragedy that unfolded in the room. That was when Lynn Harris decided she couldn't take it anymore. The worst part was she didn't think she could do anything to get rid of it.

# Part Six:

# The Well

# 1

In the small office dedicated to the check-in process to access the evidence room, Cooper filled out the form at the counter while Davis waited behind him, scrolling on his phone. Cooper glimpsed at the woman behind the counter as she kept her eyes down in the presence of the Lieutenant. He couldn't help but grin as he wrote down his full printed name and checked the time on his watch. All her attempts to hit on him seemed to have suddenly gone cold.

When he handed her the form back, thanking her and asking if they were all set, she returned a fake smile and hit the button that unlocked the heavy door with a loud buzz followed by a metallic clanking sound.

Cooper let Davis go ahead and trailed him inside the room. His boss looked left and right with innocent curiosity and disorientation. It must have been a while since he had stepped in that room, and many things had changed in the last couple of years, especially with the digitalization and the new archiving protocols for evidence.

"Have you been briefed yet?" Cooper asked as he overtook Davis to lead the way to the computer station. "I mean, on the Kroger case?"

"Yes, Tibbs gave me the generics. What the hell do you think happened there?"

"I have no idea, Harry. There are no prints, nothing that even resembles a piece of evidence. I've never seen a body like that." Cooper opened his envelope, grabbed a photo, and handed it to Davis. "Does it remind you of something?"

"Jesus Christ," Davis said with narrow eyes, grimacing at the picture. "The Hansons, of course. Please tell me you are not trying to link this to that case."

"I know how you feel about it. But look at that picture and tell me you don't see a connection. People don't just die like that, Harry. These last three, Kroger and the Hansons, seem like they had seen a monster before passing."

"I hear you. Something is off; I'm with you on that. Let's work on finding some evidence," Davis sighed.

"I asked to collect the footage from the street camera on the other side of the street. It's a long shot, literally. The camera is a hundred feet from the station, and I'm pretty sure the building will cover what we need to see, at least judging from the angle."

Davis grunted and gestured to him to go on.

Cooper logged into the system, navigated through the folders, and then exhaled with frustration.

"The files haven't been uploaded yet," Cooper said, touching his temples with quivering fingertips. "Goddamnit. Sometimes I feel we were better off without this crap," he said, pointing at the computers.

Davis was already on his phone, a device that seemed he couldn't live without. For the majority of the time he spent with Davis, Cooper noticed the phone buzzing, ringing all the time. Davis was either killing the calls with a custom message like 'In a meeting, call you ASAP' or typing furiously on it.

"Get me Kurt, please," Davis said on the phone, trying hard to practice his patience, a skill he had never quite mastered. He waited for Kurt to answer on the other side of the phone. When he did, Davis asked how long it would take for the videos to be uploaded to the system. Davis stood there listening, starting to shake his head.

"You've got two minutes to upload the files. If you can't, I expect you to get your ass down here with a laptop to show us the video. And Kurt, please confirm you understand this is not a request. It's a fucking order."

He hung up the phone before poor Kurt could confirm. Harry's face had gone red.

"Hey pal, take it easy. We'll get there."

"These fucking people, sometimes I wonder if they even know what this place does. They look like the goddamn Geek Squad from Best Buy. There's never a fucking sense of urgency. Well, I'm going to give them a sense of urgency. One way or another."

They both turned back when the door buzzed loudly again. Kurt rushed in with an open laptop in his hands. He was panting from the run, his dark straight hair stuck on his forehead pearled with sweat. The guy was so thin that a wind gust could have taken him away.

"I'm sorry, sir!" he said, trying to catch his breath. "We are having some issues on the network, hence the delay in uploading the video."

Davis stared at the guy without saying a thing, his hands clutched to his waist.

"Thanks, Kurt," Cooper finally said, grabbing the laptop from his hands. He returned to the large desk with the big monitor and sat in one of the chairs. Davis sat on the one to his left.

Cooper hit the play button on the video player and looked at the black-and-white image flickering in front of his very eyes. As expected, the camera was too far from the scene, so the abandoned building that had once served as a station covered just a tiny portion of the screen. Beyond it, near the train tracks, was the scene where the body of Kroger had been found. He hit the fast-forward button, and they kept looking for a few minutes at the cars passing by in both directions. On the very far left of the screen, the camera caught a portion of a gas station. Only one pump, an outdoor ice machine, a fenced area with barbecue propane gas tanks, and a section of the parking lot area were visible in the shot. When the digital clock at the bottom right corner of the screen, tracking the time was close to the time the train passed, Cooper resumed playing at normal speed and looked at the screen with narrow, focused eyes.

The left side of the abandoned building, from that angle, was just about covering the far right end of the gas station parking lot. If the killer had dumped the body at the scene in an attempt to stage it as a train hit, the gas station parking lot would have been the perfect spot. Of course, the killer might or might not have known about the street camera, but Cooper couldn't fathom the idea that the killer could have been aware of what was visible and what was not from the camera. Cooper watched cars getting in and out of the parking lot, then the traffic calmed down, and nothing happened for a few minutes.

"What are we hoping to find on this?" Davis asked in a surprisingly calm tone. Cooper knew he was enjoying being back on the hunt.

"Anything really. If the killer dumped the body, it must be on this tape. Unless the victim just fell from the sky."

They watched for another two minutes. Everything was still; no cars drove by or stopped by the station, and there was no movement whatsoever. Cooper was on the verge of fast-forwarding again when he saw the nose of a white SUV parked at the far end of the gas station parking lot. The lot was behind the abandoned building, but it looked like it overlapped from the camera angle. The white car pulled into one of the parking spots, the hood and the passenger door hidden behind the building.

"Here we go, here we go," Cooper said, his heart beating fast in his chest and the adrenaline rushing. He felt the spark that only that kind of discovery could provide, that sensation of having a lead, a direction, something to chase.

"The car's too far for the camera to be accepted as evidence. We cannot even get a plate from this," Davis said as he got closer, squinting at the screen as if doing that would make the image clearer and more defined.

The car was parked there for five minutes, then backed up in reverse, left the lot, and merged back onto the street, away from the camera.

One minute later in the footage, the train passed and stopped a few seconds later.

"That must be him. The white car," Davis said. "A bummer, this is all we've got."

Cooper didn't reply. He rewound to the moment the car pulled in and paused the video exactly before the vehicle's front half got hidden behind the building. He hit the printer button and retrieved the photo from it.

As he looked at the blurry contours of the white SUV, his heart accelerated, and an eerie sense of uneasiness pervaded him. His subconscious knew already, but the awareness that he had seen that car, that he knew it from somewhere, came slowly into the conscious part of his mind as if his brain was trying to lessen the shock. The face of the Hansons trapped in a grimace of profound terror, the backward-facing head of Kroger, and the bone sticking out of his throat flashed in his mind like a never-ending film that got stuck in a solitary movie theater.

As the pieces started to make some sense in his head, Cooper wasn't quite ready to accept the absurd theory that was taking shape. One thing was certain: it was about damn time to talk with Lynn Harris again to ask her what her car was doing near the crime scene where the results of horrific, murderous actions had unfolded.

# 2

Jack Sullivan left the guest room and walked to the kitchen, where he sat on one of the stools near the counter. He opened the book he had been trying to finish before that eventful morning and transcribed the words from Peter Hanson's mouth onto a blank sheet. Then he grabbed his phone and searched in the list of the most recent calls.

"Jack." The voice of Joel Kopernick sounded even more surprised than the previous time. "This is becoming a pleasant habit of yours."

"I wish I could tell you that I bring good news, Joel, but the truth is that I need your help more than ever. I hate to be a bother. Are you free to talk?"

"Oh! Please stop with that nonsense. You are not a bother. Give me one moment while I move into my office."

Jack waited, listening to the padded sounds of footsteps and a door closing in the phone. *What in the world am I doing here?* Jack asked himself. He thought about his several panels with Joel on his side, discussing spiritual paths, nature, and critical differences between religions. The two of them had shared so many stimulating thoughts over dinner. Joel Kopernick had been a gust of fresh air, a breeze in the stale air of what his previous life had gravitated around.

"Here I am. All yours, Jack."

"I'll get straight to the point. I'm in the middle of a pretty serious situation, and I need your help."

"Okay." Jack could picture Joel's face frowning with curiosity even without seeing him. His voice had an interrogative note coming from his irresistible curiosity.

"Before I get into it, would you be so kind as to try to translate something for me?"

"Uhm. Sure. From what exactly?"

"I have no idea. I have transcribed the sound as I heard it, the best I could."

There was a moment of silence on the other side of the phone, then Joel said: "I'm sure you are aware of how many Native American languages there are and how different some can be compared to others."

"I am aware. Let's hope you are pretty fluent in this one. Are you ready?"

"Hit me."

Jack looked at the notes he had taken of the meaningless words Peter Hanson had blotted out in that alien, bellowing voice that didn't belong to him. It hadn't belonged to anything in this world. Then he read the words to Joel repeatedly, with some hesitation on the accent and pronunciation at first, then more fluently as his tongue got used to the sounds. Even repeating those words, without knowing their meaning, gave him a sense of uneasiness and threat. Sure enough, that was the tone when he heard the words.

When he stopped, he could hear Joel breathing into the microphone, a slightly accelerated breathing that increased Jack's anxiety level.

"Does this make any sense to you?" Jack asked with impatience.

"Where did you hear these words?" Joel said, his voice dry and serious.

"Can you translate them for me? I'll explain everything."

"I'm not sure about the exact origin of this language, but it must be very ancient. Some sounds are coming from the Cherokee, but they are mixed with other sounds from the tribes in the northwest. But I think I get the meaning."

"What does it mean?"

"It translates to 'Stop helping. Stop helping the man. He is finished. Stop helping, or you will finish too.'"

Jack shivered at the sound of those words. The image of the black eyes gleaming, like a giant fly staring at him, crossed his mind. That gaze, so full of cold malevolence, was so empty that it made his head spin. Jack recognized the intolerable obviousness of evil. The dead and guttural voice was so coarse that he could feel it scrubbing on his skin. The thought of it made Jack cringe; his teeth clenched together.

"Where did you hear this?" Joel brought him back to reality.

"Do you remember what we discussed in our previous conversation?"

"I do indeed. I was afraid it had something to do with that. What happened?"

"I know this is going to sound crazy, Joel, but I think I need you to come over here."

"Over there?" Joel asked with a veil of amusement.

"Here, to Indiana. Look, I wouldn't ask if it wasn't important."

"Okay, okay. Would you mind giving me a little bit of background first?"

"The Hollow, the shape-shifter spirit that we talked about."

"Yes, I remember," Joel said as he recollected.

"It's here, Joel. It's in my house."

"What...what do you mean it's in your house?"

"I saw it with my own eyes. He is using my neighbor, Peter Hanson, to send me a message. And the message is what you just translated for me. I am afraid Peter is possessed."

"Can you describe exactly what you saw?"

Jack told him everything without troubling himself too much by repeating things that Joel knew already. He told him about Lynn Harris, Bill and Jane Hanson, the pendant, his own experiences and manifestations, and Peter Hanson, his attempted suicide, the mass attached to his neck, and the protruding dark veins.

Jack couldn't help but imagine how crazy he must have sounded. For years and years, he was the one who had to listen to people claiming to be possessed or witnessing in some capacity manifestations connected to a case of demonic possession. Ninety-eight percent of the cases were related to hysteria, multiple personality disorder, dissociative identity disorder, schizophrenia or other mental health disorders. All of them had been accompanied by a very high level of conviction where the victim truly believed they were possessed.

He was now the one claiming to be in front of a case of true demonic possession, and the fact that he had done his homework and excluded all other possibilities didn't make him sound any less insane.

"Jack, don't take this personally, but I have to ask," Joel said. He talked slowly, clearly still trying to process what Jack had just revealed to him. "I am assuming that you have already confirmed that we are not in front of a case of psychosis, correct?"

"I am one hundred percent sure this is not a mental health issue, Joel. This is real. This thing is real, and it is haunting us. Can you come for a few days?"

"Of course, it will take me a couple of days to get there," Joel said, and Jack remembered that his friend did not travel on airplanes.

"Thank you very much, Joel. Is there anything that I can do in the meantime? Any suggestions? I have never seen anything like this."

"Well, I honestly don't know Jack. You know I am a strong believer in the world of spirits, but I have never experienced any encounters with one in person. I have collected many testimonies of people who have, but I'm unsure what to expect."

After a brief pause that seemed to last forever, Joel said, in a serious tone:

"I can tell you this: if this spirit is a Hollow, then there might not be anything that we can do. I mean anything at all."

Jack felt his blood freezing in his veins.

"What...What do you mean?"

"The Hollow spirits are parasites. Their goal is to feed themselves from the host. From the very few stories I can recollect—in fact, there aren't very many if compared with witnesses of Wendigo manifestations for example— they move from host to host until they find the one that can guarantee him the longest survival. In the meantime, it eats. It eats until there is nothing left to eat."

*Stop helping. He is finished.*

"From the folklore, you can remember, are there any stories about people that have been able to break free from a case of possession?"

Silence on the other side of the phone.

"Give me a couple of days, and I will be there. Text me the address to this number. And, Jack?"

"Yes."

"Don't engage with this thing. Stay clear as much as you possibly can."

Jack hung up.

He texted his home address to Joel, then sat on his chair and covered his face in his hands.

*Stop helping. Or you will finish too.*

He got up and walked to the guest room.

He found Luna in the hallway. She didn't turn towards him when she heard him approaching. She kept staring inside the spare room, where the monstrous creature had manifested, whining with fear.

# 3

Cooper parked his car in front of the Harris's driveway, oblivious of blocking the white SUV that pointed in his direction. He didn't need to look at the print from the street camera on Washington Street. He knew that was the car in the footage. He felt the rush of adrenaline running in his legs, making them sore; he felt his heart racing fast as he savored the moment.

Those moments were the ones that had him fall in love with the job in the first place when he was still a newbie, an eager but inexperienced boy who survived South Chicago and escaped Roseland.

He got out of the car and lit a cigarette. Looking around, he took off his jacket and threw it on the driver's seat before closing the door. He inhaled and took a few steps forward, then turned around, unconcerned with being seen. Cooper's gut feeling was screaming at him from the first moment he talked to Lynn Harris. The light in her living room had been turned on briefly, then back off around the estimated time of death of the Hansons. Her car had been spotted near the crime scene of another murder. He didn't have any evidence to support this lead, but he wouldn't stop trying to dig deeper this time.

He walked to the white Toyota SUV along the passenger side, peeking inside. If the body of Adam Kroger was carried in the car to be dumped near the railway, there could have been traces of blood. The front seat was clean, and nothing obvious seemed to jump out to Cooper's eye. The backseat and trunk windows were tinted and reflected Cooper's features as he tried to peek inside.

In the reflection of the car window, he suddenly saw an object, a shadow growing larger and larger. He instinctively shifted to the left just in time to avoid the hit.

Cooper moved so quickly that he lost his balance, falling on his side, his forearm scratching the abrasive concrete surface of the driveway. He turned and saw the object with eyes wide open in disbelief.

The black body of what seemed to him to be a raven, was splattered against the window, exactly where his head was a few seconds before. The shiny beak was nicked due to the violence of the kamikaze attack. The body slid down the window, smearing blood on it, until it fell on the driveway with a soft thud. Still struggling to believe what just happened in front of his eyes, Cooper watched the bird convulsing on the ground with his neck bent. It flapped its wings a couple of times until life left it. He looked up and saw more ravens perched on the power lines, watching the scene.

Cooper got up and wiped the dirt off his arm. He then looked toward the Harris house and saw Lynn as she stared out of the window. It took Cooper a few moments to realize that she was staring absently. He waved his hand to catch her attention, but she didn't move. Her unblinking eyes were wide open, but she wasn't alert. She looked like she had fallen into a trance, trapped in a semi-conscious state.

Once more, Cooper realized how beautiful Lynn Harris was. Two blonde waves of hair framed her delicate features and light green eyes. Tears were running down on her tanned face.

A sense of dread and danger grew inside Cooper's mind when he approached the window she was staring from.

She flinched violently when Cooper knocked on the glass, waking her from the hypnotic state she had fallen in. She looked at him with a mix of surprise and shame. A very different look compared to the one he had seen on her when they had spoken on his previous visit. She looked lost, the portrait of an inconsolable sadness.

"Mrs. Harris," Cooper yelled from the other side of the thick double glass window. "Can we talk?" he asked, pointing at the front door on his left.

She rushed away from the window and came out of the front door as she put a sweater on her shoulders. Her eyes were alert now, filled with diffidence.

"Mrs. Harris. I'm sorry if I startled you. I thought you saw me coming up the steps."

She wiped the tears off her face.

"Can I borrow one of those?" she asked him, pointing at the pack of cigarettes in his hand.

"Of course," he said as he opened the pack and pushed one cigarette up, just enough so that she could grab it. He cupped his hands around the cigarette to block the wind and flicked the lighter.

"Thank you," she said as she took a deep draw in, slightly trembling as she exhaled the smoke.

"Are you okay, Mrs. Harris? You seem a little upset."

"I'm okay. Just spaced out, I guess."

"Huh. Spaced out. Does it happen to you often?" Cooper asked as he lit another cigarette for himself.

"Sometimes," she said, raising her head slightly to inhale.

Cooper wanted to get straight to the point, but Lynn looked much more open and willing to talk than the last time. Patience was necessary now; there was no need to prod her.

"Do you have children, Detective?" she asked without looking at him directly. The question took Cooper by surprise.

"I do. A seven-year-old boy. His name is Tyrese."

"Tyrese..." she said vacantly, looking at the ravens on the power line. "That's a nice name. Tyrese."

"I used to have a son too. Will. He's dead now," she continued; her face was a mask made of perfectly smooth and firm wax. Her features seemed perfectly still as she talked; her forehead didn't flex, and her eyebrows didn't move. Cooper couldn't tell if she had blinked once.

"I'm very sorry to hear that. That is terrible."

She nodded as she put the cigarette out on the wooded column of the porch, leaving a black mark.

"How did that happen? If you don't mind me asking?" Cooper said, hoping to keep the conversation going. He already knew Will Harris died as a result of an overdose. His mind flashed to the image of the man with the leather jacket staring at him from across the street.

"Drugs," she said absently, flicking the cigarette into her front yard. "I thought I could see him again, you know?"

Cooper chose to remain silent once again. He gave her a nod as if he really knew what she was talking about.

"I didn't care what it would take to keep him close. A mother would do anything for her child. Ask your wife, Detective; she would rip your guts out if that meant saving her child. She wouldn't even think twice."

"What are we talking about, Mrs. Harr...."

"I thought I could keep him close. That's all I wanted to do." She overrode him as her voice broke into a sob. "I thought I would find a way to make it work, but then he started to ask me to do things. I couldn't sleep. He liked it when I was afraid. I don't know why, but he did. He kept asking and asking—more and more. I couldn't anymore, so I had to let him go. I had to let him go again."

She threw herself into Cooper's arms. He held her as she let out a mournful, agonizing cry. Cooper gently backed up and had her sit on one of the wicker chairs on the porch.

"Hey, hey, hey. It's okay, Mrs. Harris. Take a few deep breaths, okay?" Cooper said as he let go of her grip and kneeled in front of her. "Where is your husband, Mrs. Harris? Is he home?"

Lynn Harris shook her head faintly as she looked straight in front of her, her gaze lost, unseeing, staring into the vastness. Cooper knew something about loss but not enough to imagine what the loss of a child would do to a human being. The thought of losing Tyrese gave him physical pain. It made him dizzy to the point that he had to stand up and look away from her. It was like imagining being on a ledge of a very tall building, looking down, then turning and jumping, watching the blue sky, feeling the gravity and the acceleration pushing the stomach up like in a roller coaster, then the hit, the blackness and...

Then wake up.

"Mrs. Harris. I cannot even imagine the pain you are going through. I really can't, and I'm so sorry for what you had to go through, but I need to ask you a few questions if you'll allow me."

She didn't say anything. She just looked at him with empty eyes.

"Okay, where were you between 10 and 11 a.m. this morning?"

The question didn't seem to provoke any emotion in her. Cooper had hoped for some sort of reaction, but there was none. To his great surprise, the person in front of him was just a shell of a beautiful woman who was once a mother, a wife, a daughter, maybe a sister. It looked like the life had been sucked out of her, like an empty coconut that leaked its precious water along the way.

"He asked me to take him, so I did," she answered dryly.

"Who? Who asked you?"

"My son."

"Your son?"

"Yes."

"Mrs. Harris, are you ok?"

"I am ok."

"Who asked you to take him?"

"My son."

"Your son is dead."

"I know."

"What makes you think it was your son?"

"He looks like him. Very similar. Not identical, though. I knew it wasn't him, but it was close enough to me."

Cooper felt goosebumps growing on his arms as a light, cool breeze came through, moving the dead leaves on the street.

"Did this person that looked like your son tell you his name?"

"It doesn't talk. But he asks through the mind, you know?" Lynn said as she raised her finger to her head.

"Like telepathy?" Cooper asked, trying to block the skepticism in his voice.

Lynn Harris didn't respond.

"Where did he ask you to take him?"

"To the old train station on Washington Street."

"What time was that?"

Lynn Harris didn't respond.

"What did you do when you arrived there?"

"He told me to stay in the car, then to leave."

"Did he get out of the car?"

"Yes."

"And what did he do?"

"He ate."

"Ate what?"

"The man that lived near the station. The beggar."

"He ate him?"

"It ate him first. Then it killed him and threw him on the tracks."

Cooper remained silent for a few seconds as he started to play with the idea that she was faking a mental breakdown.

"Can I ask you a favor, detective?"

"Of course."

"I have a terrible headache. Would you mind grabbing my ibuprofen in the foyer? It's just here to the right."

"Sure," Cooper said as he got up.

He walked into the house and turned to the right.

Cooper entered a state of disbelief as he looked around the living room. The furniture had all been moved out of the room. Symbols of men and women were drawn everywhere, on the walls, carpet, and white curtains. There were so many drawings that it looked like the room had wallpaper. Some drawings were made by scratching on the wall, some with spray cans, some others with what looked like blood. In the middle of the room, on the ground, was a picture surrounded by seven white candles, the solidified wax running down to the carpet. Without knowing exactly why, Cooper brought his hand to his holster, undoing the button and keeping his hand on the gun's grip, feeling the metallic net pattern, and getting ready for something to happen.

When he turned to the window, it was too late.

He tried to scream, to stop her, but there was no time.

He saw Lynn Harris standing up on the front porch, looking straight at him through the window, as she wrapped her mouth around the long barrel of a revolver.

Her eyes were already dead, a horror Cooper knew he would carry with him for the rest of his life. The eyes were something his comprehension couldn't grasp, not completely. They were empty and bottomless, like a well with no end. A well that led to places he didn't know existed. Places devoured by the darkness, where light was unknown. Light leaked under a door in a darkened hallway, the glow of dread seeping further into his consciousness, his mother hanging from a beam that rhythmically creaked from her weight.

The gun went off in a deafening roar that seemed amplified as the world slowed around Cooper. He watched the bullet exiting from the back of her head, bringing along a mix of brain and pieces of skull. The eyes that were already dead kept staring at him as the body fluttered in the air, like a flag on a windy day.

They changed as life left Lynn's body and her brain shut down. The dim light in her eyes disappeared, and the pupils darkened, giving her face the look of a reindeer.

Cooper ran out and called 911.

And the top of the well had been moved over, letting him stare at things he wasn't supposed to stare at.

# 4

Jack had fixed himself a humble dinner made of two slices of a few days old sourdough—nothing that a spread of butter and an oven couldn't fix—and shredded cheddar cheese on top. It reminded him of the days at the monastery, during Lent, when the vow of poverty was pushed to extremes, and the only meals served were bread and one apple per day. Compared to those days, cheddar cheese looked like a real treat.

He had brought his plate into the guest room, where he constantly monitored Peter, who seemed to have fallen into a deep sleep. He ate his meal and prepped Luna's food in her bowl. She looked at it skeptically at first, as he wasn't the man that normally fed her, but after a few seconds, she launched at her food and devoured it in a heartbeat.

Jack was looking outside the guest room window when he heard the gunshot. He had heard a few in the past few weeks when laying in bed at night, pondering whether they were fireworks or gunshots.

But this one sounded much closer.

Jack shivered. Something was wrong. He could sense the dread crawling under his skin.

Peter seemed to have a similar reflex from the bed as he started mumbling meaningless words in his sleep. At least Jack was glad to notice that his original voice had returned, replacing that ominous bellow.

Jack approached the bed—Luna jumped on it, wagging her tail, excited to hear Peter's voice again—and squinted, tilting his head to offer his ear closer to Peter.

"My jacket...call Cooper. My jacket." Peter whispered. His voice was weak and trembling. Every word came out with a pause, taking effort to pronounce. His fingers, hand, and arm struggled, trembling as if an invisible force pushed them down as he tried to raise them. Jack realized Peter was a prisoner and that every word he tried to pronounce was a small break in a hard-fought battle.

Jack rushed to the chair where he had placed Peter's belongings, and he searched his sports jacket pockets. Jack's eyebrows relaxed when his fingers touched the sharp edges of a business card. The name of Robert Cooper, Homicide Division, was printed in upper case letters. A phone number had been handwritten on it with a blue pen.

Given the fact that a phone number was already printed on the card, Jack assumed it was the extension to the detective's office. The handwritten phone number must have been a personal contact Robert Cooper had given to Peter. He left the guest room and went into the living room, looking at the card and pacing back and forth. He wondered if it was a good idea to involve the police. *What was Jack Sullivan going to tell the detective anyway? That he was caring for a man who had just attempted to hang himself in the attic? That he had decided to keep him at his place and provide medical care he didn't have any experience of while trying to fight an evil spirit that had targeted him?* That sounded like a recipe for either jail or a mental health facility.

On the other hand, whatever the reason was, it seemed important for Peter to contact him. Joel would be there in a couple of days, Jack thought. Maybe it would be easier for him to show Detective Cooper what state Peter was in and let him draw his conclusions. Sometimes the only way to believe was to see the damn thing for yourself. Jack knew the Hollow had barely started its relentless destruction process with Peter Hanson.

Taking a deep breath and exhaling with his eyes closed, Jack Sullivan looked at the card again, then started typing the numbers into his cell phone and hit the call button.

A weird glaring caught his eye as he waited for the detective to answer the call. He walked to the kitchen and gasped when he looked out of the window.

A feast of emergency vehicles was parked in front of the Harris house. The road was closed both ways by two police cars parked horizontally. The glare of the blue and red intermittent lights on the vehicles shone in the early evening as the daylight died at the horizon on the other side.

# 5

Cooper sat on the front porch chair, looking at the sun going down, out of sight. As two IMPD cars arrived, Cooper watched Lynn Harris lying lifeless on her front porch. A puddle of thick and dark red blood had formed near her head. The blood gathered in the gaps of the deck and dripped down on the soil underneath.

The forensic team arrived shortly after, followed by the coroner and another four IMPD cars. A perimeter was established. He instructed the agents to keep it quiet and to keep the vultures away from the scene as much as possible. Cooper knew the media would eventually make it there, but the later, the better. He was waiting for Frank Harris to get home. There were questions he needed to answer, and Cooper intended to have that conversation at the station as soon as possible.

This time, the gloves were off.

While the forensic team examined the body and the house, his mind returned to Lynn's words.

*The man that looked like my son.*

Those words echoed in the back of Cooper's mind as he shivered at the thought of the man with the leather jacket staring at him from the other side of the street with that inhumanly broad grin. The man looked just like the one in the picture on Lynn's bookshelf.

*He looked like my son but wasn't quite the same.*

Cooper wondered if she had been on drugs. *How could she be convinced a dead person asked her to drive to Washington Street?* The toxicology report would tell him more, but, just like for the Hansons, Cooper was sure no traces of drugs or heavy medications would be found in her blood.

Suddenly, he missed the everyday routine, the open and closed cases supported by logic, confessions, and iron-clad evidence. The Hansons, Kroger, and now Lynn Harris were all connected. The excitement for a difficult case, a different case, had already faded as the number of casualties exponentially increased by the day. All suicides, some alleged, some staged to look like that, and one unfolds right before his eyes. He needed answers and facts, and he needed them quickly.

He saw a dark gray Buick turning around the corner and slowing down as it approached the perimeter that IMPD had created.

Frank Harris got out of the car in the middle of the road, stormed out of it, and ran towards the house. His eyes were wide open with astonishment and concern. The agents let him inside the perimeter.

He looked around, confused, craving for a familiar face and explanations. When his eyes crossed Cooper's, Frank Harris rushed towards him and took a few seconds to catch his breath.

"Detective. What happened?" he asked with a broken voice. Cooper felt a wave of pity invading him. He felt numb, disconnected, the way only death could make him feel.

"Mr. Harris. I'd like you to come with me to the station."

"What happened? Where is Lynn?"

"Mr. Harris. I'm really sorry. Your wife is dead. She killed herself on the front porch. The forensic team is analyzing the scene, collecting evidence."

"What? Wait...what?"

Frank Harris crashed to the ground, rocking himself back and forth while hugging his knees, hiding his head between them. He screamed in denial, shaking his head. Cooper had seen it so many times that he felt disgusted by it. The way the brain tried to protect the body to soothe the shock going through the body when catastrophic news like that was delivered.

"Mr. Harris. I appreciate that this moment is so difficult. I'm so terribly sorry to bring such news. I will have you escorted to the police station. We need to talk privately there."

The man screamed, resisted, and insisted on seeing his wife. A yelping shriek gushed out of his throat as he called her name. When Cooper nodded, two agents dragged him to one of the cars and put him in the back seat. One of the agents patted twice on the roof. The car made a U-turn and drove away from Cooper's sight.

He took his phone out to call Davis when the phone buzzed in his hand. The number on the screen was not saved in his contacts.

Hesitantly, he answered the call.

"Cooper."

"Detective Cooper, this is Jack Sullivan. We don't know each other, but I am a neighbor of Peter Hanson."

"How did you get this number, Mr. Sullivan?"

"Peter told me to call you. He is not doing very well at the moment. He is resting at my place, across the street from his house."

Instinctively, Cooper turned around, scanning the houses on the other side of the street, across from the Hanson property.

"How can I help you, Mr. Sullivan?"

"How soon could you be here? I have some information you might find helpful for your investigation."

"How about twenty-five seconds? Just the time to cross the street."

# 6

Cooper saw the front door of the house opening as he crossed the street. The light flooded out in the driveway and mixed with the flashing light of the emergency service vehicles and the police cars parked in the street.

Standing on the doorstep was the shadow of a tall man. Cooper recognized him as he got closer to him. He was the same man he had seen the first time he interviewed Lynn Harris.

"Mr. Sullivan?" Cooper asked interrogatively as he offered the old man a handshake.

"In the flesh. Nice to meet you, Detective, and thanks for coming so quickly." The old man said. His grip was nice and firm. "What's going on there? Is everyone okay at the Harris house? Please come in. Please."

Cooper looked around, and the house was warm and cozy. The air was filled with the smell of freshly cut wood and incense. The old man offered to make him some coffee. Cooper gladly accepted. The damn day had started early, and the end of it wasn't even close. He thought about that morning when he left his house, kissing goodbye to Tyrese and Caroline, telling them he would be back for dinner. A promise he didn't know he would have to break. Not back then, when Adam Kroger and Lynn Harris were still breathing and going about their day.

The old man came back with a mug of steaming coffee and invited him to take a seat.

Cooper sat and took a sip.

"So, how can I help you, Mr. Sullivan? You said you had information for me?" Cooper cut to the chase.

"I do, Detective. Before we get into that, may I ask again what happened across the street? I wasn't sure about it a little while ago, but I think I might have heard a gunshot."

Cooper sighed.

"I am afraid I'm not at liberty to talk about that."

"Detective, I believe Lynn Harris was involved with a series of accidents." The old man mimicked the quotation marks with his finger when he pronounced the word accidents. "Now, can we speak frankly? Off the record?"

"I believe we can," Cooper said. "Please continue."

"As I said, there has been a series of accidents. as you are surely aware of: Bill and Jane Hanson, Oliver Curry, and now we also have..."

"Hang on, back the bus for me for one second. What was the second name?" Cooper was now really interested as he extracted his notebook from his pocket and clicked the tip of his pen, ready to take notes.

"Oliver Curry. I thought you knew about it. He died in May on the westside. I believe it was Avon."

Hendricks County, Cooper thought. Even if that wasn't his

jurisdiction, he wasn't proud of his lack of research on other suicides or suicide attempts after the Hansons. Honestly, he felt a slight wave of embarrassment hitting him in the face.

"Please continue."

"Of course. I was going to say that Peter attempted suicide here in my house this morning around lunch. But I stopped it in time. He is now sleeping in the guest room down the hallway," the man said, keeping his head down.

Cooper's heart started to gallop in his chest.

*What in the actual hell was going on?* He thought as he still hoped to wake up from this nightmare. He invited Jack Sullivan to continue.

"There is a connection between all these cases and Lynn Harris. At least I know there is one specifically." The man talked calmly and confidently, as if he had evidence of what he was talking about, even though Cooper couldn't imagine what kind of evidence he possessed. For what it was worth, the man could have had dementia.

But he wasn't, and Cooper knew that. He knew from the moment he had mentioned the connection to Lynn Harris. That was the same connection he was looking for since he had seen the bodies of the Hansons, since that light had turned on in Lynn's living room and then back off, captured by the security cameras. The old man didn't know that Lynn Harris was in a body bag right now, in the back of the coroner's van, waiting to be opened up and examined.

Cooper intended to keep that truth from the old man for as long as possible.

"What makes you think there is a connection between these cases?" Cooper asked with genuine curiosity.

"Well, before I go into that, I want to clarify, for the record, that Lynn Harris is involved, connected to these deaths but only indirectly. If that makes sense. She is just a vessel."

*He asked me to take him, so I did.* Those words echoed loudly in

Cooper's head, bringing a wave of dread and discomfort that he did not enjoy.

"A vessel?"

"Indeed. A vessel. She might have acted against her will. Someone demanded certain things."

"And who would that person be? How do you know that?"

"I'm not proud of what I'm about to say, but I followed Lynn Harris on one occasion from the grocery store. I had already observed some weird changes in her behavior in the past days, so when I saw her wandering aimlessly at the grocery store, I just kept her in sight and decided to see what she was up to."

"Okay," Cooper said, wanting to know more.

"And so I followed her. It didn't take me much time to realize she was also following someone. The man she was following was Oliver Curry, or so I learned the following day on the local news."

*Jesus Christ*, Cooper thought.

"I followed her until she stopped in front of his house. She didn't get out of the car. She just waited for the man to take his groceries to the house. Then, he drove away. On the following day, Oliver Curry was found dead in his house. The local news said the police didn't want to release information to the public, but rumors leaked about a possible suicide lead. The investigators could never prove it and never found the weapon he had used for it. I can't be completely sure, but I reckon the case, as of today, still remains unsolved."

Cooper shivered as the image from the Washington Street camera returned to his mind. The white SUV arrived at the gas station, parked for a few minutes, then left. He thought about the features of the Hansons and Adam Kroger, trapped in that eternal scream of hopeless terror.

"And I don't have any proof of what I am about to state," the old man continued. "But the Hansons were probably the greatest folks I have ever met, full of life and love. There is no chance in the world they decided to take their own life."

"Mr. Sullivan..."

"Please call me Jack," the old man interrupted him.

"Okay, Jack. I appreciate the information you are trying to provide here. It is a lead I'm going to check. But, just to be clear, are you suggesting that Oliver Curry, Bill, and Jane Hanson were murdered?"

"I don't suggest that. I know that. Let me ask you something, Detective. Have you had the chance to talk to Lynn Harris since the discovery of the Hansons?"

"Yes, I have," Cooper said while the image of the puddle of blood next to Lynn Harris's blonde hair flashed in his mind.

"Did you happen to notice a necklace she was wearing? A pendant she was seemingly obsessed with?"

The memory of Lynn Harris at the Hanson's crime scene re-emerged. He also remembered her playing with it but couldn't recall whether she had it on their second encounter. He was sure as hell he didn't see it on her a couple of hours before she blew her brains out.

"I actually do remember that."

"The pendant is an old relic, a talisman, Detective. She came back with it after a trip with Jane Hanson in Utah. I have reasons to believe the talisman is cursed."

"Cursed?" Cooper said, trying not to be offensive with his helplessly skeptical tone.

"Lynn Harris gave the relic to Peter; today, he was very close to killing himself."

"Mr. Sullivan, are you being serious right now? Because I have to get back to work. This is not going where I thought it would go."

"I get it. It all sounds unbelievable. But if you allow me five more minutes, I think you will change your mind."

"I doubt it. Are you trying to tell me that these people have died because of a ghost?"

"Not exactly. Not a ghost, but a powerful supernatural entity."

"Listen, I have to get goi..."

"Please, Detective. Just five minutes, and you'll be on your way."

Cooper sighed, putting his notebook back in the jacket's pocket, unable to hide the disappointment of where a promising conversation had gone.

He nodded and silently agreed to it.

"Follow me," Jack said and walked into a dark hallway. He opened a door on the right side of it, and a feeble light flooded out of it.

When the door opened, a gelid gust of air came out, invading the house and hitting him hard like a slap in the face. He felt the cold inside his bones. It reminded him of the winter days on Lake Michigan. A damp and mortal cold filled his lungs, his nose hair freezing as he breathed in.

Only this wasn't a natural cold. There was a boundary to it as if it moved in an invisible cloud of ice. He felt it on his face, arms, and chest, but not his feet. Also, there was no way it was that cold outside.

The old man disappeared into the room, projecting a long shadow on the opposite wall.

Then Cooper took a few steps forward, fighting a strange sense of uneasiness and fear. The hallway made him think of when he found his mother hanging in her room. He swallowed and breathed deeply as he entered the room. His first instinct was to turn around and get the hell out of that house. Suddenly, he felt as if he couldn't trust the old man. Then he took another step as he squinted to make sure he understood what he was looking at.

The body of Peter Hanson laid on the bed with his limbs

restrained to the bed frame. He wore only his underwear despite the arctic temperature in the room. His body shuddered lightly as if it was going through a constant tremor or a convulsion. His eyes were closed, but Cooper could see his eyeballs dancing frantically beneath the eyelids, which were purplish. His lips had turned light gray as if a layer of ash had been deposited on them.

Black and dark blue veins ran from his neck down to his core, branching out along the arms. They all pulsated as if chunks of organic material were pumped through them. A black stain, similar to what he had seen on the Harris's house siding, surrounded Peter's neck like a tumor.

"What the hell is going on here?" Cooper asked in a voice that was broken by fear. "Why is he here and not in a hospital?"

"Because he would die at the hospital. Nobody could save him there."

"Put your hands up where I can see them," Cooper shouted as he extracted his firearm from the holster and pointed it at the old man.

"Oh, you gotta be kidding me."

"I'm not going to say it twice," Cooper said, raising his voice even more.

The old man suddenly changed expression as he looked beyond the point where Cooper was standing. It took him a few moments to realize something was happening behind him.

When the smell surrounded him, it was already too late.

Cooper turned slowly as the stench of damp wood and rot assailed him, followed by the familiar sound of a thousand flies. Then, in the darkness of the hallway, he saw it. A shadow moved slightly in front of him. He felt its presence so clearly that if he extended one arm in front of him, he would touch it.

The image of the man with the leather jacket grinning at him from the other side of the street came back to him. He saw the dead eyes on Lynn's face again, the screaming features of Bill and Jane Hanson. The dots automatically connected in his mind against his logical comprehension. Cooper knew all those things were one, and one was all of them. He could hear its raspy breathing, an otherworldly growl followed by a hissing sound.

The evil stood still in front of Cooper, as tall as the ceiling.

A voice came from the other side of the room. And even without directly looking at it, Cooper knew that voice didn't belong to the old man or Peter Hanson. He turned and almost fired his gun when he saw Peter Hanson sitting up in the bed with his eyes open, even though they weren't his at all.

Dark spheres gleamed in the empty and wide sockets. Peter's mouth moved, opening and closing rhythmically. A bellowing sound came out of it. Nonsense words slowly became sounds that he recognized. Cooper looked at him with shock as the blabbing started to become clearer. It was as if Peter Hanson, or whatever that thing was, was learning to speak at that moment.

*"How....Huuuw is yhooo... How is your mother doing, Detective?"*

The hair on the back of Cooper's head pricked, and a long, cold shiver ran through his spine. The voice he was listening to came from a place of death filled with desperation and sorrow. That voice was everything he had escaped from and was now knocking furiously at his door.

Cooper stood there, watching with terrified eyes the body of Peter Hanson moving jerkily, invaded by spasms, bellowing out sounds that didn't make sense. He turned and looked at the old man, his gaze serious and focused, taking notes of something, studying the abhorrent scene like a scientist observing a new species for the first time.

At that moment, Cooper knew that everything he had told him was true, that everything that had happened to him was real, that the death of the Hansons was just a piece in a puzzle that started long before then. And all the pieces started to align in his mind, moved by a force he had never allowed himself to believe in. As he watched the pillars of his rationality crumble, Cooper stood there pointing a useless gun at a being that was clearly impossible to kill or comprehend.

Then Peter's eyes turned suddenly back to normal. As the blackness surrounding his pupils retracted and the energy that permeated his body left him, he fell back heavily on the bed. Jack Sullivan rushed to check his pulse, and Cooper placed his service 9mm back into the holster. He took a few clumsy steps back, hitting the desk behind him, then sat and crossed his hands behind his neck. *What in the actual fuck just happened?* He thought as he found himself panting, in tremendous shock.

"He's okay. But he won't hold up for long," Jack Sullivan said as he put a hand on Cooper's shoulder. Then he took a seat in front of him.

"Detective. I know all this is hard to process. But this man doesn't have the time for us to process. Do you understand what I'm saying?"

Cooper nodded without looking at him, still staring at the still body on the bed.

"I will ask you again since you failed to answer me earlier. What happened at the Harris house?"

"Lynn Harris is dead. She shot herself in the head," Cooper said without even thinking about hiding that information. The time of hiding was over.

"As I feared," Jack Sullivan said, standing up and pacing the room. "Lynn was the one that brought it here. She brought it with the pendant, and she welcomed it. The Faustian bargain. Do you follow?"

"Not really, to be honest with you."

"It is pretty common for demonic creatures to offer something that is comforting, an escape from pain and sufferance, but the evil always demands something back in return, something much more valuable than what it can offer."

"Like selling your soul to the devil?" Cooper chimed in, still unable to process the absurdity of the words that came out of his mouth.

"Exactly! Lynn Harris was going through terrible grief after she lost her son. That was the perfect occasion for the creature to relieve that pain. Like a painkiller. Extremely addictive, right?"

Cooper nodded, making a real effort to follow the old man's train of thought.

"That's how it starts. But then the evil starts demanding more and more. And there isn't a simple way to break that deal. The evil owns you. And I believe this evil, the Hollow, was using Lynn Harris to survive. This thing is like a parasite. It needs its food to survive. It needs the pain, the grief, the suffering."

"The suicides," Cooper said as another puzzle piece went in place.

"If you want to call them that. I don't know how these people died, but surely they wouldn't have ended up the way they did without the influence of the Hollow. It didn't need them just to die but to suffer in the process."

The picture of the Hansons' faces flashed in front of Cooper's eyes, the head of Adam Kroger facing backward, the empty eyes of Lynn Harris on her front porch.

"But those...you see, that was not its real goal. The real goal had always been Peter Hanson. I don't know why, but that's what my gut tells me."

"Why Peter Hanson? He had Lynn Harris. He could have entered her body, just like he did with Peter now."

"Exactly! But it didn't. Instead, it drove her to death the very moment she became useless to him."

"What do you want me to do?" Cooper asked as he sprung forward from the chair.

"We need to know what was so appetizing about Peter. If there is a way, the only way to get rid of this is to understand what he wants. A friend, Joel Kopernick, should join us soon to help."

"Whatever this Hollow thing you are talking about is doing to Peter, it doesn't seem quite done yet. At least, that's the feeling I've got. Maybe it's a process. Maybe it'll buy us some time."

"Good point. Even though every case of possession I have seen is different, there are commonalities. Like every infection, the demon needs time to work through the system."

"How do you know these things? What do you mean when you say every case of possession? Have you seen more shit like this before?"

"Just a couple of times in a lifetime. Most cases where my presence was needed were not real instances of demonic possession but rather mental illness."

"What are you? A doctor?"

"I have a degree in theology, but I once was an exorcist, son."

Cooper remained silent for a long minute while Jack Sullivan paced the room.

"You might be right about one thing, Detective. Whatever this spirit is doing, it needs time to complete it. It is waiting until the possession of Peter Hanson is complete. This could buy us valuable time, but we must use it wisely while waiting for Joel. The only person that could have given us the answers was Lynn Harris, and she is dead."

Cooper got lost in his thoughts as he tried to navigate these rather unusual investigative waters—nothing like the ones he was used to. The horizon of possibilities that stood before him in a conventional case had just broadened exponentially, giving him endless possibilities—a playground he wasn't used to playing in. Then something occurred to him. A thought that gave him a rush of adrenaline, the hope that maybe they could still know more about this entity.

"That's not entirely true."

Jack Sullivan turned to him with interrogative eyes.

"Lynn Harris was not the only person that knew about this. Her husband, Frank, is being transported to the police station as we speak. I'll go talk to him right now. In the meantime, you've got my cell if something happens."

Robert Cooper fled the room before Jack Sullivan could have a say.

# 7

A choked gasp came out of Peter's mouth as he opened his eyes. There was no sense of gravity in the suspended world where time flowed at a different speed. It was cold down in the well. He touched his neck instinctively, but the bruises and the burns from the noose were gone. There was no pain down in the well, not physical, at least. He looked down at his hands, and they were translucent, like looking in a pool of clear and trembling water. There were no sounds down in the well, but there were vibrations.

That's how he knew he wasn't alone.

He was standing, but there was no weight keeping him grounded. He saw his feet on a mat of dead leaves and twigs. He felt the soil beneath them, damp and fertile, swarming with earthworms. He felt their presence and life in a way he had never experienced before. It was like all his senses had been put through a huge amplifier.

There was a small light in front of him.

He was in a tunnel, one with a tall ceiling. Darkness surrounded him with such strength that he couldn't tell how tall the ceiling was. It could have been ten feet or a thousand. The light seemed so faint from his perspective that he could have run for years without reaching it.

*Or was it just a few steps away?*

He started walking towards it.

As he moved through the air, he felt the particles hitting his skin with terrifying clarity. They bounced against his skin, traveled forward to hit something else, then traveled back to hit him again. And he realized that his sight was only a self-imposed limit as he could see without watching.

Peter kept walking, sensing several presences on his path, suspended.

Peter Hanson couldn't help but think this was how death must have been.

A slit of light pierced through the darkness. A door opened in the infinite blackened wall. Peter entered it and found himself in the hallway of an apartment complex. Two rows of discolored vinyl doors crowded the gray walls where the plaster had chipped away, and several layers of graffiti had been spray painted. He realized he could hear again as the faint cry of a baby came to him down from the end of the hallway. He could hear the rattling sound of dishes thrown in a sink, the squeaking sound of bed springs followed by laughter and moans, couples screaming at each other, the baby crying louder, more desperately.

Then he heard it, the sound of music. It was a familiar song by Metallica that made him shiver, delivering a mix of nostalgia and anxiety. He followed it as the notes of Kirk Hammett and James Hetfield's guitars joined, filling the musty air with sadness and incredible beauty.

Tears came down from his face as he stopped in front of the second to last door to the left. The number 7 from the 217 had pivoted and was now upside down, forming a sharp L.

A neon light flickered, crackling right above his head.

He put a hand on the knob and entered. A horrible stench coming from the kitchen welcomed him. A pile of dirty, crusty dishes towered in the sink. Flies buzzed around the overflowing trash can. A man in his underpants and a white undershirt with yellow stains was passed out on the floor. An unconscious, half-naked woman laid belly down on a filthy couch. The music was loud and came from one of the rooms at the far end of the apartment.

Will Harris sat at his desk, hunched over, under the dim light of the table lamp, writing in his journal. Peter didn't need to look closer. He knew it was a song. The neck of his acoustic guitar, the same old one he used to look at jealously, stuck out from his left side. Peter listened to him gently touch the strings, trying different chords and writing them on top of the words with a pencil.

Peter knew that song would never be perfect in Will's mind. He would change it over and over until he hated it. It had always been like that. And he never realized how beautiful his first drafts were.

Will got up and turned toward him. More tears came down when he looked exactly in Peter's direction without seeing him.

It hurt. It hurt so much to see Will in that state. His face was so gaunt, making the bleak eyes bigger than they used to be. A profound sadness and desolation lived in them. And Peter felt it all as if it were his own. The vise of guilt gripped him, taking the wind out of him. *Where had he been when Will needed him the most? At a college party getting drunk or maybe trying to get laid? What was he thinking as he let the missed calls and the text messages go unanswered? Had he chosen to forget about him? And why?*

Peter tried to turn the other way when he saw Will grabbing a spoon and prepping his next shot, but he couldn't. Not watching or ignoring wasn't an option anymore. The presence that loomed behind him wouldn't let him.

*Was that his last one?* Peter wondered as he watched the heroin boiling in the spoon above the flame of Will's lighter. A single tear rolled down his cheek as he pulled the syringe plunge and pushed it back up, letting the air out.

Peter watched his dull pupils widen as he shot the liquid into his skeletal arm, leaving the syringe hanging. A tear of blood spilled out as he collapsed on the bed, looking at the ceiling for the last time.

And out of Will's mouth came his name.

"Peter," he whispered as life left his exhausted body.

As the guilt invaded him, threatening to eat him alive, the room's ceiling opened, showing the tunnel's darkness. Down in the well again, Peter wandered among the shadows of ghosts and ancient creatures crossing one another's paths, atoms colliding in a sidereal void. He felt their energy, their thoughts and their agonies. The vibrations they emanated merged and died, shattering on his flimsy matter.

Behind him, the usual presence. The Hollow loomed, perched in the darkness, watching his every step, guiding him toward the next sick attraction. Peter was terrified of it; something about its inexorability made it even more terrifying. He didn't want to be anywhere near him, yet Peter felt it connected to him in a way he wasn't quite ready to accept. It was transcendent and utterly empty. There was no compassion or empathy to be found in it. It was pure instinct and survival. There was no logic, no love, nothing remotely human. Only the insatiable hunger, the unquenchable thirst for suffering, and the ancestral malevolence. Ancient, elemental.

Another door opened in the endless tunnel—an opening leading to the woods. Peter recognized the path leading to a small creek. He had spent most of his life running in the woods near the treehouse named The Fort, location of uncountable adventures with his friends. His mom and dad stood by it, looking in his direction without seeing him. It was a hard hit, one of those that ached in the depths to see them alive. A cruel reminder of a state in which they could be no more, no matter how desperately he wanted to hug them again.

A wave of guilt assailed Peter as he struggled to breathe. So many things had been taken for granted. So many missed chances to stop and tell them he loved them, to hug them and make sure they knew. There was a sadness in their eyes, a piercing nostalgia of the times gone, of life flowing in front of impotent eyes too fast to be grabbed.

Suddenly, Peter felt a strange sense of relief, as if a boulder had been lifted off his chest. The presence behind him, the demon that wanted him to watch, to be crushed by the pain, was gone. It was just him, his parents, and his inconsolable sadness. He felt his knees trembling as he discovered this new dimension of grief where sorrow, guilt, resistance, and atrocious pain clashed with the smile of great memories and love. Peter stood in the middle of this explosive battle, whose clashes resonated in the emptiness of his subconscious, traveling in powerful shock waves.

He felt a burning feeling on his neck and fell to his knees as he struggled to breathe.

His mom and dad smiled at him, and it wasn't a horrible grin this time. It was their smiles, and it hurt; it hurt so bad that he couldn't have that anymore.

He wanted that moment to be forever.

"It's ok, baby. Look for us when you need it," his mother said to him as the world around them fell apart. The shed collapsed under the weight of falling trees.

Peter looked at the cloudless blue sky tearing apart as if it was made of cloth and someone had just stuck a knife into it, ripping its fabric.

Beyond the sky's blue was a pitch-black darkness waiting for him.

Back in the tunnel.

# 8

All the interrogation rooms in the IMPD central station downtown were located on the first underground floor. The artificial light from the old neon ceiling lamps was cold and produced a surreal atmosphere when it met the light green colored walls. There were ten interrogation rooms in total, and even though their size varied—the higher the room number, the smaller the size—what happened in the rooms was recorded every time the proximity sensors were triggered by human presence or action.

Room one was the biggest interrogation room and also Cooper's favorite one. It wasn't just because of the more comfortable chairs, the wider table in the middle of the room or the dedicated coffee station. Behind the wide mirror-like window on the northern part of the room was a badass computer room. The suspects were not just recorded, but sophisticated machine learning algorithms analyzed their facial expressions, and their voices were captured, decomposed, and further studied.

Harry Davis pushed for these technological changes in investigative work in collaboration with national security and intelligence agencies. The federal government funded the expensive equipment and resources needed to run the program to use AI to make extracting information during an interrogation more efficient and to try to build a database that would one day help prevent crimes.

Cooper hadn't been the biggest fan of these new techniques, but he was slowly coming to like some of the features that advanced software could put at the disposal of the investigators.

When he entered room number one, where he had specifically instructed the agents at the scene to put Frank Harris, Davis was already there. He sat in a chair and scrolled on his phone with his glasses low on his nose. One of the room technicians assigned to the night shift thrashed on a keyboard, the monitor in front of him displaying lines of white code on a black background.

"Finally. What took you so long?" Davis asked, visibly in distress. "Can we go one freaking day without a body, Cooper? I don't know what's happening here, but this must stop. The timing of it all is just the worst possible."

"You don't say," Cooper cut laconically and walked to the row of monitors sitting in front of the window, staring at Frank Harris as he sat in the interrogation room.

The lights in the room were strong and focused on the interrogator, who was spotlighted as if he were on stage in a comedy show. Frank's forehead was pearled with small drops of sweat as he stared at the cup of coffee on the table in front of him with empty eyes.

Cooper felt for him. He knew Frank Harris's life was pretty much over. Even though he was the only member of his family that still had the privilege of breathing. The thin thread keeping Frank Harris sane and alive after his only son Will's premature death had been completely torn apart the moment Lynn pulled the trigger, leaving him behind.

Cooper knew how delicate that thread was and what was needed of him to protect it and make it stronger. He had to go through that process himself. Peter Hanson knew now about that thread, too, but in the case of Frank Harris, the thread had given up, lacerating things that were now beyond the possibility of being repaired.

Cooper knew that Frank had nothing to do with what happened to his wife or the death of the Hansons or Adam Kroger. However, something inside himself still believed that Frank Harris was holding key information that could help shed light on this whole clusterfuck unfolding. And now, after witnessing with his very eyes the insanity of what was happening to Peter Hanson, he had even more reasons to believe something could be squeezed out of Frank Harris.

Cooper's hopes weren't high, not after seeing what he had seen at Jack Sullivan's place, and quite frankly, not after looking at the empty shell that Frank Harris was now in the monitor in front of him. He stared with the same eyes his wife had right before deciding it was all too much to keep going.

"Is the thermal camera correctly calibrated?" Cooper asked the technician as he pointed at a screen where the figure of Frank Harris was colored based on his body temperature.

"Yes, sir, I checked it twice, and everything seems to be good on the sensor side."

Cooper nodded as he massaged his chin and the right side of his face, gazing at Davis, holding a grim expression.

People or suspects who had to go through a formal interrogation typically showed increased body temperature, which intuitively made sense with an increased stress level. It wasn't a matter of deciding if someone was guilty or innocent based on body temperature; that kind of argument wouldn't stand one chance in a court of law, but it was a fact that everyone who sat in room one exhibited a higher body temperature.

Cooper had imagined that after the shocking news of his wife's suicide, the thermal camera would show Frank's temperature all over the place.

What would generally be a human figure with a lot of yellow, orange, and red colors on the thermal camera was only a bunch of blue, black, and gray. The cold colors dominating the thermal cameras meant that his average body temperature not only wasn't elevated, but it was actually lower than the average body temperature.

Cooper didn't have any reading on his heart rate or vitals, but he could bet that if those vitals were to be taken from Frank Harris, they would show bare minimum activity. The absolute essential activity that the brain needs to keep the body alive.

Everything else was gone from his eyes, conscience, and heart. Everything had been erased, like a computer that had just reset, losing all its data. The flame of life that might have once burned in the man had been reduced to sparse embers after the death of Will and were now wet coals.

Cooper talked with Davis and briefed him, omitting his visit to Jack Sullivan's house. There was a vast part of himself that still rejected everything that he had seen not even an hour earlier, let alone bringing all that in front of his boss, the most cynical and pragmatic person he knew.

They talked strategy for a few minutes about the interrogation and the best way to go about it. When the technician gave Cooper the okay, the detective walked out of the room, turned around the corner, and opened the door that entered the interrogation room. He glanced at the cameras as he walked around the table and sat in front of Frank Harris, who didn't acknowledge his presence, staring with vacant eyes at his coffee as if he was staring into an abyss.

Cooper placed his manila envelope and pocket notebook on the table, then looked at Frank Harris, hoping to get his attention.

"Mr. Harris."

No signs of life on the other side of the table.

"Mr. Harris." This time, Cooper raised his voice and snapped his thumb and index fingers together. Frank seemed to return to reality and slowly turned toward the detective with dreamy eyes.

"Do you want a refresh of that coffee, Mr. Harris?" Cooper asked softly as he glanced at the cold coffee in the disposable cup.

"No, I'm okay," Mr. Harris said hoarsely.

"Mr. Harris, I'm terribly sorry for the loss of your wife. I would like to understand more about what might have led her to do what she did. Would you be ok answering some que-"

"You cannot understand." Frank overrode him in a calm tone. Cooper shivered as he knew where the conversation was going.

"What can I not understand? What makes you think that?"

"Because you are looking, Detective, but you cannot see. Not yet. But you will see. And when that happens, it will be too late. It's always too late when we see."

"What are you talking about? See what?"

Frank Harris didn't answer. His eyes reddened again as the pain came back to him like a powerful wave.

"The things that consume us from the inside. That's what the monster craves."

Cooper scribbled something on his notebook, and goosebumps appeared on his arms as the image of the monster he had seen at Jack Sullivan's house came to his mind.

"Did a monster do this to your wife? Is that why she did what she did?"

"She was gone the day Will died. I thought she would never recover from it. And to be honest, Detective, I was gone too. There is no such thing as recovering from something like that." Frank said, then paused for a little bit. Cooper stayed silent; he wanted him to keep talking as much as possible.

"Then she went on that trip with Jane. I thought maybe she would find some joy in that. And when she came back, it looked like she was a different person. But then I learned that she had brought something home with her. A disease, she and I used to call it."

"Why now? It's been a really long time since Lynn's trip?" Cooper asked and looked at the camera. He knew that the eyes of Harry Davis were on him, probably wondering what was going on in his mind, if he had lost it just like everyone else seemed to do these days.

"When we realized that it wouldn't let us go until it had a new body, Lynn decided to give the illness to someone else. It takes time for it to choose the body. It needed to be someone who was suffering greatly. In the meantime, it needed to eat."

"Is that why Lynn drove to Curry's house?"

Frank nodded.

"When you say that your wife gave the illness to someone else, do you mean Peter Hanson?"

"Yes."

"Why? Why Peter Hanson?"

"Because she hated him. She blamed him for Will's death."

"Peter came home after learning of the death of his parents," Cooper said, thinking out loud.

"That's when she gave it to him. It lives in the necklace," Frank said, and for the first time, Cooper saw the grimace of remorse on his face.

"Did Lynn give the illness to Jane Hanson?"

"No."

"Is there a connection between your wife and Jane Hanson's death?"

"Yes."

"Can you expand on that?" Cooper asked.

"I told you. It needs to eat."

"Did your wife kill Mr. and Mrs. Hanson?"

"She didn't. She didn't choose them. The disease did."

A shiver ran through the entirety of Cooper's body as he saw Frank's facial features changing right under his eyes. His face was deformed, and his grin became monstrously broad, revealing blood-stained fangs.

"*You are next, Detective,*" Frank said with that horrible smile.

Cooper turned and looked at the glass behind him as if to signal something to Davis. By the time he turned back, Frank Harris had already moved with a quickness that didn't belong to a human being. He stood on the side of the table, staring at the mirror in front of him as if he could see through it.

"Mr. Harris, go back to your seat," Cooper ordered, feeling the holster of his gun right underneath his fingertips; his heart raced in his chest. Frank Harris, or this new version of him, didn't move a muscle and kept staring at the mirror, smiling at it and ignoring his instructions. The Hollow, Cooper thought, it's controlling him right now.

Frank sprung forward, sprinting toward the mirror with an alien quickness. He rammed into it with his head. The room shook after the terrible hit. Cooper looked horrified at Frank's self-inflicted wound; blood gushed from a deep cut on his forehead. His facial expression was still the same. No pain, no movement, no breathing. He was just an empty marionette. A body like the man that was there until a few minutes earlier. Before the monster took control.

Everything slowed down in Cooper's sight. As he reached for his gun, Frank grabbed a triangular piece of glass that had cracked after the impact and brought it to his throat. Cooper watched the haunted eyes of Frank Harris as he watched him press the glass into his neck, slashing it from left to right, hearing the noise of the tissue, the muscles, and the arteries getting torn by it. He watched a gush of blood spurting out of the wound. Frank let the glass fall to the ground and stared at Cooper with a smile painted on his face. Cooper saw the color leaving Frank's body until he collapsed in a puddle of his blood.

Three agents stormed inside the room, uselessly pointing their guns at the last member of the Harris family, dead on the floor, still grinning.

*You are next, Detective.*

The words echoed in his mind as the darkness surrounded him. He thought of Tyrese and Caroline. What if this thing could get to them? The thought of it was terrifying, and as he felt the dread flowing in his veins, Cooper realized that was exactly what the monster wanted from him.

# 9

In the darkness of his car, the tired eyes of Robert Cooper were illuminated only by the dim light of the digital dashboard. He shifted his gaze from the speed gauge to his left, where houses stared back at him with obscure, unwelcoming eyes. He ruefully shook his head, fighting against the gloom in his heart. His mind went back to Frank Harris grinning at him as he slit his throat deep from ear to ear as if he had wanted to transfer that hideous smile from his face onto the neck. He had wanted him to see it. Whatever had possessed him in that exceptional rush of madness, it wanted that image to haunt Cooper for the rest of his days. At the moment, Cooper couldn't shake that notion from his head.

But that wasn't the most terrifying part of what he had just endured. As the agents and the onsite medical personnel rushed in vain to aid Frank Harris while he bled to death onto the epoxy floor, Cooper ran back into the room behind the mirror and asked the technician to rewind and play the recording from the beginning. He felt the incredulous eyes of Davis looming on him from behind as he re-watched himself talking to Frank Harris. The man who was now dead and being carried away from the interrogation room spoke in the video with expressionless eyes. His features were still and cold. He breathed and spoke, but Cooper could have sworn the man was already dead if it wasn't for that.

He asked the technician to pause near the moment when he brought the piece of glass to his throat. Cooper saw his own terrorized features on the screen as Frank Harris ran the glass through his jugular. Frank Harris wasn't smiling at all in the tape. He didn't flinch or move. He was already dead inside. There was nothing left of him. But Cooper could have sworn he smiled at him—the same incomplete, unfinished smile of the man with the leather jacket.

He slammed on the brakes and looked at the red traffic light that had materialized in front of him. The green Holt Road sign swung on the metal cable with a squeak in the silent night.

*How is this even remotely possible?*

*You're next, Detective.*

Those words echoed in his mind with threatening power.

*This thing could get me, Caroline, or Tyrese.*

It can get whoever it desires. He shivered at the thought of it. He hit the steering wheel so hard that he almost broke his hand and screamed in the silence of the world around him.

*Was the world so unaware? Or was he so ignorant of the creatures that inhabited it? How many of these things were out there? How could he have possibly gone, in a matter of hours, from rejecting even the remote idea that such things could exist to the impossible notion that the Hollow was the only creature of its kind that existed?*

He grabbed his phone and called Caroline. He got paranoid when it took her more than three rings to answer the phone.

"Hello?"

"Caroline."

"Hey, Detective, when are you planning to be-"

"Caroline, are you and Tyrese ok?"

"Love. We are ok. Are *you* ok?" she said after a moment of silence.

"I'm alright. Listen to me, would you take Tyrese to Stacey's for a few days?"

"To Stacey?"

"Yes, love, to Stacey."

"Why would we do that? Did something happen, babe?"

"Nothing happened," he said with a shaking voice. "It is just out of precaution. Just for a few days until I figure this out."

"You are scaring me now. What is going on?"

"Just please fucking do as I say. Will you?" he shouted in the car. There was no answer on the other side.

"Please, Caroline! Will you do that for me?"

"Babe, he is in bed already. Do you want me to wake him and-"

"Yes. I want you to do that."

"Okay."

"Listen. I'm sorry. I'm just exhausted."

"It's alright, babe. I trust you. I know you can't tell me what it is, but can you promise me something?"

"Go ahead."

"Can you promise me you are alright and this is just out of your paranoia?"

"I promise you," Cooper said, trying to push away the wave of emotions that was about to hit him. He fought hard with himself to hang on just a few more seconds.

"I'll call you later, ok? Let me know when you guys make it safely there. Ok?"

"Okay, baby. I love you."

"I love you too," he said as he hung up and cried. The image of his mother hanging from the beam returned to him, so vivid that he could almost touch her cold body dangling from the squeaking rope. He knew he was back in a really dark place he had fought his whole life to escape. He knew the Hollow had targeted him. What he didn't know was how much of that gloom was his own and how much had been brought by the demon. As if it made any difference, he thought. *What difference does it fucking make?* His only hope was that he had acted early enough, sending his family away. He couldn't be sure if it would make any difference or not. If the Hollow was with or around him in any capacity, he didn't want to bring him near Caroline and Tyrese. He parked his car in front of Jack Sullivan's house. His eyes were red, and his heart ran fast while he tried to take some deep breaths to get rid of the unbearable knot that had formed in his stomach.

And he found himself praying for the first time in his life. Praying to something he had never believed in, that he still didn't believe in.

*Please keep them safe.*

*Please, hide them from this thing.*

The cold he had felt in the guest room before had now invaded the whole house. It hit him like a hard slap when Jack opened the front door and beckoned him with a tilt of his head. Cooper felt as if the blood in his veins froze instantly, and he watched his breath in the still air of that alien world made of emptiness. The whole house was soaked in the gloom and dereliction that belonged to long-forgotten places.

"How are we doing?" Cooper asked Jack as he shivered. The old man shrugged and sat on his chair in the den. He looked tired, but there was this aura around the man, a sense of focus and planning, knowledge and wisdom. It made Cooper feel they had at least a chance against this evil.

"I don't know. Did you learn something from Frank Harris?" Jack asked.

The image of Frank Harris grinning as the blood gushed out of his throat flashed in front of his eyes.

"He killed himself at the station right after I started interrogating him."

Jack Sullivan got up and brought his hands to his head, pacing the room back and forth.

"It's like an infection. It used Will's death to cling to Lynn and spread to the Hansons, to her husband. But it didn't possess them. It just used them as he waited for the perfect prey. And now that it found it, both Lynn and Frank Harris were of no use to it anymore. The thing that I don't understand is why Peter? What is the connection? It can't be random. The connection is the key."

"Revenge," Cooper said, keeping his head down.

"Revenge?"

"Frank Harris told me that his wife blamed Peter for her son's death."

Jack Sullivan's eyes opened wide with enlightenment.

"Of course, of course," Jack Sullivan muttered, then ran to the small coffee table where his notebook was and furiously flicked through the pages until it stopped on the one he was looking for.

The doorbell rang, and Peter's dog rushed to the door as Jack Sullivan looked at Cooper with interrogative eyes. He wasn't expecting anyone at that late hour.

Cooper heard the door opening, a muffled sound of words exchanged, and the door closing back. Jack returned to the living room with a skinny, short man in his sixties. He wore a black velvet cowboy hat that gleamed in the room's light. His brown leather coat was so long that it almost touched the back of his loafers. Underneath it, he wore a pair of black pants and a white shirt buttoned up all the way up. Deep expression wrinkles crossed his forehead and the area between his nose and cheeks. He was clean-shaven and had hazelnut eyes that instilled a sense of calm, trust, and innate insight. Cooper wasn't sure that was the case, but he could have sworn he was already studying him in a very subtle way, in a way that could have gone very easily unnoticed.

"Detective Cooper, let me introduce you to Joel Kopernick."

Cooper sprung forward and shook the man's hand. His grip was firm and tight.

"Mr. Kopernick. A pleasure to meet you. I didn't think you would be joining us so early," Cooper said as he glimpsed at Jack Sullivan.

"Neither did I. But that's what planes do these days. Under normal circumstances, I would have come with my horse," Joel said in a deep and kind voice.

"I still can't believe you jumped on a plane. Look at you. You've got no excuses anymore," Jack said as he came back from the kitchen with a cup of coffee.

"Don't count on it, old man. You can consider this a once-in-a-lifetime circumstance."

Cooper saw the thin Native American man glancing toward the hallway, head tilted sideways, listening like a dog on high alert as if he sensed some invisible presence coming from that way.

"I wish it wasn't," Jack said, losing the optimism in his tone as he spoke. "I really wish it wasn't such a unique circumstance."

"I know. Please show me," Joel said. It took Cooper a few seconds to realize he was talking about Peter Hanson. The knot in his stomach seemed to have grown larger at the idea of seeing what was in the guest room as his mind flashed back to the shadow of the Hollow staring at him while it pulled the strings of Peter Hanson like a puppeteer. The bellowing sound that came out of his mouth in that alien language, the empty eyes just like Lynn and Frank Harris. And then his mother, the rope, all the things left unsaid, all the questions left unanswered. Hadn't he seen enough horror on this day alone?

How much could one possibly take before peeking into the abyss of madness? It hurt to even think about going inside the room, but he had to. Something way more powerful than any of his fears demanded for him to go in there. He felt like he was in one of those video games where the story can't keep unfolding unless the player doesn't do what is required.

Jack went inside the room, followed by the dog. Joel Kopernick stood in front of the door for a while, staring at something inside the room while he let his briefcase fall on the ground with a thump. Then he walked in, keeping his gaze straight as if he was dragged into the room in a state of hypnosis.

Cooper entered last.

The emaciated body of Peter Hanson laid in front of his eyes in a state of degradation that Cooper didn't think was possible to see in such a short amount of time. He had seen the man unconscious in that bed a few hours before. He wasn't looking good then, but now it looked like the end of the road was very near. His skin had become so pale that it almost looked translucent. He must have lost something like fifty pounds in a matter of hours. Black veins had emerged on his body, like stripes at the bottom of a dried-out river. The black mass attached to his neck had doubled in size. His eyelids, now darkened, trembled rhythmically as if a light and periodic electric shock went through them. Whatever process his body was going through had accelerated exponentially, and Cooper's hopes that he could recover from it were slim.

Cooper shivered at the staggering contrast between Peter's apparent quietness and stillness and the profound mutations happening to his body. As he traveled to the edge of his dreams, something was sucking the life out of him.

He raised his eyes to the ceiling.

The room was dark, but as his eyes got used to the dim light, he saw something moving on the ceiling. A quick shadow ran across it from side to side.

This time, Cooper didn't have to wait for the stench of rot to realize that the Hollow was there with them, guarding its dormant vessel from above. He glanced at Joel and Jack, who nodded back at him to confirm they were also aware.

They walked slowly out of the room and closed the door behind them.

"Christ!" All that came out of Cooper's mouth was a whisper choked in his breathing.

Jack sighed, and their eyes met as he turned to face him. Their cautious optimism, that promising sense of focus, seemed to have dissolved in the heavy, still air of the house infested by the evil.

"What do you think, Mr. Kopernick?" Cooper asked, and once more, he felt all the impossibility of that situation. He just asked a man he barely knew what he thought about another man possessed by a demon that was feasting on everyone's pain.

The man glanced again at the hallway, ignoring Cooper's question.

It started raining.

Fat drops hit the roof, producing a ticking sound that increased in intensity. Cooper looked out the window and saw the street light distorting through the water that crawled down the glass.

"Joel." Jack Sullivan called the attention of his friend, who stood just a few feet away from him yet so distant in his focus.

"Where is the relic?" Joel asked, glancing at Jack.

"It's in the room. Peter's wearing it around his neck."

Joel brooded, then clasped a hand on his chest. "We need to begin," he said as he moved rapidly towards his briefcase. He rested it flat on the dining table and opened it, then grabbed a large volume out of it, a book that seemed so old that it barely held itself together.

The spine was pretty much gone, and twines kept the thick, yellowed pages together.

"We need to begin what?" Cooper asked.

Jack approached Cooper and put a hand on his shoulder to reassure him.

"The exorcism," Jack said, keeping his head down as if he had just said a word he wasn't proud of.

Joel approached them with the book open in his hands. Cooper saw drawings on the old pages; handwritten notes and symbols covered them.

"Jack, I'm not sure how to go about this. I've been researching since you told me about this. The elders don't want to talk about it. I don't think they had ever had to deal with anything like this before. We need to prepare. We need to start as soon as possible, but we shouldn't go about this with high expectations. We need to be prepared for the worst."

Jack Sullivan nodded as he stared off.

"What's the worst?" Cooper asked, immediately regretting the question that now sounded so infantile.

Both men looked at him with eyebrows tilted in a concerned and serious expression.

"These rituals, Detective," Jack Sullivan started in a soft voice, so close to a whisper. "They have a very high rate of failure. As a matter of fact, they fail most of the time. If we fail to cast this evil out of Peter Hanson, he will die."

Cooper stared silently and gave the man a light nod.

"He will die anyway if we don't try," he said.

Jack Sullivan smiled at him and patted him on the shoulder. "Let's prepare. Shall we? What do we know, Joel?"

"The demon will attack. Not necessarily in a physical way, but on a psychological or an emotional ground. If we offer our emotions and fears, it will take them and use them against us."

Cooper's thoughts went immediately to Caroline and Tyrese, and he felt weak and unprepared for the battle.

"The demon doesn't have power over us if we stand strong in our principles. We must not fear it. If what you told me is accurate, Jack, the Shapeshifter might not be as powerful as we think it is, not yet."

"What makes you think that?" Jack asked.

"The fact that it didn't enter the body until now. It had to feed. It had to get stronger to the point of being able to invade someone. Peter's body has deteriorated at a rate that makes me think the demon still needs strength. Otherwise, it would have used Peter in other ways. Don't you think so? Judging by his condition, it is not unreasonable to think that Peter Hanson won't be its ultimate destination. I know you thought Peter was the ultimate target, but I'm afraid I have to disagree."

"Continue." Jack gestured to him.

"It is now getting stronger as we speak. These entities have been summoned and imprisoned in a relic, the pendant in this case. Back in the day, it was a very well-known ritual among the people of the tribes that practiced witchcraft. The ritual can be repeated, but the evil needs to be cast out of the body first. It needs to be lured out of the body."

Cooper listened to the unreal conversation, bewildered. Luring a criminal out of his cove was something that he understood and could strategize. This was something that made him feel so small but glad at the same time, glad he didn't have to be the one to make decisions.

"How do we lure it out?"

"We need to offer something that it wants. Something more than what it is getting out of Peter Hanson."

# 10

Cooper stood near the window at the far end of the living room, looking outside at the unrelenting rain pouring outside. The dart of the raindrops under the streetlight and the shockwaves they produced in the potholes on the asphalt clashed profoundly with the smothering stillness of the house. Jack Sullivan and Joel Kopernick talked in whispers on the other side of the room, reading through the pages of their respective volumes, collecting their thoughts and spiritual strength as they got ready for the fight.

As he looked at Jack Sullivan wearing a pendant with a silver crucifix at the end of it, Cooper couldn't help but wonder if religion mattered at all. Could a Christian God defy a Native American evil? Was a Native American force required to beat another one of its kind? He had never been a spiritual man, but he felt stupid asking himself that question. The world had built many barriers and labels between cultures that were likely worshiping entities that couldn't care less about those labels. For much of his life, he had dealt with good people and bad people, some of them really bad. He was always a strong supporter of the uncountable shades of gray that were just part of human nature. *There is no black or white, Caroline.* The words he often said to his wife when she asked about convicts, murderers, or victims resonated in the back of his mind. It's more complicated than that, he used to respond. And yet it was black and white after all, and the dualism of the battle that was about to unfold in front of his eyes was so stark that it made him dizzy.

"It is time," Jack Sullivan said to him as he quickly moved across the room and grabbed Cooper's hands in his. "You don't have to go in if you don't feel like it," he said softly and reassuringly as he smiled at him.

"I don't know what's going to happen in that room," Cooper said in a shaky voice.

"Neither do I," Jack said. "But I can tell you one thing, and you should try to keep it in mind, no matter how hard it gets in there."

"What is it?"

"Do not engage with the demon. This evil is always looking for an escape, for a chance of weakness. Whatever negative thought it might instill in you, fight it with all your strength. Be determined not to open that door to it. And remember, just you being here is doing more than you'll ever know. The bond that we seal tonight. That is immense."

Cooper nodded, and with tears of fear mixed with ones of awareness, he followed the two men, initiating the slow procession. Joel led the group with his old book firmly in his hands, and Jack Sullivan followed, holding the cross in front of his face. Cooper trailed with his heart pounding in his chest.

He felt the energy level rising, a deep vibration of forces building up, ready to clash.

"Oh! God..." Cooper uttered when he entered the room; he gasped in wonder and felt his legs becoming soft and weak.

Peter Hanson was perched in the corner of the guest room where the walls met the ceiling, suspended seven feet above the ground. He cradled himself in a semi-fetal position, rocking his body back and forth, staring down at them with dark and empty eyes as deep and cold as caverns. His face had muted: the lips retracted, and sharp fangs were visible from the semi-opened mouth. *A feral animal,* that's what Cooper thought as he glanced at the demonic features that had appeared on his face.

"*Leave or be ready to suffer,*" the demonic voice croaked from Peter Hanson's mouth. Cooper shivered at the sound of it. The stench that came with it was intolerable, something Cooper had never experienced before. It smelled of a dead animal in the woods, covered with damp leaves and infested by maggots. For a moment, Cooper thought that leaving was indeed a fine idea. The demon looked at him, and Cooper was sure that was because he reeked with fear. He looked at Jack Sullivan, who nodded confidently in return.

And in that moment, Cooper felt the staggering impact of the old man as he stared up at the demon. What was left of a world that had once been solid and real, made of facts and logic, was wiped away. Cooper realized the magnitude of the moment and the battle setting up in front of him. He was glad to take a stand on the side of Jack Sullivan, who gave him strength and confidence. He had wondered, in the last tumultuous hours of this bewildering day, *why the monster hadn't gone after the priest. Why, of all the people it had selected, had he never tried to go after the only person who was hunting it.*? And the answer laid right in front of his eyes. There was something otherworldly about this old man. Perhaps it was his faith or his wisdom that made him look so strong in front of the vile creature. The Hollow dreaded Jack Sullivan. If the dark force that infested Peter Hanson's body seemed insurmountable, there was something just as powerful on the other side, fighting against it. Cooper wished he had seen that resolution in Lynn or Frank Harris. He wondered if it would have saved them or if they were too damaged and far beyond repair to reject the parasite. He didn't have that strength either. On the contrary, Cooper thought he would be a perfect prey for the Hollow.

Joel started chanting incomprehensible words with his eyes closed and one hand on the page of his book. The demon looked away from Cooper and in the direction of the thin man. The front of his hat hung low on his forehead.

"What should I call you?" the voice of Jack Sullivan thundered in the room. Cooper flinched at the sound of it.

The demon looked at the old man standing and hissed back at him like a cornered animal ready to defend itself with all the means at its disposal.

"What is your name?" he asked again.

The mouth of the demon, once belonging to Peter Hanson and holder of a powerful smile, opened, showing multiple rows of fangs pointing in all directions. He stretched his claws toward Jack Sullivan.

"*Na Losa Falaya,*" the demon eventually bellowed in a deep, alien voice.

Cooper noticed Joel Kopernick's features getting darker and more concerned. Whatever the demon said mustn't be good.

"What do you want?" Jack Sullivan continued with a potent tone that seemed to shake the whole room. The demon grinned and released a ragged cackle that forced Cooper to look away. When he looked back, the body that once belonged to Peter Hanson twisted and contorted unnaturally as if it was made of rubber.

"We cast you out! Leave this body in the name of Father, the Son, and the-"

And before Father Sullivan could finish, the demon let out a deafening sound. It was the sound of a million mournful voices moaning, crying, and screaming their pain. Cooper couldn't possibly explain how, but he knew that was the sound of the trapped, the people that the Hollow had fed off of, the agonizing, choked cry that dies in sorrow. Parents grieving their lost children, regrets, guilt, words that had never been spoken before it was too late, desperation, denial and illusions.

It filled the room and blasted through it like a potent wind. Something flew across the room and broke the window near the desk. Drawers opened and closed randomly. Cooper heard the snap of the door frame cracking in the middle as if a devastating invisible force was trying to rip it away from the plaster wall.

Joel's book was blown out of his hands as he struggled to keep his balance, pushed back by that unrelenting wind. Jack Sullivan held on with one hand on the bed frame, keeping his crucifix high in front of his face toward the demon, attempting to screen himself from the power of evil.

# 11

Back in the long, dark tunnel with a dizzily high ceiling, Peter Hanson walked among the shadows of those who could not escape the well. He couldn't help but wonder if this was hell. It would make sense to him. He couldn't possibly imagine a place filled with more gloom and suffering. He felt it in the shadows that passed by like a bloodhound smelling its prey from a mile away. He could almost tell that grief had a different scent than regret or guilt, and he wondered when he had become such an expert in the matter. He wondered *if the other shadows could see him or if he was already a shadow, and what did he smell like?*

The difficulty of keeping the time in the tunnel was second only to the paradoxical perception of space. The light, the opening at the end of the tunnel, was a circle as big as a penny in front of his eyes. It became visibly closer at times as he walked toward it until it started to shrink again. He would turn around, trying to walk in the other direction, toward the other end of the tunnel, to only learn the same lesson.

There was no way out of there, and the presence that forced him to walk, breathing on his neck, was always there. Peter felt it getting more and more powerful just as he got weaker and weaker. He knew he wasn't dead yet but realized he was running out of time.

Suddenly, the tunnel started to shake violently, twirls of dust dancing in front of his eyes. There wasn't a sound in the tunnel, but he felt the ground growling under his feet, the shadows stopping their eternal movement.

But most importantly, he felt the presence behind loosening its grip on him, distracted by the quake.

*Look for us when you need it the most.*

His mother's words returned to him, thawing his heart from the icy desperation it had fallen into. A thin slice of light appeared in the darkness.

A door opening.

In the multidimensional space he found himself in, it wasn't easy to judge how far away the door was from where he was, twenty feet or maybe a hundred. He couldn't possibly know, but he knew that was his chance.

He had looked for them when he needed them the most.

And they had answered.

Deep down inside him, Peter knew his parents were there, waiting behind the door.

And there was nothing that could stop him from trying to get there, even if that was the last thing he did.

So he got ready.

And he ran for it.

# 12

Cooper tried to find shelter behind the dresser, pushing against it with all his strength so it wouldn't crush him against the wall. His hand instinctively went to his gun's holster as the demon's scream raged inside the room. The bed's sheets fluttered in front of the Hollow; his mouth opened, shouting a malevolent bellowing sound.

"Father, we beg you to hear us." Cooper heard Jack Sullivan screaming from the bottom of his lungs. His voice surged in the chaos.

The demon hesitated, struck by the power of the old man. His words flung powerfully through the room as it recoiled in the corner. Joel Kopernick stood back up and resumed his native chant. Cooper realized once more the titanic presence of Jack Sullivan in the room. While his mind kept telling him that the old man didn't have supernatural powers, every part of him, deep inside, stated that the man had unearthly capacities that went well beyond the material flesh.

"That you spare us, that you can help us find relief, that you lift up our mind and spirits..."

Like a spider, the demon moved quickly across the ceiling, bending his head downward to keep its terrifying gaze on them. Jack Sullivan turned, following him with the cross shaking in his hand, but Joel didn't react quickly enough.

The Hollow swung its long arm in the air, and its claws met Joel's neck, ripping through the flesh. Joel let the book fall on the floor, blood gushing on the pages. Cooper watched him bring both his hands to his neck as his eyes widened with surprise and sudden awareness. Joel looked at Cooper before falling on his knees and then face down as the blood rushed out, collecting in a puddle.

"I command you, abhorrent spirit, to obey me to the letter..." Jack continued as tears oozed down his face.

The demon ceased its screaming, and the room became quiet again. Paralyzed against the dresser, Cooper watched with horror the evil spirit feeding from his fear and shock.

"Don't let it, Detective. Don't let it in," he heard Jack yelling at him as the monster moaned gutturally in pleasure.

"*Do you want to say something to your mom, Detective?*" The demon asked him. "*She is right here with us.*"

Cooper felt an intense pressure growing inside his chest. For a moment, he thought that was the end, that he was about to have a heart attack. The demon had stricken, and he had felt the hit very clearly. He felt angrier than he had ever felt before. What would he say to his mother right now if he had the chance to talk to her? He considered the possibility offered by the evil. Tears ran freely from his saturated eyes as he squeezed his fist hard.

Every day, he had dreamed about talking to his mother again. Some days, he dreamed about hugging her tight; others, he dreamed about spitting his hate at her, his anger for abandoning him, being selfish, and making his life so much harder. Some days, he thought about telling her about Tyrese and Caroline, of the family he had built, thinking she would be proud of him.

"I forgive her. Tell her I forgive her," Cooper said as he stood up again, facing the monster directly, looking straight in his dark, empty eyes. The pressure inside his stomach reduced, and the feeling of being robbed of his own emotions diminished. Whatever he had offered, the Hollow was not interested in it. The Hollow was now standing on the floor in front of him, carrying the emaciated body and features of Peter Hanson. Whatever it was doing, it had now stopped, as if his words had anything to do with it.

"We cast you out of this body, oh you abomination. Leave this body and obey the Lord." Jack Sullivan resumed the ritual.

The demon turned to him and hissed, recoiling in one side of the room. He was on the defense now and evidently weaker.

"I forgive you, Mom," Cooper kept going. "I forgive you, and I love you, and I miss you every day of my life." He screamed at the demon as if his mother was inside him. As if she could hear him. He didn't care if that was true or just another fantasy; imagining his mother talking to him again felt good. And for the first time, he wasn't picturing his mother the way he had found her, hanging by a rope. Her face wasn't swollen and purple from the asphyxiation, but it was her sweet and caring face tucking him in the blankets, reading a bedtime story for him, caressing his face, and kissing him goodnight on the forehead.

Cooper fell on his knees as he abandoned himself in a liberatory cry. The poison, the bad memories, and the darkness that he hosted for such a long time were slowly moving away from his mind, making room for other memories, the ones that had been buried deep down with all the rest.

The demon hissed again and stretched its arms forward, weakened and surprised. It turned around as if it was looking for something. It then looked at Cooper again, then at Jack Sullivan.

And Cooper understood that the demon was looking for a way out.

It was looking for another vessel.

The parasite was looking for a way to survive, and it was running out of options very quickly.

"I command you to leave this body and obey the word of our Father." Cooper heard Jack Sullivan screaming to the demonic creature that recoiled in the room's corner. It had killed Joel, who was never going to be a viable option as a new vessel, just as Jack Sullivan. And Cooper suddenly realized that he was the best option for the Hollow to find another vessel, another host.

Cooper fell to the ground, exhausted, while everything blurred out of his vision. The room started to spin, and he felt dizzy. The screaming and moaning resumed as the battle between Jack Sullivan and the Hollow entered its final round. He heard the buzz of flies trying to cover the booming voice of Jack Sullivan. Cooper turned his head to his right, where he saw the dead eyes of Joel Kopernick staring at him. He turned again, looking at the ceiling and its light gray paint. The reflection of the table lamp shook on it as Cooper's strength seemed to abandon him suddenly.

Please, no! No, no, no. He tried to tell himself, trying to stay conscious.

A dark shadow of a long being was now on the wall. And the shadow had eyes, much deeper and more desolated than the ones he had seen on Peter Hanson's face.

The shadow stared at him from above. As Cooper's senses abandoned him, he could still feel its malevolence, that terrible gloom.

Then, the world went dark.

# 13

Peter ran for the dim light of the door that opened in the tunnel. Behind him, the dark presence growled in anger, caught by surprise, and chased him. As he ran as hard as he could, the tunnel kept shaking violently all around him as the quake intensified. The roar of the world coming apart, breaking its foundations, reached him from behind.

Twenty feet.

The door kept opening slowly, inviting him in; the light coming out of it was orange and spread powerfully in that dark, doomed place with no gravity. Peter felt his energy depleting. The presence was close behind him, gaining ground.

A huge boulder landed right in front of him. Peter swerved at the last moment to avoid it.

Ten feet.

With his heart pounding in his chest, Peter collected the last bit of strength left in him and jumped, pushing hard on his right foot to get as much thrust as possible. He flew through the air with his arms stretched to the light. When he went through the door, he felt the warmth of the place, and all the sounds of the world were back.

He landed hard on his stomach and let out a scream of pain as his arm twisted in the fall.

He rolled onto his back with closed eyes and took a few seconds to recover. The gravity was back, the sounds were back, and the presence was gone; the trapped ones were gone, their smells. It was all gone. What remained was the beautiful sound of the waves shattering on the rocks, their foam sizzling in the distance. Peter felt the warm and fine sand in his hands, slipping through his fingers, fleeting. He smelled the seaweed and the caper bush resting on the shore. He heard the sound of the seagulls chanting in the thin air.

He opened his eyes and found himself in front of a majestic sunset. The sun approached the horizon, breaking like a yolk in the sky. It was a familiar view, and it suddenly came to him where he was and the meaning of it. He turned to his right, and his heart ached; he felt the tears filling his eyes quickly. His mom and dad walked from the umbrella, planted in the sand, toward the shore, where a ten-year-old kid was busy building a sandcastle with his small yellow bucket. They hugged and then walked to the younger version of Peter to help him out as he smiled at them.

*Look for us when you need it the most.* He thought of those words once more and finally understood their meaning, as that old memory was unlocked in his mind. His father held young Peter in his arms, and the three of them looked at old Peter and smiled at him. And just like that, the ache was gone, and the power of their love thawed his soul. Tears flowed freely down his cheeks as he smiled back. He wanted to run to them, hug them, and tell them how much he loved them. The claws of grief peeked back at him, and the sun seemed to go down quicker now.

It will never get easier. *There will never be a moment where I won't miss you or think of you*, Peter thought. But now he knew where to find them when he needed them the most. As the last sliver of the crimson sun got ready to be swallowed by the sea at the horizon, Peter saw his parents and his young self point in front of them along the shore.

Peter turned and saw a circle of light floating in the air.

An opening, another door.

The perimeter of the circular gate shone in the dusk that proclaimed the death of the day.

And with the darkness looming in the distance, the presence that haunted him was back. He saw the long and tall shadow running toward the gate. His legs went back into motion, and he started running, never diverting his gaze from his family. It was time to say goodbye once more. But this time was different; everything was different.

He ran again for the light as the tunnel swallowed the beach, sky, and sea. He was back in the tunnel, but the light at the end of it wasn't just the size of a penny now. It was right in front of him. He felt the ragged breathing of the demon behind him, the stench of rot, and the gloom it carried. When he crossed the gate, he opened his eyes and gasped, desperate for air, as if he had been holding his breath underwater for a long time.

He coughed and looked around him.

He was in a bedroom he had never seen before. Jack Sullivan screamed with his head tilted up right in front of him. On his right, Detective Cooper laid on the floor unconscious, a few feet away from a Native American man with his face resting in a puddle of blood.

It was terribly cold in the room, and he realized he was naked, except for the briefs he wore. He looked up at the ceiling and saw the demon that was chasing him. It raged against Jack Sullivan as the old man held a cross in his hands and recited words that seemed to come from a Christian ritual.

"Get back to where you belong, for the Lord commands you to," he heard him saying.

Peter felt the touch of a cold object around his neck. He grabbed the necklace and pulled it hard, breaking the clasp. Jack Sullivan saw him and nodded at him. Everything just suddenly made sense to Peter. If the demon didn't have a host, he would be forced to return to the relic that had hosted it before it was summoned out. Peter threw the pendant in the air; he looked at it gleaming in the room. Jack Sullivan grabbed it with determination and held it up as he pushed forward with his rite.

"Get back where you belong, Na Losa Falaya. The Lord orders you so. We order you so!"

For a moment, nothing happened, and Peter could see the first signs of surrender in Jack's eyes. He looked tired and seemed as if he had been battling with the demon for quite a while. He didn't seem like he could take another swing at it. Then the bellow of the demon ceased, the sound of flies buzzing suddenly stopped, and the room was filled with a surreal silence.

Peter watched dark molecules of what seemed to be black dust gathering from all around the room, twirling around and forming a whirl that started at the ceiling and gently made its way to the pendant in the shape of a twister.

He saw the eyes of the evil staring at him with hate and revengefulness.

Peter couldn't help but think about how ancient it was, how long it had been around, and when its inevitable return would be. He surely hoped to never have to deal with it again.

Just like he now knew where to find the people he loved when he needed them the most, he was sure he could just as easily find the

Hollow, waiting for him just around the corner.

When the last bit of black dust had disappeared inside the pendant, Peter fell to the ground, and before the lights went out again, he heard Luna anxiously breathing in his face, the warmth of her tongue kissing him.

Then, exhausted, he abandoned himself to the darkness.

He dozed in and out of a scattered dream. Red and blue lights flashed in the night, alternating with the blackness of his eyelids. Raindrops fell heavy on his face as three men and a woman put a transparent mask on his face. The soundless vibrations of the tunnel were still with him. He saw Will, the real Will, and then he saw Will's mother and father staring at him, spotlighted in a dark, smoky room. Flashes of men, women, and children from an ancient tribe appeared in front of his eyes as if he was watching an old reel with no audio. Then, the sound of the flies again and imploring shouts spoken in a foreign language but still utterly understandable. Women begging to have their children back, men forced to watch the unthinkable: fires, gunshots, and more screams of pain. People threw themself into a fire to save their burning children—blind desperation.

The face of the Hollow.

Then, back in the real world, he saw his chest rising and heard the sound of the defibrillator. More blur, more darkness, then the lights again, muffled sounds of people talking in agitation. And then the sound of the stretcher rolling on wet asphalt, the rhythmic bumps of the concrete blocks, then the smooth, soundless roll on the linoleum floors. More people coming, more machines, more whirring and beeping sounds. The smell of the trapped ones in the tunnel and the damp sufferance they were soaked in.

His parents were smiling at him.

The machine's beep became flat, alarms ringing, people in white gowns poking his arms with needles. A weak thread he tried to stay anchored to. He felt that he could go. If he only let go one inch on that thread, he would go. He could be with his parents again. *Is this how it ends?* Peter thought—bitter disappointment. *Luna is waiting for me. I've got a book to finish. Who's going to tell my story? Who's going to read it?*

*The world is going dark. Please turn the light back on. I want to stay.*

And the light came back on, and he heard himself gasping for air without feeling a thing—an unsettling feeling.

"Stay with me. Stay with me, Peter." He heard the detective talking from far away.

He held onto his consciousness as tight as he could.

The machine resumed its beeping, fast and irregular.

There was intense pressure on his throat, a stinging pain radiating from it. The cold of a metallic object sliding inside it. And all of a sudden, he wasn't breathing anymore. The room went quiet, and he could only hear the hissing sound of the ventilator.

He closed his eyes and let go.

# Epilogue

The fall has an odd and sudden way of vanishing; right after Halloween, the decorations are put back in a dusty box and placed in the corner of a garage or a basement. Threatened by the sure promise of the cold Indiana winter, the fall disappears, leaving a sense of incompleteness, of harsh estrangement. The buckets are still filled with candies, the harvest is saved, the days are short, and the nights are long and cold. The air is still and crisp, and the backyard's bonfire is crackling with life. The trees are bare, and the undergrowth in the woods is low and barren, pretending to die with the promise of a sweet return.

Cooper throws a bunch of twigs in the fire, flicking his cigarette butt into it too. The smoke he exhales mixes with his cold, condensed breath. He hides his chin in the neck of the winter coat.

"How's that new book coming?" he asks.

Peter smiles, staring at the hypnotic fire.

"I was thinking I should get hospitalized more often. Two weeks in bed do miracles for the writing." he laughed. "It's coming along. I think my editor will have the manuscript on his desk next week."

"Well, you can't say you don't have material for the next one," Cooper said, winking. "How are you feeling anyway? How's the recovery going?"

"Pretty decent considering the doctors told me my heart stopped twice and that they have never seen a body in such precarious conditions. They still wonder how I got in that condition, I reckon. After all, how could they possibly understand what happened."

Cooper became serious again as if the past weeks' memories had returned to him.

"Yeah. Can't blame them."

"How are Caroline and the kiddo?" Peter asked. On the day of his discharge from the hospital, Cooper showed up to drive him back home and introduced him to his family. Caroline had prepared supper for all of them.

"They are fine. Everything's going back to normal bit by bit."

"And are you fine?" Peter asked as he looked at Cooper's eyes, tired and sleep-deprived. He hadn't asked directly if he wasn't having trouble sleeping, but if Cooper had been dealing with the same dose of nightmares that Peter still faced, there wasn't reason to ask. Cooper sighed and nodded as he looked at the dark blue sky. He turned as the storm door opened with its characteristic squeaking sound.

Rosa approached them with a tray. She carried mugs of hot

chocolate- a half-melted marshmallow floating in it—the steam raised from the mugs, vanishing in the cold air.

"You surely know how to cheer up two sad souls, Rosa," Peter said.

"Thank you very much, ma'am," Cooper echoed him as he sat around the fire.

"No, no, no Mr. Peter Hanson." Rosa shook her head as he placed the tray on the small coffee table between the chairs. "Don't think that I have forgiven you yet. I can't believe you didn't call me when you needed to. I took two weeks of vacation to go see my son, and you almost died. Your mother is probably cursing me right now," she said, letting a smile slip out as she remembered her.

Peter nodded and smiled back. "I'll make it up to you, Rosa. Don't you worry. Have a seat with us. Will you?"

She glanced at the two men, still pretending to be mad, then burst into a loud laugh and joined them around the fire. They talked and laughed, evoking memories and summoning up funny stories. Tears came down with the remembrance of a time that would never be back but that, at the same time, will never really be over.

*Nothing is forever, only who we are,* Peter thought as the words of his father came back to him.

*And now you are gone, Papa,* Peter thought, as the embers fought to stay alive while the day died around them.

But you will never be gone.

Not really.

***

Jack Sullivan reached the hill's summit, trailing four men and two women, holding his hand up against the strong wind. The terrain was dusty and clayish, with shattered and smooth rocks crunching under his weight. His black coat wasn't warm enough, and his feet ached inside the once-polished dress shoes, now covered in dust. He stopped and caught his breath, for the hike had been just as strenuous as unexpected. He had imagined a graveyard by the side of a road, but when he thought of the life of Joel Kopernick, he realized how silly that expectation was. This was much more like him. It comforted him to think of him right there instead of a conventional place. He wasn't made for conventional things; quite the contrary, he had lived to fight them.

And that place fit perfectly; it checked all the boxes.

He looked ahead of him and didn't see a grave, didn't see a cross with a name on it, or a tombstone. In front of him were yellow-colored hills that extended so far at the horizon that his eye couldn't conceive the end of it. A stunning landscape of smooth shapes and perfection in the vastity of the land. And it was all clear. The land was God, and God was the land. And Joel Kopernick returned to the land. This was the place where his body had been burned, where the wind had picked his ashes and spread them, where they had always belonged.

The two women ahead of him, Joel's wife and daughter, looked at him and smiled. There was sadness in their eyes, but there was no pain. There was wisdom in them that he had seen in his old friend, and so was in the eyes of the four men who chanted ancient songs and prayers for their departed friend. Jack stopped and turned around and cried for Joel, for the friendship he had lost. He felt the guilt burdening him. Jack knew that Joel had played a fundamental role as they fought the Hollow together, but he couldn't help but feel responsible for the price Joel had paid to succeed. Deep down, Jack knew that if there were a way to go, Joel would have chosen the way of going with honor, fighting for what was right. Still, the toll remained on Jack Sullivan's heart. His mind went back to the

Derringer boy once more. He had thought about it a great deal after the exorcism of Peter Hanson. The evil was cast out, but Jack's mind could never get rid of it. The wounds were too deep to heal; they would stay open to the end of his days.

One of the men, the eldest, approached him and offered him a hint of a bow. Jack Sullivan reciprocated, offering the elder his respect.

"Joel told me of the spirit that cannot be named."

"We fought it together," Jack said, struggling to keep his gaze on the man's piercing eyes as the guilt got a hold of him once more. He had dragged Joel into that hell just as he dragged Jane Hanson into it.

"Did you bring it with you?" The elder asked, glancing at his coat pocket.

"Yes. Yes, I have it."

"Please give it to me," the man demanded dryly.

"Where are you going to put it?" Jack asked.

The elder raised his head to the sky and brooded.

"In a place where no one will find it," he eventually said. "Please give it to me."

Jack hesitated for a moment. The thought of someone else handling it gave him the chills. Not that he wanted to have anything to do with it. He just wasn't sure if he could trust this man. *Joel would tell me not to be so paranoid,* Jack thought, and that made him smile. He grabbed the small, black velvet box he kept in his coat pocket. It was one of those jewelry cases that usually contained a ring or a pair of earrings.

But not this time. This time, it was the pendant that had caused so much chaos and loss. *Not ever again,* Jack thought as he handed over the box. The elder stood there examining it, rotating it in his hands. Then he opened the lace that kept it closed and, after a quick glimpse inside, tied it back around the opening. The elder looked at Jack Sullivan and nodded slightly to thank him.

"I trust you will know what to do with it. What happened to Joel should never happen to anyone else," Jack said.

The elder nodded again. Then, he put the box in his jacket and rejoined the other man at the hill's summit.

Jack Sullivan walked to the overlook and sighed.

In the distance, a wild horse galloped through the valley. In the sacred silence of the place, he could hear the sound of the hooves hitting the ground. A cloud of dust rose behind it as he ran freely, untamable.

He envied it.

He liked to think it was Joel greeting him, showing off the freedom he had conquered at last.

# Author's note

It takes a writer to finish a manuscript, but it takes a village to make it a book.

These words have accompanied me for the whole journey, from the very first time the seed of Hollow started to germinate in the back of my mind. This story had me digging deep, in the most hidden corners of my mind, through my darkest fears and I shocked myself with what came out.

The idea for this story didn't come out all of a sudden, as it happens for most of my work. It took a slow shaping, like water tearing incessantly on a stone, carving paths into the hard surface, and ultimately revealing fragile things. Horror is an interesting genre: it can look like a niche on the surface but is probably the widest genre in literature and the reason must be anchored in the broad spectrum of human fears. Some people are scared of the dark, some others of spiders, human madness, heights. You name it.

As Hollow took shape I had to come to accept one of the things that scares me the most. Losing the people that I love, having to say goodbye to them -or not having the chance to. That was the trigger that unlocked the story inside my subconscious, and I had to let it out in small doses. I found myself thinking about that possibility over and over as I laid in bed looking at the shadows of the trees dancing on the ceiling. And just like all our demons, they like to haunt us at night, when we are more exposed, unable to rely on the comfort of the daylight, when things look bigger and stretched, just like the shadows on the ceiling.

There are countless volumes that attempt to prepare one for the demon of grief: they are often handed out by counselors in hospitals or during hospice services. They tell you about the human body getting ready to shut down, about the nature behind the process. But ultimately nothing can prepare us for the loss, the gloom and the void behind it. So we fear it, just like we fear anything that is unknown.

In the timeless dimension of grief, the air is too painful to breathe. So we try to escape it, to find distractions, to pretend to be ready to go back to normal life. In my mind this was a message I wanted to convey, through the story: our society doesn't allow us to grieve. Too many other things to do, too many things to produce, to consume. Too much work to do, or money to make and not enough time to stop and face reality. During my research, I came across a small tribe in the Indonesian mountains called Toraja. On the opposite side of the spectrum, Torajan people keep the bodies of their loved ones in their homes for a long time after their passing. The corpses are treated to food, clothes, water and even cigarettes. It is in their tradition and belief that the soul of the dead remains in the house for a long time, until it is ready to move forward.

While the practice of preserving the bodies and sitting them at the dinner table for supper might seem a little too extreme, I like to think their reasons have something to do with the time needed to process such an important natural event. Among the uncountable traditions expressed by different cultures and folklore, the one that attracted me the most was the one of the Native Americans.

And here comes the biggest dilemma I have had while writing Hollow: how do I build a story that involves Native American traditions without falling into stereotypes that will depict a wrong image of this incredible culture? Access to Native American folklore is extremely limited as the tradition is mainly transmitted orally. I was lucky enough to speak with people that had direct contact with natives, on top of my own research. I was able to ask questions about old stories, costumes and rituals. It was very challenging to find the balance between research and fiction. I didn't want to turn Hollow into an academic exercise on Native American history, yet I was drawn to this culture in a way I have never felt before.

So, long story short, I tried to merge all these elements, both traditional and fictional, to build the evil entity that dominates my story. And here comes my second message: the fitting of the Native American folklore into the narrative of Hollow is entirely fictional and does not intend to offend anyone. Quite oppositely, I wanted to expose historical facts and topics that elevate the spiritual nature of this great culture.

This book is for my family: my beautiful wife Shanea who supports me in my unconventional endeavors. This book wouldn't exist without you. Thank you Lola and Ralph, for the constant reminder of unconditional love. To my parents Pietro and Maria Gabriella and sisters Fabiola, Martine and Federica, to my father-in-law Daymon. If telling the story of Hollow has taught me anything, it is to remind people you love them, as you might not have another chance. All you have is now. I love you all, more than I'll ever be able to express.

Thank you to all the people that made Hollow a reality. Thank you, Hilary. There isn't anyone else on this planet I trust more than you when it comes to books. To Mar for taking care of my marketing struggles. Thanks Ross for the absolutely incredible art that you have produced for the cover of Hollow. Thank you to all the local bookstores that are crazy enough to put my titles on their shelves: Tomorrow Bookstore, Between The Pages, Indy Reads, Fallen Leaf Bookstore, Viewpoint Books and many more. You guys can't imagine how helpful that is for an independent author. A special thanks to Bruce Garrison for the spiritual and deep knowledge that he exposed me to. So much of this book was inspired by our long conversations. Last, but not least, thank you to the incredible community that gravitates around independent authors: book reviewers, beta readers, bookworms. Your passion is a propulsive force for the Horror and Thriller genre and it is truly changing the name of the game. Thank you to all the other incredibly talented authors I had the pleasure to meet along the way. To all the readers that have just finished reading Hollow: I hope you enjoyed it, I hope you felt it on your skin in the same way I did while I was writing it.

It takes a village to make a book. It truly does.

And I couldn't be prouder of having you all in my village.

Onto the next one.

Davide Tarsitano

June 2023

# ABOUT THE AUTHOR

Davide Tarsitano is an author of horror and dystopian novels. He was born in Cosenza, a small town in southern Italy. Tarsitano has won the 2022 Book Fest Literary Contest for Best Horror Novel and The Reader's Favorite 2022 Award in the same category. He currently lives in Indianapolis with his wife Shanea and his two dogs Lola and Ralph.

**Published works:**

The Tooth Fairy (2022)

Hollow (2023)

For more information visit

**dtarsitano.com**

Or follow him on social media:

**Instagram: @dtarsitanoofficial**

**Facebook: @Davide Tarsitano - Author**

**Twitter: @DTarsitanoO1**

**TikTok: @davidetarsitanoauthor**

**Amazon: @Davide Tarsitano**

**Goodreads: @Davide Tarsitano**

# THE TOOTH FAIRY
# A novel by Davide Tarsitano

Johnny Hawk is a successful entrepreneur in the tech field, escaping from his former life after an utter breakdown. During his trip across the country, his route crosses with Wendy Jag, a beautiful woman who works as a dentist in New Mexico. As the attraction between the two lost souls escalates furiously, they engage in a passionate and daring physical affair. For the first time in a while Johnny finds some peace and hope for the future. But he cannot imagine that behind those innocent and deep eyes Wendy is a profoundly disturbed woman, tormented by the demons of her past: a childhood made of abuses, losses and nightmares filled with darkness. As Wendy's feelings for Johnny grow stronger, the fight inside Wendy's chaotic subconscious begins.

The Tooth Fairy, a dormant and malevolent side of her personality is reawakening, silently awaiting…to take over.